Fire & Shadow

THE DARKWORLD SKINWALKER SERIES

Skin Deep

Lost Soul

Last Chance

Blood Promise

Scorched Fury

Fate's Edge

Grave Debt

Oath Bound

THE DARKWORLD SOULTRACKER SERIES

Blood Magic

Demon Kin

Blood Curse

Demon Soul

Blood Moon

Demon Bones

Blood Born

THE DARKWORLD IRIN CHRONICLES SERIES

Retribution

Requiem

Resonance

Revelation

INFINITE
INK
BOOKS

Fire & Shadow

T.G. AYER

For Dhivya- daughter and assistant

People should believe that wishes do come true
Because when we wished...We got you

GLOSSARY & PRONUNCIATION

Maya Rao – *Mah-yah* Rao (as in *now*)
Devan Rao (Dev) – *There-vin*
Leela Rao (Lee) – *Lee-lah*
Joss (Jocelyn) Cawood
Nik (Nikhil) Lucas – Nik-eel Lucas
Ria Gupta – *Ree-yah Goop-ta*
Sunita Gupta – *Sue-neeta Goop-ta*
Hardev Gupta – *Harr-dev Goop-ta*
Amber Alden
Byron Richards
Claudia Romero
Viren Sen – *Vee-ren Senn*
Yama (God of Death and Justice) – *Yah-mah*
Dharma (Yama) – *DhaR-maa*
Chandragupta (Keeper of the Book of Life) – *Chun-thra-goop-ta*
Chayya (Goddess of Shadows) – *Chah-yaa*
Varuni (Goddess of Wine & the Amrita) – *Vah-roon-nee*
Amrita – *Um (as in gum)-reeta*
Narakasura (Kas) – *NaR-gah-soora (Kass)*
Balraj – *Baal-raaj*

Priya – *Pree-yah*
Rakshasa – *Ruck-sha-sa*
Patala - *Pa-taa-lah*
Naraka – *Naa-ra-kah*
Kailas – *Ky* (as in *my*)-*laash*
Swargaloka – *Swarr-ga-law-kah*
Naga – *Nah-gah*
Visha – *Vi-shah*
Madu – *Mah-dhoo*

CHAPTER 1

Maya flinched. A thousand tiny knives of white-hot pain splintered through her skin. Her teacher's knuckles crunched against her cheekbone and she spared a fleeting thought for the beautiful bruise sure to flower across the side of her face by the next morning. It was her own fault. Her attention had strayed. Again. Not that she was very good at any form of martial arts anyway. But she did try.

She should have tried harder.

If she had, she wouldn't be lying flat on her back with the whole room spinning around her. She wouldn't be lying so close to the gym mat that she had to wonder if the odd smell came from the plastic or from the hundreds of sweaty fighting bodies traveling over it every day. Neither would she be cursing the fact that she'd be sporting this hideous bruise all the way until prom.

Darn it.

"Honey, are you okay?" Leela Rao hurried to her daughter's side, her dark hair escaping from the knot at the top of her head. She knelt and threw a narrow-eyed glance at Maya's teacher.

At least Mom cares enough to check if I'm still alive.

Maya groaned as her mom's fingers probed her cheekbone, only causing further pain. And maybe even breaking off splintered bone.

Her mom tucked a stray strand of Maya's black hair behind her ear and sat on her heels. "It's fine, nothing broken. But you will have a lovely black eye for the next few days."

"Yeah, let's see what Child Services says," Maya muttered.

She was prone to opening her mouth and spewing out words without thinking. It's what usually got her in trouble. She immediately regretted the comment and hoped her mom hadn't heard. One look at her mom's face told her otherwise. Leela frowned and shook her head, as if wanting to scold, but knowing the time and the place was entirely wrong for disciplining her daughter. Still, Maya had no intention of apologizing.

"Come on. If you're fine enough to be a smart-ass then you're fine to get back up and practice." Her Kung Fu teacher smiled, all teeth, and stuck his hand in front of Maya's face. She glared at the hand. She really had no choice so she took it and allowed him to lift her back to her feet in one fluid move. "No pain, no gain, hey Maya?"

She dusted herself off despite knowing full well no dust clung to her. She kept her eyes on the floor, not daring to look around. How many of the other students had witnessed her embarrassing knockout?

Nik was there too, somewhere within the broiling group greeting their instructors and filing out of the studio. Nik who always seemed to be around, ever since his arrival three months ago. If they didn't happen to run in the same social circles, Maya would have suspected him of stalking. But no, they went to the same school, and within days of Nik's arrival they'd shared the same martial arts class, even had a few short and awkward conversations when she'd caught him watching her and he hadn't been able to flee easily.

Nik Lucas, with his dark curling hair, strong chiseled features and deep black eyes.

Nik Lucas. The forbidden fruit.

Nope, only nice Indian boys need apply. Besides, if she'd heard it once, she'd heard it a thousand times - when she was ready for boys then she was ready for marriage. Nik remained off-limits. Too white. Not Indian enough. Whatever. Maya couldn't even allow herself the pleasure of daydreams. She'd be setting her heart up for the inevitable break.

Maya tried to stop thinking of Nik, tried to convince herself he'd probably missed the whole debacle. She resumed her position, wide stance, bent knees, weight on the balls of her feet. Her cheek stung, a reminder to keep her eyes on her teacher's hands, or rather her Sifu. She had to call him Sifu during her lessons. Them's the rules. She really wanted to grit her teeth but the blow to her cheekbone still bled icy pain into her jaw.

Maya blocked her instructor's first strike with an effortless snap of her wrist. He was going easy on her. Which meant he'd bring out the big guns soon enough. She tested her jaw, moving it side to side as she circled him. Eye to eye. Hand to hand. She hoped eating wouldn't be a problem.

Two lightning fast moves later, she froze nose to skin with his fist. He'd spared her the full impact of the punch. And he wasn't usually that generous. Maya blinked, staring at his golden-brown eyes over the edges of his knuckles. Nope, not a hint of sympathy. Nothing.

She sank into her stance again and knew it would inevitably end in trouble. This time he used a smooth roundhouse kick, and whacked her feet from under her. The bone-shattering impact with the ground left Maya in stunned agony. Way worse after the blow to her cheekbone. Way worse when her head hit the floor so hard she almost passed out.

"Dad!" Maya cried, her voice filled with unshed tears and pain.

"Sorry, honey. Are you okay?" He peered at her, a cheeky grin pasted on his face. It wasn't fair when he did that. In fact, he got away with everything because of that stupid, lopsided grin. He pushed wet strands of hair from her cheeks, his fingers moving to her neck to check her pulse. "Maybe we should call it a day, okay?"

Er . . . like I'm going to actually say no? Really Dad? She nodded, and allowed him to help her to her feet. When her knees buckled he swung her smoothly into his arms.

So embarrassing.

Sixteen years old, and her father still carried her as if she weighed the same as she had ten years ago. But she let him, and just rested her head on his chest. This time she refused to fight him.

Teacher or not, next time he'd better watch out.

MAYA'S MOM fluffed up her pillows and smiled down at her daughter. "You'll be happy to know this injury will get you out of going to temple this week."

"Why is that? Wouldn't it be better to go and show all your friends you're bringing up your daughter the traditional, well-disciplined way?" The words were out and there was nothing she could do to take them back.

"Maya," her mom gasped. But the shock melted from her face as she sat on the edge of Maya's bed. "Honey, you know we haven't brought you up in the 'traditional' way. You wouldn't be learning to fight if we did."

"So why am I? You and dad can both see how terrible I am? Why don't you let me give it up?" Maya pouted, glad they'd moved on to another topic, a safe distance from her insults to her parents..

Her mom tucked her hair behind her ear; she'd always said

Maya shouldn't hide her pretty face behind her hair. "Because you must learn to protect yourself. We need to know that you have at least some ability to defend yourself. Just in case."

"In case of what? Somerville's probably the safest suburb in the state of California. Maybe even the whole of the western seaboard," Maya grumbled. Grabbing a cushion from beside her, she began to pull at the beaded tassels. She'd been training under her dad's tutelage since she was six years old. He'd been running the school ever since her parents arrived in America when Maya was just a baby.

"Well, you just never know-" a note of hesitation in her mom's voice drew Maya's gaze. Her mom opened her mouth to say something, but a moment later the urge seemed to subside and she went silent. Then she sighed and said, "You should send up a prayer or two." Maya stared as her mom pointed a finger to the ceiling. "You probably need all the help you can get especially with a black eye that bad."

"Mom,." Maya scolded, shocked she'd suggest such a thing. "You know what I think."

"Yes, honey. I know you don't believe now. But someday soon, you may no longer have a choice. Now, get some rest." Her mom stood, gently patted Maya's cheek before leaning over to kiss her forehead. Her waist length hair, so like Maya's, swayed as she walked out of the room. At the doorway she turned and winked at her daughter. "If you don't want the gods to help you, then you'd better be prepared to help yourself."

The door closed with a snick just as the cushion Maya had been playing with hit it. Maya shook her head, chuckling. Her mom always had a way with words. Although her parents had accepted she didn't fully believe in the theology of Hinduism, her mom never failed to try her luck at convincing her every so often. Still, she was thankful they didn't force her to perform all the rituals and customs. They were less orthodox than the other parents in the community, like her friend Ria's father. But they still maintained their belief in the gods.

It's merely mythology. Not actually real.

But when her mother looked at her that way, Maya had to wonder what it really took to believe.

CHAPTER 2

"*H*oly moly, what the heck happened to you?" Ria whispered as she traced the bluish-purple splotch on Maya's cheek. She hadn't even bothered to say 'hi', just barged in, plonked herself onto the bed and stared in morbid fascination at Maya's bruise. "It looks so painful. Does it hurt?"

Maya shook her head slightly, to avoiding hitting her throbbing cheek against her friend's exploring fingers. In the next moment, Ria pressed against the darkest, most painful part of the bruise.

"Ow!" Maya howled, unable to control the volume of her pain, struggling with the throbbing agony.

"What? I thought you said it didn't hurt." Ria tried to look innocent. And failed.

"Right. Why would I admit it hurts like a hot iron against my face?"

"Because it hurts, silly." Ria smiled, long dangling earrings sparkling, hair pulled neatly away from her face.

"Don't be such a girl. You're not supposed to admit that something is painful." Ria stared at Maya, confused and partly distracted by the striking bruise. "You're not supposed to admit to being weak. That's all I'm saying."

Ria shook her head. "But you aren't strong, so doesn't that make you weak?"

"Nope. I *am* strong. It's part of my training. And . . . because I say so."

"And the shiner? What does that say? That you lost a fight with your father's fist?"

"It says I'm brave, and courageous." Maya knew she was reaching. Knew the bruise made her look like a loser. She'd feel it more at school next week. "And it was my instructor's fist."

The argument was one they'd had time and time again. Even though they'd moved to America before she was born, Ria's parents had done a great job brainwashing her into thinking women were mere objects, meant to bear children for their husbands and certainly not meant to fight. Only men did that, and men were supposedly there for protection.

Ria snorted. "The bruise says you lost the fight. I say it spells weakness. Besides, girls shouldn't be fighting. Or learning to fight."

There she went again.

"And which male chauvinist told you that?" Maya pierced her friend with narrowed eyes. She wanted to ask what happened when Ria's father raised his hand against her, as he'd done all her life. Who protected her then? But Maya bit her tongue.

"My mother, you idiot." Her friend's kohl-lined eyes went flat. Maya knew a lie when she saw one.

Ria's dad was pure, unadulterated male chauvinism in a neat and tidy Indian package. Her poor mom would have been in deep trouble if she hadn't had a son after Ria. Thankfully, Ria's two little brothers served to remove the attention from her lack of maleness. God knew, they'd probably be arranging a marriage for her soon.

Just the thought made Maya want to grit her teeth again.

"Really, Maya. You and your dad should be more careful with your sparring sessions. Girls are not built to fight like guys. Look at what happened to you; a black eye? Are you seriously going to continue learning martial arts now?"

Maya nodded. "Yup, as soon as the bruise heals."

She hid a smile at the expression on Ria's face. Her friend's cheeks flamed and her eyes glittered. Boy was she mad, but instead of yelling at Maya as she usually did, she took a deep breath and looked out the window.

"Well, who am I to tell you how to take care of yourself when it's abundantly clear you're doing a perfectly good job on your own."

Maya heard the hurt in her friend's voice. And she understood. Ria just didn't want anything to happen to her. Of the two friends, Maya had always been stronger, and she'd always been the one to take care of Ria. Good thing their families attended the same temple so they saw a little more of each other at cultural functions. A little taste of Indian tradition in suburban America. Ria was the only reason Maya agreed to go to any of them.

"Ria." Maya waited for her friend to turn and face her. Then she smiled. "Thank you. For worrying about me and even for bossing me around."

That drew a small smile from Ria and she walked over to the bed to perch on its edge. "Promise me you'll take care of yourself? Please."

Maya nodded. "Pinky swear."

Ria giggled and both girls locked pinkies and smiled at each other for a moment.

"It's getting late. Let's go." Maya pulled her hair around her face, hoping the fall of black curls would hide her cheekbones until they got into the darkened movie theater.

～

"Hey, you two. You've been let out on parole?" Maya and Ria turned to make space for Joss as she snuck under the red plastic barrier.

"Hey." Both girls smiled and Maya waited. Joss was sure to have an interesting reaction to the bruise.

"Woah! What the hell happened to you?" Joss's eyes narrowed, as if she expected Maya to come up with some fantastic lie, reminding Maya that Joss hadn't turned up for class so she'd missed the knockout session.

Joss, or Jocelyn Cawood, a name she loved to ignore, had joined Dev Rao's martial arts school two years ago and Maya often enjoyed a sparring session with her friend. She also enjoyed a good dose of envy as Joss seemed to pick stuff up so much faster than Maya.

"Sparring accident. I wasn't concentrating. Didn't duck fast enough." Maya moved backwards, tilting her head so her hair covered most of her face.

"Sheesh." Joss wrinkled her nose and leaned closer. "Does it hurt as bad as it looks?"

Maya shrugged, not eager to continue the discussion with so many people around. Turning to face the cashier, she caught sight of Nik standing in the next line, and whipped her head away, hoping he hadn't seen her staring.

Lately, she'd been seeing Nik around far too much. Not that she minded. She saw a confidence in his eyes, like he was stronger than he looked, and sometimes like he knew more than he let on. He managed to fit in and yet stand out all at the same time. His crooked smile and those broad shoulders were certainly easy on the eye.

A quick glance back at him revealed he'd spotted her. And he stared at her, the slightest hint of a grin at his lips. Ugh! Lips she had no right even thinking about.

He took a tiny step toward her, his mouth opening as if he meant to say something, but the line moved ahead and Maya followed, ignoring Nik and whatever he'd been about to say. She didn't have a chance in hell with a guy like him. Besides, she was here for movies, not boys.

～

THE MOVIE ENDED up being lame. A slasher flick which made Maya want to laugh hysterically instead of scream. Whatever happened to her normal human reaction to scary stuff? None of it seemed scary to her, although her friends both screamed on cue.

Exiting the theatre, the three girls slowed to a stop as Joss's cellphone vibrated. While Joss dug into her pocket, Maya scanned the crowds surging from the doors of the cinema for one tall, dark-headed form, trying to appear nonchalant.

"Hey, you guys wanna go to Amber's party Saturday night?" Joss said after checking her texts.

"I didn't know we were invited." Maya kept her voice bland and uninterested. Ria stiffened beside her.

Ria never went to parties. She wasn't ever allowed.

Maya hardly went either. She hated the cool parties.

She rarely received an invitation to any of them and even if she did go she wasn't part of the popular crowd. Besides, it was too much of an effort to fit in. Too much of an effort to pretend to be something she wasn't.

And, under no circumstances did Maya qualify as cool.

So, when Joss tossed Maya her cellphone to read Amber Alden's text invitation, there were two reasons she didn't want to go.

Her ghastly bruise would still be around. Who'd want to pitch up looking like someone had used her as a punching bag?

And because she wouldn't fit in with Amber's crowd. She didn't feel up to making such a huge effort. Didn't feel up to inventing some elaborate cover story just to get out of the house.

Didn't feel up to pretending she understood what went on in Amber's pretty dark head to even bother to extend the invitation to Ria and Maya.

Too hard.

Maya handed back the phone and shook her head.

"Aw, come on Maya. You cannot seriously be telling me you plan to snub the only invitation you have ever - and I will repeat - ever received from Amber." Joss's voice almost broke.

This was one of the times Maya wondered why her blonde, blue-eyed friend even bothered to spend any time with them. Sure, they'd been together since kindergarten but Joss had always been popular, while Maya and Ria were, and always would be, outcast.

But Joss was right. Being ostracized almost always began with a 'No'. And since Maya and Ria had absolutely zero chance of obtaining permission to join the cheer-leading squad - with all those tiny little skirts revealing the girls *thighs* for everyone to see - they couldn't risk declining.

"I'll help you pick something to wear if you like?" Joss offered, smiling, already knowing she'd beaten Maya into submission.

"Fine, I'll make a plan. And thanks for the offer, but I think I can figure out what to wear all by myself." Maya relented, but she had a feeling this was a bad idea.

Maybe the years of being told how bad modern society was had ingrained itself in Maya's consciousness. All those years being told by her family how easily a girl could ruin her reputation, and lose her precious chance of finding a decent husband. Or maybe Maya's conscience was stronger than her need to rebel.

In the end, she knew it was a bad idea. A very bad idea.

CHAPTER 3

*B*etween the inventive lies to her parents and the multiple wardrobe changes, and the repeated attempts to hide the fading, but still hideous, purple and yellow bruise on her cheek, Maya was exhausted even before she arrived at Amber Alden's mansion. Everything about the place, including its clean modern lines and miles and miles of glass, screamed Maya didn't belong. The threatening wrought iron gates, the curving stone driveway. Even the door at the entrance opened out wide enough for a semi to pass through.

And yet here she was.

Her stomach rolled.

Some huge butterflies there. Maya still wondered about Amber's reasons for inviting her. But she didn't linger on those thoughts. The house vibrated; laughter and music making the ground rumble beneath her feet.

At the last minute, she'd donned a pair of dark blue jeans and a strappy sequined top that belonged to a fancy Indian outfit. A bit raunchy, but Bollywood set the trend and if she wore Indian attire it was okay to display everything from below the boobs to the hips. But not thighs. Or knees. Even ankles were semi-taboo, depending on who made the rules.

Someone swayed past. A guy, hands tattooed all the way to his black painted fingernails, held the wall for support. Maya watched him stumble into the garden, retch and fall straight into a blooming rose bush. Her stomach did a nosedive. *Nobody mentioned anything about alcohol.*

A voice in her head laughed at her, the sound echoing in her mind. *So what am I? Naive? Stupid? Of course, there's alcohol. It's a popular party, rich kids, college students.* Maya sighed, walked through the enormous doorway and promised herself she was going to take this opportunity by the horns.

Whatever that meant.

She paused, lost in a huge hallway, lost in her decision to enter this place, and totally losing the argument against staying. Fortunately, within the next few seconds, Joss rushed in through a small set of doors and things began to look up a bit.

"Hey, you made it." Joss grinned, her tongue-bar peeking at Maya, reflecting the light in a slightly macabre déjà vu kind of way

Relief flooded Maya's veins. Was she so insecure that the mere sight of Joss made her relax? Joss, the bearer of Amber's special invitation, the reason Maya was here in the first place. The reason she'd lied to her parents, who now believed she and Joss were having a little innocent sleepover at Joss's cavernous, empty house.

Joss slung her arm around Maya's shoulder and pulled her into the kitchen, waving her hand at nothing and everything in the chrome and cherry-wood room. "Get a drink, whatever you like."

The bench-top overflowed with every alcoholic drink under the sun. The myriad colors were pretty in a barbaric kind of way. A large silver pedal bin stood beneath a refuse rainbow, filled to the brim, dozens of empty bottles strewn beside it.

Maya tread water in the sea of her ignorance.

But Joss came to her rescue, handing her a glass of blue booze. Maya tried to sip the contents with an air of nonchalance, hoping to exude experience. No such luck. She obliterated the effect when she choked and spluttered on the first sip. She cleared her throat and took a good swallow. The blue heat seared its way down her throat and she struggled for air and struggled to swallow and couldn't believe she'd sunk to such a terrible low.

Rules, rules, breaking all the rules. Liquid heat gouged burning fingernails all the way to her stomach.

"Thanks," Maya said, the word scorching in the wake of the blue blaze. *Wait. What am I to be thankful for again? Suicide by internal first-degree burns?*

Searing flames licked her insides, sensuous and languorous and so hot.

She blinked and gasped.

"No problem," Joss said. She giggled before slugging a deep red drink, a drink too red, too thick, and Maya felt her throat close. "Amber left these for us. Said they were a special 'thank you' for accepting her invitation."

"Nice of her." Maya rolled her eyes, feeling them wobble. Amber didn't inspire even the slightest bit of affection in her and no gift, alcoholic or otherwise, could warm her heart towards Miss Popularity.

"Yeah. Very nice of her. See, I told you Amber was nice," said Joss nodding so hard her blonde locks fell forward almost hiding her pretty oval face.

Maya glared at her, eyes narrowed, but Joss paid little attention. Joss shoved her hair out of her face and her words tumbled over her swollen lips, swollen words swirling like the liquid in her glass. Joss swayed, her turbulent balance at odds with the unmoving floor. She swept a glance around the room, eyes glazed, reality glazed, nodded for no apparent reason, and then dragged a stool to the counter almost tipping herself and it over each other. She shoved a few bottles aside to make room for her elbows.

A mean chill constricted Maya's gut, a chill with a knife-edge of fear. Here, in this strange house overflowing with kids who were almost nasty, always indifferent, and Maya's one ally swayed before her, wasted. Sixteen and wasted for god's sake. The tiny thrill of excitement she'd experienced on entering the party had long since faded, consumed by reality one intoxicating drop at a time.

Maya blinked and lost focus and missed a breath. Strange, inexplicable warmth licked at muscles now too relaxed, too calm. Heat filled her body, a heady awareness of soft limbs and melting bone, and the odd and distant thunder rumbling beneath her ribs and in her skull. Fire broke the floodgates, and burned a gentle path to Maya's fingertips, and left a thrum in her ears and in her heart and in her throat.

Maya shook her head. *No, I won't allow anything to spoil this for me.* She blinked away the heaviness in her eyelids, and tensed her upper arms, but they felt wrong. A heavy sleepy sludge had invaded her muscles, had pushed through her defenses. She gasped, gripped by a sudden wave of fear, but no sound left her twisting throat.

"Joss." Maya shook Joss's arm as her friend's eyelids drooped and she began to slide off the stool. Joss's eyes shot open. She stared at Maya, and stared more. All blank innocence and cheerful smiles, though she failed to hide the fleeting confusion, the equally fleeting suspicion. "You don't have to shout. I can hear you just fine."

Maya deliberated, chewed her lip, and scanned the kitchen. She stared through the gap in the doorway opening on a dark and sweaty, heaving throng. Bass shook the house, hammered the walls and throbbed beneath her ribs.

She had to get Joss out. A house full of drunken kids was no place for a teenage girl to pass out. Maya wanted to release the laughter building in her throat. Wanted it all to be terribly funny, funny because her judgment had let her down so badly. Wanted the gnawing teeth in her gut to be wrong. But her instinct refused to back down. And, right then, Joss's safety outweighed Maya's suspicions.

Getting Joss home should be easy.

Getting Joss home would have been easy, had Maya been in full possession of all her faculties.

Tingling.

That was it. Her entire body, fingertips included, tingled as if millions of tiny fire-ants were kissing every inch of her skin.

The ants themselves would have been bearable, but the way the kitchen twisted and tilted affected Maya more. The floor bucked beneath her feet and her throat contracted. The ants and the twisting scared her. Terrified her. Maya's glass sat on the counter, blue melting ice cubes reflected the bland kitchen fluorescent light.

What the hell was in that drink?

Blood thundered in her ears as Maya tried her best to keep focused. Joss had been drinking the cocktail far longer than her. Made sense she'd be far more under the dubious influence of the drink. Alcohol. Definitely alcohol. Nice-tasting stuff, if you went for stuff like that, but alcohol nevertheless.

I'm so dead when I get home. Maya's dad had the nostrils of a shark - he could smell lies, fear and alcohol within a five mile radius.

So dead.

Half-walking half-carrying Joss, Maya made it to her car, maneuvering her semi-conscious friend into the back seat. She almost dropped Joss twice as her fingers began to lose all feeling. Thank goodness for the old blanket she kept in the car. Usually fulfilling its purpose at the park or beside the river, it now covered her silly, intoxicated friend, hiding her in darkness and shadows.

Maya straightened.

Too quickly.

Blood rushed to her head, and the world continued its spinning even though she was pretty sure both feet were still on the ground. Maya swallowed several times, gulping, hoping to hold onto the contents of her stomach. She suspected that, in itself, wasn't a good idea considering the contents of her stomach were causing all her problems.

She had one foot inside the car, about to get in and drive Joss home when strong fingers dug into her arm, the points of sharp nails driving their vicious edges into her bare skin.

"Where are you going, Maya? You just got here," Amber said, her voice sweet and cloying, the black ringlets of her hair glistening in the garden lights. Her almond eyes gleamed, and Maya wondered where in the ancestry Amber proudly traced all the way back to the wilds of Kenya, had there been an injection of Asian eyes.

"So, where is Joss?" Maya blinked as Amber's voice simmered, so mellow and so gentle Maya would have missed the pure deceit if it weren't for the slightest tightening of the girl's dark eyes, and the strength of her grip on Maya's arm.

"No idea. I couldn't find her." The lie flowed, so smooth and believable, off Maya's tongue. Amber's gaze flicked to the passenger seat then back to Maya's face.

Maya took a breath to steady herself and caught a whiff of the strangest scent she'd ever smelled in her life. Something between warm blood and spices. The rich coppery odor churned her stomach again, and this time it threatened to free its contents. Ugh! The stink of rotting meat clawed at her gut. Maya was no vegetarian, but this stench, this concentration of raw-flesh scent, lodged at the back of her throat and filling her nostrils, made her dizzy with nausea.

Fear doused Maya's hope of getting Joss home. Strange. Why was Amber objecting to her leaving? Maya, the unimportant kid, who went ignored most of the time. Instinct told her to pull away from Amber's grip, but a weird heat filtered through her. The alcohol, no doubt.

Maya blinked. A tingling warmth spread from Amber's flesh into her own body. And suddenly Maya wanted to laugh at how ridiculous she was being. It occurred to her how judgmental she was being of Amber. *I'm so incredibly lucky to be invited in the first place. Joss would be okay sleeping it off in the car, wouldn't she?* While the world righted itself inch by painful inch, Maya smiled. *Amber might actually be a very nice person after all.*

Maya blinked again- struggling with thoughts in her head that didn't seem right. *What is wrong with me?*

She swallowed again. Hard.

Maya squeezed her eyes shut, then snapped them open when everything around her began to spin while her stomach spun in the opposite direction.

Okay, eyes wide open is the safest bet.

She let Amber walk her back into the house. And smiled a fake smile at Amber, still wondering at her sudden change in attitude. Then Maya admonished herself. She shouldn't be so ungrateful; the girl had welcomed her into her home after all. Hadn't she just furthered Maya's position in the popularity stakes with her generous invitation?

Of course, going with Amber wasn't a bad idea.

*M*aya stepped into the foyer, swallowing a bubble of nervous excitement. Nik leaned against a wall near the stairs, dark hair curling onto his shoulders. His nonchalant slouch didn't fool her. His black eyes stared right through her as if he knew something she didn't.

Her Nik-based musings were short-lived as Amber tightened her grip, steering her to the left. Maya avoided Nik's gaze and turned, submitting to Amber's direction. And found herself staring right into the brightest blue eyes she'd ever seen. Electric blue and purely predatory. She knew him from school. One of the kids who always hung around with Amber. Someone's boyfriend or ex-boyfriend or something. He had those searching eyes that made her want to take a long, long shower.

Amber pushed her toward the guy. "Maya. Meet Byron. Byron, Maya's going to *entertain* you this evening." Her words and her tone sent shivers up and down Maya's spine. Byron grinned. *Yeah, definitely one of the guys who always gets what he wants.* The gleam in his eyes spelled a whole lot of danger.

He snaked his arm around Maya's waist. She drew on her

inner strength just to control the urge to shudder. His hand lay cool, serpentine against the stress-induced heat of her own skin.

Skin which crawled at the contact.

He *felt* venomous. Even his blue eyes seemed unnatural. All wrong. And he was also under the mistaken impression he had the right to touch her, hold her. A ripple of fear skittered up her spine, soft thunder, ominous and unrelenting.

"Come on, baby. Why don't we go outside? A little fresh air?" He had to shout over the music blasted from various speakers dotting the living rooms on either side of the foyer. He squeezed Maya to his hip. A message. He was simply not taking no for an answer.

"Listen, bud. I don't think so." Maya stepped away from the odious boy, shrugging him off even as he reached to pull her back, his fingers closing around her arm like talons, digging sharp and deep. She stared down at his fingers but his hand was just a hand. Yet her skin screamed with pure agony as if five knives dug their way into her flesh. She shook her head, swaying on her feet.

Hallucinations? Not good. Not good at all.

"Maya, Maya. Come on. Why are you acting like a kid? This *is* a big kid's party." Amber still stood beside her, watching them with steely grey eyes. Cold and metallic, they shone a dull silver. How had she never registered Amber's strange eyes? She'd thought they were dark, but she must have been mistaken.

Amber leaned closer, the meat and smoky, spicy scent engulfing Maya. The stench drowned her thoughts and stole her senses, leaving her to deal with another wave of nausea.

Amber spoke into her ear, loud but not so loud anyone else would be able to hear. An island of privacy within a crowd. "Why don't you keep Byron *company*? Or I might have to go search for Joss. She's missing all the fun. I know a few guys here who think she's pretty hot."

Maya stared back into Amber's metallic eyes. The subtle threat lurked beneath her innocent words. Clear enough.

Go with Byron.

Or Joss is in deep shit.

Whatever happened tonight, Maya couldn't leave without endangering Joss as well. Blood thundered in her head. A waterfall of rapid and terrifying reality, so loud she barely heard Amber's coy giggle as a trio of cheerleaders passed by, whispering into Amber's ear as they went. Barely registered Amber bump into her as the girls hugged each other and moved on.

Maya's heart tightened when she understood the silent warning in the flirtatious sound, the steely threat in Amber's eyes as they held hers for the barest moment. *Have fun or else.*

Then, Byron's cold arm snaked around her waist for the second time. His fingers sank into the soft skin at her hip, with just a hint of super-sharp penetration. Maya looked down at her hand, now red from Byron's grip. The surface intact, not broken, not bleeding as she'd expected. Fear was making her imagination go wild.

This time she couldn't shrug him off. Couldn't run. Terror ensnared her. No point even trying to defend herself against the cold creep. No point going over all the moves in her mind. Heel into instep. Punch to groin. Gouge eyes. Whatever.

None of it mattered.

Maya's breath came in small puffs. Standing in the hall, being groped by Byron, she scanned the two rooms, left and right. Nik was gone. Would he have saved her anyway? This was his crowd, and she was the outsider.

"Come. Let's go outside," Byron spoke in her ear. His voice loud and cutting. His breath moved across her cheek, hot and fetid. Worse than alcohol. Like something had crawled in there and died a long time ago. Maya shuddered and winced as his lips touched her temple.

The cold softness freaked her out.

He pulled her through the dark, crowded room, jostling dancers and couples in various stages of making out. Maya tensed, but the lack of light wasn't the reason for the sense of darkness creeping into her bones. Perhaps it was the intense spicy bloody odor still coiling around her, but something was wrong. Maya's heart pounded harder. She knew Byron had felt her pulse race when he threw her a knowing smile that curled at the corner of his lip, and said volumes as his thumb dug into her waist, then drew small circles on her skin.

Outside, the air bathed Maya's face, welcoming, and fresh. But she still smelled spicy blood with every breath she took. Byron pulled her to a lounger at the pool and sat, tugging her hard to sit beside him. His silence rippled along her spine sending slivers of fear into her bones. Fear that intensified when he smiled. He placed his hand on her knee and Maya jumped.

She shot to her feet.

Had to make an excuse. Anything to get out of there. *Am I seriously contemplating going through this for Joss?*

"Er . . . I think I need to use the bathroom." Maya turned to walk back into the house when Byron grabbed her arm, digging deeper into her flesh. Hard enough to surely leave bruises.

"There's a bathroom in the pool-house. It's closer." He knew. He stared at her, eyes flat. Maya was stumped. No way out, so she trailed after him.

What now?

Safely inside, Maya lowered herself to the edge of the large bathtub. Her hands and knees shook. Maybe if she called her dad or her mom. She considered the possibility of permanent grounding a better choice than what surely lay ahead of her. Maya dug in her bag for her cellphone but came up empty. Where had she left it? The damned phone had definitely been in her bag the entire time.

An image flitted through her head. Amber bumping into her when the cheerleaders had passed them in the hall. Amber pressing close to her, as if they were best buddies. Maya's heart plummeted.

Amber had taken the phone.

Byron banged on the door, scaring the living crap out of her. Maya gripped her handbag within stricken fingers.

"What's taking you so long? Do I need to call Amber?" Byron growled.

Maya stalked to the door and flung it open. She had every intention of shoving past him and getting the hell away. Joss would still be in the car so if she ran fast enough she'd get there before Byron.

Byron was ready for her.

Maya tried to run past him, but he slammed his palm into her chest. She stumbled backward, her hip hitting the basin with a solid thwack. Her body ached but her gaze remained on Byron. He kept his head down, looking at her out of the top of his eyes. Like a bull, readying himself to charge straight at her. She expected smoke to rise from his nose soon.

The scent of blood and spice floated thick on the air. Cloying. Maya felt like she was drowning just on the odor. Her heart beat faster than anything she'd ever experienced. Sweat beaded on her forehead. Her hands shook and burned with an inexplicable, spreading heat. And the strange and unfamiliar sensation coursing within her veins? Adrenaline or fear?

Byron closed the distance between them in the blink of an eye. His hand spread around her neck before Maya could move. Before she could think. Even before she realized there was nowhere to go. He lifted her by the throat, her feet dangling at least a foot off the floor.

He was so strong, so frighteningly strong. His fingers dug deep. Maya tried to cough.

Tried to breathe.

Darkness enveloped her, thick smoky darkness shrouded her. Hazy. She kicked her useless feet. Ragged jerky movements. She was going to pass out. Then she'd be at Byron's mercy. No way. Not happening. But the flickerings of unconsciousness began to seep into the edges of her vision.

Fear streamed through her and then, with the last reserves of energy, she kicked hard at Byron's knee. Hard enough to break it. A satisfying crack echoed across the tiled bathroom. Byron hunched over his knee, releasing his grip on her throat. Maya gasped, sucking air into her starved lungs, stumbling away from him, but he growled. Like a rabid animal.

Fear spun Maya around on stricken feet. Facing her attacker, she could see his next move. He barreled straight at her. And for all her training, she did the one thing her dad always said never to do. She ducked her head and hid her face, hands out, as if she could fend off this vicious attacker merely with her bare palms.

Maya sensed the heat on her skin before she saw it.

Byron was on fire. A living column of shimmering orange flames. She couldn't breathe. Was afraid to breathe. *How did that happen?* She glanced around the bathroom as panic filled her veins, her fear taking on a whole new level of hysteria. She had to put the fire out. She edged around Byron as he clawed at the melting skin of his face. She reached the basin and hesitated. *Was water really the best thing to douse the flames? Would I do him more harm than good?*

She turned to the faucet and froze. In the mirror, she watched the burning reflection of Byron disappear. He was there one moment and gone the next, only a few burnt shards of fabric left to say he'd even existed.

Maya gasped as she remembered the last thing she'd seen before Byron became nothing: brilliant blue eyes turning a frighteningly blood-red.

And Nik, holding the doorknob, staring at the empty space on the floor behind her.

CHAPTER 5

*B*efore Maya could think of a good excuse, Nik grabbed her shoulder giving her a rough little shake, his eyes tight with concern. The room had begun to take on a nice fuzzy darkness, while little spots of starlights sparked at the edge of her vision. Perhaps he was more observant than she was. It was probably a bad idea to faint here in the pool-house bathroom; right after Byron disappeared in a column of fiery flames. Nik seemed to know this too.

Maya's clothes hung in tatters where Byron had grabbed at her, her face swollen where he'd hit her hard enough to knock her into next Tuesday. She winced at the pain lancing through her ribs. Had Byron cracked them where he'd slammed his beefy forearm into her? He certainly hadn't felt the need to hold back.

She frowned. Wanted to figure out what the hell just happened. Why Byron had attacked her was easily answered. But why he'd disappeared wreathed in flames still remained a mystery.

Nik's warm arms offered comfort, but Maya rejected him, shoving at his hands, needing her space, needing air. He shook her again. And at last, she started to breathe.

"No time for you to hyper-ventilate or go hysterical on me okay?" Nik spoke softly in Maya's ear, keeping her upright with a firm arm gripping her waist. He leaned her against the wash-basin, shrugged off his jacket and wrapped the warm leather around her shoulders. "We have to get you out of here as quickly and quietly as possible."

"You followed us here?" Maya frowned, her brain foggy from near asphyxiation. She blinked and concentrated on Nik, pretty sure she hadn't seen him creeping around after them. And maybe she was concentrating on him too much because suddenly all she wanted was to rest her cheek against his oh-so-inviting chest.

Get a grip Maya.

Nik's voice broke through her forbidden thoughts. "I was trying to keep an eye on you. Then you both disappeared and I had to search the house. It took me too long to get here. I'm sorry."

He fingered the bruise on her throbbing cheek. Good thing her dad's shiner remained well hidden beneath layers of makeup or she'd have a matching pair. One of these days she just had to stop this habit of getting punched in the face.

"Can you walk?"

Maya stared at Nik not sure if her legs would hold her, wanting to ask for help, but wondering why Nik even bothered. Was this another con to take advantage of her, another trick a la Amber? Right this minute, she refused to accept his kindness, if that's what it was. Maya stiffened within Nik's grasp.

"You have to try. It would attract too much attention if I had to carry you. And we really need to get moving. Amber could be looking for the two of you even now."

The heated urgency in Nik's voice seemed too real, too visceral to be an act. He ran his long fingers through his hair, making it stand up at all angles. And even though her heart hammered because of Byron's attack, she had to tamp down the urge to run her own fingers through Nik's hair and fix the mess.

What the hell is wrong with you, Maya?

"I'm sure I can manage," she finally responded, her voice dry and dead. No way was she letting him carry her. And the thought of Amber chilled her to the bone. The girl had deliberately set her up. What kind of person does something like that? Maya didn't want to think about what could have happened if Byron hadn't turned into a six-foot wall of flame.

She pushed Nik back, standing upright, forcing her gelatinous muscles to bear her weight. She stared down at the ruined fabric of her top. One strap hung broken, ripped at the seam. Beads had unraveled everywhere, turning the beautifully intricate patterns into a mess of bare fabric, partial patterns and random blobs of the remaining beading. She'd left her jacket in the car and she'd have to accept Nik's if she intended to make it out of the house without drawing attention to her state of disrepair.

Maya scanned the bathroom for her handbag, then retrieved it from where it had landed beside the toilet, pulled the strap over her shoulder and gave her reflection a cursory glance. She ran her hands through her thick straight black hair. There, now she was presentable. Sort of.

If she moved quickly, maybe nobody would see her. Maybe. She turned and marched out of the room, out of the poolhouse. Nik remained by her side, keeping up with her.

"Smile," he said, as his eyes flicked to the door to the living room still packed with music and dancers. "You're supposed to be having a good time here."

He threw an arm over her shoulder. Maya pasted a grin on her face, knowing she probably looked quite maniacal, and not caring in the least. She didn't feel much like smiling. Not after the whole Byron thing. Not while Nik's arm remained around her, so close she breathed in the scent of him.

She scanned Nik's face. *Why is he helping me? What were his motives?* But he was helping her to get out of Amber's house.

Away from the horror of Byron's remains in the pool house, if papery blackened bits counted as remains.

"Thank you," she said to Nik, meeting his eyes straight on. "For helping me."

He shrugged, scanning the garden, his shoulders stiff, muscles tense. "Don't thank me yet. We still have to get the hell out of here."

They turned and walked past the pool, entering the dark throbbing mass of bodies inside the front room. The music pounded and darkness embraced the writhing bodies filling the room, hiding those who lounged at the edge of the dance floor. Despite its comforting veil, fear bubbled in Maya's veins. What if Amber or one of her minions saw them?

But they made it outside without incident, shutting the monstrous door behind them, leaving behind the music and the mayhem. At the car, Maya sighed and leaned against the vehicle, relieved to see Joss still passed out in the back seat. So Amber hadn't known where she was after all.

She'd played Maya from the start. Anger rose within Maya's gut and her fists clenched. But there was no point being furious with Amber now. Not that she was likely to run on back inside and punch out the girl's lights in revenge. Better to leave now.

Maya was about to get into the driver's seat when Nik put a hand on her arm and stopped her. "I'll drive. You're in no shape to get behind the wheel, anyway."

She glared at him, taking in the strain around his eyes, the hard set to his chin, as if he'd seen something that pissed him off and he was just reigning in the anger. Maya scowled. She didn't really care what he was thinking. Right now, she wasn't in the mood to be babied.

She shrugged his hand off. "I'm not drunk!"

"Maybe you're not drunk but you *are* in shock." Nik's face remained clear, his expression firm. "I don't mind. I'll drop you at home and take a walk back to my place."

A sudden weariness overtook Maya. Why bother fighting when all he was doing was helping? She sighed, scrambled over the gearshift and buckled up, keeping an eye on the doors to Amber's house. They remained shut, but she imagined Amber and her accomplices would come pouring out at any moment, to prevent them from getting away.

Such a drama-queen thought. But after the evening she'd just had, Maya suspected it was a real possibility.

She watched Nik, her arms leaden, her heart still throbbing and hurting, as he backed the car out of the space and drove through the gates. "Not that I don't appreciate it or anything, but why are you helping me? We barely know each other." Maya had noticed Nik the day he arrived at Couldrey Hunt High. And maybe it had been her imagination but she felt certain he'd noticed her too, considering it had taken him mere days to enroll at her dad's martial arts studio.

"You needed help. And it was clear nobody else there would bother to help you. Everyone is too concerned with what Amber can do for their social status." A hint of anger showed through in his voice, his fingers tightening on the steering wheel.

His words rang true but there was something beneath them. What wasn't he telling her? Then a memory slipped into place. Still fresh and horrific but enough to beg questions.

"You weren't surprised were you?" Maya asked, her narrowed gaze trained on Nik, but all she got was a cute Nik frown for her efforts. "When you stood at the bathroom doorway…you weren't surprised to see him burning."

Her voice lowered to almost a whisper. "Nik? What just happened? What happened to Byron?"

She stared out the window, wrapping her arms around her icy body. It wasn't a cold night but ice settled on her skin, seeping into her flesh and bones, seeping slowly into her heart. The darkness made a mirror out of the window and she saw a frightened, injured girl staring back at her.

"Can I please get hysterical now?"

Nik chuckled.

"What was it? Some sort of spontaneous combustion thing?" Maya asked, desperate to know why Byron had attacked her, both physically and emotionally. Though she'd tried to defend herself, she'd been helpless. Then he'd disappeared in a burst of flame.

"It's worse than that," came Nik's dry response.

"You're crazy. What could possibly be worse than spontaneous combustion?" she asked, shaking her head.

"Nope, not crazy. I just know what I saw."

"Which was?" Her question held more than a hint of a challenge. As if she dared him to make up some ridiculously unbelievable story.

"It was you. You killed him."

CHAPTER 6

A thick silence followed as Maya stared at Nik incredulously.

"Now I know you're crazy. What the hell do you think I am? Some kind of fire-wielding magician or something?" Maya laughed, the sound high-pitched and almost painful.

And suddenly she didn't want to stop laughing. But something told her if she started she probably wouldn't be able to stop. So she clamped her mouth shut and gnawed at the inside of her cheek.

"Something like that." Not the response she'd expected. Or wanted. He was supposed to say she was being silly.

"This is not funny, you know," Maya said.

Anger slowly built up inside her. Sure, he'd saved her sorry hide but did he really think she'd accept his ridiculous explanation? That she can burn things up at the drop of her hand?

"I'm not joking. You need to speak to your parents about it." Nik held her gaze, his eyes dark, foreboding, and insistent.

"Are you insane?"

Telling her parents would mean she'd have to admit she'd

gone to the party. They thought she was at Joss's watching old movies and eating marshmallows like they used to do eons ago.

Nik's eyes narrowed as he studied her face. "I take it your parents have no idea where you are right now."

"Really? You really think my parents would've given me a free pass to go to this kind of party? No freakin' way. Besides, it isn't any of your business. We don't even know each other." Maya crossed her arms and stared out of the window again, avoiding his all-knowing eyes.

"It's my business because I'm going to take you home after we drop off Joss."

"Look, I appreciate your help but-"

"Hey, what's going on?" Joss groaned as she sat up in the back seat. She stared from Maya to Nik and back again. "Maya, what's Nik doing driving your car? And what am I doing here?"

"You were wasted. I put you in the car to sleep it off," Maya bit back, still annoyed Joss hadn't had the sense to control her alcohol.

"But I barely had anything to drink." Joss frowned, and Maya knew she was searching her memory trying to recall the drinks she'd consumed. Then Joss nodded, blue eyes still unfocused. "Yup, some kind of juice, then the drink Amber gave me. I wanted your first big party to be fun. Really. I didn't drink enough to be so drunk I'd pass out."

"Who made the drinks?" asked Nik softly.

Joss's eyes filled with tears of horror as the magnitude of what had happened sank in. "Amber."

"So Amber drugged Joss so she could get to me?" Maya asked Nik. "What did she want with me?"

"What are you two talking about? What happened to you?" Joss leaned forward shaking Maya's shoulder.

"Amber found me at the car and stopped me from leaving. She threatened you. And forced me to go with Byron." Maya kept her voice expressionless. She still felt dead inside thinking about what could have happened.

"She what? What happened, Maya? Please tell me he didn't-"

"No, he didn't do anything to me. Just punched me up a bit. And Nik saved me." Maya looked at Nik who seemed to understand she didn't want Joss to know about Byron's fiery exit.

"I'm so sorry, Maya. So sorry." Joss sobbed, tears rolling down her cheeks. "If I hadn't convinced you to go this wouldn't have happened."

"It's nobody's fault, Joss. You couldn't know what Amber was up to." Maya spoke the words but knew deep down she did lay some of the blame at Joss's feet.

And of course, some of it lay at her own. Hadn't she been the one so excited about the party she'd hardly slept, had changed her clothing at least fifteen times? No, not only Joss's fault.

"We'll drop you off first, then Nik will take me home."

Joss nodded. "Okay, but weren't you supposed to stay with me tonight?"

"I think Maya needs to go home and at least put some ice on her cheek." Nik examined Joss in the rear view mirror.

"What happened?" she asked and gasped as Maya turned toward her to show off Byron's handiwork. "Ohmygod. Did Byron do that? Wait until I get my hands on that loser."

Maya turned in her seat. "And what will you do? Punch him? Put a hit on him? Drive-by shooting maybe? Oh wait, maybe burn him at the stake?" Fury surged through her veins. "You go home and get some rest. God knows what they put in your drink. I'm going home. I think I may need to see a doctor too."

"Where else do you hurt?" Nik asked, frowning.

Maya ran her hand gently along her ribs. "Here, somewhere."

Before Nik responded Joss asked sharply "What's wrong with your ribs?"

"Byron punched me in my abdomen and chest. I think he may have broken one of my ribs."

"You have any trouble breathing?" Nik asked.

"I can breathe fine most of the time. Just every now and then I struggle to take a deep breath."

"Breathe deeply in and out. Slowly. If you can't breathe properly you may have a punctured lung and we'd have to take you straight to the hospital."

Maya did as she was told. Thankfully, it seemed her lungs were intact. For now.

A few minutes later, they dropped off Joss, waiting until she got safely inside her house. The silence in the car hung heavy between Nik and Maya. And deep in that silence, she wondered again why he was helping her.

Even though Maya had spent plenty of time sneaking peeks at Nik and nurturing her little crush, the truth was they hardly knew each other in the first place. It took only a few more minutes to get Maya home. A few more minutes of deep silence. A few more minutes of wondering if she was making a big mistake by going home.

Nik got out of the car and waited for her to come around. Maya took the keys, locked the car, and stood staring at him as she clutched her handbag to her ruined top. He stared back. Said nothing. She wanted to say thank you, wanted him to stay and comfort her again. She was beginning to miss the warmth of his arm around her, supporting her.

Then he turned and walked off.

"Tell them," Nik called out over his shoulder as he disappeared down the street toward his house.

Maya braced herself and walked to the entrance. She froze before the door, her hand refusing to slip the key into the lock. Panic surged through her.

How could she tell her Mom and Dad the whole story and live through seeing the disappointment in their eyes? She wondered if she should avoid talking about this evening at all.

But the decision was taken out of her hands when the door to her house opened as she was about to unlock it.

She swallowed hard and stared straight into her father's eyes.

"Maya?" Dev Rao eyed his daughter, a worried frown marring his forehead. "Is Joss okay?"

"Yeah Dad, Joss's fine," Maya said, suddenly exhausted as adrenaline fled her body. She walked into the darkened house and stood in the foyer. Her muscles tightened and instinct told her to head for her room. Just leave it and go to bed. Maybe it's better left for the morning. Maybe she would see things differently in the bright light of a new day.

"Are you okay, honey?"

"Yes. I'm fine. I just wanted to come home. That's all."

Maya moved to the staircase hoping to make a quick getaway. Big mistake. A shaft of light from the street lamp at the curb shone into the foyer. And onto her bruised cheek.

"Maya."

Her dad's golden brown eyes looked darker than usual, his voice loud and stern. When he got like this there was no getting away. Maya sighed and turned to him, knowing he'd be reaching for the light-switch.

The hall-light blazed. Maya's dad took her chin in his hand, his fingers stiff and yet gentle. He turned her face to study the imprint of Byron's fist. She swallowed hard. No getting out of it now.

"Dad, I need to talk to you and Mom. Now." Maya's voice broke on the last word. All the stress and fear of the day threatened to overwhelm her. Threatened to turn her into a bawling mess.

Maya's dad threw her a worried glance, ran a hand into his pitch-black hair, then took the stairs with leaden feet, still sneaking glances back at her and frowning as he went. She made it to the sitting room on legs threatening to give way any second, muscles tight and sore. She kicked off her heels and curled up against the silky cushions to wait. She squeezed her quivering hands, hoping they would stop shaking.

Footsteps and voices floated to her from the stairs. Maya heard them talking, her mom questioning her dad, tone filled with worry.

"Honey, are you all right? What's wrong?" Maya's mom looked back and forth between father and daughter. Her face revealed the strain of her worry, pale and drawn. She fiddled with the buttons of her silk pajamas as if she needed to keep her hands busy.

Maya's dad switched on the sitting room light. She kept her eyes down as her mom gasped at the sight of the bruise. It was worse than the sparring injury she'd received. Mostly because Byron had intended to hurt her. Her mom walked to Maya. Her steps were slow and careful, as she sat beside her injured daughter, as if afraid to jar her. She reached out and tucked stray strands of hair behind Maya's ear, inspecting the damaged skin.

"Who did this? What happened? You'd better start talking, young lady, or I swear I will-" She drew in a breath and twisted her lips in frustration.

On a surreal level Maya felt grateful, despite the severity of the situation her mom remained under control and willing to listen. In reality, exhaustion weighed Maya's body down. She needed to get this confrontation over with.

"I wasn't at Joss's," she confessed and waited for the backlash. But both her parents were silent, and waiting. Her father still stood a few feet away, a couch between himself and Maya, as if he needed the protection. "I lied about going to Joss's. We both went to Amber Alden's party."

CHAPTER 7

"*Maya.*" Disapproval etched her mother's voice as she spoke the name. But the disappointment in her voice hit hardest.

There would be ramifications for her lies, but for now, her parents had to know exactly what happened. If they thought her crazy, they were free to admit her to the nearest house of crazies.

"Something strange happened to Joss at the party. When I got there she looked totally drunk."

MAYA'S MOM STIFFENED, and frowned at her. It probably only occurred to her then the party had been one of the un-chaperoned kind. But although her expression hardened, she still said nothing.

"I took her to the car. I was about to bring her home when Amber spotted me. Something was so strange about Amber. She seemed cold, so . . . vicious. She forced me to go with Byron, one of the guys from school. And she threatened me with Joss. It was the way she looked at me. I knew she meant to arrange for someone to hurt Joss, maybe rape her even while she remained unconscious or something, if I didn't do what she said."

Both Maya's parents stared at her in shocked silence. Her dad drew in a ragged breath, then wiped his face, as if the action could wipe the worry off his features. "So she forced you into a situation because Joss was irresponsible enough to get drunk?" asked her father, his eyes dark with anger.

"No, that's just the thing. Joss didn't drink. Okay, she'd had one alcoholic drink. Same as me. Not enough to knock her out. One drink. Nik thinks Amber spiked them."

"Why would she do that? And what was Nik doing there?" asked her mom before her face froze with shock. "Did you say you were drinking? How could you do that? First, you lie and go to this party and then you drink alcohol? What were you think-"

"Lee, let's leave that alone for now. Maya has more to tell us, don't you, Maya?" Her dad spoke, his eyes unreadable, his fingers gripping the back of the couch. "So, what was Nik doing there?"

"He was invited. He's actually much higher on the popularity scale than I am. And he saved my life. Byron did this to me," Maya said. She pointed at her face. "Would've done way more but something happened."

"What happened?" Leela gripped her daughter's arms, looking very likely to shake her if Maya didn't talk fast.

"Byron got really abusive. He punched me and I think he broke one of my ribs too." She fingered the spot. "It got so bad I started to panic. Then he came at me. Sorry Dad, but I didn't do anything you taught me. I just hid my face and warded him off with my palms."

Maya laughed and shook her head, the sound hollow and bitter as it echoed through the silent room.

"That's when he burst into flames and disappeared."

"What!" Both her parents asked simultaneously.

"Nik thinks *I* did it."

Her parents exchanged a strange glance. Fingers of worry

trailed up and down Maya's spine. "What?" Maya asked, panic welling up within her. They were supposed to say it wasn't possible, not stare at each other like they'd both been caught stealing cookies from the cookie jar. "What are you not telling me?"

"Maya, we need to talk," said her dad.

"What more do we need to talk about. I've told you everything," Maya said.

"Okay, Maya." Her dad came around and sat on the couch, and Maya leaned back. *Always a bad sign when Dad looks all serious..* "You're not a normal kid."

"Tell me something I don't know," she mumbled. Maya looked up, feeling slightly guilty in case he'd heard her. Her mom had, and she shook her head, disapproval in her eyes, but neither reacted.

Bad sign.

"It's really hard to tell you this, but you understand the concept of reincarnation, so we can start there."

Maya nodded, sensing something momentous about to happen.

"Before you were born, your mother and I lived in a remote forest region in India. We belong to a very devout group of Kali followers."

Maya stiffened. They really thought this was the time to bombard her with religious crap? "Dad, you know I don't believe all that stuff right? It's just mythology."

Her dad nodded, and the act of patience went further to unsettle Maya than a screaming fit would've ever done. "I understand, but you need to listen to what I have to say. Whatever your beliefs or doubts, you need to put them aside until I'm done."

His voice held a tired, almost weary edge to it, so Maya clamped her jaws shut and prayed they'd stay shut until he finished.

He seemed to take her silence as agreement and continued. "Our enclave was run and guided by Mother Radha. She was our guiding light and when she became ill, many of the followers began to doubt we'd be able to continue our work."

He paused and shook his head. Maya turned to her mom. A strange, faraway expression flickered across her mom's face, as if some distant memory had reached its fingers out to her, grabbing hold and weaving the memories around her.

Her dad continued, gazing off into the past. "When Mother was on her death-bed, she asked our Goddess for one gift. She begged with her dying words to live again. To live so she may serve the Dark Goddess. Nobody could have guessed her wish had been granted. We tried to continue without her, but many of the older followers began to leave, to go out into the world to serve the greater purpose. We'd thought of leaving too. But we had to wait. For you."

He looked at Maya, leaning forward and propping his elbows on his knees. She tensed, but the small reminiscing smile on his face calmed her. "When you were born, we waited only until you were healthy and strong. We missed Mother far too much. But we found we had another reason to leave."

Maya played with the fringe of the silk cushion she clutched in her stiff hands. Her dad walked over and sat on the other side of her, as if being closer to her might make her listen. He didn't need to. She was listening well enough.

"The compound is situated high in the mountains, in the wilds. One day we checked on you, expecting to find you fast asleep in your crib. Only we got more than a surprise. You were awake, sitting up in your bed, talking to a pile of ash. We would have thought it strange if we hadn't known the pile of ash had once been a cobra. We found the molted skin near the window." Dev shook his head as if even after all these years he still found it difficult to believe.

Maya blinked, still unsure where this little tale was headed.

"It was you. You had killed the snake. Ten months old, barely able to walk and you'd recognized the threat and incinerated the cobra." Her mom spoke, nodding, urging Maya to accept, to understand.

Dev cleared his throat. "Then the new leader of the enclave came rushing into our home claiming she'd had a dream. One that told her Mother had been reincarnated and who the child was. She'd stood in our doorway staring at you. The pile of cobra ash confirmed it to all of us."

"So you think I'm the reincarnation of your leader?" Maya was still processing the fact her parents had admitted to be followers of the Goddess Kali. Only the mention of the pile of ash that had once been a cobra encouraged her to pay closer attention.

"We *know* you are her," Maya's mom spoke, her tone gentle, tender.

"Apart from the woman's dream did you have anything solid?" Maya stared at her parents skeptically, beginning to doubt they were in possession of any sanity at all.

"We didn't need confirmation. We had enough trouble trying to control your growing power. You burned stuff up left, right, and center. Before long, we decided to bind your power. For your safety and for the safety of those around you."

Yeah, Byron would have a thing or two to say about that.

"We always knew there would be a time when we'd need to tell you the truth, but we hadn't expected it to be this soon. The bindings were strong, they should've held well enough," Her mom hesitated. "Was there anything else that happened, anything that could've made you ill? Did you feel dizzy or nauseous at all?"

Maya nodded. "Yeah, I felt dizzy and a bit ill but that was because of the alcohol. Although, I only drank half the glass. I stopped because I felt so weird."

"Yes, we will talk about *that* later." Leela's voice spelled trouble. Boy, was she in for it. When her mom got mad she got really, really mad.

"That's probably the reason. The binding must've been easier to breach with the alcohol in her system." Her dad nodded, seeming satisfied with his assumption. But Maya was too busy wondering what her punishment would be for this additional transgression. First lying, then drinking. Not to mention murder, however weird the circumstances.

"So, it *was* me, then?" Maya still had trouble accepting she'd killed Byron. How could this happen? Her dad nodded, sharing a knowing glance with her mom who's head bobbed up and down as well. "Unfortunately, that's a yes."

"Why?" Maya asked, then burst into tears.

It had been too much, had taken its toll slowly. From the stress of lying to the weakening effects of the alcohol to the fear of possible rape by Byron. Knowing she'd been the one to end his life should've been more satisfying given his intentions had never been of the gentlemanly kind.

But all she was able to process was she'd just killed someone. Maya shivered within the circle of her mother's arms. She hadn't even felt her mom move.

"There is more, of course," her dad said.

"Of course." Maya couldn't hold back her snark, but the hiccups and the high squeak she emitted spoiled the effect.

"Something must have sparked it. You drank half a glass and it seems alcohol has a strong effect on you."

"Well, Nik suspects the alcohol was drugged. Maybe that's why I felt so weird?" Maya offered, leaning forward out of the security of her mom's embrace.

"It could be the alcohol and drugs broke the wards. Just in case, is there anything else you can think off?" Her dad frowned, then asked, "Any strange odors?"

"Now that you mention it, yes. I kept smelling this weird stench. Like blood and spices. Horrible. It filled my lungs it was so strong." Maya's looked from one parent to the other and both were nodding, their expressions more serious now than ever. "What? What happened?"

"We knew this day would come." Her dad sighed, the sound

weary, as if he was finally giving in to something. Beside her, Leela echoed her husband. "It's the scent of a Rakshasa."

"Which is supposed to mean what to me, exactly?" Maya asked, one eyebrow rose. She really hated the mythology. With her limited knowledge of what a Rakshasa was, she preferred her dad to spell it out for her.

Dev Rao took a deep breath. "Demons to you, kid. They possess the bodies of innocent people whenever they want to obtain something specific. They kill for pleasure too. But mostly they do their master's bidding. They're never very good at self-management."

"So you're saying Byron was a demon." Maya absorbed the idea, turning it over in her mind. "So what would they have wanted with me? Why would they want to kill me?"

"Well, that's easy. The entire demon population probably wants to kill you. They always have - ever since you were born."

"And why is that?" Maya asked, barely able to stop herself from snapping.

"Because you're the only living human who possesses the power to scent a Rakshasa."

CHAPTER 8

"You are kidding right?" asked Maya. They'd blown the whole thing way out of proportion here. How did they expect her to swallow this crap when she didn't even believe Rakshasa's existed in the first place? They might as well have revealed vampires really did exist and she was really a vampire hunter.

And yet, the memory of the scent of putrid meat teased her nostrils. An odor she'd smelled when Byron had been close. Accepting Byron was a demon got just a little easier for Maya. Crazy, but easier.

"I'm sorry honey, this is a shock for you but it's very real. So real we've been hiding you your entire life. If this was an attack on you, an attempt to either abduct or kill you then we need to take action." Maya began to worry as she looked at her father's face. The gravity in his tone, the sadness gleaming in his eyes, an expression she'd never seen before.

"This isn't happening." Maya shook her head. She refused to accept it. It couldn't be true. All she'd wanted was to have a normal, all-American life. Why were they trying to force her to believe this nonsense. "No! I won't listen to any more."

She pushed off the sofa, away from her parents. Multi-colored cushions scattered in a mess of reds and golds. Maya didn't care. She half ran, half limped to the stairs, all thought of the possibly broken rib gone, her only desire to escape to her room before her tears spilled. To get away from them.

She turned at the stairs. "I don't believe this, and you know what? I don't think I ever will believe it. It's a myth. Stories people tell. None of it is true. And I am not going to get caught up in it. You believe if you want to. I certainly am not." She flung the words back at them, flung their faith in their faces too. Too late to take the words back now.

Maya glared at her parents who stared back, surprised at her outburst. Her mother's dark eyes were moist and ringed with worry, while her dad's expression remained perplexed. Oddly, neither her mom nor her dad looked as furious as she'd expected.

A thin ripple of guilt ran through her, but she didn't give in. She refused to give in. What were they trying to do to her anyway? Make her lose her mind? Take her over to the dark side?

She ran up the stairs two at a time, and entered her room with the intention of slamming her door shut. She never got the satisfaction.

Maya took one step into her bedroom.

Then the world spun and she fainted.

MAYA OPENED her eyes and had to shut them again quickly. A bright, white light lit the room, and it hurt. Through scrunched eyes she caught a glimpse of overly colorful, patterned curtains. A machine let out a constant beep and behind her paper crackled like soft little lightning strikes. She stiffened, and turned slowly. Something about having her back to someone she couldn't identify made her uncomfortable.

But she relaxed as soon as she saw her mom, propped up in a

metal chair, face scrunched up as if trying hard to process what she was reading from the rumpled newspaper in her hands.

"Hi, Mom." Her words came in two soft croaks but Leela heard. She came to Maya, leaning against bed, kissing her cheek, bringing a waft of pine scented cleaning product with her.

"Hey baby." She leaned her elbows on the bed beside Maya. "How are you feeling?"

"Sore. And thirsty," Maya replied. "What happened? Where am I?"

"You're in the hospital. I believe you fainted," her mom said, grinning. "You just proved you *are* a girl."

Maya smiled. It was an old joke. At six years old, Maya had announced only girls faint. She swore she'd never, ever faint simply because she wasn't a *girl*.

"Don't get used to it. It's just a passing phase." Maya laughed and then cringed as pain flashed through her torso.

"Be careful, honey. You had a punctured lung. You must've been short of breath at some point but you never noticed it. The doctors said it would take four to six weeks to heal but I think you'll be fine. You've always been a fast healer." Maya wouldn't have thought anything except she heard a strange, high-pitched lilt at the end of her mom's sentences. What was her mom keeping from her?

"Mom?" asked Maya, "What is it?"

"It's nothing really, honey. You should concentrate on getting better. Nothing else matters at this point."

"Come on, Mom. There's something you want to tell me. Why can't you say it and be done?" said Maya, now exasperated.

"Because your mother has been through a whole lot this evening." Maya's dad walked in bearing two steaming paper cups. The scent of coffee filled the air. He handed one to her mom and turned kind and caring eyes to Maya. Eyes now slightly sad. "What she needs to say is not something any mother should ever need to say to her child. Especially when it's something that child does not want to hear."

"Oh, Dad. Not the whole mythology nonsense again."

"Yes, Maya. This is serious. More serious now you've landed yourself in hospital."

"Dad, it wasn't my fault. I didn't give myself the broken rib." Her voice rose as anger brought a flush of heat to Maya's face.

"Yes, we understand that but if you hadn't gone to that party this wouldn't have happened."

Maya's mom broke in. "Something like this was bound to happen at some point. We hadn't planned on cotton-balling her for her whole life you know." She turned to Maya. "At some point you will need to come to terms with the truth."

"You didn't." Maya glared at her mom. "Didn't you bind my powers in the first place?"

"We'd only meant the wards to last until you were capable of defending yourself. Now that they're broken we have to face this together, and accept it together." Leela took hold of her daughter's hand, but all Maya wanted to do was pull it away. She couldn't accept her mother's comfort. Too many thoughts filled her head. But she left her hand locked within her moms, and waited for her to continue. "I can understand it's hard to believe but power comes in many forms to so many different people. You need to accept it and learn it, to protect yourself and to protect your family. Besides, a gift like this is not something you should ever spurn. The giver of that gift might not be happy with rejection either."

"What are you saying, Mom?"

"What your mother is trying to say is *you* are special. Whether you want to believe it or not, you possess a unique power. You hold within you the power to destroy demons, to track them, and to kill them. And that very power is what makes you vulnerable because you're a novice. You're unable to control your power at all. So far, we've protected you, but it's clear we can no longer be

your sole protection. It's time you learned to protect yourself."
Dev paused as he stood beside his wife. "Maybe keeping the truth
from you for so long was wrong. And I'm sorry. But what's done
is done, and at this point you know the truth, you have the power
and you really no longer have a choice. Because your ability to
kill the Rakshasas will always put you in mortal danger."

MAYA TURNED ONTO HER SIDE. The room was silent; the emptiness of the small, clinical space amplified by the absence of her
parents. She'd never been afraid to be alone before, but now, with
everything they'd revealed, she felt utterly insecure, flinching at
the shadows, tensing every so often as footsteps went back and
forth in the passage outside her door.

Not that she really believed them, though. It was way too far-
fetched. Kali and Rakshasas? Demons. Yeah, she totally believed
in demons. Maya scoffed in silence, drifting into an uneasy sleep.

MAYA AWOKE one harsh breath at a time. The room felt different.
Warmer, denser than the usual recycled air-conditioner air. Her
body alerted her that something was terribly wrong. Exhaustion
weighed down her bones, perspiration lathered her forehead. A
forehead so hot she wondered what happened. She'd been fine
when she'd gone to sleep. The doctor had come in and checked
her, and she'd been fine. They'd said she could go home as long as
she took it easy, no strenuous activity.

Maya placed her hand at her rib, and snatched it away as if
she dipped it into molten lava. Neither the absence of pain in her
ribs, nor the absence of bandages shocked her. What made her
body stiffen was the presence of a garment she was dead sure she
hadn't been wearing when she'd fallen asleep.

She knew what a sari was, how the fabric felt, and how it draped around a woman's body. And Maya knew she was wearing one. How was that even possible? She reached for the light and her heart sank when her searching fingers came up empty.

No light, no nightstand.

In that moment of whirling panic Maya would've sprung to her feet and rushed to the door. But her body forced her to move slowly, one aching, quivering limb at a time. Her heart thumped in her chest. She'd never felt this sick in her life. Shivering, shaking, so hot she swore she'd begun to melt. At last, she got her legs to do as they were told and move until she was able to sit upright. Her pointed toes searched for the little stool beside the bed. Nothing. Her heels bumped solid ground almost at the same level of the mattress.

Maya blinked in the darkness. Her first experience of utter black blindness. She decided she didn't like this feeling at all. *Where the hell was the darned light, and what happened to the bed?*

Getting to her feet was a lot harder than the decision. She spent a while on her knees, willing her weak limbs to take her weight.

She wiped at her forehead, swatting away the rivulets of sweat trailing at her hairline. Her breath came in short sharp bursts, the effort taxing both her body and her lungs. She froze, and took another breath. There it was. Maya smelled incense. Sandalwood incense. And burning camphor.

Something was very, very wrong here.

She was desperate for light now, desperate to see where she was. More than anything Maya was desperate for help. She tried to call out, to scream. She heard movement. Someone must have heard her. Help was coming. A quivering light floated toward her, so eerie for a second she freaked out.

Until a face came into view, lit from below and distorted by the flickering flame. The features appeared demonic, so scary the hairs on Maya's neck stood on end and she felt the fingers of a chill through the heated fever. The woman spoke in hushed tones, kohl-lined eyes filled with concern and what Maya could've sworn was grief.

A deep red sari hugged her body, the color bleeding into the shadows. Most definitely not a nurse. Maya stepped backward, away from the apparition, sure the woman was something from her nightmares. And as she fell, her heart stammered almost to a halt.

Before she passed out, two things stuck out clearly; spot-lighted in her mind.

The flickering oil-lamp threw its shivering light upon stone walls and large stone columns reaching high toward the ceiling, higher than the little light could go. Hand-carved stone walls.

And, as she fell, arms flung out before her, Maya had her first look at her hands. An old metal bangle encircled one wrist, reflecting the yellow lamplight. Old frail hands, skin so papery thin it lay upon the bone of her arm as if her flesh had vanished.

They were not Maya's hands.

CHAPTER 9

The lock clicked, and the door sighed open. Aunt Claudia stepped into the room, a wry smile on her face as she leaned against the door and took in Maya's forlorn expression.

"Trust you to sneak out of the house to go to a party and end up smokin' a dude."

"Very funny." Maya tried not to smile, but it had always been difficult to sulk around Claudia.

Claudia Romero, a close friend of Maya's mom, and more of a big sister to Maya. She was so close to the Rao's she might as well have been family. From babysitter, to friend and confidant in sixteen years, Claudia was still easier to confide in than her mom. Although she'd get a motherly rebuke if she put a foot wrong.

As it was, Maya found it strange Claudia wasn't as pissed off with her as her parents. Perhaps she wasn't entirely aware of the whole demon situation.

Maya stiffened, shock paralyzed her limbs as she stared at Claudia. Claudia's dark doe eyes stared blandly back at her.

"What did you say?" Maya kept her voice low enough to cover the wobble of fear.

"What do you mean?" Claudia walked to the bed and sat beside Maya. She placed a small gift bag on the covers over Maya's knees.

"You just said 'smokin' a dude'. What did you mean by that?" Maya ignored the gift even though she ached to open it.

Claudia leaned closer, until their faces were a mere foot apart, and asked, "What did you want me to mean by that?"

Maya shook her head. "Stop trying to confuse me. Why did you say that? What do you know?"

"I know enough."

"Enough to know I killed someone?" asked Maya, her voice like granite. "Enough to know it's not that big a deal 'cos the dude I 'smoked' happened to be a demon?"

"Yup."

Maya wasn't sure if she wanted to scream or cry. Perhaps both would make her feel better. She bit her lip, stemming the wave of self-pity about to engulf her.

"No way are you going to wuss out on me now, chica. We have serious business to attend to."

The sharp, stern command stopped the tears that had been so ready to fall. "What do you mean?"

Maya's heart fell as she realized Claudia might know exactly what was going on.

"What I mean is we need to get you ready. Stronger. Tougher."

"So you know about the demon?" Maya cut in. "What do you know?"

"I know everything, chica. I know about your powers, about how your parents bound those powers for your protection. I know who you are, and who you were." Claudia took Maya's hands in hers, and squeezed them, and the mere meeting of skin began to relax the confused girl inside Maya. "You have the same eyes, you know?"

"Same as whom?" Maya asked, fearing the answer.

"Same as Mother." Claudia nodded, lost in thought for a few minutes.

"How did you know her?"

"She trained me. She was my teacher and my mentor, my mother and my friend. She left many broken hearts behind when she died." Claudia laid her palm on Maya's cheek. "And we see her in you, shining so brightly there is no question. The same spunk, the same strength."

Maya shrugged the palm off and rose from the bed. She walked to the window to stare outside, where the trees were red and gold, and the sky was a cool clear blue.

"So you're one of them?" Maya nodded at the door to her room. "A Kali follower like them?"

Claudia's face fell, and for a moment Maya wished she could take back her tone of contempt. Too late. Besides, she was pretty sure she meant it.

"Yes I am, chica." Claudia rose, joined Maya, and curled up on the window seat. "What do you know of Kali?"

"Enough."

"What exactly do you know?"

"Enough to know I can't bear the thought of all of you guys following those . . . ancient . . . illogical beliefs. All that blood-sucking makes me sick."

Maya refused to look at Claudia, instead inspecting the silent street outside, the fallen leaves gathered in untidy piles beneath the trees lining the path. She turned only when the sound of laughter disturbed her.

Claudia was well into her laughing fit, tears welling in her eyes, one hand clamped over her mouth.

"What's so darned funny?" asked Maya.

"You." Claudia managed the single syllable between hiccups of laughter as she tried to regain control.

Maya clenched her teeth, then immediately unclenched them

as pain spiked into her cheekbone. Byron's blow still hurt like the blazes.

"I'm sorry Maya. It's just I never, ever thought I'd hear those words coming from you. And especially when you consider who you are."

Maya took a deep breath. "Okay then. So who am I?"

Claudia sighed, at last in control of her giggles. "You, Maya Rao, are the Hand of Kali. The living embodiment of the power of the Dark Goddess."

"Cue the dramatic music," said Maya, raising an eyebrow.

"Come on, Maya. I'm trying to tell you the truth here," Claudia snapped. And Maya looked away. She had no intention of apologizing. Not when the entire family seemed to have been in cahoots her entire life, keeping the truth from her.

"So, when you were babysitting, what were you doing exactly? Demon watching? Or watching me for power spurts?"

"To be honest, I was doing both. We've had you hidden pretty well. Until now. The question is, how did they find you?"

"Care to tell me who *they* are?" snapped Maya.

"The Rakshasas. They are the demons who roam the earth. They are and always will be around. Many of them, but not all, are monsters who roam to kill. They knew about you a long time ago. The Hand of Kali. That's what you were called ever since your reincarnation was confirmed."

"The Hand of Kali. So what does the Hand do then?" asked Maya, repulsed and yet intrigued. She'd felt the rush of energy run through her body in the seconds before Byron had been incinerated. She had to admit it if only to herself; if this whole power thing was real, it was safer to get a handle on it, rather than to have it control her.

"The power to scent the blood of a Rakshasa. The Power to create and control fire. And the power to-"

"The power to kill the demons," said her dad as he entered the room.

Maya watched as he sent Claudia a look far too stern, almost bordering on a reprimand. She blinked in shock as she watched Claudia lower her eyes, a silent apology for some unknown transgression.

"I'm sorry to interrupt you girls. Maya, when you came home last night you mentioned Nik believed *you* had turned the demon into flames?"

Maya nodded.

"How well do you know him?"

"Not that well. He's always around. We aren't friends or anything." As she spoke, Maya blushed and was glad her darker skin hid the rosiness.

"And he arrived to help you after the demon disappeared?"

"No, he arrived as Byron was burning up. Nik saw him go from flames to ashes." Maya frowned. "But Dad, how would Nik have known? Is he one you your followers too?"

Maya cringed at the thought. Not another nice guy falling into the clutches of mythology. Although twisted within her own dilemma, Maya didn't miss the fleeting expression on his face. A meaningful twist of guilt that had nothing to do with Maya's health and everything to do with the enigmatic Nik Lucas.

An odd expression flickered over Dev's face. Then it was gone. "Maya, I know you must feel like we've been keeping you in the dark but remember this knowledge is given with a responsibility that, until now, you've been too young to bear. We've discussed it and we agree. It's time for a full-scale training effort. Your rib should be healed before the week is out. In that time Claudia, your mother and I will get you up to speed on the theory."

"Theory?"

"Yes, Demon culture, sub-culture and social interaction. Methods of killing. Methods of armed combat. The truth behind the old myths and legends. And above all, the teachings of our Dark Goddess."

"So you're telling me you'll be turning me into a Kali follower?"

"Maya, whether you like it or not you *are* a follower of the Goddess. Our job is to teach you everything we can in the time we have. You need to know everything. There's nothing we can do about the info dump, but we have to be prepared. Just in case."

"You think they will try again?"

"Yes, I do. That's why you're not to be left alone at any point in time."

"So you guys have powers too?"

Dev frowned, then nodded. "If by powers you mean can we fight the demons, then yes."

"No, I meant can any of you guys smell them and turn them into flames like I can?"

"No Maya, only *you* can. You are the conduit to Kali's power. And, as much as you might not want to hear this, we are not here to protect you."

Maya's dad rose and came to stop in front of her. He held her by the shoulders, squeezing in reassurance.

"You are here to protect *us*."

CHAPTER 10

The sky bled orange and red and yellow and the colors danced to the sound of the waves. There was something so visceral about a sunset over the ocean. The waves, breaking on the shore, retreating, then reaching back again, and again. It was Maya's favorite place.

After almost a week confined to her room, Maya was finally able to walk on her own. She'd demanded a trip to the beach. It was annoying to be tailed constantly, to be dropped off like a little child, watched from the hillside parking lot. She refused to glance up at her mom waiting in the car, to acknowledge she wasn't alone. That would spoil everything.

The sand beside her shifted, and someone dumped themselves next to her. She didn't look. Knew before he sat down it was him. He had a unique scent. Some exotic, spicy fragrance he wore. No doubt he knew it drove the girls crazy.

Maya blushed and stared as the evening sky darkened, still grasping at the disappearing splotches of brilliant ruby. She suspected her mom or dad had arranged this and made a mental note to thank them. This meant she probably wasn't waiting for

Maya any longer. A quick glance up the hill confirmed her mom's Audi was gone.

"How you holding up?" Nik asked. Maya sneaked a peek. His elbows rested on raised knees and he kept his eyes on the skyline too.

"As well as can be expected under the circumstances," Maya mumbled. "Who told you?"

"Your dad paid me a visit."

"Did he try and kung-fu your ass?"

"Pretty much. I survived. Then we had a long talk. So it's all fine," Nik chuckled "I'm glad you're still alive."

Nik met her eyes, a question hovered there. Or an expectation.

"Okay, I'll say it . . . thank you for saving my life." Maya bit the words out as if each one were a poisoned gumdrop.

"What are you thanking me for?" Genuine puzzlement creased his forehead. "You are the one who killed that demon's ass."

Maya thought about it for a while. True, Nik had arrived a little too late to be of much use. Had Byron meant to rape her she'd be having a totally different conversation right now. Instead, she had to accept he was really a demon, not the nasty linebacker she'd thought he was.

"But how did you know it was me who did that to Byron?" Maya had been dying to ask Nik that question. "When you got to the pool-house he was already on fire. You didn't see a thing."

Nik linked his fingers, deep in thought. He'd heard her question and Maya hoped he wasn't trying to make up some bland excuse.

"I can see them," he answered at last, ending his sentence on a sigh.

"See whom?" Maya hesitated.

"The Rakshasas. I can see them. It's okay Maya. I know all about them," Nik reassured her.

"So what, are you also one of them?" She pinned him with an inquisitorial stare.

"Them?" He stared at her. His expression arctic. What had she said to make him go cold on her so suddenly?

She didn't find his evasiveness at all funny. "The Kali followers."

His eyes warmed and he relaxed, but his face remained blank. "I am, and I'm not. It's hard to explain. My allegiance lies with another god, although I would bow to the Dark Goddess in a flash."

"So to whom do you owe your allegiance?" Maya gritted her teeth. Why was it so darned difficult to get a straight answer from anyone?

When he finally answered she expected Nik to lie, and glared at him, daring him. But he blinked and smiled. "My allegiance is to Lord Yama."

Around them the beach was silent, sand shifted at Maya's feet in the warm breeze.

"Yama as in the God of the Dead?"

"Yes, the Lord of the Underworld. That Yama."

His voice rang with a deep reverence and yet the respect was edged with a hint of anger or impatience. Almost a petulance Maya couldn't understand. She shook her head, unable to believe that the whole crazy mess could get any worse. "Okay where are the hidden cameras?"

"What?" Nik twisted about, looking around and behind them.

Maya laughed, more at herself than at the confused boy. "Nothing. It's just a joke."

Nik shook his head. "Maya, I was sent here to protect you. That is my job."

The words stung, but they made sense too. He'd been there, everywhere she'd gone. Ever since he'd first arrived.

"I am here to help you. To train and to learn. Whatever it is you need. You're important, not only to Kali but to the rest of the pantheon too. Yama wants me to ensure your safety. Yama's word is law and I usually do what I am told."

"So all the time you've been in Somerville you've been on surveillance duty?" The question came out clipped and cold.

Nik nodded. "I guess you could call it that. Moving into a big house in a rich neighborhood almost guarantees entry into the popular crowd. In my case, it worked well. And Amber honed in on me. She'd been possessed when I first met her. At first I thought she'd recognize me, but she didn't."

"So why did you think she would recognize you?"

"I'm not sure. I thought at first the Rakshasas would smell me or something but they were oblivious. I watched them. I was tempted to get close, but I had no idea who they were working for and if I'd be walking straight into a trap. I couldn't take the chance. Especially since my main task was to find you, Maya, and keep you safe." Nik was silent for a moment before continuing, "The presence of the Rakshasas told us you were in danger. But we thought your power was latent, and it wouldn't reveal you even if they tried anything. That's why I kept close at Amber's party. We still have no idea who these demons are working for."

"So you've encountered them before?" Maya asked.

"Of course. They work in the palace in Patala. I've known them all my life."

"You grew up with them?" Maya's skin rippled with anger.

Nik turned to face her. "The Rakshasas are a race. They all have different allegiances. Some give their allegiance to demon kings of the other underworld planes, some still worship Ravana, and some have even thrown off the mantle of servitude and now live in the human world, side by side with humans who haven't the faintest idea who they really are."

"So do you track them down?" Maya asked, shocked that demons were allowed to live among humans. Surely it shouldn't be allowed.

"Why? They have as much a right to a life as you and I. We do keep an eye on them though. And the hell hounds know when one of them goes off the rails."

The sky had darkened, now more black than red or orange, and the gentle breeze had turned frosty, nipping at Maya's bare, sand-covered toes.

She shook her head, trying to fathom how she felt about all the people who populated her world. Parents who'd hidden her true nature from her for her entire life. A Mexican woman and a good old American boy who served Kali and Yama. Who was she to deny the existence of mythology anyway? Maya sighed. For every time she'd ever scoffed at the legends, or criticized the traditions. She sighed for every time she'd sneered at her parent's ancient, dusty old beliefs.

Maya laughed silently. Was she really taking this so calmly, when all she wanted was to throw herself onto the sand and scream and kick and yell and cry out her frustrations.

But it was the deep, burning fear inside her that worried her more than anything. The fear of the power she contained within her. The fear of what she could do with all that power. The fear of whom she was meant to be and of how little control she had left in her sorry life.

If this was all true then she was in deep doody.

CHAPTER 11

$\mathcal{M}$aya sat on the backyard steps, dusting her feet, and her sneakers. Sand seemed to have gotten everywhere. The screen door opened and shut behind her and her dad dropped onto the step beside her.

"Thanks, Dad."

"What for honey?"

"For telling Nik to come over."

"Well now that I know he's not here to abduct, maim or kill you . . . . He seems okay. Just be careful who you trust, okay?"

"Sure. Maybe we need to draw up a rule book." When her dad frowned she said, "Rules for Maya. No life, no friends, kill demons, don't trust anyone."

"Maya!" he admonished. "Whatever rules we have are only there for your protection. Once you know what you're doing you'll be fine."

Maya scowled. Nothing her dad said made any difference to how she felt. Everyone seemed so busy trying to control her they'd all forgotten she should have a choice in the whole business, seeing as *her* life and *her* power were the problems.

"And we never said you can't have friends now, did we?"

"I guess not. But what if having anyone over meant they'd be in trouble? What if they get mixed up in this whole mess?"

Her dad ruffled her hair. "You seem to have a pretty good set of brains in that head of yours. There is some truth to that, Maya. It's up to you of course, but there's nothing stopping you from finding a good balance. You have to be-"

"Be careful. Yeah, I know." Maya sighed and got to her feet, dusting her rear. She turned to go back into the house when her dad touched her arm.

"Your mother and I are really proud of you. I wanted you to know that. You've had a lot to deal with in the last few days, and I wish you'd never had to experience any of it. We tried to protect you as best as we could but we knew the time would come when you'd need to take the power and use it."

"Thanks." Maya didn't want to hear any of what he was saying. It made her realize the truth of his words. But she never wanted any of this. Why did it have to happen to her?

THE GYM WAS SILENT, all classes canceled for this particular session. Only Maya's parents and Claudia were present.

Maya stared at the weapon her mom now held within her elegant hands. Leela moved around the mat, foot sweeping the floor, graceful and beautiful. She twirled and twisted her strange weapon in a lazy snaking dance, swirling like a Capoeira dancer, a deadly one at that.

It was an ancient Indian weapon called the Madu. Really a pair of shield, with twin antelope horns melded together to form a natural double-ended piercing weapon, dangerous enough for its points to slice through human skin, slash open a jugular or rip out intestines.

They gleamed, so dark brown they were almost black. The horns held a unique beauty as they spiraled until they reached their deadly points. And Maya ached to hold them in her hands. She could almost feel her knees soften, willing her to sink lower, to grab the horns and wield them as her mom was now doing.

Her mom came to the end of her lesson and handed the weapon over to Maya, who spent precious seconds tracing reverent fingers over the horns. The solid, ridged smoothness of the Madu was entrancing. She glanced up, guilty and ready to accept her scolding for delaying the lessons but her mom merely stared at her, eyes gleaming with pride, and Maya felt the thrill of satisfaction rise within her.

Maya smiled. She walked to the center of the mat and assumed her stance, repeating as many of the movements she could remember. Forward thrust on bent knees, low sweep around the body, backward kick, backward thrust. Like dancing, only deadlier and far easier to hurt oneself with a wrong move. At least with her dad's nunchuks, she'd end up with a bunch of purple bruises rather than gaping, bloody wounds.

And Maya found it hard to assimilate she was enjoying this training more than she'd ever enjoyed a sparring session with her dad.

Because she had enough power to send him flying on his ass if she wanted. And she was so untrained she could easily incinerate him if she made the wrong move. The most annoying part of this whole training process was nobody was willing to begin her training on controlling her fire.

Maya was dead set on changing that.

"Joss called again. And Ria," her mom said as she cleared the table after Friday dinner. "They've called several times this week, Maya. You planning on returning the calls at all?"

Maya was unsure what she wanted to do. She glanced up at her mom shaking her head. Then she avoided her eyes, busying herself with scraping remnants of butter chicken from the plates, stacking the dishwasher.

"You have to speak to them, Maya. They're your friends and they care about you. And what will you say to them when you return to school next week?" Her mom walked to her, placing a tender arm around her shoulder and asked, "Do you blame Joss?"

Maya shook her head. "No Mom, I don't. I could hardly be angry at her, even if she was partly to blame for the situation. If she hadn't insisted I go to that party. If she hadn't drunk what Amber had given her. Or given it to me . . . ." She sighed, pretty certain there were too many ifs and hindsight seemed to make everything so simple. "But no, she's not to blame."

She stared out the window, listening to cicadas sing outside in the warm evening air. Soon the weather would change, and like the weather, everything around her seemed to continue. The world didn't stand still because Maya Rao suddenly discovered she was a freaking demon-killer.

"Maya, it's what we have to deal with now. The reality is these demons have infiltrated the town. The Rakshasa who possessed Byron wouldn't have worked alone. If they'd meant to take you, they could still be around somewhere. And until we know exactly what it is that they want, we are staying put."

"So we aren't leaving town, then?" Maya wasn't sure if she was relieved or upset at the news. It seemed the most logical step, to leave the town and its demons behind.

"It hardly makes sense until we know what they want. They have ways of finding the people they are after and it wouldn't matter where we go, we'd be prolonging the inevitable."

"Better to stay and fight then." Maya sighed. *This is so not a good idea.* "I'm worried, Mom. I'm afraid of how desperate these demons are and who they would pick to possess to get close to me again. Joss and Ria are normal human beings. They can hardly be expected to protect themselves. Would they even know they were possessed?"

Leela shook her head. "No, I don't think that's the way it works. The demon is absorbed into the person, they have no idea what they are doing is out of character."

"And once they are possessed can we get the demon out of them? Can we save the person?"

"Sometimes. And it depends on the circumstances too." Maya's mom smiled tenderly at her. "You're worried about Byron aren't you?"

Maya nodded. "I killed a boy, Mom. It doesn't matter if he was possessed, I killed him. No more Byron. What about his parents? They don't have a son anymore."

"I know it's hard, honey. But you did what you had to do, you had to protect yourself. And who knows if the demon would've left Byron's body intact. Sometimes the demons wreak havoc with the mind of their host. Sometimes they leave behind a shell of the person." Leela shuddered. "The longer they stay the worse the result. And sometimes they just come and go. We never know. That's why we're so glad we have you. Now we have someone who can help us fight them."

Maya heard what her mom said but her mind was on Ria and Joss. "What if they use the girls to get close to me?"

Her mom nodded. "That's a possibility. Is that why you're ignoring their calls?"

Maya smiled, glad to confide in her mother. Strangely enough, it was her parents she now relied on. Two weeks ago, all she wanted was to get as far away from the claustrophobic arms of their parental devotion. So many rules to follow, so many things to think about. Until recently the rules regarding boys, parties and revealing clothing had applied.

Until the whole demon incineration thing.

Would the rules change now she was this all-powerful demon hunter? And what did her future have in store for her?

CHAPTER 12

The abandoned underground parking lot seemed the safest place when working with potentially destructive balls of fire. Concrete blocks were a damn sight more comforting than a wooden house or even a lonely forest filled with very flammable trees.

Maya looked around and gritted her teeth. She found it odd of all the people in her life to train her right now, it happened to be Yama's stooge.

"You know, you don't really have to bother with this. My dad can help me practice." Maya offered, hoping he'd agree and drive her straight back home.

"I know you don't think I have to but I really do. The last thing I need is for you to be lacking in knowledge."

"Knowledge?" Maya glared at him. "What do I need to know other than the fact that I can roast a person with my hands?"

"Yes, knowledge." Nik's face darkened. "Tell me, how much do you know about Rakshasas?"

"I can kill them and they stink."

Nik remained silent for a moment. "So you've been able to

smell the demons from the start, right Maya?" When she nodded he continued, "Has your ability gotten stronger?"

"I don't think so, not that I've noticed. At Amber's I smelled the Rakshasa scent around Amber at the car. But the scent on Byron was so strong… decaying meat and spices." Maya fell silent as she digested each memory, and went back and forth trying to compare it with the Byron-demon who'd attacked her. "The scent on Byron was cloying, but not as powerful as the Amber-demon."

"It could be you had no idea what the odor was with Byron and perhaps with Amber you were distracted by the fighting and maybe even in shock," Nik said, almost to himself. "Or it could be your power to scent the demon blood is getting stronger. And this might actually be a good thing."

"Yeah…a good thing." Maya mumbled. She was annoyed with Nik. More than annoyed. Not that he had the power to create fire with his own hands but he seemed to think he could boss her around well enough. She wondered what he did in his role as minion to a god.

"Come on Maya, concentrate." His voice echoed within the empty parking garage.

She sighed and took up her position again. Breathed deep, even though the rib still hurt a little. She held out her hand, palm facing her imaginary opponent and concentrated.

Nothing.

"You know what? I think this is a waste of everyone's time." Maya dusted her palms together, anger vibrating through her like little volcanic waves. "You're probably all wrong. Maybe I'm not this . . . this reincarnated version of Mother Radha. Maybe you guys are wrong."

Nik stared at her as she gasped for breath, the tirade taking more out of her than the last hour of her so-called training.

"Are you done?"

"What?"

"Are you done already?" Nik repeated his question, his eyes

cold, flinty. "Are you done feeling sorry for your poor little self? Are you done going over all the bad things that have ever happened to poor little Maya?"

As Nik spoke he stepped close, and the closer he got the more Maya seethed. His words bit at her, like gigantic crows pecking bloody bites out of her flesh. She hated him so much right then. The object of the biggest crush she'd ever had, now the object of such violent rage she could easily have-

Maya gasped as she flew through the air. She landed on her butt, coughing and spluttering inside a huge dust-cloud. Stunned, she waited until her head stopped spinning and the parking garage righted itself, before she tried to get back on her feet.

She blinked the dust from her eyes as it settled around her.

"Nik?" Maya called out and her voice bounced around the building.

The sounds of scrabbling echoed behind her words and Maya ran headlong toward it, tripping over her own feet in the dust-engulfed semi-darkness. She stopped in horror as Nik slapped at the flames merrily burning on the arm of his jacket.

She froze, dead certain she'd hurt him somehow, unable to bear his wrath. Worse, his pain.

"Did I do that?" She hoped he'd just say no.

"Now that's what I'm talking about. Good job, Maya." Nik laughed and coughed at the same time.

"Are you demented? I could've killed you!" Maya snapped, horrified gaze trained on disappearing flames.

"No, you wouldn't have killed me because I actually know what I'm doing."

Maya scowled at Nik, disappointed now he hadn't received so much as a singe.

"I had to get you in . . . what do you call it . . . the zone? When Byron attacked you it wasn't just the alcohol allowing you to access your power. It was the base of power inside you."

She frowned. A small part of her saw how sexy he happened

to look even when he smudged soot on his cheek as he dusted himself off.

"Where did your power come from? Just now, you would've felt parts of your body heat up, or vibrate or just feel odd or different."

Maya thought back to the strange dizziness she'd experienced, an odd vertigo pushing her off-balance and it hadn't helped when she'd been thrown backward. She touched her chest, recalling the heat which had pooled there, beneath her sternum, like a boiling river of anxiety, only controlled and almost solid.

"My head. I felt almost dizzy but strange. And my chest. It felt weird, sort of hot."

Nik nodded. "Anything else?"

"And my abdomen. The heat was similar to the one in my chest. What's all this about?"

"They are your Chakras. Where you draw your energies from. Your head is the Crown chakra which controls the spiritual aspect of the power." Nik reached out a hand, placed his finger in the middle of Maya's forehead. Right where her third eye should be, not that she put much stock in third eyes anyway. She so wanted to swat his arm away but a part of her wanted to hear him out too. And she was becoming very aware of Nik, especially where his skin touched hers.

"Your chest is the Heart Chakra, where you connect with the emotional aspect of the energy." Nik moved his annoying finger to her chest laying it against the bare skin revealed at the neck-line of her filthy tee shirt. He'd soon feel the thumping of her foolish heart beneath his finger. Nik had no idea what he was doing to her. His finger lay over her heart, the same heart that thumped harder and harder because he stood so close, touching her.

"And the abdomen area is your Solar Plexus Chakra." Nik blandly poked the finger into her belly. She'd known it was coming. His nearness disturbed her, the heat of his finger through the fabric of her worn tee shirt made her clench the muscles in her abdomen against the intrusive digit. "Oddly enough this is where your thinking happens."

"Are you serious? My brain is in my stomach?" Maya scoffed. *Yeah, the same stomach currently doing somersaults as all the places Nik touched now seem to burn with need.*

Nik shook his head. "From the looks of it, that is where the problem lies. You're thinking far too much. It's why I had to engage your thoughts, focus them on your anger so you would feel a solid need to manifest it. That's where the Fire comes in."

"So the Fire is the manifestation of my anger?"

Nik nodded. "Anger and rage yes, but the Fire will manifest with most of your intense emotional peaks. The Kali Fire will flow, in tune with your body. Happiness and passion are also possible peaks."

Maya blushed at the word passion and hoped he'd change the subject quickly. Passion was the last thing she needed to discuss considering she was alone with him. Her parents had bound the parking garage when they'd arrived but then they'd left them. Alone.

"Right, now use your Chakras to direct your power. Aim at the far wall. You want to create enough energy to propel the flame all the way to the wall," Nik said as he took up a position close behind her. He looped an arm around her and placed his palm against her abdomen. Maya swallowed a gasp. The thin fabric did nothing to prevent the heat searing into her body from his skin. How the heck did he expect her to concentrate while he touched her? "Right, now breathe."

Maya breathed, realizing too late breathing itself meant her body moved against the hot hand on her tummy. How she wished he'd remove his hand. But then again she didn't. Instead, she concentrated on breathing, trying her best to ignore his touch, and failing miserably.

"Now focus as much energy as possible and let it loose," he

said. Maya thought he'd remove his hand but he hadn't. She gulped, closed her eyes and tried to focus. Head, heart, abdomen. Heat began to build but Maya wasn't exactly sure what type of heat. The boiling warmth didn't resemble an angry heat at all. Instead, it simmered and bubbled, becoming hotter and hotter, threatening to burst into a million smoldering pieces. Maya held out her hand and let the pulsing heat fly.

A gigantic ball of fire exploded from her palm, and flew across the empty parking garage. The spinning spheres of flame generated so much energy as it left her palm she flew backward again, but she didn't fall on her butt. She fell with Nik. He took it in stride, grabbing her in his arms and rolling with the momentum of the explosion.

Maya lay flat on her back as she glanced up at Nik. They both looked at the far wall where her ball of fire had emblazoned a large burn mark. Maya laughed, thrilled she'd succeeded at last. Nik joined, laughing and happy after being so surly and stern the last few hours.

But the laughter died out slowly as Maya became aware of their position. She lay on the ground, her body almost entirely covered by Nik's, and it wasn't his weight making it hard for her to breathe.

Nik's face hovered inches above her, his gaze landing on her lips and staying there a bit longer than necessary. She sucked in a breath and only seemed to close the distance between them.

He let out a sigh, almost a growl and the warmth of his breath trailed across Maya's face. She needed air, managed a breath that was more a sob. Then Nik's lips closed over hers and Maya couldn't breathe anymore. She found she didn't care if she never breathed again.

Suspended in time, heat and passion set them ablaze. They said everything with a kiss that could never be said with words.

Nik pulled away, staring deep into Maya's eyes. And his soft lips claimed hers again and she forgot where they were and why they were in the abandoned parking garage in the first place. All that mattered was the passion overflowing between them and nothing could pull them apart.

At last, to Maya's chagrin, it was Nik who pulled away, his dark eyes impossibly darker. "I'm so sorry," he said, an expression much like regret creasing his features.

Maya flinched. "What's there to be sorry about?" She shoved him away and scrambled to her feet dusting herself off. "It was just a kiss. Don't worry about it." Maya hid her hurt with an empty smile. "Are we done with the lessons?"

"Yes. We've done enough for the day." Nik's face darkened as he rose to his feet, but Maya didn't care to figure out what he was thinking.

She walked off toward the exit, grabbed her bag and waited. "Right then, let's get going."

As Nik neared the door Maya shoved it open, holding it wide only long enough for him to pass through, then she let it slam shut. The door clanged, shaking the frame and spewing dust across the floor, the sound almost a death knell to Maya's damaged heart.

No. This has nothing to do with my heart. It's just my stupid ego that's hurt.

I'll get over it.

CHAPTER 13

When the doorbell chimed Maya's stomach clenched as she sat cross-legged at the foot of her bed, applying salve to her scraped knuckles. She froze.

Idiot. Afraid of a mere doorbell. Doesn't bode well for hand-to-hand combat with a Rakshasa, does it? Yeah, but it's Nik you're more afraid of than demons.

Maya waited.

And when two sets of footsteps climbed up the stairs, she knew who had come to visit. Her heart jumped, a certain joy adding to the thump of dread.

"Hey, stranger," Joss said as she entered the room, Ria trailing behind her. Joss flung herself onto a bright green beanbag near the window while Ria perched beside Maya, and inspected her injuries.

"So, how did you get these?" Ria asked, shaking her head and sending her long earrings shivering.

"With those." Maya nodded at her dresser where her set of Madus now sat. She'd insisted on keeping them with her, the weapons already so much a part of the new Maya that the idea of another person fighting with them made her want to cringe.

"Yikes. What in God's name are those?" Ria relinquished Maya's hand and walked to the dresser as if walking toward a poisonous snake, as if sensing danger but entranced nonetheless.

"They're Madus. Ancient Asian weapons made from antelope horns. It's mainly used as a shield but it's pretty awesome as a weapon too."

Ria shook her head. "I've never heard of anything like this. Where did you get it?"

"My dad gave them to me. They're small enough to conceal or keep in my bag, and deadly enough in case . . ."

"Yeah, how are you feeling after that?" Ria asked, shooting a critical glance at Joss who sat on the beanbag in silence. Maya understood Joss's reticence now. Joss had brought Ria up to speed. And either she felt guilty or Ria had forced her guilt to the surface. Maya would happily bet her money on both options. "How's the rib?"

"Better, healed in fact."

"That was quick. What, do you have super healing powers then?" Ria smiled.

You have no idea.

Maya snuck a glance at Joss, whose eyes remained trained on her cellphone. Her heart gave a discomforting thump against her ribs; to think this all began with a stupid text message.

"I'm fine. Nothing happened that couldn't be fixed, so don't worry about me." Maya hoped her words would satisfy Ria.

Ria who was so sensitive, so particular too. She had the power of a mother hidden within her tiny frame. And she could nag the ear off a fish. Worst of all, she never strayed one inch from the strictest of traditional law.

Maya, on the other hand, stayed as far from traditional or stereotypical as possible. Besides, she didn't mind so much if Ria was orthodox Hindu, but it was the way she allowed herself to fall under her father's chauvinistic dominance, the way she accepted being nothing more than a chattel, or a workhorse. In

Mr. Gupta's eyes, she'd never count for much and he wasn't shy about saying so. Maya forced her thoughts elsewhere; pondering Ria's predicament frustrated her no end. Especially knowing the girl would never do anything to get free herself.

She got off the bed and strolled to the window seat beside the beanbag. She secretly adored the lime green silk chair, with its band of gold embroidery and its random golden paisley patterns. Who would've thought one could Indianize a lame old beanbag?

Maya didn't miss the tightening of Joss's muscles or the way her friend avoided her eyes. Poor Joss. She had no idea what she'd gotten mixed up in.

The buzz of Ria's phone was a welcome disturbance to the rising discomfort.

"Sorry Maya. I have to go home. My mom said I can't be long. I have chores." Ria gave them a sad smile. "You girls have fun for me."

ALONE, Joss turned to Maya, her eyes filled with tears.

"I'm so sorry Maya. I had no idea-"

"Come on Joss, we're fine. It's okay." Maya responded unsure of what exactly Joss knew about the incident.

"What do you remember?"

"Well, I recall drinking the cocktail Amber brought. I thought they'd be fine . . . I mean . . ."

"Were they sealed? Were the tops still on?"

"No." Joss glanced at Maya, her eyes glimmering behind anguished tears. She crawled off the bag and onto the window seat beside Maya where she tucked her hand into Maya's arm in a half- hearted attempt at a hug. "I'm so sorry."

"Joss, it's fine. You're fine, I'm fine. We just need to figure out why she did this to us." Maya patted her hand, a tender spark of joy flitting through her at the depth of their friendship.

"Well, that's pretty obvious, don't you think?" Joss said, her voice brittle. "Byron wanted to get laid."

Maya knew better, but hesitated, unsure of how much truth Joss could handle.

"Look, I got away. So no harm done."

Joss lifted Maya's hand into hers, closed her finger into a fist and inspected Maya's scrapes and bruises.

"Not thanks to me." Her friend's voice broke on a high pitched, teary note. "If it hadn't been for Nik ..."

"How much did he tell you?" Maya was curious. What did Nik tell everyone? Was he trying to make himself look like a savior? Maya admonished herself. It was an unfair thought. However she felt about Nik right now, she knew he'd never do that. Her stomach did a tiny flip as a memory of their encounter in the parking garage flashed before her eyes. Then she wiped it away. She'd seen the regret in his eyes. The kiss sure meant more to her than it ever did to him. Which made her the fool? Maya focused on what Joss was saying.

"Only that Byron ran off as soon as Nik walked into the pool-house." Joss shook her head. "The bastard knew he'd done something wrong. Did you know he's missing? Probably couldn't handle the heat, especially after what he did."

So people thought Byron had run off, afraid of the conse-quences. Maya heaved a silent sigh of relief. At least nobody was about to point a finger at her. *When Byron doesn't surface everyone will just assume he ran away for good. Hopefully.* Byron had never been the nicest of people, but Maya still felt incredibly guilty for killing him.

"He hurt you Maya, he should go to jail. I still don't under-stand the type of person who would hurt a girl like that."

"Amber and Byron manipulated both of us. The minute we walked into Amber's house we were doomed. We played right into their hands and it's exactly what they wanted. Yes, who knows what could've happened if Nik hadn't come looking for me. But you've got to stop blaming yourself. *You* are as much a victim as I am. They drugged you. You were defenseless."

"Thank you for saving me. I don't know what I would've done if they-" Joss burst into tears. Maya's heart clenched. The whole incident had affected Joss too. The knowledge she'd been drugged, incapacitated, and unable to defend herself. The knowledge of how vulnerable she'd been had shocked the poor girl. Worse was probably knowing how close she'd come to being attacked while unconscious.

But would Amber have carried out her threat? Would there have been a point if all the demons had wanted was Maya herself?

"We're fine, okay?" said Maya.

Joss nodded and the girls sat in silence, the moon and stars brightening the inky sky outside. Clenching her fist, Maya contemplated the very realistic possibility the Rakshasas might not give up easily and that no matter how she looked at it, both Joss and Ria were in danger.

CHAPTER 14

That night Maya's dreams were filled with flames.

She opened her eyes, her muscles awash with a strange lightness. She rose from the bed and made her way downstairs. The house simmered in silence, streams of silver moonlight sneaking through the blinds, cutting swathes of magical light along the dark wood floors.

When she blinked the silvery glow disappeared and sinuous shadows danced across the walls as if the moon was alight with white fire. Maya padded to the front door and flung it open, eager to see what caused the shadows, uncaring of the dangers she might invite into her home.

She'd already stepped outside, one foot almost down the first stair when she stopped in her tracks, suspended in horror.

The whole world was ablaze. Orange and red and yellow flames roared and danced, eating away the homes, the cars, and even melting the tar on the street.

"Put out the fire, Maya." A honeyed voice whispered in her ear. Maya didn't fear the voice. Perhaps she knew its owner meant her no harm. Perhaps she'd heard such a voice somewhere before. She obeyed and took two more steps, away from the house and closer to the fire.

The flames threw a blanket of warmth around her. The urgency of time pressed upon her. Whatever she was meant to do had to happen soon.

"Use your power and put out the fire, Maya." The voice rang in her ears. No longer a honeyed whisper, the strong female tones clanged, loud, unavoidable and yet still nonthreatening.

Maya extended her arms, ready to try when she stiffened. In her dreamy calm she hadn't registered she'd only ever used her power to *create* or manipulate fire. Never to kill a blaze. The knowledge froze her to the ground and the flames crept close, eating at the sidewalk and the trees in her front yard.

Mrs. Finnegan's jacaranda roared into a wild blaze, and across the street, flames engulfed one house at a time.

"I don't know how," Maya whispered, her words stolen on a gust of heated wind.

"Maya, put out the fire, child." The voice was firm and Maya sensed its owner would soon lose patience with her. The thought of her anger filled Maya with dread. Some sense within her feared displeasing the invisible speaker. But the terror wasn't of retaliation, rather of disappointment.

"I don't know how," Maya cried, tears filling her eyes and dripping down her cheeks unchecked. Oddly, the tumultuous heat around her hadn't evaporated any moisture from her face.

She wanted to turn but found she couldn't move. The fire had reached a foot from where she stood.

"Yes, you do. Find it deep within yourself. You have the power. You need to accept your ability before you can master it."

Maya tried to look around her. She'd glimpsed a woman beside her. A woman with bright black eyes and bluish skin. A woman who exuded warmth and a deep sense of love. But Maya was still unable to turn to her. To face her.

"Maya, Hand of Kali. I have granted your wish. Do not make

me regret it." The woman whispered, her voice echoing within the roar of the oncoming flames.

An empty silence followed, leaving Maya bereft. Her attention returned to the rustling of the fire at her feet as they sucked the air from her lungs and threatened to engulf her whole.

She screamed, but the roaring flames swallowed the sound. She tried to concentrate, tried to draw on what she'd learned. Perhaps if she imagined drawing the flames into her body she might douse the raging blaze.

She held out her hands, taking the few seconds to calm herself and focus on the fire. She whirled the power inside her then sent it to her fingertips where it spun, tiny invisible whirlwinds.

She turned her palms to the fire and concentrated on urging the flames into her hand, to suck the vicious fingers of heat away. A rush of energy hit her head on and she stepped back, holding onto her concentration and onto the open link to the fire. Maya drew strength from deep within her. Perhaps it was those Chakras Nik had been going on about, but she wasn't sure. It wasn't the time to analyze now.

The heat around her lessened and she studied the street, aware the flames had backed away, retreating, defeated. She tried to close off the power, concentrating on the whirling energy inside her, but it didn't work. More and more flames were sucked into her body, swirling within her like living fire.

The heat consumed her and she shivered with fear. Unable to stop the steady stream of power, she panicked, tried to move her hands away. The sudden movement pulled her out of the link with the Fire energy but the fire inside her body continued to rage.

Soon she was ablaze, every inch of her skin. From afar, she saw herself, fire raging all over her body, even her hair bright and blazing in the now dark night.

The molten heat seared her from inside out and she began to

scream, an agonizing, pitiful keening as flames sought their way through her pores.

With a sudden rush of heat and a choked off squeak Maya woke up.

Just a dream. You idiot, it was just a dream.

Her pulse raced and she took deep breaths trying to calm down. As her heartbeat slowed and she settled her jittery fingers, she smiled into the darkness. She'd panicked over a mere dream. She reached for the nightstand, to switch the light on. Swinging her legs onto the floor, she headed for the bathroom, desperate for water. In the mirror, she appeared normal. She didn't even look like she'd awakened from a nightmare.

Maya shook her head, filled a glass and walked back into her room. She reached for the covers as she went to set the water down on her nightstand.

The glass dropped to the floor shattering into a million tiny daggers.

The entire surface of her bed, except for the spot she slept on, was blackened, scorched to a fine ebony dust.

MAYA SHIVERED, despite the heat still simmering on her skin. She watched her parents clean up broken glass, strip down the bed and inspect the mattress.

"It's ruined." Her dad shook his head. "Wow, you have some kind of power there, honey."

"Dev, she could've been killed and all you can think about is the extent of her power," her mom said, her expression filled with disapproval.

Maya's dad glanced at her, and winked. She smiled, understanding him completely. Yes, she may have been killed. But yes, this power was beyond anything she'd ever thought she'd possess.

"It just means you need to train really hard, Maya," he said, his placating tone entirely aimed at his scolding wife.

They lugged the ruined mattress out to the guest room and brought in the spare mattress. After they made the bed, all three sat down, staring at each other.

"Can you tell us what happened, honey?" said Leela.

"I was dreaming . . . . It was just a dream."

"Clearly it wasn't." Dev raised his eyebrows, but his eyes still twinkled a little too merrily for the occasion.

Maya related the entire dream, grateful she recalled everything. Usually when she woke from a particularly scary nightmare, she had to think hard to retain the memory of it. The longer she remained awake the harder it became to remember.

Not this time though. This time she remembered every detail.

Her dad exchanged a glance with her mom. "I'm no dream therapist, but I have two guesses. It's either your mind telling you that you have so much potential with your power…so much left to learn. Or it means the Dark Goddess has paid you a visit, to tell you something important about your power."

"Huh? What would that be?"

"You don't only have the power to create fire, you also have the ability to destroy it."

CHAPTER 15

The first Monday back at school was decidedly strange. Amber and her crew were predictable. Death-stares that required no weapons to be lethal. Maya scoffed. As if mere stares would affect her. But she remained aware Amber had caused her entire demon-smoking debacle. Aware too, the girl had gone to such lengths to orchestrate the whole evening. Maya planned to keep a solid eye on her from now on.

Ria and Joss gravitated to Maya and soon the girls trudged from class to class almost as if nothing had ever happened. Teachers nodded vaguely at Maya as if discussions included more than Byron's attack. Kids stared too. Some frowned, some gawked. Weird.

At lunch, the trio found a spot beneath a shedding tree, away from the rest of the tables.

"What's going on?" asked Maya. "People are staring, they're all acting real weird today."

Both Joss and Ria shrugged, a poor attempt to avoid the question.

"What? What the hell is happening here?"

Ria blushed, but was the first to speak, again throwing an all-your-fault glare at Joss who had the grace to provide a returning blush. "They think Byron did more than just beat you up."

"What? But . . . Nik corroborated my story. We were clear on that. Nothing else happened. He never got the chance." Maya's face burned. *What would people who believed that story think of her?*

Maya bristled. Why should she care? Sure, she needed to be concerned about her parent's reputation in the town, but the important people knew the truth. Didn't they?

"You don't believe it, do you?" Maya asked Ria. When her friend didn't answer, Maya hovered between panic and rage. "Ria!"

"What? Oh . . . no. Of course not. You said nothing happened. I believe you." But Ria's gazed sat somewhere in the vicinity of Maya's ear and her heart sank like a rusted anchor, prepared to hold her down until she drowned in a sea of her own pitiful tears. How could Ria actually believe such a thing? "Heads up. We have incoming."

"Huh?" Maya asked, confused as Ria's warning tugged her out of her cesspit of self-pity.

"Amber is coming over," Ria said.

Maya stiffened. What would she want? To gloat. Or make fun of her?

"Hey, Maya," Amber said, smiling, her honey eyes glittering in the sunlight. Odd seeing Amber stand before her so calm and steady, when she'd never been known to sit still. Even that funny thing she did, flicking the elephant-bead bracelet on her arm with one manicured fingernail. Amber's grandmother hailed from Kenya, and the ivory piece was an heirloom. Today, Amber's hands remained unnaturally still.

"Hey, Amber," said Maya, keeping her tone polite as she deliberately unclenched her hands.

"How are you doing, Maya?" said Amber, her voice rich and loud.

Maya offered a hesitant smile. For a moment, the strong scent of rancid meat distracted her. "I'm good." She gave Amber a second, harder inspection.

"We heard about Byron. I'm really sorry. I feel so responsible. If I hadn't invited you the whole horrible thing wouldn't have happened."

Maya could tell everyone heard it. The note of insincerity in Amber's voice. The lack of emotion as she spoke the words as if reading from a script. Maya cringed. The whole apology routine was probably a setup anyway. She forced herself to nod and smile.

Be nice. And maybe she will go away and leave you alone.

"You wouldn't happen to know where Byron is, by the way?"

There it was. Maya had expected some underlying reason for this conversation. Amber wanted to embarrass her in front of the school.

"Do you know where he is?" A hint of urgency edged Amber's voice. A lilt of desperation that implied Amber really needed to know where the demon had gone. Why the heck was she so desperate to know?

"I'm sorry. I have no idea where he is." Maya was careful to keep her tone as neutral as possible.

"Thanks for dropping by Amber." Joss sent the girl a tight smile that said plainly *You're done now so you can leave.*

Amber stared at the trio of girls, then stalked off. Maya held herself stiff against the deepest need to sigh in relief. She sensed eyes on her. She couldn't afford to show any kind of weakness.

"What was that all about?" Joss stared at Amber's back as she returned to her group of minions.

"No idea," Maya answered, but it was a lie. She knew what Amber wanted. She wanted exactly what she asked. Where was Byron?

The girls split up after school, each going their own way. Maya walked, deep in thought, passing big piles of rust-colored leaves as she went. Contemplating the new rules of her new life, the new purpose she now had, she almost missed the buzzing of her cellphone.

She fished the phone out of her jeans pocket, skimming the incoming text from Ria.

Had to go back to school. Come keep me company. I'll be at my locker.

Strange text, but Maya spun on her heel and headed back to the now eerily silent building. At least the main doors were still unlocked. She pushed through and strode down the hallway, her sneakers squeaking on the linoleum floor. It didn't take long to get to the bank of lockers housing Ria's locker, but the place sat silent and empty.

Maya scanned the hall. Nobody in sight, not a sound to indicate the place was occupied.

And yet.

She sniffed. The strange odor again. Rich blood and spicy incense. A heady, nauseating mixture burning at the back of Maya's throat. She swallowed to keep from throwing up all over herself.

A wave of cold spiked down her spine. The hairs on her neck prickled. She wasn't alone.

The strong smell of blood curled around her, assaulting her nostrils. Maya turned, almost expecting to see Byron, revived. The living dead come back to take his revenge. But it wasn't Byron who'd brought her to the darkened school, all alone and defenseless.

Amber stood in the middle of the hallway, her head tilted slightly to the right, tight curls shadowing the side of her face, shading her eyes in sinister darkness. It used to be a signature cute tilt that said *I'm popular and you really really want to be like me.* Today the pose seemed weird. As if Amber no longer had control of her body.

Maya clicked her tongue under her breath. Amber had come up behind her so quickly she hadn't had time to remove the

Madu from her bag. Now she slipped her hand beneath the flap of the satchel, hoping the dim light would hide the movement.

"I wouldn't do that if I were you," said Amber, her voice sounding a little off-color.

About to respond with a rude remark, Maya met Amber's eyes. And clamped her jaws shut in shock. Amber's eyes glowed the hot red of molten lava.

CHAPTER 16

Maya didn't stop. The point of the horn brushed against her seeking fingertips and Maya groped for the weapon, dragging it forth and dropping the satchel off her shoulder. She needed to be unhindered and ignored the contents of the bag as they scattered across the floor.

Only two practice sessions didn't give Maya the skill of a true warrior but she knew enough to defend herself and probably enough to damage her opponent with her vicious horns.

She hoped.

In the darkened silence of the school hall Maya faced the Rakshasa who possessed the body of Amber. It made sense; the two demons had worked together to drug Joss and force Maya into the house.

Maya faced a pissed-off demon looking for her partner.

As far as Maya could tell, Amber had brought no weapon with her, had held nothing within her hands, nor had she drawn anything from a pocket or sleeve. Yet now she held knives. Gleaming, deadly, sharp knives.

It took precious seconds for Maya to process the knives weren't separate weapons. They were merely extensions to

Amber's body. Every fingernail ended in a sharp, silver edged claw, and Maya now stared at ten deadly weapons capable of shredding her to pieces.

They circled each other, and Amber struck first. Maya swayed out of the way, arching as far back as possible, and prayed it was enough. She felt the air move against the skin of her abdomen, heard the fabric of her jacket rip as Amber's nails tore into the garment.

Maya didn't wait. She jumped and swirled, a roundhouse kick ending in a swipe with the Madu at the demon. Amber side-stepped the attack, raising her eyebrow in an *is-that-all-you-got?* look. Maya gritted her teeth in frustration. Of course, it wouldn't end so easily. What had she been thinking?

Amber came at her again and again, until pain raced through Maya's arm, followed closely by a warm moisture seeping into her sleeve. She'd been hit. No time to inspect injuries. Maya backpedaled, and tripped over the strap of her abandoned satchel. She slumped to the floor and watched Amber race at her, taking full advantage of Maya's clumsy misstep.

Amber fell onto Maya, the demon's aim clearly to pin her to the ground. Maya had other ideas. She'd tucked her foot close to her body as she fell, angling toward the demon as she attacked. At just the right moment, Maya lifted the sole of her foot, planted it into Amber's stomach and used the force of her landing to flip the other girl and throw her over.

The demon flew, the momentum of Maya's fall and the impact of the two girls enough to propel the Amber-demon across the hall into another bank of lockers a few feet away.

Amber grunted, and rose, holding her stomach.

"What the hell do you want?" Maya shouted, getting back up so she could protect herself better.

Amber laughed and her voice echoed, a deep spine-chilling variation freezing Maya's blood. "We want *you*, Maya. We want you."

"Well *you* are going to have to try harder. I'm no easy catch," said Maya, wondering at the folly of challenging the Rakshasa. Too late now.

"Don't you worry Maya Rao. We have your scent now. We have finally found you."

"What do you want from me?"

"What do we want? Surely you know." The demon laughed and for one awful moment Maya thought she saw the horrible deep red of the Rakshasa's true face. "We want your soul."

Maya frowned. Her parents hadn't said anything about the Rakshasas wanting her soul. *Perhaps there's more to this attack than even Mom and Dad know.*

The demon seemed to gain stamina merely from her statement. She attacked again. Renewed by determination and fear, Maya settled into a comfortable rhythm. She owned the Madus. They balanced within her palms, part of her body.

Only one problem - the Rakshasa possessed the same comfort with her own weapons. She swiped Maya with the back of her hand, the blow sending her crashing into a line of lockers. A few doors snapped opened, spilling their contents into the path of the demon.

Slightly stunned from the impact, Maya blinked a few times. Her heart pounded in desperation. She had no time to waste being knocked out. She jumped back to her feet keeping a bead on Amber who came barreling at her, swiping left and right with her clawed hands.

Maya used the Madus to defend the attack, stepped a little to her right and planted a kick straight into Amber's ribs. They both heard the crack, but Amber seemed unconcerned. Of course. This was only the body of the host. Most likely the demon would find another to possess.

Maya remembered Ria and the strange text luring her to the empty school.

"How did you get Ria's phone?"

The demon laughed, an almost baritone chuckle, so out of place within the tiny frame of the beautiful Amber.

"Where is Ria? What have you done to her?"

The Rakshasa may have hurt Ria. Spurred by that rage, furious that the demons were targeting friends, Maya attacked.

She spun on the ball of her foot, keeping clear of the fingertips of blades. Maya surged forward, feigning a move to the right, which the demon blocked with ease. Maya dodged fast to the left, slicing the angry tip of her weapon across Amber's bared jugular.

Blood spurted in a long red stream, the spray decorating the lockers and walls. The Amber-demon fell to the floor, clutching her neck. The Rakshasa brightness in her eyes faded. Maya couldn't take her eyes off the dying girl. She watched until her eyes returned to their warm hazel, and until the brief flickering of life faded.

Maya's first instinct was to close the girl's eyes, but a strange heated breeze brushed against her and she stiffened. She turned, and out of the corner of her eye she glimpsed the raw form of the demon. But when Maya faced it head-on it seemed shrouded in strange creeping shadows.

The Rakshasa growled, so loud and angry, the sound rattling the windows and sending the open doors of the lockers swaying back and forth. She hurled herself at Maya, the heat of its rage almost singeing Maya's cheeks.

Maya stepped back and fell, her heel catching on a fat marker from her bag. The demon kept coming, ten deadly blades on a collision course with Maya's chest.

And then the demon was swallowed by streams of shadow, disintegrating into blackness and Maya hit the ground, still in one piece.

CHAPTER 17

Maya shivered on the cold floor as dark wispy shadows swirled and faded into nothingness. Still in shock, she pulled herself to sit upright, scanning the hallways in case the demon was hiding in a shadowy corner. She needed to get up, and get out of the school before anyone found her there.

She stared again at the shadows. Something still felt wrong. Amber lay dead, her cold corpse blood-drenched on the hall floor, her blood decorating the walls in ghastly patterns.

The blood was enough to make Maya want to vomit. She shivered at the heady, revolting scent and forced her limbs to act, to drag herself back to stand on her shaking legs.

Maya turned to gather the contents of her bag, and froze. The dusky shadows beside the lockers shifted. As she stared, the wisps of shadow darkened, coalesced into a small, seemingly fragile woman.

Maya jerked her weapons about, ready to attack, as depleting adrenaline spiked back into her veins.

"You need not fear me, child," she said, her voice soft, and honey-warm, her deep brown eyes delicately almond shaped.

Even her smile radiated beauty. Nothing like the coldness of dark shadows from which she'd emerged.

Maya, hands shaking, refused to relax until she knew who her newest opponent was. She remained in attack mode and asked, "Who are you?"

"I am Chayya. Goddess of the Shadows and of the Shade."

Maya's mouth formed a small and silent 'o' and Chayya's pale pink lips turned up in a kind smile. Maya frowned, trying to recall if she'd ever heard of Chayya, but she drew a blank. Maybe she was one of the more obscure gods. Come to think of it, Maya had never heard of a goddess of shadows.

Maya scanned Chayya's face. She looked young for a goddess but then again what did Maya really know about gods and goddesses? Chayya stepped toward Maya, her long hair swaying behind her, hands tattooed in intricate henna patterns.

Maya stiffened but the goddess seemed unfazed. "Maya, I am here to help. There is not much time." Chayya glanced around at the bloodied walls and the corpse at Maya's feet. "We need to hurry and get you out of here."

In one smooth movement, Chayya grabbed the hanging end of her dark blue sari, swung it around her and tucked into the front of her skirt. It was the most mundane of actions but it brought Maya back to her senses.

Chayya chuckled before kneeling to help gather Maya's books and stationery from the floor. "This attire is not suitable for battle, but it will do for now. Come child. Get your things. We should leave now."

"I can't. I have to find someone." Maya shuddered, fearing what the demon may have done to Ria.

"We do not have time."

"I don't have a choice." Maya's body iced over, and heated up again just as fast. She had been disrespectful to a Goddess. Never mind her previous inclination to scoff at the mythology, the real thing was standing right in front of her, challenging her to disbelieve. "I'm sorry. My friend's life may be in danger."

"Very well. I shall call on the shadows to help. We do not have time to waste."

Maya frowned but continued searching the floor for her stuff. She grabbed her makeup bag, using it to deposit anything drenched in Amber's blood. Done, she rose to watch Chayya who now stood, arms akimbo, eyes closed.

Chayya murmured words beneath her breath, the rhythm and tone reminding Maya of a priest's incantations. Her heart thumped double time. Smoky shadows swam from corners and crevices in the hallway, speeding toward the goddess who called to them. They gathered around Chayya, spinning in a vortex of nothingness until they exploded in a hundred different directions as if orchestrated to instantaneously burst off down the hallways and into classrooms.

"Never mind them now, let them do their work," said Chayya, as if she'd just sent a group of kids off to play. Maya wouldn't have been surprised had the goddess dusted her hands together, satisfied her work was done. She watched Chayya out of the corner of her eye, wondering if all the gods and goddesses looked as young as she did. Must be nice to appear twenty-five forever. Maya pulled herself from her thoughts as Chayya asked, "Do you have everything?"

Maya nodded. "Why did you come?"

"You needed help, Maya. I have been charged with watching over you. And with supplying you with a little bit of education too. And so I came."

"How did you know I needed help? And why do you want to help me?"

"Because you are special. You are someone we have waited for. For a very long time the world has been in dire need of a person with strength, knowledge and power."

"And you think *I* am this person." Although Maya refrained

from injecting her self-contempt into her question, some of her emotion leaked through.

"Knowledge is gained from experience Maya. You have only just come into this power. Thus you need patience and tenacity."

Maya nodded, her mind drifting to the possible danger that Ria could be in. All because of her. How much good was she when she risked her friends lives just by knowing them?

They were ready to leave and Maya flinched as pain filtered through her forearm where the demon had wounded her. She was about to ask how long the shadows would take to search the place when little patches of foggy darkness flitted back and encircled the goddess. They came from every direction, converging on her like a million black moths to a living flame.

"She is not anywhere within this building Maya." Chayya's voice reverberated around the hall, echoing into the darkness.

"How can you be sure?"

"The shadows know life from death. They would know if your friend were here."

Dread seeped through Maya's veins like lethargic molasses. "And if she weren't alive?"

"Then they would sense her too. Every living thing has a life force and even when death comes, a certain living spirit remains until the body is disposed of," Chayya said, her voice gentle. "Do not worry Maya, your friend is not here and she is not dead. It means we need to search elsewhere. Come, let us leave this place."

Amber's corpse lay shrouded in inky shadows, steeped in cool, curdling blood, the story of her violent death told on the red-streaked walls around her.

The goddess and the girl turned and disintegrated into nothingness and shadows.

~

MAYA BLINKED as Chayya deposited her in front of Ria's house.

She felt slightly queasy from the whole disappearing and reappearing experience. She wasn't entirely sure she wanted to ever do that again. Teleportation certainly wasn't all it was cracked up to be.

Chayya glanced up at the Gupta's house. "This is where your friend is."

"That's great, thank you." Maya grinned and made to move to the front steps when Chayya touched her arm.

"I do not think you want to go there."

"Why not?" Maya tugged her hand away, trying not to be obviously rude.

"I sense the Rakshasa inside. It would be unwise for you to engage the demon while your friend's parents are present."

"Okay, I won't go barging in then. I need to make sure Ria is okay."

Chayya didn't reply. She nodded, and disintegrated into shadows.

Maya took a deep breath and bounded up the stairs to the Gupta's front door. She jabbed the bell, her stomach doing cartwheels. The Gupta's doorbell chimed, playing a popular Indian tune. Maya scowled. Ria's father really needed to step into the modern age. She tapped her foot, hardly able to wait until someone opened up.

At last, she was greeted by Ria's mother who bore the harried expression of a harried wife. Strands of hair escaped the bun tied low at the back of her head, a bright red dot broke the frown lines on her forehead and a smear of flour streaked across her cheek. Of course, no male member of their household would answer the door. Ria's dad had strange rules.

Mrs. Gupta beckoned Maya inside, a tense smile broke the sober lines on her face. "Hello, Maya."

"Hello Auntie Sunita. Is Ria home?"

Ria's mom peeked over her shoulder into the sitting room where Maya was certain Mr. Gupta sat, paying close attention to their conversation. She looked back at Maya, a sadness darkening her pretty green eyes as she shook her head. "Ria is home but she has chores. Can I give her a message?"

Maya was relieved despite being given the old Gupta runaround. At least Ria was home and safe.

"That's alright Auntie. I'll speak to her tomorrow."

Maya turned to leave and caught a glimpse of Ria in the front room. She stood beside the table lamp, the light casting shadows across her face. Maya's stomach twisted with dread. Something was wrong.

She backed away, walking home as fast as she could, trying to convince herself she'd imagined Ria's cold sneer and gleaming red eyes.

CHAPTER 18

The Rao household was silent. Shock settled like the first snow flurry, slowly cooling its occupants into a bland and emotionless silence, one step away from mourning. Maya saw the look on her mom's face; the pained expression of a woman who desperately needed to cry but who held herself in check so as not to upset her daughter.

When her eyes fell on Maya's bloodied arm she left the room for a few seconds to return with bandages and towels. At least she had something to do as Maya hadn't wasted time telling her family the whole sordid story. The ambush and Amber's death were expected pieces of her gory tale, the demon's escape wasn't. But the presence of the Goddess of Shadows sent the entire room into silence.

Maya didn't have time to grill her parents on why they were so worried about Chayya. She'd saved Maya's life so she couldn't understand the strange fear she'd seen in their eyes.

Claudia and Nik arrived soon after. Nik stuck around more for Maya's benefit than anyone else and she appreciated her parent's thoughtfulness although she wasn't entirely sure she wanted him around. But she was way too full of worry for Ria to be bothered with him right now.

"This is very unexpected," said Nik as he sat in the sofa opposite Maya. Her stomach tightened. He'd chosen the seat furthest from her. Clearly, he wanted some distance. Exactly what Maya wanted. Wasn't it?

"What? That the demon lured me into the school, attacked me, then ran off and possessed my friend?" Maya bit out, her tone bordering on icy.

"What?" Four voices asked in unison, sounding much like a ghostly acapella troupe.

"The demon has Ria."

"Maya. Explain please before we expire from shock." Her dad's voice soft and calm, as if she were a wild horse to be broken.

"It knew Ria is my friend. Obviously, she knew. Amber . . . or the demon . . . she used Ria's cell phone to lure me back to the school. But Ria wasn't there. Chayya searched for her-"

"Chayya looked for her?" Nik asked, managing to achieve a raised eyebrow expression without raising an eyebrow.

"Yeah, you have no idea . . ."

Maya's dad cleared his throat, bringing the two young people back to the conversation.

"Right. Okay, so I went straight to Ria's house after leaving school, and asked for her. Auntie Sunita said she was busy but as I turned to leave I saw Ria . . . and she had . . ." Maya stopped speaking. It hurt too much. The knowledge Ria could die stabbed her like a hot poker.

"Maya, chica, what did you see?" Claudia asked, her voice gentle as all eyes watched as Maya struggled with her pain and fear.

"Ria had red eyes, just like Amber's were at the school."

Maya swallowed hard and then burst into tears.

After she'd cried and relaxed somewhat Maya cleared her throat. "So what are we going to do about Ria?"

"Apart from breaking into the house, abducting her, and performing a spell by force, you mean?" Done with dressing Maya's wounds Leela folded her arms and sank into the cushions, dejected.

Maya scowled.

"She is secure in that house you know," said Maya's father. "Not much chance of storming the fort."

"Tell me about it," said Maya, dozens of memories flooding back of times Ria had not been permitted to do the usual kid social thing, like movies, concerts and parties, and even study dates. "Maharaja Gupta is a tyrannical ruler."

Everyone laughed, a strained, tight version of the real thing. Mr. Gupta's stringent control over his family was no secret, and as Maya watched her father's jaw clench, she acknowledged the adults saw much the same thing in the overbearing man's attitude as she did. The laughter died, and everyone gradually switched back to sober and worried.

THE NEXT MORNING ARRIVED, bleak and dull. The dressings on her cuts were changed and Maya was relieved to see they were thin slits in her flesh that would heal over soon enough. She had to force herself to go to school. But despite knowing it would seem strange if she were absent on this day of all days, the temptation to head off to some abandoned piece of land and use the trees for target practice almost won.

Maya gritted her teeth and jogged up the sidewalk to the entrance to the school. A strange buzz electrified the area. All around the stairs and the doorways, little clumps of students spoke in hushed tones.

Maya knew what they were talking about. She knew.

She was so deep in the black mire of her thoughts she entered the school's front doors and walked straight into Joss.

"Hey, I was just coming out to look for you." Maya's eyes narrowed as she examined Joss's decidedly green-gilled expression.

"What's the matter?" Maya asked, offering the most appropriate response considering she should be ignorant of the whole debacle, like everyone else.

"One of the halls is cordoned off." Joss answered, taking a deep breath of the outside air, and a couple steps away from the entrance. "Also happens to be the hall with our lockers. Means we can't get to them." As she talked, she walked down a few more stairs and leaned against the balustrade that hemmed in the stairway.

"Cordoned off?" Another appropriate response.

"The police are all over the place, yellow tape everywhere. The hall has seen better days, that I can tell you."

Maya needed to see for herself. "Will you be okay outside here for a few minutes?"

Joss nodded.

"I won't be long, okay?"

Joss nodded again, seeming happy enough to sit and wait for Maya.

Maya ran up the stairs and entered the building. The buzz intensified inside and she strode to the hall, scanning the corners for lurking shadows. Her heart thudded but thankfully no wisps of darkness lurked there.

She turned the corner.

The hallway looked pretty much the same as last night. Streaks of dried blood were painted across the walls, and along the floor. A pool of blood marked the spot where Amber had fallen and bled to death.

Maya guessed that Amber's body had been discovered either late the previous night or early this morning. A few uniformed men and women dotted the passage, swabbing and taking photographs, studying and talking. More hushed tones.

"Excuse me, Miss. If you need something from your locker you're just going to have to manage without it for today." A voice broke through Maya's thoughts. She turned to the source.

A police officer glared at her, as if her very presence created a disturbance. In a cool, flat voice, he warned her to stay away from the hall. Something about investigating a student homicide.

Maya retreated, leaving the grisly, blood-drenched hallway, swallowing hard as she walked. She felt like what she was - a criminal. Amber's blood streaked the walls and floor and it had all been her fault. Maya didn't care that the Rakshasa had started the whole thing.

If it hadn't been for her, Amber would still be alive.

She passed clusters of gossiping students as she headed back to Joss. The student body seemed to be abuzz with the news, as if the means and method of the death of a fellow student outweighed the actual death.

Near the front doors, a group of Amber's friends jostled Maya as she passed. All the girls bore the same brand of pained, red-eyed, fake grief.

Maya snorted in silence, passing by as invisible as always. Amber was never the most likable person. And Maya's seeming ability to blend into the schools walls and floors had, on more than one occasion, allowed her to be privy to the worst Amber-related gossip.

In reality, the dead girl's friends simply hated her guts. And now they cried for her. Maya didn't understand it. However it was painted, and no matter how horrible Amber had been, she hadn't deserved what happened to her.

The day had warmed a bit and the sun bathed Maya's face and head as she pushed through the doors. Joss glanced up at her and smiled, looking less green.

"Feeling better?" Maya asked.

"Yeah. Much." She shot Maya a sheepish smile. "Sorry."

Maya opened her mouth to make a joke out of the whole episode because both girls knew Joss wasn't going to live this down, when the hair at the back of Maya's neck rose, sparking little stabs of electricity down her spine.

And the odor of blood and spice scented the air.

Maya glanced up at the entrance to the school and sure enough, there stood Ria.

Or rather, the Rakshasa who had control of her poor friend's body. Ria stared at her, her eyes flicking from Joss to Maya, her lips curled in contempt.

She stared straight at Maya then glanced back at the doorway, meeting Maya's eyes again with a frigid glare. A spark of triumph flared in her dark eyes, eyes for the briefest moment glowed a faint amber.

"What the heck was that?" asked Joss, gripping Maya's arm.

"What?" Maya responded, frowning both at her shock and Joss's grip on her arm – the arm the demon had split open.

Joss glanced at her face, then at her upper arm where Joss's fingers dug into her flesh, nails and all. With a sheepish, uncertain expression clouding her features, she released her grip and said, "Nothing. I thought I saw something but it's way too weird." As she spoke, she stared up at Ria, an odd look marring her profile, as if she expected the other girl to sprout another head.

Maya said nothing, unsure of how to respond, especially when her heart thudded with the possibility that Joss had seen Ria's eyes glow. Maya hadn't even known it was possible for normal people to see a Rakshasa's true form.

All the while Ria stood at the top of the stairs, unmoving as if entranced. Kids walking in and out of the school parted for her, like water around a rock in a stream. But it was her dead, cold stare that chilled Maya to the bone.

"Maybe we need to speak to Ria."

"I really don't think so Maya, not after the way she just looked at us. I'm no sucker for punishment okay?"

Joss met Maya's eyes and Maya knew nothing she said would change her mind. Ria had her well and truly spooked.

"Fine, I'll go myself," Maya said a little too sharply.

But even before she took the first step toward the Ria-demon, the Rakshasa disappeared, merging with the crowds, gone before Maya could get to her.

CHAPTER 19

When the doorbell chimed the last person Maya expected was Ria's father. Maya's dad answered the door, and was left there, his greeting falling onto deaf ears as Mr. Gupta stalked past him, brushing his meaty shoulders against him, his chubby cheeks pink and moist. He stomped into the living room with Ria in tow. Ria whose face and arms were covered in purpling bruises.

Maya's mother and Claudia rose from the couch where they'd been talking. Now they stared, visibly horrified by the poor girl's injuries. Did they, like Maya, also fear the obnoxious man may have brought a demon into the Rao home? Maya lowered the volume on the movie she'd been watching.

"Ria?" Maya stood up, wanting Ria to look up at her so she could see if the Rakshasa was still in control.

"Don't you dare speak to her! You've done enough damage to my family already." Mr. Gupta's black eyes speared Maya's, like she was some disgusting thing stuck on the sole of his shoe.

Maya stared at the red-faced man. Every instinct told her not to speak, not to talk back. He was an adult, after all, and good little Indian girls knew how to be respectful. But she couldn't control her need to know what was going on.

"What do you mean? I haven't done anything!"

Mr. Gupta laughed, the harsh bark spattering Maya's cheek with drops of spittle. "Pretend all you want but the entire town knows exactly what you are. And it's certainly not a lady!"

Maya wiped her face, repulsed by the warm moisture, but she couldn't linger on her distaste for Mr. Gupta's body fluids. She was desperate to find out what he meant, why and how he could have hurt his own child so badly. Not that he hadn't hit Ria before, but previous instances had left her with a black eye or a sprained wrist, not leaving her looking like she'd been used as a punching bag.

Ria watched in silence, a shadow of a smirk on her lips. That one little curl of her mouth confirmed the demon was still inside Maya's friend's body. What was the Rakshasa up to? What had she done to make Mr. Gupta so angry he'd hurt his daughter this way?

"Now, Gupta. What are you trying to say?" Maya's father asked, his voice an octave higher as his anger built at the other man's insults.

"What I am trying to say Rao, is you've spoiled and coddled your daughter far too much! She's an embarrassment to the entire community and you'd better do something about it. Soon."

"You're not making any sense."

"Sense? What doesn't make sense is how you can condone her behavior. Surely, you don't approve of her consorting with the Richards boy? Interesting cover story too. You really think we believe that nonsense about him beating her up?"

At first Maya was a tad confused. Richard's boy? Then it dawned on her - Byron.

"What was it, Maya? A lover's quarrel? And now nobody can find the boy? Not to mention the horrible death of that Alden girl."

"Come on, Gupta. Maya couldn't have had anything to do with that boy's disappearance or the Alden girl's death," Maya's father responded with iron control but a vein beat blue and angry at his temple. "I hardly think you really believe the things you're saying."

"Oh yes, I believe it. And why do I believe it? Because I had a nice long talk with my daughter. That is how. Ria's behavior and attitude has gone from bad to worse. And your daughter's influence has been the sole cause. I understand some people are unable to enforce proper discipline in their homes," Mr. Gupta glanced at Dev, criticism clear in his fiery eyes. "But please don't make your inability to control your daughter my problem."

Ria's father faced Maya, his flabby cheeks wobbling with anger, his eyes flashing the depth of his dislike. "I came here tonight to tell that girl to stay away from Ria. I don't want her in my house. I don't want them to even know each other. I know it may not be in your nature to respect the wishes of an adult but Ria certainly will. Won't you, Ria?"

He'd held onto Ria's arm throughout the entire conversation as if he suspected she might run for her life. Maya would have, had she been in Ria's shoes, but Ria herself? No, Ria wouldn't have run. Now, he shook his daughter's arm, his fingers clasped so hard into her skin it seemed very likely the pudgy digits would sink right into her reddened flesh.

"Insolent girl." Gupta turned to his captivated audience pointing an uplifted palm at Ria. "See, how she doesn't answer. She has learned to be disrespectful from Maya. But I will no longer tolerate it."

He turned and stamped out of the living room, and out of the house dragging Ria with him. A car door slammed, then another and the vehicle took off, speeding down the street.

"Things are getting a bit too exciting around here these days," remarked Leela, as if the infuriated man had been nothing more than a courier delivery guy.

"Did you see the way she looked at me?" Maya whispered.

Her father nodded. "So what do you think that was all about?" he said.

"The demon has control of Ria's body. I think she pushed Mr. Gupta to the edge knowing he would blame me. Probably knowing she can get into the house that way."

"Even if she entered, the house is warded, right from the foundations up. No way would she have been able to stay here, or take anyone's body." Dev Rao sighed, weary and worried.

"Then she will try to find another way to get to Maya," said Claudia. "I'll go check the wards."

"Wait, I'll join you," said Maya's mother.

The two women left the room. At least they had a purpose. Maya hated being useless in this situation. But what did she know about warding a house against evil anyway?

Maya decided to ask the big question. The subject everyone seemed to be avoiding at all costs.

"So . . . about Chayya."

Her father glanced at her, a worried expression painted on his face.

"See! What's that look for? What do you guys know that you're all keeping from me? Is she some evil god or something?"

"Okay Maya, no need to get upset," her dad placated her. "It's not Chayya herself we are worried about. It's the fact that a god, any god, is here in this town, that is a concern."

"Why? Surely, she was here to help. She didn't seem like she was threatening my life or anything."

"No, what is a concern is that the gods only get involved for two reasons. Mischief, which I don't think applies in this case, or . . ."

"Or?" prompted Maya.

"Or it means big time crap is about to hit the fan," said Dev.

"Alright. Now what?" asked Maya, frustrated. They seemed to keep going in circles.

"No idea."

CHAPTER 20

The next evening, with Ria's possession still on her mind, Maya disappeared to the silent gym, determined to try and make more valuable use of her time. A lot better than sitting in her room replaying the memory of a certain kiss and how horribly it had ended. Or the messy death of Amber.

Soon she was immersed in the moves of her latest routine. She loved the silence of the studio when all the teachers and students had left after training. The cloth of her sleeves labored against her sides as she performed each move, the sound swift and harsh. Her feet moved rapidly against the plastic mats, rubbing the floor in short sharp strokes. The burst of flames rushing in small roars spurting from her hands like little red and orange flamethrowers.

Odd how she'd never enjoyed her Kung Fu training and yet now when she combined the art with her Fire practice, she seemed to have developed a deeper appreciation for it. She still didn't believe she was much good at the martial arts, but at least she enjoyed the sessions rather than gritting her teeth the entire time.

Maya paused in her workout, an odd sound reaching her ears,

loud enough to break her concentration. The bright fluorescents of the studio brought everything into stark contrast. Beyond the windows, the last dregs of daylight had fled the sky.

Although she strained to listen, Maya heard nothing. *Dad will be back soon to fetch me.*

Scared of being alone, Rao?

She scowled, shaking off the paranoia. The stupid inner voice was right, she'd become overly cautious, borderline paranoid. The week had crawled by, each day a visceral sign of how much her world had changed. Ria's absence from school had served as a constant reminder that their trio was down to a duo because one of them was currently possessed by a demon.

Even Joss was subdued. Whether her encounter with Ria had dampened her usual joy for life, or whether she sensed the carnage in the air, Maya had no idea. Besides, she had little time left for messing around. Training followed every day of school, hours of backbreaking, finger-blistering, eyebrow singeing practice.

And though Maya's improvement was consistent and strong she often wondered what the purpose was to it all. Chayya had disappeared, and the demon in control of Ria had retreated to the shadows. It would have been so easy to pretend nothing bad had ever happened.

There.

The sound came again, a scrabbling of paws and claws at the door to the studio. Maya sighed, relieved she hadn't imagined it, but annoyed at being disturbed at all. She'd finally reached the stage in her fire training where she was able to send out small controlled bursts of flame. She practiced her accuracy on dozens of targets set up around the gym. Right now, she had to douse the flames of them before she went searching for strange noises.

Learning to absorb the fire had been much harder than actually producing one. Maya concentrated, pulling the energy toward her, sucking the power out of the hot flame before it entered her body. Or was it her mind? She was still unsure where the flame went. She made a mental note to check with Nik.

When Maya opened the door, the entrance fell silent. She clicked her tongue, more annoyed now than ever as she searched the blackness hanging from the moonless sky. A strange foulness filled the air, as if rotten garbage littered the street.

She wrinkled her nose and retreated into the room. She was about to lock up when a vicious growl erupted from the darkness beside the door. She'd seen Chayya's shadows coalesce and dissipate but these dark and oily blobs were no mild shades. A viciousness in the rumble of the sound sent blades of ice deep into Maya's veins.

She froze, struggling to see anything within the night. Beads of nervous sweat coated Maya's forehead as she forced her body to behave, to cease its shuddering.

No fear.

Don't be afraid. Animals can smell fear.

Whatever lurked outside in the black night knew she was terrified.

She moved her fingers again, a fragment of an inch-hardly much considering the door stood wide open. But the unseen creature growled, the sound sending waves of terror into her bones. The street remained silent, no lights shone. The nearest streetlights were out too. As if everything had fled from the presence of the invisible evil lurking outside.

Now what?

She couldn't close the door, and she couldn't run. Did it mean she had to stay and die? But Maya gritted her teeth, knowing and feeling the power of the fire coursing through her veins. She could defend herself. If she could smoke a friggin' demon she could darn well smoke whatever creepy animal stood outside.

Bring it on.

A monstrous dog sprang from the darkness, its haunches as high as Maya's shoulders. It growled again, jowls shivering, spittle dripping from gaping pink jaws, four eyes glaring. All this she processed in slow motion as it took mere seconds for the dog to land on her, and even less for both Maya and the creature to hit the ground.

Its paws slammed into her chest, sending shards of agony into her body. The amount of pain made Maya look down at her chest. Blood. Too much of it for Maya to believe everything would be okay.

She examined the dog's blood-drenched paws and shivered at the sight of its enlarged, and deadly sharp claws. Just like the Rakshasa's.

Wait a freaking minute. Four eyes?

It was a demon dog.

But Maya refused to take it lying down. The beast backed off and watched her, its head tilted slightly to one side as if it listened to the voice of an absent master. She stared at the beast, eyeballs-to-eyeballs, and rose inch by tiny inch to her feet. She would have run except a second growl stopped Maya in her tracks.

Another monstrous dog stood behind her, within her line of sight. Maya wanted to cry. Until she remembered she had a pretty strong power herself. She just needed to produce the bursts of fire without giving herself away.

Maya concentrated on the steady panting and the gleaming black eyes, searching deep inside herself for the fire. Heat rose in tiny waves from her gut. The solar plexus Chakra Nik had mentioned. The heat built up steadily until its molten fire broiled. At last, Maya readied her hand turning it ever so slowly to face her palm to the animal, keeping a steady eye on him.

Maya sent a burst of fire straight at the dog in front of her, dashing out the door as soon as the flame left her hand. Behind her, the dog yelped and whined, in pain at the mercy of her fire.

She ran, leaving the gym behind, knowing she couldn't outrun those hideous monsters but trying anyway.

The clatter of claws on the blacktop confirmed the second creature was hot on her heels. She stayed focused, and sped off. As fast as she'd ever run in her life. But it wasn't enough.

The dog caught up to her, ran beside her for as long as it took to swipe at Maya's leg, knock it out from under her and send her tumbling onto the sidewalk.

Her chest burned with the wounds from the first dog and now her calf was surely split wide open.

They were intelligent enough to know the best way to bring her down. Who sent these animals to kill her? Someone must want her dead.

Badly.

Maya had no energy left to produce her fire. No other means of self-defense except to run and *that* was no longer a viable option. But she could use her body and her strength to beat the beast.

She waited as the animal drew closer, as it stood over her, staring at her face. It bent its head and sniffed her skin. The dog nuzzled her injured calf, and whined, pushing her leg with its huge wet nose. The nose drifted up to her neck where the dog nudged her again, sniffing and whining and pawing the concrete. Agitated about something, the creature didn't see her bring her leg up.

Maya kicked it straight in the ribs, and the dog howled in pain. She got to her feet, glared at the animal now whining piteously on its side. She would have to kill it. Whoever had sent it would either send more or come here himself to retrieve the monster.

Yes, she had to kill it. And she could harness her firepower now that she had her breath back, not to mention the surge of adrenaline rushing though her body.

Maya focused her mind, and concentrated on the crying animal. For the briefest instant pity tugged at her heart until the burn of her injuries reminded her they were here to kill her ass.

The fire built inside her again, stronger this time and more focused.

She stepped back, aimed her hands at the dog and pushed the heat through her fingers, expecting the pulse of energy to shoot through her arms.

Nothing happened.

Maya stared at her hands, scowling at them. What had gone wrong? She was positive she'd done everything right. Had the energy been greater, it would have killed the animal.

A breeze lifted Maya's hair, throwing loose strands across her face and a hand grasped her forearm.

"Maya. Leave the poor dog alone. It is not here to harm you," a woman said behind her.

Maya spun on her heel, ready to counter the woman's ridiculous statement with the proof of her injuries. But when she turned, all words left her throat.

A woman stood there, shrouded in a blood red sari, her hands adorned with golden jewelry. Maya had seen enough pictures and statues in her lifetime to know who the woman was. Her black hair flared out behind her in a wavy sea, all the way to her waist. The most distinctive part of her though, was the color of her skin. Her entire body was the color of a deep blue sea.

The Goddess Kali stood before Maya.

CHAPTER 21

$\mathcal{M}$aya couldn't help but stare. Strange. The bluish tinge to her skin didn't even clash with her pitch-black hair or the red of her garment. Maya was a little disappointed to see the goddess only had one pair of arms. She'd expected four at the very least. Still, she was even more beautiful than Chayya.

"Hello, Maya. I had hoped we would meet under better circumstances but I believe you need me, and so does Sabala, it seems," said Kali, throwing a wry glance at the prone dog.

"Sabala?" Maya hadn't imagined her first meeting with the Goddess of Death to be this mundane. In fact, she hadn't envisioned meeting the Dark Goddess at all. Somehow, even her encounter with Chayya hadn't prepared her for this.

"Yes, this is Sabala." Kali was already tending to the dog, who still lay writhing in agony on the concrete.

Harden up, mutt. You ripped me to shreds and you don't see me crying like a baby, do you?

Soon the dog got to his feet, nuzzling Kali's legs in gratitude. More like adoration. Without his hideous growl, he resembled a four-eyed, muscle-bound Doberman, vicious teeth and all. He trotted over to Maya, who flinched and remembered to hold still. It wasn't because she was afraid of dogs in general. Her trepidation was due to Sabala's very recent attempt to rip her to pieces.

"His brother Syama is back there." Kali pointed a dainty finger at the gym. "Syama and Sabala are the dogs of the Underworld. The dogs of Patala."

"They belong to Yama?" asked Maya.

"Yes, they are his guard dogs…his search dogs. The dogs and others like them roam your world seeking those who have escaped their fate. They also, come to hunt the Rakshasas and return them to Patala where Yama can deal with their fates."

"Why do they want me?" Maya swayed on her feet, about ready to collapse.

"They do not want you. They seek the creature that has marked you." At Maya's frown Kali continued, "They seek the Rakshasa who has escaped her death. The one who has taken your friend. And of course, they track the demons by odor. The scent of the Rakshasa remained on your body after your battle."

"Ria? These dogs are looking for the demon who has taken over Ria?" Maya shivered, the horror of how Ria could die made her head spin. "If they find Ria they'll kill her."

"No, Maya. I will not let that happen," Kali replied, her tone firm.

"Who sent them?"

"Yama. Or to be specific, whoever is in charge of the Hellhounds. The dogs get their orders and then set out to fulfill them." Kali turned and led the way back to the open door of the studio. The lights blazed a bright welcome from the shadowy darkness of the street. As they entered the gym, the streetlights flickered and switched on one at a time.

Maya thought of Nik who should've been passing the information to Yama. But really, she had no idea how these things worked. No real idea how Nik communicated with his boss in Patala.

Kali knelt beside the other dog. Maya recalled its name. Syama. Both the animals were identical, not a hair different from each other.

"So the Rakshasa should have died? What happened?"

"That is what we need to find out. Chayya has told me the demon possessed your friends." The beast twitched then shook his head and sneezed. He moved one paw at a time and got to his feet, and proceeded to nuzzle the golden edge of Kali's blood-red sari in much the same manner as his brother had.

Maya didn't deny that Amber had been her friend. At this point, it was hardly necessary. The girl was dead anyway. And probably never responsible for the whole Byron episode either.

"So what will they do now? Won't Yama be angry that they haven't done their job? Or whoever it is they report to?" asked Maya.

Both the dogs turned to look at Kali, the same expression of expectation mirrored on their faces, as if they'd understood Maya's question and also sought the answer.

"I will speak to Yama. They must go home now." The dogs whined, pawing at the carpet in protest. Perhaps they feared their master. "No nonsense, you two. Off you go. And do not fear, I shall send Yama the news so he is not angered by your failure."

Both animals, the monsters that had lurked in the shadows and scared the living daylights out of Maya, the creatures who had ripped the skin at her chest and cut her leg open, now jumped up and down, spinning and chasing their tails like puppies beneath the benevolent gaze of the Dark Goddess.

Maya had to smile. The sight was such a happy one it was easy to forget how quickly the beasts could have killed her.

The dogs turned in unison, and ran to Maya, running circles around her too, nuzzled her legs and then sped off out the open door, into the night. Before they crossed the blacktop both animals disappeared.

Maya faced Kali, eager to know how she intended to help Ria.

Her head spun as she moved and her vision clouded as she opened her mouth to speak. She fell to her knees instead, her legs unable to carry her, her body overcome by blood loss and shock.

MAYA STIRRED, her breath coming in raspy gusts. Pain lay on her chest, burning strands of it etched into her living flesh. Shards of memories drifted to her.

"Kali," she whispered.

"Yes, honey, the goddess will help you. Pray to her," Leela said, but Maya wanted to laugh. She knew her mom assumed her words were only prayers. What else would she think they were?

Perhaps it was all a dream.

"Stay still, Maya. You've lost too much blood. And you have to tell us what happened."

"The dogs, they attacked me. And Kali came to save me."

"What dogs, honey?" asked her mom.

"Leave her."

Maya heard the voice and relaxed on her pillow. Just the rhythm and tone of Kali's voice was enough to send waves of calm through her body, relaxing her tense and tired muscles. Kali leaned over her, in much the same way she'd done with Sabala and Syama.

The goddess laid a palm upon her heated forehead, then sat beside her. Kali lifted her hand off the bed and smiled at her. The goddess was beauty personified. How had she ever thought her a hideous depiction of blood and sacrifice? How ignorant had Maya been to scoff at the beauty of this love now passing through her.

Kali healed her body, repairing the damage done by Yama's pets. Maya sighed as the pain faded away, as the muscles loosened and healed. She thought of Ria and a shaft of fear rushed through her heart. She prayed her friend would remain safe.

Once Maya got better she had to find a way to free Ria from the hold of the Rakshasa.

For now, she had to heal. Strength meant she'd have the power to fight the Ria-demon.

Her eyes drifted closed and she sank into a deep sleep. Beyond the reach of pain and sorrow.

But not beyond the reach of dreams.

CHAPTER 22

*E*ven the air seemed to know something momentous was about to happen. It seemed to know, too, that this event was not a happy one, for it hung, unmoving, dense and heavy with incense and the rich odor of frankincense. The priestesses burned them incessantly, hoping to drive away the evil spirits and demons sure to be lurking in the darkness at times like these. Shadows curled around the pillars of the temple hall, slithering in sinuous blackness, disappearing into nothing high above their heads.

Mother was dying.

Her breath came in shallow, uneven waves. The buttery light from the oil-lamps shuddered, gleaming, reflecting against the gold threads in the fabric of her crumpled, sweat-ridden sari, like tiny golden, ghostly fireflies. Her drenched red cotton sari lay plastered to her emaciated form, and her dying body resembled a bloodied corpse.

Her chest rose and fell, the movement so fleeting that many times the priestesses leaned over her, to place a cheek close to her mouth hoping for a whisper of heated breath to confirm she still lived, she still breathed. The fevers had turned her body into a mere shadow of the once-strong, once-vibrant Mother.

Against the rich burgundy of the fabric, her skin looked sallow, papery thin, and burned with fever. Such a fever her dark cheeks were rosy with the blush of it.

She groaned and turned to the statue of the Dark Goddess, her pallet conveniently placed within the inner sanctum of the temple. In the outer room, the priestesses began to sing. Soft and low, the rhythm of their voices and the heartbeat of music soothed both ear and mind, entrancing. The sweet melody rose, joined by cymbals and the methodic beat of drums. Music of devotion, music to move to and dance to. Music for life, not this pathetic excuse for what was left of the high priestess of the temple.

The Mother blinked, a tear gathered in her eye, burning with the heat of fever and regret, pooling as she struggled to swallow and breathe and clutch the last seconds of her life to her breast. The tear escaped from her eye as she clasped her hands to her heart and prayed, muttering ancient chants.

Would her prayers be heard?

Would the music of her daughters guide her prayers to the feet of the Dark Goddess?

The Mother gathered her will and her faith, and pushed herself upright, struggling to stay seated even though she shouldn't have the strength to do more than raise her head a few inches off her sodden pillow.

The dried ropes of the pallet cracked and groaned beneath her. She transferred her weight to her weak legs, legs shuddering with the effort, promising to give way if she so much as blinked.

The Mother shivered, bent over, body so heavy, so tired. She held on to the bed frame, and then a nearby pillar, for support. The pillar felt hot, it burned her fingertips, seared her palms. Or perhaps her own body emitted the intense heat. She ignored it, the way she ignored the sparks from the ceremonial fires, when they sometimes spat their flaming embers at her as she prayed.

She shuffled forward, one pillar at a time, urging her feet to move, one heated inch and then the next, until she reached the foot of the statue. The form of the Dark Goddess shone, pure unadorned stone. The marble gleamed the deep blue of the dark waters of the sea. No garments hid her body from view, no garlands shrouded her, just the single slim rope of marigolds carved into the stone itself. The face of the goddess was beauty incomparable, hair flung out behind her, hanging down her back and over her shoulders. No red blood dripped from her mouth or coated her tongue.

This temple did not glorify the Dark Goddess's power. Only her purpose.

Her power was subtle.

Her purpose was infinite.

Like the simple stone carving itself. Severed demon heads emerged, skillfully formed from blue marble, their ghastly teeth and glaring eyes neither shocking, nor fearful.

The Mother imbued her power in the followers who came to train under her, men and women who sought her teaching, and travelled from the furthest ends of the Earth to learn at her feet, who learned the skills and arts of the Dark Goddess. Who stayed and practiced, and left the temple grounds. Sometimes they returned but mostly they did the work of the Dark Goddess in silence, with no desire for glory or prizes.

Sinking to the uneven stone floor, the Mother's breath left her lips in a heated, achingly tired sigh. Palms flat on the stone she slipped to her knees, her spine coiled, small puffs of breath forced in and out of her fever-weakened lungs. Soon she sat cross-legged, knees ablaze with the fever fire, before the gleaming marble statue.

She pleaded with her goddess.

Her time had come but she had not fulfilled her deepest

desire. A lifetime spent training those who would serve. A lifetime without reprieve. The Mother had never gone out into the world to serve the Dark Goddess. That which she had always wanted but the goddess had not allowed.

Perhaps now she will give me a chance, thought the Mother. *Perhaps now I shall be able to serve her with my strength, serve her as a warrior, not as a teacher.*

Perhaps.

CHAPTER 23

Maya blinked, awakening to the sound of birds in the trees, and a kid tooting a bicycle horn and screaming with laughter. Outside the house, the world went by as normal. But inside the Rao household emotional chaos was the order of the day.

A soft knock on the door ushered in Maya's parents. The smiles they gave her seemed weak, lukewarm, their faces looked drawn and tired. She could so easily ignore them. All she really wanted to do was turn her back to them and demand to be alone. She was so over all the lies, all the subterfuge. For so many years they'd kept the truth to themselves, lies and smoke behind fake smiles.

"Honey, are you okay?" Leela lay a meal tray over Maya's legs. Some kind of soup and buttered rolls. Maya wanted to laugh. They were feeding her invalid food when she'd just been healed by a goddess who shouldn't exist. A thrum of guilt simmered inside her.

Maya nodded and paid close attention to her soup. The silence in the room thickened much like the meal itself. She lifted her chin and caught the glance Dev and Leela exchanged. Unsure, guilty.

"What the matter with you guys?"

There was that look again. "Nothing, honey. We are fine. Just worried about you." Maya's dad moved closer and sat on the edge of the bed, but she could tell he barely allowed his weight to settle into the mattress. As if the slightest movement would hurt her in some way.

She lay back against the pillows, tired to the bone. "I can tell something is wrong."

"Nothing is wrong," said Leela, pulling the chair from the dressing table toward the bed. "It's not every day we have an audience with a goddess."

Maya snorted. "I'd have thought you guys would've taken it way better than me."

"You would think," said her dad with a wry grin on his face. "We knew the time would come. We didn't realize it would come so soon."

"I can handle it, Dad," Maya said with a soft sigh.

"I'm sure you can. It's just not that easy to watch your daughter arrive home ripped apart."

"I'm fine now," Maya hoped he'd change the subject. She frowned, as an odd shuffling filtered into the room. "So what did she tell you?"

Something, Maya wasn't entirely sure what, made her unwilling to say Kali's name out loud. She felt uneasy, as if the mere mention of her name would summon the goddess. Maya still wasn't sure how she felt about her, so better she stayed absent until Maya gathered her wits.

"Kali-Ma was very clear in her instructions. We are meant to train you and protect you as well as we can." Dev looked at her, exchanged a nervous glance with her mom and then looked over his shoulder at the door. He turned back to meet Maya's eyes and for a brief second she could have sworn she saw a flicker of guilt.

"What is it, Dad?"

"Kali was keen for you to have the ultimate protection-"

"Those were her words actually, *ultimate protection*," said her mother.

Maya's dad eyed her, a touch of amused impatience on his face. "So in order for you to have the best possible protection she left behind a guard."

Maya snorted, and studied the orange sludge in her bowl again.

Do they really expect me to eat this?

"She was happy since you know the guard you'll be comfortable having him around." When Maya's dad shifted on the mattress and shared that strange look with her mom again, she knew for certain something was up.

"What's wrong with you two? What are you keeping from me?" She glared at them, eyes narrowed, although even the small muscular effort was beginning to tire her.

"Dev, you may as well tell her, she's going to find out anyway."

Maya wanted to be annoyed, but she couldn't gather up the energy. She shook her head and snorted. "Yeah Dev, tell me," Maya mumbled.

Her dad grinned. "The goddess left Sabala behind to protect you. He will guard you day and night. She was adamant he's not to leave your side."

The sound at the door made sense now. The soft keening filtering through from the other side was a dog's muted whine. Maya shuddered, the agony in her wounds as fresh as when the mutt had inflicted them.

She was so horrified at the prospect of the hellish beast entering her room she stared at the door in silence, willing it not to open.

"Are you alright, honey?" asked her mother, almost whispering. Was she afraid for Maya or the beast?

"You're going to have to accept him at some point. The

goddess gave us these instructions. And I'm guessing the dog knows what his duty is. There is no declining this offer," Dev said. Maya recognized his "Dad being reasonable" tone.

"That dog is not just a dog, Dad. He is a hellhound. A dog from hell. One who, only a few hours ago, tried to kill me." Maya's voice rose, every second word inching a note higher as she spoke, until it cracked on the last syllable.

Her dad stood, and she knew the argument was over. "Honey, it's now or later or tomorrow. It's inevitable. You're not going to be able to leave this house without him you know."

Through the discussion and the fears of the dog from hell, Maya had forgotten she wasn't a helpless little girl. She had power. And she'd defended herself pretty well against Sabala and Syama. She guessed she could handle him if he stepped out of line.

Still, she wasn't jumping for joy.

A soft scratching came from the other side of the door and Maya cringed. Was he gouging those horribly sharp nails into her bedroom door, or was he scraping the wood floors instead?

Maya's dad spared her one last glance before he stepped to the door and turned the knob, allowing Sabala to enter. If ever she'd seen a dog imbued with majesty it was this one. He entered, head high, eyes locking with Maya's. She could have sworn he gave her a small nod, as if acknowledging that she'd relented to his presence.

His pelt gleamed ebony, like his four eyes. But before he lowered his head Maya caught a glimmer of amber from those obsidian eyes. Like a ring around the darkness. Not as bad as Amber's demonic eyes but it still had the power to creep Maya out.

He turned to glance at her parents. Maya snorted. Both looked ready to bow or kneel before the creature.

He is not a god, people!

But Sabala merely gave them a quick once-over, then turned

his head back to Maya. He moved closer, nails clicking on the polished floor, then silent as he stepped onto the small rug beside her bed.

He lowered his haunches and remained as still as a statue. Maya could have sworn he didn't even breathe. She sighed. Maybe if she pretended he was really a statue she'd get through this whole thing much easier.

Staring at the dog, Maya's muscles twinged, her body remembering the fiery heat of the injury Sabala had inflicted. She gritted her teeth. The urge to break the dog's neck washed over her and startled her, shoving Maya out of this strange funk.

She sighed again.

Sure, he'd attacked but he'd had his reasons. Now he obeyed his mistress. Who knew if he was happy with the job himself. Maybe he hated his assignment as much as Maya despised it.

She stared and he stared back.

Stalemate.

CHAPTER 24

The door closed softly behind Maya's parents as they left her alone with the silently staring Sabala. Huge glassy black eyes stared at her - all four of them. The ringing of Maya's cell-phone barely penetrated her studious haze.

Sabala blinked.

Maya blinked.

And the link between them broke as Sabala's lip rose with a flash of pink flesh and hideously sharp canines. He looked at the phone and Maya grabbed it, answering it quickly before he reacted further. She had no idea what he would've done. The dark gleam in his eyes didn't bode well for Maya or her phone.

To think she was stuck with this abhorrent creature until Kali was good and ready to call him off. Ugh!

Maya glanced at the number on the phone.

Joss.

And before she knew it, the insistent voice on the other end of the call announced her imminent arrival. No amount of cajoling or excuses helped. Maya had always known the girl was stubborn.

Now what? Maya wondered as she stared at her phone, then

quickly hid it under her pillow before Sabala got any ideas. Joss had cut the call while Maya tried to convince her that coming over was a bad idea.

She stared at Sabala. *Any bright ideas, pooch?*

How do I explain my state of recovery? Then it hit her. Kali had repaired the damage her guard dog had inflicted. Maya was fine. She sat up and lifted her shirt, inspected the skin on her abdomen. A few dark welts remained, where, not too long ago, the flesh had been ripped apart, dripping blood all over her agonized self. Even the wound on her arm from the Amber-Rakshasa was fully healed, not a trace of the cuts left.

Maya lay back amongst the pillows. What were her parents thinking? Were they happy? That in the end they'd raised their reincarnated Mother? Was that what gave them satisfaction? Or were they glad to have Maya for Maya herself? Her heart twinged as she considered the possibility that they loved their Mother more.

Maya shook her head, and Sabala turned to stare at her. Then one dark, velvety ear lifted, a movement so graceful it didn't really fit his deadly profile. He glanced at the door and tilted it slightly, as if listening to a faraway conversation.

Maya sighed. Joss was on her way up.

A knock on her door a few seconds later confirmed it. And so did Sabala with his soft growl.

"Behave yourself, pooch. You try to hurt her and your ass is mine," Maya said, staring into all four of Sabala's eyes. But she couldn't assume he'd even understood her. She turned to the closed door, where a second, softer knock emanated, and hollered for Joss to come right in.

Joss sauntered in, eyebrows raised to her hairline. As per usual, her silky blond hair hung in a waterfall of pale at her back, gorgeous blue eyes glaring at Maya. She shoved her hair away from her face and pink and blue nail polish gleamed, while a bracelet chock full of charms jangled.

"What's going on with you?" She stepped into the room, shut the door with her heel, and dropped her bag on the dresser. She faced Maya, hand on her hips as if the mere stance would ensure an answer.

"I'm fine and you?" Maya responded, her tone dry and one eyebrow matching Joss's.

At least Joss had the grace to look slightly abashed. "Sorry, but I hate when you go AWOL like that."

"Yeah, being ill can do that to a person." Maya smiled, suddenly tired of the spy routine, tired of all the lies.

Joss took a step closer. Charms jingled. Sabala didn't move. *Was he even breathing?* "Your mom said you hurt your spine?"

Awesome story, Mom. I wouldn't have thought of anything better myself.

Joss reached Maya's bedside, passed the silent Sabala, and perched on the edge of Maya's bed, her back to the great big dog. *How had she not seen him?*

"So, are you feeling better? Are you able to walk?" Joss seemed eager to try and remove Maya from the house.

Maya wasn't sure how to answer that. Clearly, her mom hadn't thought it necessary to compare notes before telling Joss what happened to her. But she didn't need to worry too much about her story. Sabala understood exactly what Joss intended and it seemed he didn't agree with such girlish needs as fun and entertainment, not to mention freedom.

Sabala growled.

Low and soft at first. And Maya watched as the black fur at his throat vibrated with the sound. The rumbling growl reverberated around the room annoying Maya's inner ear, as if the hellhound snarled from inside her own body. She shuddered and Joss stiffened, her eyes widening as Maya's gaze flitted from her stricken face to the dog's threatening dark eyes.

Joss swiveled around to glance behind her and let out a strangled shriek, something halfway between a squawk and a squeal.

She stood up in shock, but her horror seemed to have robbed her legs of the ability to hold her weight and she tripped, pedaling backward to regain her balance. Her heel caught in the fringe of the handmade rug beside Maya's bed and she hit the floor.

Hard.

It was funny. So funny that Maya actually giggled. And that set her off. Maya kept seeing poor Joss flailing about and falling, and kept hearing her hysterical shriek and it was way too funny. Maya laughed and laughed and the sight of Joss still sitting on the floor, eyes wide in horror and fear didn't suppress her mirth one iota.

Only when Sabala took a step toward Joss did Maya stop laughing. In fact, the single movement sobered her up almost instantly.

"Touch her and I will tear you apart with my bare hands." Maya's voice rang clear and neutral but nonthreatening.

She meant every word.

Joss glanced at Maya, horror still eking the color from her face, and lining her eyes with the stress of her fear. Sabala growled again, low and threatening. And Joss quickly transferred her attention back to the hellhound.

Joss shuddered and Maya watched her, aware that her poor friend would have realized this mutt wasn't an average dog, what with him having two pairs of eyes and all.

Was it possible to have the goddess wipe her friend's memory? Maya stared at Joss's face, her heart thudding in her chest, guilt more than fear increasing her heartbeat.

She was amazed Joss hadn't fainted from the shock of it. Maya's gaze flicked to the demonic dog and back to Joss and she wanted to laugh again. Joss had her eyes shut tight. She slowly relaxed her scrunched up muscles and opened one eye in a strange grimace.

Bet she's hoping she imagined the whole four-eyed giant dog thing.
Sorry Joss, no such luck.

Sabala had snuck up closer to Joss, but despite his proximity as he examined Maya's poor friend, his manner seemed curious.

A strange sound echoed around the room, a deep whine repeating over and over, edged with a hint of hysteria. Joss was hyperventilating.

Fabulous.

Maya shuffled over to the edge of the bed but Sabala got to Joss first with one small step. He licked the side of Joss's face, in one slobbery move. Maya froze, Joss stopped hyperventilating and Sabala stepped away, job done.

The dog returned to the foot of Maya's bed, turned around twice in place, then sat back on his haunches. He remained there, unmoving, as if nothing had happened.

Joss remained frozen, backed up against Maya's nightstand.

"Maya?"

"Yes, Joss."

"You have some major explaining to do."

Maya nodded.

Joss nodded.

And Maya hoped to god she wasn't about to make the biggest mistake of her life.

$\mathcal{C}$oming clean with Joss wasn't as difficult as Maya had expected. As soon as she opened her mouth everything started to tumble out. And while her mouth moved, Maya kept wondering if this was a big mistake. Would Joss laugh at her, think she was nuts? Then Sabala turned his head toward Maya, as if he could read her mind and was asking her if she thought her friend was blind.

Throughout Maya's monologue, the hellhound had sat, still and silent as a statue, only moving his eyes to look at her and then at Joss who'd peeled herself off the floor and joined Maya on the bed. Maya wondered if she'd chosen the comfort of the bed for its distance from Sabala. And decided she was probably right when Joss whimpered the moment the dog turned to her.

Maya held her hand, instinctively, wanting to reassure her, knowing Joss could tug it away in disgust. But thankfully, she didn't. Instead, she grasped it tighter.

Maya finished up with an explanation of Sabala, and ended on a rushed and ridiculous introduction.

"Sabala meet Joss. Joss meet Sabala."

Joss rolled her eyes and Maya sighed, relieved. At least she wasn't bawling, or backing away slowly, or rocking back and forth, ready for the funny farm.

"So when were you planning on telling me all this, exactly?" Joss speared Maya with her baby blues.

"Never."

"Woah, way to go with the sensitivity, girl!" Joss cried, pretending to be offended.

"Look, this is hardly the sort of thing I wanted to tell either you or Ria. But now that Ria is possessed-"

"What? Who has possessed Ria?" Joss frowned.

"There are these demons called Rakshasas. They can take over a persons body." Joss stared at Maya then her eyes took on a faraway expression." Joss?"

"So these demons. When they take over a persons body do they have eyes like fire?" Joss was pale as she waited for Maya to answer."

Maya nodded."

"I see."

"I'm sorry. I know it's a lot to process. And . . . well you just met Sabala. I really had no choice after that, did I?"

"Nope. No choice at all." Joss glared at the giant dog, who stared back with all four of his eyes. "It's actually pretty cool, you know that?"

"And you're actually pretty crazy, you know that?" Maya responded, wondering when Joss would ever do anything Maya expected.

"Come on Maya, you cannot tell me there isn't at least one fiber of your being that thinks it's frigging cool to throw balls of fire and have a giant guard dog to guard your precious booty?"

Maya merely grunted, shimmying further up against the headboard. "There's a couple more things you should know."

"You're kidding me right? After everything you've told me? There's more? Because I don't think I can handle more-"

"Shut up and listen will you." Maya admonished her but couldn't help laughing. Instinctively Maya grabbed her ribs, expecting pain to rip through her abdomen. Nothing happened.

"Yes ma'am," Joss answered meekly.

"This power I have, the power to create fire? It's mine for a reason." Maya found it really difficult to say the words. Almost as if she hadn't yet earned the right. "A long time ago there was a priestess who trained the Children of Kali in their arts. But she'd been so bound to her work she hadn't fulfilled her one true desire. To serve Kali herself. To be on the front lines. So she prayed for that privilege. And Kali allowed her one more incarnation to serve. And her reincarnation is me."

"Huh?" Joss looked cross-eyed. "So you're really an old priestess?'

"Joss! I am the *reincarnation* of the Holy Mother Radha." Maya tried to be serious but Joss grinned and Maya ended up just grinning back.

"You know that sounds so strange coming from your lips." Joss said as she slowly slid off the opposite side of the bed from where Sabala sat at attention.

"What do you mean?" Maya watched, amused as Joss tiptoed toward the dresser, picked up her bag and glided to the door.

"Well, weren't you the girl who told me, not two months ago, that she couldn't understand why her parents expected her to believe in gods who don't exist?" Joss reached the door, her face at last regaining some color. She wiggled her pink and blue fingernails at Maya and smiled. "I have to go, now. I'll speak to you later."

Joss's words left Maya stunned as the door clicked shut. How had she forgotten her words and thoughts so easily? How could she have forgotten how much she'd despised the traditions, how she'd avoided anything to do with India and being Indian. And she'd been ashamed of her parents, too.

Now more than ever before, she was certain she didn't deserve any of this.

Joss left Maya to contend with her own inner turmoil. She seemed to have taken the whole reincarnation business well enough, although Maya couldn't be entirely sure until she saw Joss again.

If she saw her again.

What if she thought Maya was totally cuckoo and was merely playing along? What if she dumped Maya because she couldn't deal with the revelation? What if she convinced herself Sabala was just a figment of her imagination?

A buzzing sound emanated from under Maya's pillow and she twisted around, digging under the bedclothes for her phone. A message from Joss. Maya's heart pounded. Joss was probably texting to say Maya was crazy and she needed serious help. Maya's hand shook as she pondered if she should read the text or ignore it altogether. *Do I really need to lose another friend? I've already lost Ria.*

Maya swallowed hard, and checked the message. And heaved a sigh of relief as she read the words through a film of tears.

"Get some rest. I'll be by later to talk more. And keep an eye on that dog - I don't trust him."

Maya laughed out loud at that. Funny. Joss had countered all Maya's doubts with one text. Maya sighed and lay back on the pillows. Her eyes filled with tears again as her thoughts drifted to Ria. She really needed to learn more about the effect a Rakshasa had on the humans they possessed. Maya wanted her friend back

A KNOCK SOUNDED on the door and it swung open. Leela stood there, a slight smile on her face as she let Nik into the room. Maya glared at her. Nik in her bedroom? Really? Maya couldn't

even remember if she still had her PJ's on. *How embarrassing. Mom is going to get an earful when Nik leaves, that's for sure.*

But all thoughts of whining at her mom went flying out the window as soon as she looked at Sabala.

As Nik entered, Sabala rose from his post at the foot of Maya's bed, and faced Nik. Her heart clenched assuming Nik was done for, terrified the dog would tear him to pieces. But instead, her mouth fell open as Sabala lowered the front half of his body, and bowed his head. The dog was kneeling before Nik. Beyond hysterical.

Nik gave the hellhound a nod and walked toward the window. At that, Sabala rose and returned to settle on his haunches at his previous post. The dog's eyes remained lowered though, as if he still made some sort of obeisance to Nik. The dude certainly had some power over the beast.

Maya's visitor stared outside in silence. He hadn't even greeted her yet. What was with him?

This was the first time he'd made her uncomfortable since he'd save her butt at Amber's house. Well not to mention that kiss

. . .

"Nik."

"Maya."

They spoke together and Maya felt like a dork. The room seemed claustrophobic, and the thought of Nik in her bedroom still made her feel weird.

"Why don't we go downstairs. I could really do with some fresh air and orange juice," she said, smiling a little too brightly, too late to check what she wore. Thankfully, she was well prepared in a comfy tracksuit instead of her rabbit PJ's.

"Sure," Nik replied, his eyes stormy, capped by a multitude of frown lines. What was the matter with him? He walked toward Maya, holding out his hand to help her up. And though his offer was kind, his expression remained distant.

Maya waved him away. "I'm fine, I can manage, thanks." When did they become so formal? Her heart clenched as Nik's distance became an almost tangible accusation. Everyone seemed to be leaving her.

Maya blinked. Well not exactly. It was only Ria who'd left and it wasn't her choice, really. And Maya had no time for self-pity. Things were happening around her she had absolutely no control over, but right now she intended to walk downstairs and get herself some juice.

She led the way, her legs feeling strong and definitely not as wobbly as she would've expected given the severity of her injuries. Kali seemed to have done an amazing job with the healing. Maya was impressed.

As she got to the top of the stairs she heard a clack on the wood floor beside her. Sabala trotted with Maya and she would've been grateful if he hadn't reached his snout out and whacked the back of her knee with it. In mid-stride he kicked her leg out from under her. Maya tripped, almost falling to the floor before she caught herself with a gasp.

"What the hell are you doing?" She snapped at the dog. Sabala stared back as if he'd done nothing wrong.

"He's just doing his job, Maya."

"Yeah, I suppose tripping me at the top of the stairs so I can go tumbling down to my death is Sabala's way of keeping me safe, right?"

A strange silence hung in the air during which Nik stared at Sabala, almost in contemplation. Maya raised an eyebrow when the dog tilted his head, and stared back at Nik, an innocent look in his eyes.

"He didn't mean to frighten you or trip you up. He was warning you of the danger," Nik answered after their staring match ended. So weird. And Nik really ought to pay less attention to the mutt. Frankly, the dog was beginning to annoy her.

"Yeah well, he did almost throw me down the stairs so if he wants to help he'd better not try that trick again."

"I don't think he will."

Maya laughed, "So what, you're now a dog-whisperer?"

Nik shrugged and looked uncomfortable again.

Strange.

CHAPTER 26

They headed downstairs and Maya absorbed the bright sunlight streaming into the kitchen. Her Mom sat at the table. She glanced up as they walked in. "Hey, you two. Want a bite to eat?" she turned the page of a recipe book, eyes flicking across words. Something Moroccan for dinner tonight Maya guessed.

She shook her head, "Just some juice. I'll get it."

Her mom nodded then looked at Nik as Maya turned to the fridge. Maya frowned. *What was going on?* They were looking at each other strangely. Maya glanced back in time to see her mom widen her eyes and throw a skewed nod in Maya's direction as if urging Nik to talk to her. She waited until her mom turned back to her.

Leela almost flinched when she saw Maya had been watching their interplay, then covered it so well Maya could easily have thought she'd imagined the whole thing. Except for the pink tinge of guilt on her mom's cheeks.

Leela rose, pushing her chair back. She hesitated, eyes flicking around the table. She grabbed the book, tucked it under her arm and walked stiffly out of the kitchen.

"What the hell was that all about?" Maya grumbled, returning to the fridge for a pitcher of orange juice.

"Your mom is worried about you." Nik's tone was almost admonishing and Maya stiffened. Was he suddenly judging her for some reason?

Maya dumped the pitcher on the table, letting in make a loud thunk as the glass hit the wood surface. She didn't care when the liquid sloshed back and forth so hard it spilled onto the gleaming oak. *Why should I care? It kinda mirrors my life, right? Here I am, living just fine and then one day, bang, firepower from a goddess who shouldn't exist. Excuse me if I don't jump for joy.*

She grabbed two glasses from the cupboard behind her, this time restraining the urge to slam them onto the table. They'd shatter and she couldn't be bothered cleaning up broken glass. She slid onto a stool and waited as Nik seated himself opposite her.

Nik leaned forward and grabbed the pitcher, pouring the juice into each of their glasses.

He placed a glass in front of Maya and she took it, not bothering to thank him. She sipped, staring at the puddle of orange mess. Cleaning it up seemed like a mistake. So weird, but in a way, it represented her life. She shoved away from the table, her chair almost tipping over as she reached for the roll of paper towels and viciously wiped up the spilled liquid. Nik watched in silence as she toed the pedal on the bin and threw the sodden towels away.

Only when she sat back down did he ask, "Feel better?"

"No."

"Well you might want to summon a little more of that armor of anger." Maya's head shot up and she stared at his face. What the hell did he mean? "You're going to need it for what I am about to tell you."

Maya sighed. "Come on Nik, you can cut the melodramatics

and just spill it." She knew what he meant to say. That he needed to leave, he couldn't continue to spend time with a freak like her. Even if he knew the score, how could anyone stay knowing what a bagful of fun she was to be around? It was only good luck Joss hadn't died of horror and disbelief.

"This is not easy to say."

She stared at his face, her eyebrows raised, waiting.

Nik sat back, blew out a gust of breath. He rose to his feet, and began pacing the floor. He was making her dizzy so she stared at her juice instead.

"Okay, look. The thing is . . . you don't know me."

Maya let out a soft laugh. Who was he kidding? She knew very well who he was, but when he met her eyes, her heart twisted with worry. Something was really troubling him, so much his eyes swirled with an amber smoke, sending shivers down her spine. There she went hallucinating again.

She blinked a few times and when she glanced at Nik again the wisps of smoke were gone, replaced by Nik's dark and worried frown. The fridge thunked and clanked, then settled. Maya waited.

"Well?" she asked at last, suddenly gripped by fear. She didn't like this new, uncertain, fear-filled Nik.

"What I'm going to tell you now is something I had no intention of ever saying. Not to you at any rate." Nik fell into the chair opposite her, running his hands through his hair, making it stick up in a multitude of adorable directions. "But it's been getting a bit too complicated."

Anger and hurt flared within Maya's veins, taking her by surprise until she realized what was happening here. He really was leaving her, wasn't he? And he'd been keeping secrets. He was going to reveal he has a girlfriend, or that he had to leave and never come back.

"You don't have to worry about me, Nik," she said, her voice stony and cold as the words left her lips. "I'm fine, with or without you. I'm sure it's hard to tell me whatever it is you want to tell me, but get on with it and get it done." Her fingers gripped the glass so tight her knuckles shone white. Memories of the regret on his face after they kissed flitted across her mind, the hurt still fresh and raw.

But she didn't care. She focused on his expression, the red tinge of guilt so similar to her mother's she began to wonder what exactly was going on. Whatever he struggled to tell her was something her mom already knew. And Maya was the last to find out?

"I've been here too long, and I have to leave." Her gaze snapped to his so fast her neck hurt. She was right. "No, Maya, I am coming back. I won't leave you, unless you want me to."

"Why would I want you to leave?" Maya frowned, searching his face for a hint of why he was acting so strangely. Sure, she was angry with him. She'd been upset he'd regretted kissing her. She'd seen it so clearly in his eyes. But it didn't mean she wanted him gone. "You saved my life, you've been teaching me so much." She stopped speaking. The more she talked about how much Nik had come to matter in her life, the more difficult it would be for him to leave.

Nik walked toward Maya, placed his hands on her arms. The moment his skin touched hers, heat surged into her body. He stared into her face, his eyes troubled, struggling with whatever inner turmoil he battled. He grabbed her close, held onto her so tightly she could barely breathe. And she didn't want him to ever let go.

He sighed and his chest rose beneath Maya's cheek as she stood entwined within his arms. Then his cheek pressed against hers, the skin fiery hot and almost sparking. Maya struggled to take another breath. She was going to pass out just from a hug. Ridiculous. Amazing. Heat spiked her blood, running through her body like a drug, burning her up from inside.

Nik's breathing sounded harsh, erratic in her ear and he pulled away a little. Maya frowned, wanting so badly to wipe away whatever troubled him so much he couldn't find the words to tell her. And when he closed the distance between them, his lips claimed hers in a burst of hunger matched spark for spark by her own.

How did she ever think he'd regretted their first kiss? How could anyone regret such a pure emotion?

With a groan Nik ended the kiss, his lips leaving hers reluctantly. He held her face in his hands, lifting her chin so she could see into his eyes. "When you hear what I have to say you may want me to go right this minute."

"Maybe you should talk first, and let me make my own decisions."

"Fine." Nik's lips turned up in a wry smile. "I need to return home for a while. My father has summoned me."

"Summoned you? Sounds like he is some kind of king or something." Maya said, laughing, the tendrils of heat generated by the kiss slowly dissipating. But the seriousness in his eyes killed her humor and silence fell upon the kitchen. The sun still shone brightly, unaware Nik was about to break her heart and Maya could tell he had no idea how to make a clean break.

"He is a king." Nik's words chilled her blood.

"You are kidding right?" Maya shook her head. "Look Nik, you don't have to make up elaborate stories to leave."

"No, you don't understand. My father really is a king."

"Okay." She nodded, humoring him, still curious where he meant to take this line of revelation. "So, king of what country?"

"Well technically it's not a country. More like a realm."

"Nik, be serious. What the hell does that mean? A realm?" Maya almost laughed but things were no longer amusing her. Her heart hurt with the extent Nik was going to in order to leave without making himself feel bad.

"I am serious. Please hear me out." She wanted to yell at him that she'd been the one waiting all this while and he'd been the one waffling with his big revelation. Instead, she met his gaze with a raised eyebrow and silence and he seemed to take it as agreement on her part, because he continued. "My father is the king of Patala, the realm of the Underworld."

CHAPTER 27

"What?" Now she felt the urge to laugh. The crazy kind of laugh that made her feel like if she started, she'd never stop. Maya stared at the face of the boy to whom she'd secretly given her heart, and shook her head in disbelief. Nik was nuts. "Patala? You are making fun of me aren't you? Patala is the Underworld. You're seriously telling me Yama is your dad? Come on Nik, stop playing games."

"No, Maya. Just listen to me."

"No, this is crazy Nik. What are you thinking? That I will swallow your lies so you can leave me with a clear conscience?"

"Maya, listen to me." Nik grabbed Maya's shoulders, and gave her a small shake. But she wasn't listening to him anymore, she couldn't even look at his face. Tears gathered in her eyes, and she blinked against the burning.

How fitting.

Anger and hurt fought for control of her heart. She couldn't accept his lies, his betrayal. He had to almost yell to get her attention again. "Maya."

When she felt the warmth in his hands she stilled.

When she glanced up, and met his eyes she froze, ice smothering her veins, fear skating across her breath.

Nik's eyes glowed a hot amber.

The fiery glow of a Rakshasa's eyes.

Maya shivered, and yet she felt hot all over. Heat traced fiery fingers inside her skull, and out her ears. It would've been so much better had he been joking. Or lying. Maya would've accepted the lie sooner than this horrible truth.

Nik was a Rakshasa.

A bloody demon, from the underworld.

Son of a king? Maya wanted to laugh. As if she cared one whit about the King of Patala or his coward of a son.

The kitchen spun around Maya and heated anger gave way momentarily to the urge to throw up. She gulped and breathed and blinked. Anything to keep the contents of her stomach safely inside her body. Rage was reason enough.

But how could this be real? He must be joking.

Maya looked up and met Nik's eyes and all her questions died a quick death on her dry lips. The molten amber of a Rakshasa eyes stared back at her. As calm as you please.

How dare he stand there and look at me as if his revelation was nothing major?

"Maya. I know you don't want to listen to what I have to say and I can understand. I should have come clean a long time ago. I had many opportunities, I have to admit. But I let each one slide. Because this is what I was afraid of." Nik grasped Maya's arms, his amber eyes now back to his normal black, the contours of his face dark with worry. She shrugged off his hands. Maya felt no sympathy. None at all. "I knew you would be upset and you have every right to be. So let me give you my message and I will leave."

Maya glared at Nik and took a step back. She didn't want to hear anything he had to say. Not really. But a tiny part of her burned with curiosity. What was so all-fired important that Nik would risk Maya's anger and break her heart all in one evening?

Nik gave an almost imperceptible nod, taking her silence for acquiescence. "Yama needs your help." He walked to the other side of the table, toying with his glass of juice.

Maya snorted. "Really? That's rich. He's a god and he needs my help?"

"You don't know how special you are. You're the Hand of Kali, the blessed one. And for now, *you* are the only one who can help us."

"Us?" Maya bristled. "I thought you said Yama wanted my help?" And even as Maya asked the question she was aware of how ridiculous it sounded, especially coming from her own mouth. Yama, the god of the Underworld, the Lord of Patala, the Master of Death, a god who shouldn't exist because gods were just myths and everyone really needed to get with the program. But yet she'd accepted Chayya's help, submitted to Kali's ministrations, fought a demon and stared a hellhound in the face. *What's Yama, to add to the pile of the unbelievable?*

"What affects Yama, affects us all. Well, it affects us in Patala and Heaven first, but soon it will affect the human world too."

Maya tightened her grip on her glass. Only when she felt the heat beneath the pads of her fingers did she release the glass before she melted it right there in front of them. *Control, Maya. Control.*

"My father sent me here to guide and protect you. To help you hone your fire skill, and to give you a message. He also sent his hounds to be your guards and your guides."

"Eh? You mean the dogs that mauled me?"

"Maya, you know they only attacked because of the scent of the Rakshasa."

"Yeah, I guess I'll have to take your word for it." Nik winced at her words, but Maya felt not an ounce of sympathy for him. Deep inside she wanted him to hurt. As much as she was hurting. "So what is it Yama wants me to do?"

"He wishes for you to visit Patala and meet with him as soon as you're ready."

"What?" Maya laughed, the sound cold and unamused as it passed her tightened lips.

"Yama understands such a decision may take time for you to make. As such, he will wait for you to come to him. But please know the problem he has does get worse as time ticks by."

"Oh, so I'm to take my time to make a decision to see him, but be quick about it?"

"Something like that." A gleam of amusement flickered in Nik's eyes, doused quickly by Maya as she glared at him. She saw nothing amusing about this entire situation. Given an ultimatum by the god of death was not the most pleasant experience.

"What if I decline his invitation?" Maya asked, her chin lifted an inch, her spine straight and defiant.

"I don't believe that's an option."

"So you're really saying I don't have a choice. I have to see Yama, no matter what."

"You do have a choice. But the problem we face is so great should you refuse, it will be the one decision which you will regret." Nik sat slightly back in his stool, as if he knew Maya's fury would follow.

"Decision I will regret?" asked Maya, her voice rising as she leaned forward, pressing against the table edge. "Decision I will regret? You don't know the future. You have no idea how many decisions I already regret. Take Ria for instance."

As Maya spoke, her hands grew hotter as heat twirled and swirled before her. Within her head, and within her heart, fire grew, and flame burned, fed by a rising, uncontrollable rage. Ria may be lost to her and all Nik could think about was himself and his precious needs?

And it happened without a thought. The fire burgeoned out of control, flashing forth from her palm. A bright blaze of white and orange flew across the table, straight through the pitcher of orange juice, straight at Nik.

Time slowed as Maya followed the path traced by the blast of fire; the scorched and blistered blacked wood, the glistening glob of melted glass, puddled and sizzling mixed with boiled juice setting off a rich and fermented steam.

And lastly, Nik with is amber eyes burning as hot as the flame she'd thrown.

Nik holding his arm where Maya had burned him.

Maya swallowed, her hands burned, the palms throbbing in time with her thudding heart. Tears ached in her throat, and she wanted to apologize but no words left her lips. She stared at him, her eyes huge, shocked.

But Nik seemed to know. He seemed to see despite how sorry she was she wouldn't apologize. His beautiful eyes grazed her face, a deep sadness set in them.

Then he disappeared.

CHAPTER 28

The kitchen fell silent.

A sharp clacking on the terracotta tiles announced Sabala's entry into the deathly quiet room. At least the hellhound had respected Maya's privacy enough to wait outside while she had her mental breakdown.

He stopped beside her, staring up at her tight features, as if expecting her to do something. "What?" she snapped.

The hound walked around the table and sniffed the ground, appearing to follow Nik's scent until he stopped at the spot where Nik had disappeared. Sabala tipped his head to one side, and looked at Maya, his glassy eyes huge - he seemed disappointed in her.

Maya didn't have the energy to react to that. Sabala was disappointed in her. *So what? I didn't ask for any of this. This is not even my fight.*

And yet a part of her laughed hysterically as she tried to absolve herself of some of her guilt.

"Maya, honey, what happened?" Leela drew up close, an arm already extended to comfort her child, but Maya shrugged her off, taking a step away. She knew how it looked. Like a stupid tantrum gone wrong. "Maya?" This time Leela's voice, brisk and sharp, demanded an answer.

"Nik." Maya spoke the name and struggled to keep her tears from falling. She ground her jaw. He didn't deserve her tears. "He is such a liar."

"What did he tell you?" Leela turned Maya around and met her gaze head on. But Maya hesitated. Her mom sounded too calm. Too prepared.

"Did you know?" Suspicion zinged through Maya's head.

"I-" Leela hesitated, her eyes flicking over to Sabala sitting stock still on the other side of the scorched table. The dog simply stared back at the two women, eyes black and glossy. "Look, Maya. It's complicated. But yes, we knew."

"Complicated? How complicated was it that you couldn't just tell me the truth?" Maya's voice quivered, echoing the deep betrayal cutting to her soul.

Leela's face fell when she heard her daughter's pain. She took a step forward, then stopped. Perhaps she feared another rejection or, perhaps she knew Maya needed time to absorb it all. "When Nik arrived, he told us why he was here. So yes, we knew for a while. We meant to tell you, but -"

"But what? You thought it was okay to lie to your silly little naive child? That she would just accept everything you tell -"

"No, Maya. You weren't ready. And we were hoping you would be ready soon. We just didn't expect the Rakshasas to attack you."

For a moment rage surged within Maya, a molten river of fury. Was her mom actually telling her it was her own fault they'd kept such vital information from her? Maya opened her mouth to speak but Leela cut her off.

"Now, don't you go getting that look, Maya. What happened was the Rakshasas. Nik hadn't expected to see them right here in town. They were here before him. He had to make sure you were safe. So he asked us to wait before we told you."

"So you just listened to him? You kept the truth from me because he asked you to? You listened to him instead of thinking of me?"

"We thought he was right at the time. And to be honest, we still think it was the right choice. You were in danger. More danger from the day you manifested your Fire. We had to make sure you weren't discovered."

"Discovered by whom?" Maya's voice rose, louder than necessary, louder than was respectful but she didn't particularly care about respect right now. "If you mean the demons, then that's pretty stupid don't you think? You had a demon right here in this house, you colluded with him all this time. How could you have been protecting me when you welcomed a Rakshasa right into the family? He trained me for god's sake!"

Leela laughed as she absorbed Maya's words. "You mean Nik? He's not a demon."

"Mom! Has he gotten to you too? Didn't you see his eyes? He has Rakshasa eyes." Maya sobbed the last few syllables, then gulped for breath.

"Maya, don't be silly. Nik is the son of Yama. He is a god in his own right." Leela stepped around the table. She gripped Maya's elbows. "Listen to me. Nik is safe, he is your protector. He is NOT a demon." Leela paused as Maya's words hit her with their full impact. "His eyes? You think because his eyes glow like the Rakshasas that he is one of them?"

Maya didn't answer, but her silence was enough.

"He has all the power of the Rakshasas and more. He is so powerful no demon would try to cross his path. They fear him Maya, because his job is to punish them. He is their jailer as much as his father is."

Maya shook her head. It was all too much. Her eyes traced the blackened wood. Her fire had -

"But I hurt him. How invincible is he that my Fire burned his arm."

"You hurt him?" Leela's voice rose a few decibels, consternation and admonition a confused mix in her expression.

"Well, I was angry. And it was an accident." Maya hugged herself harder.

"The only reason you were able to hurt him is because your Fire is getting stronger. You're the daughter of the dark goddess, and your power is manifesting. It also means you may just be more powerful than he is right now."

Maya snorted. "I'm more powerful than the son of a god?"

"The daughter of Kali is meant to be all-powerful. That's what you are."

"Thanks Mom. I think I've had about enough melodrama for one evening. None of this is supposed to even be happening." Maya's voice became strident as on the last few words she uttered. She turned and rushed out of the kitchen, leaving Leela watching, silent.

At the stairs, Maya spared one glance toward the kitchen. Sabala followed after her, his pace, slow and regal. Certainly, he didn't feel the need to rush after her.

Maya ran up the stairs, her palms remembering the sizzle of heat and power she'd sent.

Power.

Such a heady thing.

~

MAYA DESPERATELY WANTED to slam her door, if anything just to vent her anger. But Sabala had followed her upstairs. She could shut him out of the room but something made her leave the door ajar for him.

She flopped onto her bed, disgusted with herself. And with everyone else at the moment. So many lies. It was getting harder to distinguish the lies from the truth anymore.

Before she could continue feeling sorry for herself or

continue feeding her anger, Maya's phone beeped. She stiffened, her fingers reaching for the cell so fast she almost dropped it.

The text message tone was Ria's.

Maya flipped the phone open to read the message. But the screen glowed blank. She frowned, checked the details and confirmed she did get the text, and it really was blank. What was Ria up to? Or was it the demon? Was she trying to call Maya to her?

Maya clicked the phone shut. Only one thing for it. She bounced up from the bed, feeling better than ever, not a twinge or a spasm of pain. She rummaged in her closet, threw on a pair of jeans and a sweater and headed out the room.

Only to be stopped dead in her tracks by a large black hellhound.

Damn, I forgot about the mutt. Now what?

The dog eyed her, as if he knew exactly what she was planning.

"Fine, you can come, but if you ever tell -" Maya laughed out loud, feeling waves of hysteria ebb and flow. What was she thinking? That Sabala would snitch? Then again, he did belong to Yama, the god of the underworld. Who knew what he could and couldn't do.

Maya shook her head. If Sabala had a way to tell someone what she was up to then so be it. She'd cross that bridge when she came to it.

Maya slipped silently down the stairs. No sign of her mom - probably filling in her dad on the day's developments. As she passed through the kitchen the burned tabletop glared its accusation at her. So did the melted pitcher, which sat right where she'd left it, solidified in many places with the orange juice still inside air pockets around the mass of misshapen glass.

A monument to Maya's fury.

Maya hurried out into the darkness, almost jogging the two streets to Ria's house. Sabala followed a short distance behind, as if merely observing her activity. *Well he'd better stay out of my way if he knows what's good for him.*

The house was quiet enough, despite being ablaze with lights. Even Ria's room glowed brightly.

On many an occasion in the past and the not so recent past, Maya had snuck into Ria's room. On days when her friend had been grounded for the pettiest of reasons, like forgetting to bring in the washing, or dropping half a dozen eggs on the kitchen floor. Things Maya's parents would've scowled at and forgotten about because they were mistakes or accidents.

But Mr. Gupta ruled his family exactly the way an overstuffed rooster would. Once, Maya had climbed the trellis and snuck into Ria's bedroom to find her friend trying to cover up her black eye with concealer. That night was the first time Maya ever wanted to kill someone. Her blood had boiled and she'd forced herself to shut her mouth only because she knew by then Ria would never report it, never complain, never stand up for herself.

Sometimes Maya wondered if Ria believed she deserved the treatment her father dished out.

CHAPTER 29

Now Maya scaled the trellis again hidden by a thick, old oak, and hoping she hadn't grown too big for the simple wooden screen covered in pink bougainvillea.

The trellis held and Maya grabbed onto the sill, and lifted herself high enough to peek inside. The drapes were ajar, the room brightly lit. Ria lay on the bed, deathly still.

Maya lifted the sash window, sending a prayer it wasn't locked. Whenever Ria would send her those special texts saying she needed her, she always left the window unlatched.

Thankfully, this was one of those times. Either that, or the demon was smarter than Maya gave her credit.

Maya shoved the window, wincing as it groaned loudly. But Ria didn't move. Opening it only wide enough for her to slip in, Maya dived through the gap and tucked and rolled into the room. She hunkered down below the sill, eyes darting to the door. Shut tight. Good.

On the bed, Ria still looked asleep.

For now, Maya was safe.

Muffled voices emanated from somewhere in the house. Maya didn't think anyone would be in any position to force the

Ria-demon to do anything she didn't want. From Ria's beaten body, it was clear the demon cared little for the damage she did to her current vessel.

And now, Ria sleeping so peacefully, hardly looked like a girl possessed. Her chest rose and fell, which was comforting. Somehow, Maya saw that simple body function as a reassurance she could still save Ria.

Maya's heart pounded against her ribs, the sound so loud in her ears it hampered her hearing. She had to calm down. And quick. No telling what the consequence would be if she were to get caught.

She wasn't sure which would be worse, getting caught by the Rakshasa or facing Mr. Gupta's wrath.

She crawled over to kneel beside the bed, and stayed low. In case the door opened, Maya could duck down and hide. "Ria," she called to the sleeping girl. When Ria didn't respond Maya called again, this time a tiny bit louder. "Ria, wake up."

Ria stirred, then turned her head slowly to face Maya. The sheets crinkled as she moved, the sound flat in the silent room. Ria didn't give her usually, toothy grin. Her blank eyes stared at Maya. No emotion flickered there, no recognition. Nothing.

Maya hesitated. "Ria, you okay?"

Ria sat up. The movement was fluid and fast, as if her body was controlled by something else; robotic, sudden and lacking the aspect of Ria which made her who she was. Maya gasped, almost choked as she swallowed.

She fell back flat on her butt, and stayed there. She didn't dare to make a move. Ria sat still, staring straight ahead so Maya couldn't see her eyes anymore. Her hands lay flat on the white bedspread, her fingers painfully thin. Maya clenched her own fingers to stop the shivers of fear coursing through them.

But she bit her cheek. *No time to get scared. If it's the demon, I will have to fight her. Certainly can't do that messing about on my ass.*

"Ria," Maya whispered, promising herself she won't call out

again. If Ria didn't respond then no one was home and Maya had to get out of there.

But Ria turned toward her. "Maya, you came." She got on her knees and she smiled her special Ria smile dissolving all of Maya's fears.

Maya scooted onto the bed and grabbed Ria, surprised when her friend hugged her back so hard she thought she heard a rib crack. "Are you alright? Is everything all right?" Maya asked, stiffening. She couldn't mention the demon to Ria. What exactly did one know when one was possessed?

"I've been ill . . . I think," Ria said, rubbing her upper arms, where a rash of goose bumps pebbled her skin.

"Don't you remember anything?" Maya sat beside her, close enough to comfort the girl, but far enough to run for it if the Rakshasa should put in an appearance. It still seems strange and slightly surreal to think Ria was free from possession just like that. They were now sitting at the foot of the bed and Maya turned her head to look at her friend, patting her back a little in an attempt to comfort her.

Something caught Maya's eye. At the bedside table sat a brass tray, filled with lamps and containers, a bowl of frankincense and one of white ash. Maya felt dread fill her from head to toe. The tray itself only meant Ria's family had been praying for her. Maya's mom had told her once frankincense had powers beyond human understanding. She said the smoke had the ability to banish demons and dark spirits and it had properties capable of clearing a person's mind.

Maya sniffed and sure enough, a faint memory of the scent lingered in the air. As if even a good airing wouldn't erase the sweet fragrance.

"No. It's been hazy. Like I've been drugged or something. My mom said I hadn't been given any sedatives or anything but I'm not sure." Ria picked at one of the little purple silk bows sewn randomly into the coverlet.

"How do you feel now?" Unsure of what to say, Maya's mind buzzed. So. It seemed like the Gupta's were treating the whole thing like a possession. And it looked like whatever they'd done had worked. Ria seemed herself, if a little confused. Maybe they'd really banished the Rakshasa.

"I'm fine, Maya. Thanks for coming." Ria's forehead crinkled. "How come my father allowed you in? I remember him being very angry with you for some reason."

"He didn't," Maya replied, her tone dry. She nodded at the open window. "I used the other entrance."

"Oh." Ria smiled.

"So, why did you call me? Do you need something? Can I do anything for you?"

"What do you mean?" Ria frowned, and smoothed her hair over her head. "I didn't call you."

"What? You didn't send me a blank text?"

"No. You mean like the ones I used to send you a long time ago?" asked Ria, her face red with memories and embarrassment.

Maya nodded

"I'm sorry Maya, I don't remember sending you any text. But the way I've been feeling these last few days I can't promise I didn't."

A trill of fear zipped through Maya. Had Ria really sent the message? Or had the demon set a very clever trap?

But Ria looked fine. No trace of the Rakshasa at all. Not in Ria's demeanor, not even in her face and eyes.

And Maya had work to do. At least she'd been able to confirm Ria was well.

"Okay, you're fine. That's good. If you need me for anything text me okay?" Maya said as she rose to her feet, her mind already touching on Nik's message and what she intended to do about Yama's summons.

Pain fired up her arm as something dug into her wrist. Maya

gasped and tried to yank her hand away, turning to Ria, aware now that her friend held on to her with a vice grip.

No. Not Ria.

The demon. It had to be. Maya's arm throbbed, intermittent flares spiking her with debilitating pain. Only then did she look at her wrist, daring to take her eyes of Ria's placid expression.

Ria's fingers curved around her hand. And her nails- thick, long, blackened nails, dug deep into Maya's flesh, drawing blood. Lots of blood. Scattered red droplets stained the white bedspread. Maya tried to pull away but Ria held on, refusing to release her.

"Ria!" Maya yelled, pushing off the bed, trying to get closer to the window. Ria followed silently, her nails still buried within Maya's arm. "Let go of me."

But Ria's eyes remained blank. She was either unaware or fine with it. Maya doubted it was the latter. Ria didn't have a mean bone in her body.

Blood pooled at Maya's arm welling and dripping down her fingers and onto the paisley patterned carpet. This was bad. Not the blood. The demon. And Maya was alone. Sabala was outside, no way for him to help her. And other than him, nobody knew where she'd gone.

Smart move Maya. Real smart move.

CHAPTER 30

"What do you want, you evil bi-"

"We want you, Maya, daughter of Kali. We want you and your Fire." The words wound around Maya like a lullaby, gently singing her into compliance. But the pain served a different purpose- it helped her pull herself out of the intoxicating hold of the Rakshasa. "Come with us, child of fire. Come with us and be one of us."

Anger surged through Maya as she stared the demon down. Now she could see its amber eyes, behind Ria's own dark eyes, moving beneath the shell that was once her closest friend in the world. "Like hell I will. Now let me go."

"You must come, or we will have to hurt you."

"You just let me go or *I* will have to hurt you!" Maya hissed, afraid to scream but desperately wanting to howl her anger at the demon.

The Rakshasa laughed and the sound echoed around the room, as if it were a real thing, bouncing off the walls and coming straight back. Maya frowned. A familiar odor drifted to her. Masked slightly by the frankincense, the rich spicy smell of blood lingered, gaining strength minute by minute.

How had the Rakshasa gotten away with it for so long? There'd been no smell when she'd hugged Ria only moments ago. The room didn't reek of it either. *Had the demon left for a while, leaving Ria conscious enough to call me to her?*

The demon's laughter died away, and Maya was now desperate to free herself. The Rakshasa's claws went deep, probably an inch into Maya's flesh. No getting those out of her fast and safe. The more she pulled against the demon's grip the harder it held on.

At her wits end, Maya almost sobbed in agony and despair. Almost. But she had a way to get free. Maya remembered her Fire. The power constantly simmered beneath her skin at her fingers, and her palms. Maya felt it surge within her veins, always at her beck and call, always waiting.

She called the Fire to her left hand, trying to guide it, to collect it in her palm. She had to direct it at the demon's fingers.

"Daughter of Fire, what will it be? Will you come quietly or do I have to kill your friend to make you?" Ria smiled and it sent shudders up and down Maya's body. Even though she knew it wasn't Ria who spoke.

The fire grew in Maya's hand, the conflagration burning and yet her skin remained unhurt.

"You waste my time, human girl!" The Rakshasa screamed and stepped toward Maya, the movement so intimidating Maya lost her concentration and a little bit of her control of her fire. The demon raised Maya's arm, holding in front of her face to watch as it dug its nails deeper into Maya's skin.

As the collected fire dissipated Maya desperately called it back, hoping against hope it would return. And fast. The odor of the demon enveloped Maya, pulling at her senses with fingers of ecstasy. So easy to give in, so easy to stop fighting.

But Maya fought to hold it back. She held her breath, tried to clear her mind, concentrate on bringing back the Fire. She could feel it building up again, damming against her flesh, pulsing in heated waves against her palms. But the drug-like odor of the Rakshasa had weakened her control. Sapped her strength too, and it was harder than it had ever been to keep control of the Fire.

"Very well." Ria's eyes stared back at Maya, and yet she saw the demon's face too, like one of those strange trick pictures where if one looked hard enough the picture became something else entirely.

And in the next instant the fire was ready, the heat overflowed and Maya's Chakra opened, channeling the flames straight out of her palm. She aimed at the hand of the Ria-demon, knowing she would hurt her friend, knowing she had no choice but still hating herself for it.

Maya opened her fingers, setting the flame free.

Molten heat streaked forth, at last unleashed, untethered. Maya gasped, struggling for breath as the power and the force of the fire channeled through her body, pulsing through her muscle and bone, coursing through her veins.

The flame flew at the demon's fingers, enveloping her forearm. And the demon screamed. A sound that pierced Maya's eardrums, hurt her deep inside her solar plexus. The fire seared her arm, but she paid little attention to the effect of the flame on her skin.

Maya's body was just a vessel for the Fire. It seemed unable to harm her flesh or bone, not that it meant she felt no agony. Her attention remained fixed on the Ria-demon's arms. The Rakshasa's screams were sure to bring Ria's family rushing into the room soon. But even the possibility of being found by Ria's father didn't concern Maya.

She focused on the blistered, boiling skin on Ria's forearm and fingers. Maya had burned her friend's hand. The demon was similarly affected, its screams of anger transitioned to howls of agony as the demonic nails erupted in flames. It released Maya's arm, thrusting her away, the action sending stabbing knives of pain deep into each of Maya's now open, angry wounds.

The Rakshasa, still screamed in agony. But all Maya saw was Ria's hand, burned beyond recognition. And the creature beneath Ria's skin.

Maya felt light-headed. Seeing the amber eyes of the demon behind Ria's eyes was one thing. It had given her the awareness the demon was still there. But now, the burning Fire revealed the Rakshasa beneath the body she wore.

Skin shriveled, dark and dead, the hand of a burned corpse. Maya shuddered, and wanted to cry. The Fire had drained her. Never before had she needed to draw the fire twice. Never before had she been faced with the double terror.

The Rakshasa barreled straight at Maya and she backpedaled instinct taking over. But she refused to only react. This demon wasn't going to have the upper hand. No way.

Maya's brain flicked through a series of moves her dad had taught her, and she hit out at the oncoming creature, slamming her hand straight into the demon's throat.

The Ria-demon choked and spluttered, skidding to a stop as Maya spun about to keep an eye on it. With her back to the door, Maya felt vulnerable. Then she wanted to laugh. She was face to face with a deadly Rakshasa but she was more afraid of Mr. Gupta's reaction.

The demon came at her again and this time Maya wasn't ready. The impact sent her flying backward to land flat on her back pinned by the Ria-demon. Ria was barely recognizable anymore. Her hair had come undone. Silky, neatly combed hair, held back by her usual barrette- all gone, replace by tousled knotted, almost oily looking limp strands, hiding most of her face.

She hovered over Maya like something from a horror movie and Maya was suitably terrified. A shout sounded somewhere in the house. The noise had alerted the Guptas and they would soon be here.

The sounds were closer now, on the landing and someone struggled at the lock outside. But they couldn't get in. Somewhere, within her fear, Maya knew the demon still straddled her but the Rakshasa's attention was solely directed at the door. With one arm outstretched, she seemed to be holding the door shut.

"Ria! Open this door immediately," Mr. Gupta shouted. "I swear if you don't open the door this minute I will break it down and then you will see."

Silence followed as the group outside the door waited for Ria to open up.

"Ria," he roared again, and something large and solid hit the door. And it would have cracked and broken in two if it hadn't been for the Rakshasa's power to keep it shut.

Maya took the opportunity. As the demon stared at the door, attention and concentration focused on the entrance to the room, Maya drew her fire again. This time it came smoothly, like a silky liquid, summoned with her mind, and conducted through her body.

The Fire sluiced from her hand, and even though her arm remained beneath one of the Rakshasa's knees, her palm was free. Free to throw the full force of the flames upon it.

And as Maya thought of her friend, a fist of ice closed over her heart. She was going to kill Ria.

CHAPTER 31

But what would Ria really be once the demon discarded her body? Or would she even be left alive at all? Her burns were bad, and the Rakshasa continued to draw more and more energy from her.

Maya had to make the decision. Kill the demon and possibly Ria at the same time or let the demon kill Maya. It all came down to self-preservation. And Maya refused to do it. She couldn't, if it meant the tiniest possibility Ria would survive this horrible ordeal, then no way could Maya unleash her fire on her.

And in the next breath, the demon took control. The door remained locked and the demon placed both her hands around Maya's neck and squeezed. It didn't take long before Maya struggled to breathe. The edges of her vision darkened, the image of the Rakshasa began to blur. She fell slowly into oblivion, having lost her chance to kill the creature.

A howl rent the air, the sound coming loud and sharp straight through the open window. Sabala. The demon looked over its shoulder at the window, distracted by the call of the hellhound. Maya saw it stiffen, amber eyes swirled with fear. Its fingers loosened their hold.

And Maya let the fire loose.

The demon ignited. A living fire, a conflagration burning from the floor and almost to the ceiling. The Rakshasa screeched, anger, frustration, agony and desperation all balled up in one terrible scream.

Maya scrambled backward away from the demon pyre. And away from Ria as she burned alive. The screams, grated on Maya's ears, gouging at her heart and Maya felt bile rising in her throat. Hot tears singed her eyelids. What had she done?

Behind the burning demon the door shuddered, the Guptas not giving up their quest to enter Ria's room. The yelling and screaming outside couldn't compare to the deafening screeching of the dying Rakshasa. Nor could it compare to the keening in Maya's heart as she watched her best friend burn to death right in front of her.

Smoke began to fill the room, stinging Maya's eyes. And the demon pyre collapsed, Ria's body falling to the ground in a burning heap.

Then two things happened at once. The door flew open, and Mr. Gupta came tumbling inside yelling Ria's name, his face boiling, seething with fury at his daughter. Another man followed, features Maya couldn't identify in the smoke-filled room.

A pair of hands grasped Maya from behind, hauling her bodily toward the window. She glanced back, ready to draw her fire and incinerate her attacker.

Chayya glared at her and grabbed her arm. "Come we must leave now."

But they were too late to dive outside. The smoke thinned, wafting out the open window and the wide-open room door.

"Ria." Mrs. Gupta screamed and ran to her daughter. At the same time, Maya looked behind her, horrified to know Ria's mother could see what remained of her beautiful child.

Maya stood transfixed as the smoke cleared to reveal Ria,

unconscious on the floor, her simple white kurta scorched and smoking, her skin unblemished. She took in the scene: Mrs. Gupta, the red dot on her forehead smeared garishly across her face, Mr. Gupta out of breath, puffing in and out. Maya could tell he was unsure how to react. How could he be angry with an unconscious daughter?

He looked up.

Straight at Maya.

But he didn't react. He didn't see her. Instead he looked at the open window, right though Maya.

Chayya shoved Maya into the darkness behind the drapes.

"Maya, we have to get out of here, now."

"Why didn't he see me?"

"I am the ruler of the shadows," Chayya said, and winked as she peered around the curtains.

Maya remembered Ria. "She wasn't hurt." She shook ahead, unable to believe it. "Ria, she was unhurt, I saw it."

"Yes, Maya, your friend will be free from any bodily injuries she may have received while the Rakshasa was using her body."

"So she'll be fine?"

"I do not know. And we do need to leave. Now." Chayya nodded at the room and lifted a finger to her lips.

Maya stiffened and she heard Mr. Gupta's slippers slap their way to the open window. He poked a head outside, then retracted it, staring around the room. As if on second thought he pulled the opposite drape away from the wall and turned to do the same to the one hiding Maya and the Shadow Goddess.

And again, it was as if neither Chayya nor Maya were even there. Mr. Gupta shoved the fabric aside and it billowed forward, taking swirling clouds of smoke with it. He coughed, frowning as he stared straight at Maya. To be on the safe side Maya held her breath. Now she wished she hadn't as Ria's father was taking too long to complete his inspection. What did he expect to see?

At last, he returned to his weeping wife. "What's wrong with her?" he grunted as he waited for a reply.

All he got was his wife's sobs.

"Uncle, she may need a doctor. It looks like she is in some sort of coma."

"What? How did that happen? What's wrong with this girl?"

"I can't tell," came the other voice. "There doesn't seem to be anything physical."

"You saying she's mad? You mean I'm going to have to put her in a mental home? What will people say? What did I ever do to deserve this stupid child? And now we won't be able to get rid of her. Nobody will want to marry her."

Maya's mouth hung open as she listened to Mr. Gupta's tirade. Of course, he had no idea what his child had been through, how close she'd just come to death. But then he'd never cared much for his sweet daughter. He'd always seen her as a commodity. Now he lamented being unable to get rid of her. Maya was glad her poor friend was unconscious and hadn't heard her father's words.

But something told Maya that Ria knew very well how little her father cared for her as a person. Maya's eyes filled with tears. A simple comparison between their parents told her she probably had the best parents ever. Something she hardly ever acknowledged.

"Come Maya, we must leave," Chayya whispered, nodding again at the open window.

Maya followed her outside, sitting on the sill to take one last look at her friend. The young man who'd checked Ria's vitals, now carried her to the bed while her father looked on, an expression of disgust on his face.

Fire burned in Maya's hand and in her heart.

Maya and the goddess of shadows slipped quietly out the window and tiptoed to the trellis. Chayya floated down while Maya struggled to make her way to the sidewalk, snagging her hair on the tree and pulling loose countless number of purple blossoms.

Sabala waited, his expression almost disappointed as Maya set foot on solid ground. "Come. We are unseen for now. Let us get far from this place."

CHAPTER 32

As Maya and Sabala ran the two streets home, the distant song of sirens closed in.

Maya held her injured hand to her chest and her steps slowed as she drew closer to her house. Her parents would've wondered what had happened to her, but if they were worried they would've called. Was her mom giving her time to think, time to cool down? Maya's heart still beat furiously, the whole scene in Ria's room replaying itself over and over again every few minutes.

Sabala clacked along beside her. Once in a while, he exhaled through his nose as if about to sneeze but decided at the last minute he didn't need to. Chayya followed within the darkness, one moment visible, the next shrouded in shadows thrown onto the sidewalk by the trees and the leaves and the dark clouds skidding across the moonless sky. The goddess hadn't spoken since they left Ria's house.

Chayya didn't need to speak to her for Maya to know she'd been stupid, and hasty. Just because she had arrived in time to save Maya's ass didn't mean the whole escapade was justified, no matter what Maya's intentions had been. But somewhere within the fiasco there'd been a tiny bit of success. Maya had killed the demon. Removed it right from Ria's living body.

It still gave her chills- the sight of Ria burning, eaten by white-hot flame. The sight of Ria's hand, skin melted, flesh burned off, revealing the shriveled arm of the Rakshasa, had been horrific enough. But Maya had died a thousand deaths when she'd seen Ria on fire.

In the end Ria had survived, and she'd been fine, not a burn in sight. But Maya still felt responsible. Because despite her friend's lack of physical injury, she emerged from her possession by the demon catatonic. Unable to walk or talk, unable to be herself. Who knew if she would ever regain consciousness?

Maya shivered to think about the consequences of Ria's condition. With the kind of father Ria had she'd end up hidden away in some institution somewhere far away where she'd be unable to sully her father's pride or his reputation. And Ria's mother would stand by, powerless to do anything to help her daughter, as powerless as she had always been and always would be as a Gupta bride.

Maya glanced around, to be sure she and Chayya were still alone on the street. It wouldn't be good for her reputation to be seen having conversations with shadows. All was clear so she asked, "Is there something we can do for Ria?"

From within the veil of darkness and shadow, the goddess Chayya sighed. Maya blinked as a light breeze kissed her cheek and for the briefest moment, she was sure Chayya danced around her in the dark.

Chayya spoke from the air right beside her. "Maya, you have seen what happened to your friend Ria. It is not uncommon. It happens all the time to people all over the world, every time a Rakshasa possesses a human body. They absorb life like a parasite. And more often than not, they leave behind the husk of a person, a corpse at best. It has become more and more common in recent times. We should be grateful she has come through the possession alive."

"Alive? You call that alive? She's a vegetable." Maya choked off the words, taking a breath and then another before blinking hard at the tears threatening to mess with her composure.

"Would you rather she be dead?" came the enigmatic response. "It can be arranged if you wish. If you feel she will suffer you can request she be taken now and not when her allotted time arrives."

Maya stared at the air beside her, stopping in her tracks, a sob and a moan stuck in her throat. "You seriously think I'd prefer Ria dead?"

"No, Maya. I am merely advising you that you have an option. If you ask I will see to it the request is received by Lord Yama."

Maya chewed on her lower lip. "So you're on speaking terms with Yama?"

"Yes. I go where shadows live. From the snow-capped mountains to the depths of the underworld, wherever a shadow is cast you will find me or my servants. I know all the gods in all the realms, all the rulers in all the lands." Chayya raised her hand waving it in a circular motion which Maya assumed indicated the realms and lands the goddess knew.

How poetic

Chayya's movement drew specks of shadows from the inky night around her, little drops of darkness that spun into a tiny tornado of blackness. The goddess dropped her hand and the shadows scurried away disappearing in the time it took to blink.

Maya shook her head, directing her attention to Chayya again. "So you can speak to him for me?"

"Maya, do you really wish for him to take your friend now?"

"No. That's not what I meant." Maya thought about how best to approach the goddess with her idea. "Could you speak to him on my behalf? Ask him what I need to do to bring Ria back."

"Maya, you do know you can ask him yourself. You are much

more likely to get a positive result than if you were to send an emissary." Chayya's words floated to Maya on the shadows. A silence followed, stretching out as Maya struggled to think of how to convince the goddess to help her. "Lord Yama has already sent for you Maya. He is a just and generous god, but it would not be wise to keep him waiting. We are all depending on your answer."

Chayya's words chilled Maya to the bone. "What do you mean *you all?*" Maya frowned. Nik had mentioned something similar. That whatever Yama wanted from her would affect everyone else in the world too. "What's going on that's now suddenly my problem to solve?"

"Maya, I am afraid I cannot speak of it. Lord Yama will tell you himself. But what you need to know is the whole world depends on this. The fate of the world is reliant on your choices."

"Thanks a lot for the pressure," Maya mumbled, unhappy Chayya was taking up where Nik left off.

"Come, you must speak to your parents as soon as possible. You must tell them about your friend."

Maya walked the rest of the way in silence, wondering what was so darned important her decision could make or break the existence of the world. It all sounded a bit far-fetched and dramatic for her.

A tiny part of her was dying to know what this big secret was. Why was it she had to go all the way to visit Yama anyway? It seemed to Maya the gods had the ability to travel wherever and whenever they liked. Hadn't Kali visited her? *And Chayya's been hanging around quite a bit too.*

How would Maya even get to Patala anyway? And what happened to all of this just being make-believe? Just being stories to teach people lessons to live better and more righteous lives?

Well if these gods really exist, and that depends entirely on whether or not I am still sane, then they can darned well help Ria.

In an instant, she made her decision. Sure, she'll go to see

Lord Yama, but he'd better have justice for Ria or else Maya wouldn't do a damned thing to help him.

Maya let out a breath she hadn't even realized she'd been holding.

A weight lifted from her shoulders. Now, at least she had hope she was doing the right thing, first for Ria and then for the god of the underworld.

CHAPTER 33

The house was brightly lit and voices drifted to Maya from the kitchen as she entered the empty foyer. Sabala walked sedately inside and Maya shut the door behind him. Chayya had been silent for so long Maya assumed she'd gone off to wherever shadow goddesses go when not saving the lives of idiotic human girls.

Maya trudged into the kitchen, her back stiff, her bloodied arm hanging innocently beside her, ready to cop all the flack she knew waited for her. By now, her mom would have filled her dad in on all the afternoon's action. But the room was a bustle of comfortable banter as her dad toiled over a steaming pot and her mom and Claudia fiddled with vegetables at the scorched table. Maya's heart thumped as the scene set her off-balance.

Claudia looked up, and grinned at Maya. She raised one eyebrow, glanced pointedly at the burn mark on the table right next to her hand, and rolled her eyes. Maya grinned back. Trust Claudia to find it funny. Still it did seem strange she wasn't receiving a thorough scolding.

"Hey, honey." Her mom twisted around and smiled at Maya. But the smile ebbed and Maya knew the whole Nik/Yama debacle wasn't totally resolved. Not for Maya at any rate. "Where have you been?"

"Ria's," Maya answered.

"Oh hey, Maya," Dev called from the stove. "Your mother's been filling me in on the happenings of the day. We do need to talk, honey. You okay to wait until dinner or you want to hash it out- Wait a minute, did you say you went to Ria's?"

Everyone stared at Maya with worry and consternation thwarting their jovial expressions, the banter of minutes ago now silent. Maya sighed and pulled up a stool. Her legs refused to hold her any longer- especially when she had to report on the whole Ria-burning incident.

"Yeah, I went to Ria's. She sent me one of our special code texts. We used to do this a long time ago. Ria would send me a blank text and I'd go over."

"Why the blank text?" Claudia asked, holding her hands up in apology. "Sorry, just curious."

"Years ago, before Ria's mom had her brothers, Ria's dad used to use her as a punching bag." Maya's voice was bland, her emotions dead, as she watched the color drain from Claudia's face.

"I'm sorry, Maya." Claudia's hand fluttered to her throat as she shifted in her seat.

"It's okay. I used to go to comfort her. Sometimes she just needed a hug and some support. Her father would lock her in her room and most times he'd forbid her mom from going to Ria at all." Maya ran her finger along the little valley she'd scorched into the table. Her skin came away black with soot. She held her finger and thumb together, smudging the dark color between her fingers. "So I always went. Every time she texted. This time when I saw the text, I think a part of me was on automatic. But the other part felt guilty because I knew the Rakshasa was trying to get to me through Ria. I guess I thought I owed it to her to go."

In the silence that followed, Maya deliberated on how to tell the story.

"Maya, start at the start and end at the end," said her father. She looked up and caught his wink. He'd always said that, ever since she was a little girl. When something troubled her and she didn't have the faintest idea how to tell him he always said the same thing. So now, she started at the start.

She told them everything, then waited while they absorbed the events. "Oh and I did managed to come away with a little souvenir." Maya lifted her injured arm to the table, the clotted blood in stark contrast to her almost bloodless skin. She knew they were all in shock when they didn't immediately fire questions or admonitions at her.

Then, in a sudden burst of activity, Leela had grabbed a first aid kit and together with Claudia began to clean out and bandage the cuts. Thankfully, they didn't ask any further questions about the wound itself.

"So we have no idea if Ria will recover?" asked Maya's father, his pot on the stove all but forgotten. It seemed he spoke more to himself than anyone else.

"Well, I plan to ask for help with that," said Maya. She stood, not really caring the chair dragged on the wood floor.

"What do you mean? Who could help Ria now?" asked Claudia as she toed the pedal on the trashcan and threw away bloodied swabs and bits of bandages. She looked from Maya's mom to her dad and Maya began to wonder if perhaps they hadn't shared the information of Nik's parentage with Claudia. Strange. Maya sent a questioning glance at her mother, who returned it with sad nod.

Maya turned to Claudia. "Nik's father wants to see me. Apparently he needs my help with something."

"Nik's father?" Claudia asked, her face darkening. "What does Nik's father have to do with anything?"

"He is Yama, Lord of the Underworld etcetera etcetera," Maya said, waving her hand about.

Claudia's lips formed a silent 'o'. She drew in a breath, opened her mouth to speak, but no sound came out. Then she clamped her jaw shut, glared at Maya's mom and asked, "You don't look very surprised at all Leela. Why don't I know any of this?"

Poor Claudia looked confused and furious and that wasn't a very safe combination in anyone. "I'm sorry. I couldn't tell you, Claude. I wanted to, but Nik made us promise not to tell anyone about it. Even Maya didn't know until this afternoon."

"Maya still doesn't know what's going on, so don't feel bad Claudia." Maya couldn't resist the jab at her parents, and she felt a stab of satisfaction when the expression on her mother's face fell. Maya was still angry with them but her displeasure slowly faded.

"So what now, Maya? What are you planning on doing?" Maya's dad had given up on cooking apparently, pulled the pot off the heat and come to stand beside her mother.

"Well, the next logical step is to see Yama." Maya sighed. *Yup. That sigh was the sigh of a person with the weight of the world on their shoulders. And why does it have to be me?*

"And how are you planning on getting there?" Claudia raised her eyebrows, leaning back in the chair, folding her arms tight against her body. Maya knew what it meant. Claudia was worried. *Yeah, I'm worried too. No, scratch that, I'm terrified. So you have company, Claudia.*

"That's a very good question," Maya said, wondering herself how she was meant to make that particular trip.

The air moved beside Maya and everyone else in the room froze. Shadows twisted and twirled, every color from darkest pitch to a deep smoky grey. Slowly, the smoke coalesced into Chayya, whose beauty seemed to be all the more evident in the bright kitchen.

CHAPTER 34

"Hello, Maya," the goddess said. She turned her attention to Maya's parents, bestowing them with a regal nod. "You must be Maya's mother and father." They both nodded, no doubt as taken aback as Maya had been when Chayya had first appeared to her.

Chayya threw a quick glance at Claudia. "And who are you?"

The muscles in Claudia's face tightened, and her dark eyes darkened as she glared back at Chayya. Maya marveled at how Claudia could completely disregard the fact that an honest-to-goodness, in-the-flesh goddess stood before her. "My name is Claudia and I'm a Kali follower like Lee and Dev here." Claudia bit out the words. As each fell, it became potently clear she did not like Chayya.

Maya had no time to think about what was happening between Chayya and Claudia, as interesting as it would be to nut that out. She had to figure out how to get to Yama. Ria's future depended on it. "Look, guys, I need to-" a text pinged through on her phone and she grabbed it, flipping it open to check if the message was from Ria. Maya's parents and Claudia were most certainly on the same wavelength as Maya. All three leaned forward, waiting. "Oh, it's Joss."

Almost as one, they sat back, as disappointed as Maya. "It's not really as if Ria is going to call. She was unconscious when I left her." Maya's words were more for herself than anyone else, as she stared at Joss's message, wondering if she could get away with avoiding it.

The phone pinged again. *Are you home?*

Maya sighed, then texted back. *Yes.*

When she didn't get a response she shut the phone and turned her attention to the kitchen and the broiling antagonism Claudia made no effort to hide. Maya threw her mom a glare, flicking a glance at Claudia but from her mother's shrug Maya knew she had no idea either.

From the looks of things they were wasting time. Maya needed to see Yama and Chayya was the best person to tell her how. So she asked, "How do I get to Patala?"

"Maya, I don't think you should be hasty about this," said Claudia, and both Maya's parents frowned. "Ria is unconscious, yes, but that doesn't mean you need to go the Underworld of all places."

Maya opened her mouth to respond but didn't get the chance. Instead, Chayya spoke. "It is understandable you are concerned about Maya's safety. But Yama has requested Maya's presence. As such, she will be completely safe in her travels to his abode."

"And pray tell how will she get there?" Claudia asked, her forehead a mass of creases, her eyes dark and glaring.

Chayya answered with an enigmatic smile. "I control the shadows, and I can move through them from realm to realm. It will be a simple feat to take Maya to Patala."

Claudia's expression fell, and her cheeks tinged pink. Maya felt sorry for her. But what had possessed her to challenge a goddess?

Chayya continued, "It is good you decided to go. Lord Yama should not be made to wait."

"Maya, I know going is probably the best thing to do, but are you sure you want to do this?" Maya's dad walked to her, placing a hand on her shoulder. "I know you feel responsible for Ria but her situation is not your fault at all. You shouldn't be making a decision based on saving Ria. If you go, you need to be sure that decision is for you and you alone."

Maya nodded, but kept silent. *Ria is my responsibility and I will fix it no matter what I have to do.* But she plastered on a smile and bobbed her head again. "Yes, Dad. I know what I'm doing. Frankly, I don't think I have much of a choice, really. Both Nik and Chayya have reminded me that the fate of the world depends on my decision. What kind of a choice is that?" Maya shrugged.

"Well, I agree you do need to see why Yama needs you. It may be important." He turned to Chayya and asked, "But why Maya? What does a powerful god like Yama need with Maya? How do we know she is not walking into danger?"

"You cannot know what will happen when she gets there. Nobody does. Everything depends on what Maya agrees to do once Lord Yama has spoken," Chayya replied, her face expressionless.

Claudia shot the shadow goddess a stiff glare, and Maya understood her need. Chayya hadn't been in the least bit helpful. But it was funny watching the two of them battle each other in silence; Claudia with her outright dislike and Chayya with her enigmatic, unaffected expression.

"Well, I'm coming with you, Maya," said Claudia.

Maya stared at Claudia, then sent an inquiring glance at her parents. What had gotten into her?

"Claude, we need you here. This time Maya needs to do this on her own. We have to let her go. And I'm sure the goddess Chayya will take good care of Maya," Maya's mom said, with a tiny bit more emphasis on the word goddess.

Then Chayya went and made it worse. "Your enthusiasm is appreciated, but I can only transport one person and that is Maya." It was as if the goddess enjoyed goading Claudia. Perhaps the dislike was mutual? But weren't gods meant to be impartial?

"What about Nik?" Maya asked. When Chayya frowned, Maya continued, "Is he not returning?"

"I presume he will return. But it is perhaps unwise to wait."

"That's fine, Maya. If Nik comes we'll tell him you left to see his father as he requested."

Maya nodded and sent an apologetic glance to Claudia before walking to Chayya's side. "What do you need me to do?"

"Be still and hold onto my hand. That is all." Chayya smiled, her face shimmering, as if her entire body was made of light.

A thought hit Maya. "Sabala," she blurted out the name, scanning the kitchen for the four-eyed creature. He still sat by the door, regal and silent and watchful.

"Sabala can come and go as he wishes. He has his own ability to travel to and from Patala."

"So he can also take me to Yama?"

"No, the hound has power only for himself. He is not strong enough to transport another living being."

"Oh," said Maya. "Living?"

"Yes, in most cases when the hounds are sent out to retrieve humans or demons they do not return with a living burden. They are killers after all." Chayya's face revealed not one iota of emotion.

Okay then. Maya wished she hadn't asked in the first place.

She sighed, resigning herself to leaving with Chayya. A small part of her regretted alienating Nik, and she wondered if he was angry with her. She assumed so, since he hadn't returned after she'd hurt him with her fire. Well, she certainly couldn't stick around waiting for Nik to pop into the room. She had to simply get on with things. "Fine. Maybe we should get going?"

Chayya turned and beckoned Maya to come to her.

"Oh, hang on," said Maya, before dashing into the foyer. She dug around in the closet and retrieved her satchel. It held her set of Madu, and she thought it was probably a good idea to keep it with her at all times. Who knew if she might need more than her fire power to help her out? She trotted back into the kitchen. "Right, I'm good to go."

CHAPTER 35

The moment Maya touched Chayya's hand she began to disintegrate, as if the shadows within her body were suddenly freed and meant to escape forever. She spent a few scary minutes wondering if she had just made a huge mistake. What if Chayya was working for the demons all along? What if the shadow goddess took her straight to the controller of the Rakshasa's, whoever had sent them for Maya?

Too late now.

They arrived within a whirlwind of shadows and swirling color. Maya felt slightly strange and a bit dizzy. The journey had lasted mere moments and yet Maya felt like she'd been put through a wringer.

The first thing she noticed was the scent of incense. The soft fragrance of sandalwood filled the air, and somewhere in the distance, someone played a stringed instrument - violin or sitar?

Maya scanned the room in which they'd arrived. Pillars of rich cream marble surrounded them, vibrant paintings drawn directly onto the walls, sculptures of dancers emerged from the solid stone as if at any moment they would step onto the floor and begin their dancing.

Maya and the shadow goddess stood beside a handful of brightly colored silk cushions that should have seemed gaudy, even garish, but right here in this decadent room sedate colors would have made no statement at all.

"Where are we?" whispered Maya.

"We are within the palace of Lord Yama. Wait here while I find out if he can see you now." Chayya walked away, slipping through a pair of gigantic bronze doors. Light reflected on the carvings as the door swung shut behind the goddess, leaving Maya alone in the massive room.

Such opulence didn't seem like it belonged in the underworld. Maya had expected subterranean passages and burning pits, not silk cushions and random trays filled with sweetmeats. Now she eyed a brass platter piled high with tempting pastries and desserts, her mouth beginning to water as she struggled to remember when she'd last eaten.

But she hesitated. Who knew what would happen if she ate something down here. Look at Persephone; stuck in Hades because she couldn't control her hunger. And maybe Greek mythology wasn't the best comparison considering. Either way Maya turned her attention away from the platter and its tempting treats.

She spun on her heel and began to pace. How long was Chayya going to be anyway? And why did she have to wait when Yama had summoned her? A pillar blocked her way so she spun around to walk back and stopped in her tracks.

The air before her twisted and swirled not unlike the whirlwind of shadows created when Chayya had brought her to Patala. Maya gasped as a face appeared in the swirling mist then dissolved and disappeared again. She could have sworn she'd seen Joss in the spinning darkness.

And then she was sure.

Joss appeared, gasping and letting out the odd shriek. She stumbled out of the whirling air, her arms flailing as she tried to regain her balance, her eyes goggling as she stared around her. Maya bit back a giggle.

Joss was followed closely by Nik and Maya's heart gave a little jump at the sight of him. She'd missed him.

Something brushed past Maya's leg and a glance down confirmed Sabala had arrived with them.

"Ohmygod, ohmygod, ohmygod," Joss said repeating the words over and over as she patted her body down as if verifying all parts were still intact. "Ohmygod, Nik, you didn't tell me the trip was going to be so hellish," Joss gasped again holding on to the nearest pillar for support.

"Well you were the one who insisted on coming," answered Nik, not in the least apologetic.

"Come on, Joss it wasn't that bad," said Maya.

Joss shrieked scraping her blond curls from her face as she stared at Maya. "Ohmygod, Maya, that was insane." Joss let the pillar go and stumbled over to Maya, grasping her into a breath-squeezing hug. "Ohmyfreaking - Oh. I guess I shouldn't be cursing right?"

Beside Joss, Nik looked like he was choking. Joss and Maya shared a curious glance but before either one of them could ask him anything, he burst out laughing. "Joss, has anyone ever told you you're too funny for your own good?"

"No, Nik. That would be impolite." Joss glared at Nik, then frowned. "And yes, I did insist on coming because there's no way I'm planning on leaving Maya here, wherever here is. Where are we, by the way?"

"This is the waiting area in the palace of Yama the king of the Underworld, otherwise known as the Lord of Justice." Nik inclined his head and it seemed as if the tiny gesture was a regal bow instead of the slightest of movements.

"Ooookay." Joss tried to stand up straighter, but Maya noticed the wobble in her knees.

"Joss, maybe you need to sit down. Before you fall down,"

Maya said, grinning at her kooky friend. And that's all it took to bring Maya to her senses.

She rounded on Nik. "What the hell were you thinking bringing her here?"

"She wanted to come," Nik replied, totally calm as he leaned against a gold veined pillar.

"Yes, she actually wanted to come," said Joss. "And she can take care of herself too."

Maya glanced over her shoulder, "Joss stay out of this. It's between Nik and me." She turned back to Nik. "You should have known better. What if something happens to her?"

"What do you mean? What's this something that could happen to me?" Joss asked.

"Maya, Joss explained to me how she feels, and why she needs to come with you. You saved her life, and she believes she owes you a life debt. I am not in a position to deny someone's request in such a case," Nik said, raising an eyebrow.

"But she is helpless, and human, and you brought her down here," Maya snapped.

"Maya, I'm not helpless and you know it. And Nik only did what I asked." Somehow, Joss had gotten back to her feet and stood between Maya and Nik as if that would make a difference to Maya's hurt and rage.

"But the problem is he knows better." Maya crossed her arms and glared at Nik.

"Maya, look, I can take care of myself."

"In the Underworld? In hell? Sure you learned martial arts with me but how, pray tell, will you fend off a demon with a hankering for your blood?"

Joss laughed, and turned to meet Nik's eyes. "What is she talking about?"

"Yes, son of Yama, do enlighten her."

"Yes, do enlight- what did you just call him?" Joss almost

choked on her question as she spun around and stared at Maya's face.

"Joss, meet Nik, son of Yama, Prince of the Underworld." Maya knew as she made the introduction if Nik so much as moved a hair on his head that looked like he would give his little arrogant bow, she would flame his ass.

Joss's head swiveled back to face Nik, and she took a deep breath. "So if you're the son of Yama, then . . . ." Joss twirled a finger around Nik's head like a baton. "Then why do you look all pale and stuff? You do lack a good percentage of melanin for an Indian god-prince-being, you know."

Despite the shock running through her body, or maybe because of it, Maya knew she'd heard right. *That's just Joss, say what she wants and think afterward.* But kids at school, even parents, were a whole other ball game when compared to god-prince-beings.

Maya watched in silence. Waited for Nik's reaction. How well did she really know Nik? Would he react like a regular guy or would he be angered by a mere human being so direct with a demi-god? And when did Maya begin to think of him as more than human anyway?

But all Nik did was laugh. "You do have a point, Joss." He nodded, and pushed off the wall. Maya's heart thudded and even Joss took a tiny step back. "When I arrived in town I used this disguise only because I felt it was the best way to fit in. I believe I made the right decision. Right, Maya?"

Maya just nodded. Yes, he'd made the right decision and he'd been at the right place at the right time to save her ass from being Rakshasa toast.

"So, do we get a peek at what you really look like?" asked Joss, voicing Maya's own thoughts.

"I suppose there is no longer a need for this disguise." Nik nodded, his expression quite serious. His face shimmered, like a mirage, wavering as if there but not really there. The shimmering stopped and the real Nik grinned at the two girls.

"Ah, there you are." Joss nodded. Apparently, she approved, although Maya couldn't tell he'd changed much except for his skin color and maybe the shape of his nose.

"Does the color of your eyes change too?" Maya asked, a scattering of ice in her tone.

Nik's smile evaporated.

"What do you mean Maya?" Joss said, frowning as she leaned forward to inspect Nik's dark eyes. "His eyes are still the same."

"It's nothing Joss," Maya answered softly, and changed the subject. "Now Nik, do tell us how long we have to wait to see your father?"

"I'll go check," he said, not meeting Maya's eyes as he turned on his heel and almost walked right into a swathe of shadows slowly coalescing into Chayya.

Chayya blinked and sidestepped the oncoming Nik before he could do more than blink himself. "Lord Yama is away. He will be back shortly and I've been told he will summon you immediately. Maya, I have some things I need to do but I will also return soon. I will assist you with whatever task Yama sets out for you." Chayya gave a little sideways nod of her head and disappeared.

CHAPTER 36

Maya clicked her tongue and spun around. The urge to kick something filled her to overflowing but given the choice between solid pillars and fluffy silk cushions, the need remained thwarted. Instead she threw herself down onto a pile of silk and fluff, and twirled her fingers around a golden tassel sprouting from the corners of numerous pillows.

Nik cleared his throat. "Perhaps you would like to join me in a sparring session, Maya. Maybe we can get some fine-tuning done while we wait?"

What is he up to? Maya watched him with narrowed eyes. Then she admonished herself. Just because he'd kept his identity from her, didn't mean he'd lied to her about everything or that he'd continue to lie to her even now, did it?

Maya hitched her satchel higher onto her shoulder and started to follow Nik as he strode toward a set of doors on the opposite wall in the waiting hall. She stopped, and glanced back at Joss who'd popped a bright orange delicacy into her mouth and looked like a chipmunk missing one nut-filled cheek.

Joss, her eyes wide, nodded vigorously. She took two steps to Maya then turned around and headed for the platter, grabbed a handful of sweetmeats, and jogged back to catch up as Nik left the room. Maya shook her head and arched her eyebrow at her friend's over laden hand. Joss responded with an unrepentant shrug and vigorous chewing.

They headed down a few passageways, walls hand-painted and trimmed with gold and jewels, lit by rows of oil lamps with large steady golden flames. More opulence in the belly of the world. *People up top sure need to rethink where they really want to go in the afterlife. What would heaven be like if hell looks like this?*

Nik made a hard left and flung open a pair of carved wooden doors. Inside, a large open rectangular area stood bordered by simple marble columns. The walls beyond the pillars shone and glinted with an array of weapons. Some Maya recognized. The rest she had to assume were from other cultures from around the planet. Even a set of Madus flickered in the lamplight, only these were tipped with vicious-looking gold spikes. These Madus meant business.

Maya dropped her satchel onto the ground, waving Joss to a safe corner. "Best if you stay near a pillar. If you see fire coming at you, please duck."

"Why?" Joss swallowed the last of the orange syrup soaked goodness. "What's going on?"

"I've got some practicing to do. Nik seems to think I will need it and I have to agree with him. So for now I practice. And I'm not one hundred percent on aim so be ready to duck."

"Oookay." Joss looked worried but said nothing. She even seemed to have lost interest in the sweets as she wiped a piece of marble tile clean and placed them carefully onto the surface. Maya felt sorry for her but there was no time to waste playing babysitter to Joss. She'd insisted on coming with so she had to take care of herself and stay out of the way.

Maya walked up to Nik and waited.

"Right. Now, we treat the fire as if it is a ball. First catch and throw the ball of flames. This will help you also learn to catch any streak of fire aimed at you and allow you to return it back to the thrower if necessary."

Maya nodded. Sounded interesting.

"Now, soften your stance. You know most of what you need already with the basics of your martial arts training."

Maya snorted. "I'm not very good at Kung Fu you know."

"It's all about feeling and enjoying the movement, knowing your body and controlling it. Nothing to it really. Feel the fire, move with it, control it. Don't let the fire control you."

Okay, let's do this.

Soon Nik was throwing balls of fire at Maya, which she caught and returned to him in elegant, effortless movements, as if she were meant to be doing exactly this all her life. The soft push and pull of the Kung Fu moves were there in her stance and her hand and foot gestures. She used her body and the technique to catch and throw the flaming balls.

"Let's kick it up a notch." Maya blinked at Nik's slang but he'd certainly spent long enough with humans, especially in her hometown, to know how people speak. And she had to admit she liked the way he oscillated between casual and formal speech.

She focused in time as a bolt of fire streaked toward her, faster and hotter than anything Nik had thrown before. Her previous movements were like a silken dance, now she felt like an unstrung puppet. Maya missed the first blast of fire. She cringed at the resulting shriek behind her.

But she didn't get a chance to check on poor Joss as another streak of flame flared at her. She kept her eyes on it and threw her hands out to catch it as it passed. All it did was slow down a tiny bit then pass through her fingers. But Maya had felt the tug of the flames, as if it would only take a little more to stop the fire in its tracks.

"Again, and feel the fire. Concentrate."

But Maya barely heard Nik anymore. This time she watched the ball of flame again, watched its trajectory. She had to use its own momentum to turn it and send it back at Nik. And this time she reached out and enveloped the fire within her hands. She moved a step back with the fireball, turned her body and the trajectory of the flame. She used the force of the path of the fire to redirect it right at Nik.

He hadn't expected it.

The fireball hit him square in the gut. He backpedaled, lost his balance and fell on his butt. Joss squealed and Maya gasped as she ran forward and began dusting away the flames before realizing too late he was unharmed.

Maya knelt beside him. Nik grabbed her fingers and in the distance she heard his voice, but it was the warmth of his hands she absorbed and the scent of his skin she inhaled. She had to pay attention. This was the worst time ever to be thinking of anything romantic. "I'm fine Maya. Fire does not harm me. And besides, you used my own fire against me. That is only meant to stun an opponent, not take him down."

She cleared her throat. "Right, so *my* fire can damage an opponent, but *their* fire will only stun them a bit?"

Maya hoped she'd successfully covered her emotional distraction. "When do I deal with the real stuff?"

"Whenever you're ready," Nik answered, his dark eyes growing darker as he kept them trained on Maya's face.

"But won't that actually mean you might get hurt?"

"Of course it does, but I wouldn't worry about *my* safety, Maya."

"Woah, Nik, you immortal or something?" said Joss.

"I am. But given the circumstances I think I may not have to bother with immortality for very much longer." Nik's voice held a trace of bitterness, sending a shiver up Maya's spine.

"What do you mean?" Maya frowned She suspected she wouldn't get anything out of him. The serious crease to Nik's forehead made Maya wonder if this had something to do with Yama's soon to be revealed problem.

"Sorry Maya, my father will tell you. We are not allowed to talk about it."

"Oh, is it some big secret?"

"Yes, it's a secret. So you'll have to wait until later to find out more." Nik gave her an apologetic smile and took a few steps away. "Want to keep going?"

"Well, as long as you can keep up," Maya shot back.

Nik covered everything they'd done so far, and paused to watch Maya catch a streak of fire in her hands. "Kill it," he said softly.

"What?" Maya frowned, confused at this new instruction.

"Kill it, extinguish it."

"I know what you meant," Maya responded, her voice dry and defensive. "But how am I supposed to do that?"

"Use your mind, pull the energy from the fire. Something like the way you create your fire, but in the reverse. The essence of your power is really your ability to create from nothing. If you use the same concept you should be able to take the flames and make them nothing." And he didn't give Maya any time to think, just sent a flash of fire at her and grinned.

Maya caught the fire, turning like she had before but this time she didn't send the fire back to Nik. Instead, she held the heat and flame within her palms. At first, she was unsure what to do with it. Should she literally squash it or was there something more she needed to do? But she played a hunch and placed pressure onto the fire, forcing her fingers onto the flames.

Bad idea.

The fire exploded in her hands. Maya coughed and spluttered, waving away the smoke from her face.

Nik was still grinning.

"I guess pressure isn't a good idea." Maya smiled wryly and blinked against the smoke. She dusted herself off and said, "Let's do this again."

Maya's second attempt was more of a success, with the fire making a hollow popping sound as it went out.

"Right, so this time, take the fire, kill it, and send a blast of your own fire, make it look like it's one movement. This will deceive your opponent into thinking the fire is his own and he won't try to avoid it."

Maya dropped into her stance, and waited, following Nik's instructions, effortlessly creating a ball of flame and directing it at Nik. It all went well until she was about to let the fire fly at him. She hesitated. She had a sudden vision of Nik being incinerated right in front of her eyes.

She shouldn't have hesitated.

And it wasn't Nik who was in danger from the flames.

Maya's arm was on fire.

CHAPTER 37

Her arm was ablaze and her torso soon followed. Before she knew it her entire body burned. She was so shocked that for a moment she remained unsure what to do. Joss's shrieks brought her to her senses. Joss drew abreast of Maya and stared at her face, shock, horror, and fascination contorting her poor friends features.

"Maya," yelled Joss. "What in god's name is going on?"

"I'm fine Joss, just keep away." But Maya wasn't fine. She had no idea how to put out the fire. Terrified she met Nik's eyes and the moment her gaze made contact, she could tell he knew.

He moved toward Maya, waving Joss away with one hand. "Right, there's nothing to it. Just calm down, get your heartbeat to a comfortable level again. Panic won't hurt you specifically, but it will maintain the fire. So breathe and relax. Now bring your palms together. Breathe in and out and try to guide the heat toward your palms. Channel the fire to your hands - you'll have better control. Right now it's feeding off your body and your Kali power and you need to disconnect it or it will drain your energy."

With Nik's words buzzing in her ears, Maya tried to concentrate. She felt the ebb and flow of the fire course through her veins, molten lava, liquid flame. She felt the seductive pull of the heat against her body, tugging at her breath, almost lulling her into a drunken ecstasy.

"Maya."

The single word brought Maya to her senses. She stiffened, hardening herself against the fire. She threw her hands out before her, opening her palms, wrists together, like an open bowl ready to catch whatever flew past.

With a breath, she channeled the energy within her veins, urging it to filter through her muscles, through her blood, into her hands. Perspiration gathered on Maya's forehead, the effort taxing both her mind and her body. She tugged at it, almost spent, and then she felt the energy slowly following the path to her hands. But it was like tethering an eel. The moment she thought she had control the power back lashed and fled back inside her, filling her up, the fire flaring hot and red.

"That was good. Go again." Nik's instruction was calm and firm and comforting. Under any other circumstances, Maya's hackles would have risen and she would have resisted his direction. Not now though. This time she absorbed his words, channeled the strength behind them.

She tried again, deliberately keeping her thoughts as far from her previous failed attempt as possible. Her confidence had been nicely obliterated. No sense in replaying it in her memory. Maya breathed in and cleared her mind and started fresh.

The second round proved more difficult, taxing her body and her strength more than before. Sweat dripped down Maya's spine. Her muscles quivered with the strain of pushing the energy through her body. At last, the power gathered within Maya's arms, still bucking and straining against the hold of her mind, but Maya refused to let go. If she managed it once she'd be able to practice and finally control the fire without breaking a sweat.

When it felt like the pulsing energy would engulf her once

more, when she sensed the tiniest waver in the energy level of the surging power, only then did Maya make her final move. Only then did she push the heat into her hands, felt it flare in the center of her palms, felt it burn.

Maya stared into the flames rising and crackling from her palms, stared at fire that had, only minutes ago, coursed through her own veins. With a soft sigh, Maya squeezed her fist and deadened the fire.

"Well done, Maya," Nik closed in on her and grabbed her shoulder, squeezing it encouragingly. Joss came closer too but all she did was stare. Maya wanted to giggle. Poor Joss looked shell-shocked.

"That was great. So what else?"

"Nothing else. You are summoned." Chayya materialized behind Joss, and didn't waste any time ending the session. She brooked no argument either, just walked off, leading the small contingent out the door. Maya hurried to grab her satchel, staring with a jealous eye at the spike-ended Madus on the wall as she passed.

Maybe next time

Someday soon, all of this is going to seem normal and fine and real. Someday soon.

Maya entered a set of double doors.

Well maybe not.

The doors themselves were made from gold, molded and carved with scenes from ancient scripts; kings being carried on palanquins, giant elephants, generals in chariots and battles, even the Churning of the Oceans; the story of the origins of the universe. Not to mention the doors were at least fifteen feet high.

Maya gulped, her legs leading her forward while her mind rebelled against what her eyes showed her. Gold and jewels decorated the room, tapestries and paintings covered the walls, a riot of color and majesty filled the silent hall. As the small group moved forward the only sound to be heard was a loud scratching as if an implement scraped back and forth across the surface of a piece of paper.

A few steps more brought them to a set of three stairs. Each stone stair again carved and edged in gold. At the top sat two men. One leaned over a large book, leaned so far over it seemed his spine must have grown into that specific shape.

The other man exuded such a power and magnetism Maya was in no doubt he was the formidable Lord of Justice, Dharma, also known as Yama, Lord of Death. He sat comfortably within an enormous golden throne, the arms curved outward like gigantic pillows, the backrest rising above his head inscribed with Sanskrit and other scripts Maya didn't recognize.

His tanned skin gleamed, a perfect foil for his coal dark eyes. He wore his mustache thick and caterpillar-like, much the same as Ria's father. The memory of her friend pulled Maya back to the present and back to her reason for being here.

Yama beckoned Maya forward. Light from the hundreds of little lamps around the room glinted on the fine gold threads in the fabric of his robe. Maya shuffled closer but didn't dare to place a foot on the steps. The last thing she wanted was to offend the god of justice for whatever reason.

"The Hand of Kali, Maya Rao. Patala welcomes you." Yama's voice boomed out into the hall and he rose to his feet, placed his hands together and bowed to Maya. Shocked, Maya was totally unsure what to do and looked around for some guidance from Chayya or Nik, but both were also bowing to Maya. Joss goggled, as confused as Maya.

What in god's name is going on here?

CHAPTER 38

"Maya, I see you are confused by our obeisance. Know that it is to the benevolent soul of the Mother Radha that we pay our respects. In your life as Radha, you were an exemplary soul. You are perhaps too young to understand this but someday I do hope your eyes will be opened to the beautiful soul you were in your previous life." Yama still spoke with such reverence Maya felt slightly uncomfortable.

Mother Radha seemed incomparable. How was Maya ever going to live up to her? Or to herself, rather. Maya shook her head slightly. It was confusing trying to figure herself out.

Despite the uncomfortable quiet, Yama sat back and studied Maya, rubbing his chin as the silence seethed. Nik cleared his throat.

"Very well, let us begin," said Yama. "You do not need to leave, Lady Chayya."

Maya turned to see Chayya stop in her tracks. She faced Yama again, a curious expression in her eyes but she said nothing. Joss, though, looked like she was about to ask if she should stay or go.

"Everyone stays. I do believe you come as a - Nik what is it the modern folk say- a bundle-"

"A package." Nik smiled.

"- ah, yes, a package deal. Now, I assume we have your undivided attention." The silence answered in affirmative and Yama continued. "Maya, your presence has been requested as you are the only person alive who is capable of completing this task. The gods are growing weaker every day, and will continue to weaken until we can retrieve Varuni."

"Varuni?"

"My apologies, Maya. Perhaps I ought to start at the beginning." Yama cleared his throat. "A long time ago the goddess Varuni, the keeper of the Amrita, was stolen from us. In the time that passed, the gods grew weaker, their power fading. Slowly becoming mortal."

Yama rose from his throne, and began to pace, as if the story took too great a toll for him to take sitting down. "In recent times we discovered who took Varuni, and we knew then that you, the Hand of Kali, were perfect for this task. We need you to go to Swargaloka. There you will find Narakasura, the demon King."

Maya gasped. Even she knew who Narakasura was. "But I thought he'd been killed?"

"In a sense, yes. But even a demon can gain sway over his god. Narakasura was granted the chance to live again. Perhaps it was believed he would make up for what he'd done, make up for the evils of his past."

"I guess he didn't hold up his end of the bargain," said Maya.

For a moment, she thought she saw a flicker of sadness on the god's face but it disappeared so fast she couldn't be sure. "No, he did not. Narakasura renewed his challenge to the gods with a vengeance. This time he was more strategic. He stole the goddess from her abode in the celestial ocean. He took her to Swargaloka. None of the gods were able to challenge him simply because of Varuni. Nobody dared to endanger her life in any way. And since that day Narakasura has remained at Swargaloka, with Varuni."

Maya frowned. "How long has he kept her captive?"

"It has been a hundred years. Not long in terms of the length of our lives. But in these years, the gods have ailed and grown frail and tired, becoming more and more mortal each day. For a long time when we thought there would be no saving us from the future without the Drink of Immortality, but the goddess Kali convinced us to have patience. That the day would soon come when a human girl would raise her hand and wield the power of Kali." Maya met Nik's eyes and he gave her an encouraging nod. She turned her attention back to Yama. "That human girl will release us from the destiny the demon Narakasura had written for us."

"And that human girl is me?" Maya knew the answer. She just wanted to hear him say it again. So she knew she hadn't imagined the whole thing.

"Yes, Maya. You are still young, and have a while to go before you gain experience in life and in battle, but unfortunately we do need to call on you now." Yama returned to his throne, resting his elbows on the armrests of his golden seat. "Nikhil has told me of some of your experiences in your town. Someone knows where and who you are. For that reason, we simply have no choice. The gods are unable to protect you for much longer. Of course it does not help when more and more people are losing their faith in us every day."

It was as if the last sentence was meant for Maya. It went straight to her heart and her conscience. She was one of those very people who had no longer believed. She was one of those people who had no longer prayed to the gods. But could she really change because Yama said so? Sure, she stood before a living breathing god, but what did it change except to know the mythology was true? Could she bring herself to prostrate herself before the gods just because they were gods?

Maya's head began to hurt as she turned the thoughts over and over in her mind. "What do you need me to do, my lord?" she asked softly. The scribe continued to scratch words into the pages, pausing only to dip his pen into a bottle of ink, before continuing in silence.

"You must go to Swargaloka, and bring Varuni back to us. At whatever cost."

Chayya gasped and Nik stiffened beside Maya.

"What do you mean, my lord? You said *whatever cost*?" Chayya said, shadows swirling around her face and darkening her eyes.

"It means just that, Lady Chayya. This is no easy task. Neither is it one to be abandoned for any reason. Maya must retrieve Varuni. Or die trying."

The hall went silent. Even the scribe had stopped his scratching.

Ice sluiced through Maya's veins, the ice of reality. So this was it. "Well, if I'm putting my life on the line then I get to ask for something in return, right?" Maya lifted her chin, not caring in the least if her request would seem presumptuous. To heck with presumptuous. She was about to embark on a journey which might well take her life. If she came back dead, or not at all, she wanted to be sure her wish was granted.

"I want to make a request for my friend, Ria."

"Ah, yes, the child who was possessed by the Rakshasa."

"You know about that?"

"Yes, my dear, there is little that is demon related that I do not know." Yama leaned forward in his seat. "I may not always be able or allowed to interfere in such matters but news does travel to my ears."

"Then can you save her? Make her well again?"

"It depends."

"On what?" Maya's head grew hot. Not a good sign. She felt like she was bargaining for a night out and about to have her parents come up with a very inventive way of saying *no*.

Yama looked over at the scribe, who had during the ensuing discussion, continued his scratching. "What say you, Lord Chandragupta? What does the life of Ria Gupta say to you?"

The old man lifted his head and Maya almost gasped to find he was neither young nor aged. As he straightened, he seemed to grow more attractive, younger, more congenial. Chandragupta stood aside, and placed the golden pen beside the book. He spoke a few silent words over the pages which began to turn on their own.

The tome itself was a monstrosity. Maya had first assumed the book lay upon a golden table. But on closer inspection, she found the enormous book sat directly on the floor, its covers made entirely of gold, its pages seemingly never ending.

Now those pages spun like the cards on a huge Rolodex, fluttering on and on until at last they sighed to a stop and fell open. Chandragupta leaned over the page, placed a finger on its surface and moved the digit slowly downward as if searching a list for Ria's name. At last he stopped, and raised his head. "A good soul, and an obedient child. A hard life, abused by her father. Her mother too, bears the responsibility of turning a blind eye for her own safety. Low self-esteem."

"Sins?" asked Yama.

Maya's gaze flew to the god. What did he mean *sins*? Ria had barely lived long enough to sin.

"Minor sins. Lies to her parents usually due to peer pressure and a wish to have some life enjoyment. Also lies as a means of gaining comfort. Disobedience toward her father - this is related to her refusal to marry the man her father has chosen for her."

Maya felt her knees buckle. She'd suspected Mr. Gupta would someday arrange a marriage for Ria, but not in her wildest imagination did she expect it to be this soon.

"Many of these lies may be excused, or the punishments for them reduced," said Yama. "And perhaps most of them could be erased as a result of her experience at the hands of the Rakshasa. That would certainly have been painful enough to warrant a justified payment for her sins."

Maya's ears throbbed and Yama's words seemed to come to

her from a distance. What were they talking about? Ria had never done anything wrong in her life. Did they really mean people were punished for every single sin they ever committed in a lifetime? And how did they know all that anyway?

Yama continued. "But even if we erase them all she will still face her punishment when she does finally get here sometime in the future."

"What do you mean?" A flurry of fear flitted up and down Maya's spine.

"We can only give your friend a second chance, not give her a lifetime of immunity against her sins."

"Oh, I see." Maya nodded. "So what happens now?"

"Well, we can make it so that once you return, Nikhil will accompany you and help transition Ria to her second life chance."

"And what if I don't make it back?"

Yama paused to look at Maya. He sat back, stroking his beard while an odd expression darkened his face. She hoped it meant he approved of her stubborn streak.

CHAPTER 39

The door to the hall opened and someone, servant, soldier or guard, entered, hurrying to Yama. Maya stepped away from the dais, and Joss took the opportunity to slip her hand into the crook of Maya's arm. "You don't have to do this you know," she said softly, her eyes pinched and worried.

"Of course I have to." Maya smiled sadly.

"No Maya, you don't owe anyone anything. This is your life. You don't have to do any of this."

In a way, Maya saw the sense in Joss's words. She nodded. "I know, I don't have an obligation to do anything for Yama or for any of the gods for that matter. They seem to need me. But I feel like I have to do what they want. I do feel obligated."

"This is all my fault," Joss said, wringing her hands. "If I hadn't goaded you into going to that stupid party, and if I hadn't taken that stupid drink from Amber, and if-"

"Filling up on If Soup, Joss?" Maya shook her head and gave her friend a squeeze. "Is that why you came with Nik?"

"Yes," Joss replied. After a short pause she said, "And no. I came because I couldn't let you do this by yourself. Yes, I do feel guilty because I helped those demon things to lure you out in the open but I came to help you. And your mom also told me more about what happened to Ria. I think she meant to discourage me but it made me all the more sure I wanted to come with you."

"Yes. Ria." Maya pushed Joss with her arm. "At least now she has a chance at a new life. When we get home everything will go back to normal. And if I don't return, you promise to make him keep his end of the bargain." Maya tipped her head at Yama, who remained engrossed with the messenger.

"Oh yeah, sure. I'm supposed to take on the god of death?"

"Promise me." The hard edge to Maya's voice brooked no argument on the part of her now meek friend.

"Okay, I promise."

A short silence went by as Joss patted her pockets, Maya assumed in search of sweets.

"Joss?" Maya asked, looking ahead at the dais, keeping her gaze off Joss's face.

"Yes, Maya."

"Have you been putting on weight?"

"Umm, you could say that."

"What's going on?"

"I happen to like food."

"You also used to happen to like your skinny jeans, and your belly button ring."

"Let me tell you the skinny on skinny jeans." Joss leaned closer, although she kept her eyes straight ahead. "The wearing of said jeans requires said wearer to hold her breath. A lot. If you hold your breath for too long you can faint. Fainting is not a good look. Worse, holding your breath makes it hard to eat. And eating is important."

Maya chuckled.

"What about the guys? You once told me being skinny guaranteed male interest, because skinny means sexy."

"Well firstly, male interest isn't all it's cracked up to be, and any guy who looks my way better be more interested in me as a person than in the size of my ass."

"Preach it sister," said Maya. She nodded, feeling a rise of emotion clogging her throat. Joss had been there for her for so many years and though recent times had caused her to wonder at the merits of their friendship, it seemed she was mistaken to have questioned Joss at all.

At last, the messenger left and Yama beckoned the group forward. Even Chayya had all but faded into the shadows. They moved in silence, and like Maya, probably feeling the finality of the moment. This was it.

The god's voice rang out. "As a boon to you for risking your life to help the gods I am willing to ensure your friend Ria is given her second chance anyway."

Maya remained silent, contemplating the idea. Yama was giving her a huge reward, something she didn't think many people received. She didn't want to appear demanding or ungrateful in the face of Yama's generosity.

But she stood her ground. "As long as Ria gets her chance even if I don't make it back."

"It is done. You have my word, Maya Rao." Yama inclined his head and Maya hoped it meant he wasn't mad at her rudeness or her insistence in getting what she wanted. "Nikhil will help you prepare for your journey."

Maya shifted, turning to leave when Yama spoke again. "And remember, Maya. The gods are depending on you for their survival."

"I understand, my lord."

Talk about irony.

"SO WHERE TO FROM HERE?" asked Maya, as the group left Yama's hall. The pressure of Yama's presence dissipated but did nothing for the weight of the task on her shoulders.

"Well, first we eat and rest, and then we set out in the morning," Nik answered.

"Do we really have time to waste?" Maya snapped, impatient to just get on with it. The longer they took, the longer it would take to restore Ria to health again.

"Maya, when was the last time you slept? Or had a decent meal? How efficient will you be in a fight if you're falling down with hunger and fatigue? You may be the Hand of Kali but you are still human, you know." He raised an eyebrow. "And besides, Varuni has been held captive for a hundred years. I don't think one more day will make much difference."

Maya couldn't argue with his common sense, considering sleep seemed a distant memory, but she still didn't see the point in waiting.

"So, what can we expect when we get there?" Joss asked.

Maya admonished herself silently. She should have been the one asking that particular question instead of concentrating on the weight of Yama's request.

"Well, the planes of existence are divided into the upper and lower planes, of which there are seven in total. Earth or mortal living is the first of the upper planes, while Swargaloka is the third plane of consciousness."

"So it's like another dimension or something," Joss asked, frowning.

"Exactly the right idea." Nik nodded and so did Chayya. "It is a kind of paradise, where people go before they are reincarnated into their next lives."

"Er, so people who go to Swargaloka, are they spirits or ghosts or something?" asked Maya. She'd heard somewhere that a person's soul went to the higher planes, stepping further up the levels as they lived more righteous lives, but she'd always wondered in what capacity they went there. Were they little lights with intelligence and consciousness floating around?

"They're the spirit or the essence or soul of the person. But they are corporeal. The life they live in any of the celestial planes are lived in solid existence. Each soul still retains the ability to travel between the planes."

"So how will we, living beings as opposed to spirits, be able to travel through?"

"For a living human it can take many decades to reach a higher consciousness allowing one to enter Swargaloka while still alive. But you gain entry because we will take you there."

Maya nodded, feeling slightly overwhelmed.

Before she could say anything else, Chayya spoke. "I shall meet you here after you have rested." She gave the group a regal nod and then the goddess disintegrated into multicolored streaks of shadow and was soon nothing but a wisp of grey in the air.

"Come ladies, I will show you your rooms. You can freshen up and rest."

"Nik, we left home at dinnertime. What time is it here?" asked Maya as they walked onto a terrace. The balcony on one side opened out onto a large, lush garden where the high-pitched call of peacocks could be heard, interspersed with the almost mournful wails of a band of whip-poor-wills.

"Considering we have no sunrise or sunset here in Patala, we work on Kailas time so it's just after 5pm."

"What's Kailas?" asked Joss as Maya digested the information. A thousand questions sizzled in her brain but she knew she'd have plenty of time to ask them all. Something told her she wasn't going home very soon.

"Kailas is the center of the world. It's the abode of Lord Shiva and an important religious location for Hinduism, Buddhism and Jainism," Nik said.

"Like the Vatican City? Or Mecca?" Joss asked.

"Something like that, only without the pilgrimage."

"Why do people not go there if it's such a holy place?"

"Because the mountain cannot be climbed. The shape of the rock faces make it impossible to scale. Many people have tried but each time they realize it can't be done. And perhaps they decide it is something best left alone."

"So where exactly is the mountain?" Joss asked as the group walked along the passage. Maya trailed behind, running her fingers on the stone balconies, tracing the shapes of the dancing girls carved into the pillars placed every few meters.

"It's in Tibet. So technically it falls under the governance of China."

"Oh. Okay. Have you been there?"

"Yes, a few times."

"What's it like?"

"Beautiful. From the outside it looks desolate, barren. But there are two lakes set within the mountain, the land is lush and Lord Shiva's palace is nothing short of majestic. Think Angkor Wat in white marble."

Maya watched Nik as he spoke about a mountain that had existed as a mere figment of her imagination, a tale to be told to believers. A tale to be believed by the devout. How had it never occurred to her to find out if Mount Kailas really existed? Through the years her parents had made attempts to educate her on Hinduism and the myths and legends. Although to most people in their community, the gods were real, they were never anything but just stories to Maya.

And Maya's parents had never forced her to believe. They told the tales, gave her the books, and left it at that. Maya assumed they hadn't forced her to accept the beliefs because they knew one day all her disbelief would evaporate in a puff of smoke.

A little warning might have been nice.

Before long they passed the unusual garden - Maya had to still accept the concept of a garden in the underworld - and entered a plush seating area. Numerous doors opened off the large room, and as Nik led them to the first one on the right, Maya began to long for a bed. Seemed odd that until this moment the idea of rest felt wrong. Now all she wanted to do was cuddle down into a soft mattress and yawn herself into slumber.

Nik waved Joss into the first room and Maya caught a glimpse of rich greens and shimmering purple silks. Maya almost giggled as they left Joss to squeal over her beautiful sleeping quarters. A few steps more and Maya was shown into a large room, deep burgundies, reds and yellows enveloped her in an explosion of rich vibrant color.

"Rest. I'll get some food sent up to you later on."

"Thanks, Nik," said Maya as he turned to leave. Maya hesitated, still unsure of why Nik helped her at all, but she didn't ask the question. Gone were the days when she would have blurted it out, uncaring of whether it hurt his feelings or not.

"It is my duty, but it is also my pleasure." Nik bowed and closed the door behind him, leaving the glow of his smile still warm on Maya.

Her heart thudded as he left the room. A part of her wanted to call him back, wanted to talk to him, and tell him she wasn't angry anymore. But maybe for the moment the best thing was to leave it alone.

Instead, she inspected the room, the floor to ceiling, satin-curtained four-poster bed, pillars carved with dancing girls and peacocks and rushing streams. The walls all hand painted in rich colors depicting scenes Maya knew were from the ancient texts like the Ramayana.

Everywhere brass vases and lamps sparkled with lights and the subtle scent of incense bathed the air. When Maya landed on the mattress it was soft and comfortable, definitely not cheap hotel comfort. She pulled the silken comforter over her body and curled up right there. She stared up at the fabric swathed on the inside of the top of the four-poster, listened to the squawk of the peacocks in the distance and the trickling of water.

Nik had said rest. And although she resisted the idea because it felt like time wasted, maybe rest was in order. After all, tomorrow would be the day she stole a goddess from a demon.

CHAPTER 40

The threads of exhaustion had just begun to weave themselves around Maya, almost lulling her to sleep when a knock sounded at the door. She pushed off the bed, then sat back hard with shock as the door opened and a girl strode into the room, and began to set up a place at a small table by the open window. Maya had grown used to the scent of the Rakshasas and there was no denying the serving girl was one of them. Maya's throat closed.

Maya barely heard the demon-girl telling her to enjoy her meal. The girl appeared not to notice Maya's rudeness, nor did she wait for Maya's response. A quick bow and she was gone.

Maya walked to the table, more interested in the food than she cared to admit, given it had been served to her by a Rakshasa. Stuffed parathas - probably potatoes, and a tall glass of what looked like mango lassi. Fragrant rice and spicy tandoori chicken. A mouthwatering dinner served in hell.

At first Maya hesitated, remembering her meal had been delivered by a demon, but it didn't take long before hunger won out and she polished the meal off lightning fast.

It was, in the end, only enough to take the edge off, so Maya began to look forward to dinner more than she expected. She leaned back, sinking in the cushion filled seat, listening to the trickling of water again. Maya shot to her feet. Water. Water might mean somewhere to bathe.

She followed the sound around a wooden screen and stopped short in shock and delight. A small pool occupied half the closed off area. A statue of a dancing girl poured water into a bath set into the floor, a little larger than a spa bath. Rose petals and holy basil floated on the top of the water and a scent lingered reminding Maya of sweetmeat and prayers.

She bent to touch the liquid. Steam rose from the pretty, flower filled surface and her fingers sank into delicious warmth. Maya wasted no further time. She chucked off her clothes, flinging them on the bed and headed straight in. Only after she sank into the enticing warmth did she think of towels and robes.

At the side of the pool sat a little tray with a pair of decanters, and what looked like a loofah. Maya smelled the contents of each - rose water and sandalwood essence. Both delightful and fragrant. A bar of soap lay on a separate tray and Maya used it to wash. Nothing untoward happened, and Maya relaxed, soaking in water that remained strangely clean despite the soap and oils. In the end, she gave in and washed her hair too, lathering the sandalwood and soap and rosewater until her hair was squeaky clean.

Maya emerged from the water to find a pile of towels at the side of the pool, and a fresh skirt and top laid out on her bed. Her jeans and other clothes were gone. Maya's heart thumped as she grabbed for her satchel where she'd dropped it. She didn't trust the Rakshasa servants even if they were loyal to Yama. She breathed a sigh of relief to find everything inside untouched.

She pulled on underwear then dressed in the clothing that seemed far more comfortable than jeans anyway. She'd just slipped on her skirt when the door flew open and Joss bounced in.

"Ohmygosh, Maya, did you see the pool? And the food? Oh wasn't that drink delish? And who would have expected a laundry service in the underworld?"

"Laundry service?"

"Yes, the serving girl told me when she took my clothes away. Good thing she said so 'cos I was about to fight her for it." Maya wanted to laugh at the image of Joss fighting a demon. A sobering thought.

"Joss, did the serving girl seem odd to you?"

"No, she seemed fine. Shy, but still friendly. Why?"

"Because she's a Rakshasa and I don't really have a soft spot for demons."

"Oh," said Joss. Then she shrugged, "Well she was nice and she didn't seem too dangerous to me. You have to relax, Maya. Do you really think Nik would put you in a position where you're in danger?"

Maya shook her head. "I don't think he would but he's grown up with these demons around him. To me, they're the creatures who want to kill me."

Maya remembered what Joss had said about fighting. She got up and faced Joss. "At least *I* can defend myself with my fire. You need to practice your moves. It's a little different in a real fight from the controlled environment of the studio."

"What?" Joss looked like she was about to choke.

"Yes, don't look at me all surprised. You must know you'll need to fight someone at some point. I thought you said you came to help me? How will you help if I have to keep watching over you all the time? I need to know you'll be fine and that you're confident you can defend yourself. Besides, you've always been good at sparring."

Joss sat still for a moment. "Okay, what do you need me to do?"

Maya decided the best course of action with Joss was to go through everything they'd learned in Kung Fu so they spent the next half hour revising. She watched jealously as Joss moved easily, performed all her strokes so fluidly. Maya sighed. *Ah well I never was very good at martial arts anyway.*

Joss fell onto a heap of cushions scattered around a low table near one of the room windows. "That was amazing," she said.

"Yes, you're a natural, Joss. You've always been a natural. I think we can get Nik to find you a weapon you'll be comfortable with," said Maya, determined not to let her own stupid jealously affect her friend's enjoyment of her talent. *At least Joss can defend herself in a fight. That's the most important thing.*

"Maya, you know, I have to tell you again how sorry I am."

"Come on, Joss. We've been over this already."

"No, I mean it. All this that's happening to you? It's huge. It can't be easy to have so much to suddenly live up to, to be told you were this amazing human being in a previous life."

"Nope. It's not easy. I often wonder if they were maybe mistaken." Maya laughed. "I'm not anything like Mother Radha. She seems so incredibly good and kind, so generous and loving and wise. I'm far from any of those things."

"Don't be silly Maya, you're everything she is. You have to realize it. And you will, sooner or later. Look at you and Ria."

"You mean look at how I put Ria in danger and got her possessed by a demon?" asked Maya, bitterness lacing her voice and her heart.

"That was definitely not your fault Maya. And you've done everything possible to help her. Even bargaining with the god of death. See, you'd sacrifice your own life to make Ria well and that's the mark of a true friend and an amazing human being."

"Yeah, still. I wish she hadn't gotten involved. And what about you Joss? Now you're also mixed up in this mess." Maya paused. "Wait a minute, where do your parents think you are?"

"Come on Maya. They think I'm going away with your family for a few days. Your parents agreed to cover for me in case mine come looking, which we both know they won't."

The nonchalant, uncaring expression on Joss's face didn't fool Maya. Joss's absentee parents never really cared what their daughter did. Right now, they were happy as long as she stayed out of their hair. Maya remembered meeting them the first time, many years ago. They'd barely even acknowledged Maya, looked right through her when she'd entered their house and been shown to their daughter's room. It struck her early on they weren't home even when they were.

It only made Maya more certain no matter how much she felt her parents interfered and tried to control her life, she preferred it that way. At least it showed they cared. Joss's parents, on the other hand, cared so little they had no idea how they hurt their child.

"So you forgive me, right?"

"For what?"

"For starting this whole mess. If it hadn't been for me the demons wouldn't have got there filthy demonic nails into you or Ria."

"Shut up, Joss."

"Fine," Joss answered and pouted. "Have it your way."

A knock on the door interrupted their banter. Maya called out for the visitor to enter. The double doors opened, ushering Nik inside.

Joss yawned. A little too well timed for Maya's liking. She threw her friend a dark look but Joss ignored her and said. "You guys chat. I'm going back to bed. I'm way too tired to keep my eyes open." She fluttered her fingers at them and sauntered out of the room.

Leaving Nik and Maya alone.

The silence felt thick, slowly becoming awkward, making Maya just want to claim exhaustion herself. So many things had happened, so many words said and not said.

Maya was about to say goodnight when Nik spoke. "Would you like to see the gardens?"

That was the last thing she'd expected and it caught her off-guard. "Sure. But what can you see in this darkness?" she asked gazing out the door and into the garden shrouded in shadows.

"Well, if you don't come you'll never know." Nik gave Maya a cheeky grin and she laughed softly. He looked so sexy, smiling at her, his eyes all crinkled up. How could she refuse?

"Okay, now I'm curious. Lead on."

Nik led her along the balcony toward a curved stone stairway leading into the densely planted garden below. The cobbled path, lit by flame torches every few feet, wound its way deeper into the trees.

Maya remained silent. She was afraid to break the spell woven around them. She had to admit she enjoyed the time alone, just walking, and no talking. With so much ahead of her the next day, she certainly didn't need the added stress of tension between her and Nik. Maya crossed her fingers at her side and sent up a prayer for nothing to mess up the evening.

With her hand tucked within the crook of Nik's arm, she breathed in the rich fragrance of jasmine and roses, listened to the call of the peacocks, and gazed up at the gem-studded rock ceiling high above them.

At last, their stroll came to a halt and Nik slowed as they entered a large circular garden. A marble fountain claimed the center, a stone dancing girl endlessly poured water from the fat pitcher in her arms.

Nik led Maya to a nearby stone seat. She sat, taking in the trees and the soothing sound of running water.

"This is so beautiful." Maya sighed deeply. "I can't believe this actually exists way down here . . . wherever it is we are."

Nik chuckled beside her, his dark eyes lighting up as he smiled. It never failed to take her by surprise how one little smile from him could turn her stomach upside down and make her breath come just that bit faster.

He leaned forward, elbows on his knees, steepling his fingers.

"Tell me something." When Maya stared at him, questions in the curves of her eyebrows he asked, "How do you feel about this rescue mission? Do you have any doubts?"

"Nope, no doubts. I agreed to do it so I have no intention of backing out." Maya sighed. "But I still wonder if you guys could have gotten all of this totally wrong. How sure can you be I am the right person for the job?"

"We are certain, Maya. And Kali's very presence around you when you were hurt is enough confirmation that you belong to her." Nik stared at Maya with a strange look in his eyes. He threw his arm across her shoulders and gave her a quick squeeze. "Don't worry. I'll be right there with you."

Maya's answer never got past her lips. He was too close to her, his body and thigh pressed up against her so close she could barely breathe. All she managed was a nod but when he didn't respond she looked up.

The moment their eyes met Maya felt her stomach tighten. The intensity in his expression held her attention. So much she barely noticed as he closed the distance between them. His mouth claimed hers before she could take another struggling breath.

Maya lost herself in the heat of his lips, in the depth of the passion of that kiss. Her heart beat so fast and hard she felt sure he'd hear it soon. His hand snaked to the back of her head bringing her closer, deepening the kiss and stealing all her breath. Maya reached up and threw her arms around his neck, needing to hold on to something.

Probably a good thing she was seated; her legs would certainly not have held her up if she'd been standing. Nik pulled back, and they both gasped for breath in the heat between their mouths. Maya told herself it was time to pull away, time to put some space between them. They were in a garden for god's sake. Who knew who was watching?

But all she could do was look at his mouth and hope he'd kiss her again. And it was as if nothing could keep them apart. They were drawn together as if nothing else mattered but that next kiss.

Not so long ago Maya would have snorted with hysterical laughter had someone told her she'd be kissed with such mindless passion. It just wouldn't have seemed possible she'd have the power to move someone this way. And that was the crux of it. She could tell Nik was as much moved by the kiss as she was.

The rustling of feathers and the loud call of a peacock close by pulled them apart reluctantly. With one last tender kiss, Nik sat back and glared at the intruder.

"Shoo," he said, waving away the beautiful bird.

"No, don't." Maya grabbed his hand. "He's so beautiful."

"Yeah, nice to look at but nosy and noisy as hell." Nik snorted.

Maya laughed. "No he's amazing. Look at those colors. And isn't he a proud fellow too?"

Nik held Maya's hand as she spoke and the warmth of his fingers crept all the way into her stomach with lightning speed.

She cleared her throat. "Pity though."

"What's a pity?"

"That the dude is the one who's gorgeous. I feel sorry for the girl peacocks."

"True. They can get ignored sometimes. Dull brown is not the most eye-catching of colors."

Maya chuckled as the peacock turned and circled the fountain, head held high as if he knew they'd been talking about him. "Showoff," she called but he paid no attention, just continued strutting until he came right back to Maya's side.

"Shoo," Nik waved the bird off. "This girl is mine. Go find yourself a girl of your own.

Maya flushed at his words. He'd referred to her as his girl. But what did that really mean between a human and a demigod? What would be the future for their relationship?

And just like that, the spell was broken. The threads of those warm and crazy feelings still lingered inside Maya, but reality had returned and her immediate future had no place for making out, let alone a romance.

They walked back, fingers still entwined, their steps slowing as they got closer to Maya's room. Nik paused outside her door, and Maya met his eyes. He seemed as uncertain as she was and she wasn't sure how good that was.

He smiled and stepped away until their threaded fingers could no longer keep hold.

For the next few moments all was right with the world and with the underworld.

All was right until Maya awoke the next morning.

CHAPTER 41

Maya rose and found breakfast on her bedside table and a peacock on her balcony. She'd slept well and was grateful for the toast and yogurt to fill her hungry belly. Although no sun shone, there seemed to be an abundance of light outside.

A quick soothing bath got her moving and she was dressed and ready, having found her freshly laundered clothes hanging over a chair near the dressing table. Maya gave the beautiful room one last glance and closed the door behind her.

Joss waited in the foyer and threw Maya a bright grin. "You're finally awake sleepyhead."

"What? Did I oversleep?"

"No, I woke up way too early. Those darned peacocks sure know how to make a racket," Joss grumbled.

Nik walked in, a serious expression darkening his features. Half a dozen white-garbed Rakshasa guards accompanied him.

"What's wrong?" asked Maya.

"Nothing I can do anything about really, I'm just worried...if you're ready." A stab of doubt ripped through Maya and must have shown on her face. "It's not you Maya. Believe me I wouldn't expect you to take this mission on if you weren't ready."

"I'll be fine." Maya offered.

Joss snorted.

Nik turned on his heel. "Right, let us get going."

Maya and Joss followed him out of the room and they soon regrouped in the waiting hall in which they'd arrived the previous day. This time the platters were empty and Maya had to hide her smile at the disappointment on Joss's face.

Chayya appeared within seconds and dusted herself off as she approached Maya. "Are you ready, Maya?"

"As I'll ever be." The muscles in Maya's neck and shoulders bunched as her tension mounted. She had to take a few deep calming breaths before her heart rate resembled something close to normal.

Nik joined Maya handing her a bag. "Weapons. Share them between the two of you but they must be on your person at all time or you may not have them when you arrive."

Maya withdrew four vicious looking daggers and a couple of short swords. She shared them along with their sheaths, between her and Joss, feeling much more comfortable now Joss had the means to defend herself.

"Maya." Maya glanced over her shoulder to see Nik holding out the set of deadly-looking Madus and a small bottle of dark blue liquid. "Here, these are for you. They're gold-tipped, and this is a special poison you release into the tips."

"What type of poison?" Maya asked, as she took the Madus and bottle, worried again. What if she ended up dying by her own weapon in a fight?

"It is Visha, the venom of the naga Vasuki."

"You mean the same serpent Vasuki the gods used as a rope to churn the Oceans? The same poison Lord Shiva swallowed that made his throat blue?" Maya wanted to scoff; she wanted to laugh out loud at how preposterous it all sounded. But how could she possibly laugh when she was holding this conversation with the son of Yama the god of the Underworld, while walking along a corridor in a palace in Patala in the actual Underworld. Not laughable, not preposterous. It was really happening. Or this was some amazing dream.

Nik strode beside her. "Yes, the same. Keep it safe and use it only when absolutely necessary. Naga poison is deadly to anyone but Vasuki's particular brand is lethal to demons."

Maya nodded and held tightly onto the Madu, staring at the little bottle of death.

"Okay, everyone ready?" Nods all around got Nik moving out the hall and into a smaller room not far down the passage.

The sound of footsteps hurried toward them and Maya turned to see a demon guard rushing to the group. Maya had gotten used to the other guard's respectful demeanor, so she didn't miss the leader who spent more than a few moments staring almost viciously at her as she approached. And when Maya met her gaze, the demon quickly looked ahead at Nik. Maya frowned, studying the girl-demons beautiful features, her almond shaped eyes, high cheekbones. *If there weren't any laws that demons should be ugly, then this demon sure broke them all.*

She listened, fascinated as the vowels and the consonants of the ancient language fell from the lips of the prince of the underworld. The lyrical tones of the Sanskrit tongue rode on the air while the Rakshasa guard nodded sagely at intervals, hands clutching at swords, jaws clenching. At the head of the small regiment, the beautiful demon stood, fairly vibrating with passion and vehemence.

This would probably be when they salute their general prince all together in one smooth movement.

But nobody moved.

A voice broke into Maya's thoughts. "Your Highness, is there anything you would have us do?" Maya glanced over and confirmed the voice belonged to the female demon with the vicious stare.

"Yes, Priya," said Nik, beckoning her.

Priya hustled past, making an effort to brush against Maya, forcing her to take a step away from Nik to make space for the darkly beautiful Rakshasa. She held some type of scroll and began to unroll it. "We have the goddess Varuni's exact location within the palace, Your Highness," she said, holding up the map.

But Maya didn't miss the movement of Nik's hand as he tucked his palm tablet back into his pocket. Of course, the prince of Patala had been brought up in the modern world; naturally he'd have an affinity for modern technology. And yet it still surprised Maya. *A demigod using a tablet. So weird.*

And Nik rose a bit more in her estimation. He cared enough for his subordinate's feelings not to flash his electronics and make Priya's efforts look unnecessary or less in any way. Not that Maya cared much for the state of the demon's feelings. Being shoved aside was enough of a reminder the Rakshasa didn't like her. Maya cared even less what she thought. The demon had tried and failed to hide the venom in her eyes far too many times for Maya to be under any misconception that Priya was a potential ally.

Holding both her tongue and her temper, Maya waited to be told the location of the hapless goddess she'd come to save.

Priya ran a finger across what Maya gathered was a map of the palace. "She is being kept here." She stabbed a spot, and Maya clenched her jaw, impatient to see the layout for herself so she could get the job done and get home. She hadn't forgotten Ria, despite the churning upheaval of the last few days. "The guards at the door work in six hour intervals and there is always a man outside, so that is not the best way in." Priya ended with an almost triumphant glare at Maya.

Maya gritted her teeth.

Really, what was she thinking to allow the Rakshasa to affect her at all? She needed to keep her wits about her, particularly because she didn't trust Priya. The rest of the royal guard seemed amiable enough, not that any of them had so much as looked at Maya. They must have rules against fraternizing with the Hand of Kali, considering she was deadly to them.

"All the rooms on the same floor of the goddess's chamber are currently unoccupied, so any one will be a suitable way in," said Priya as she rolled up her map, stowing it into her shoulder bag without allowing Maya or anyone else a view of the layout.

Again, Maya had to force herself to unclench her jaw. Seriously, the demon seemed to know all her buttons right now. She needed to stop allowing a mere Rakshasa to affect her, especially one she could probably kill with the slightest flick of her wrist.

Really, Maya. Get a grip.

"Thank you Priya. That will be all. Maya will retrieve the goddess." Nik appeared oblivious to the demon-human tensions wound so tightly around him. It was a wonder Chayya or Joss hadn't jabbed Maya in her own ribs in the last few minutes.

"But she isn't trained for this. We have trackers, and archers and warriors in our guard." Priya faced Nik head on with both her beauty and the fire of indignation in her eyes.

Well tough, demon. I'm the Hand of Kali so you'd better get used to it.

Yet, another voice whispered in her mind.

"Priya, you know as well as I do that we can't get in. None of us, demon or god, can get past Narakasura's wards." Nik spoke kindly but Priya's face paled. She nodded, looking almost nervous as her head moved up and down.

"Could I have the map please?" Maya kept the venom from her question. *I'm the hand of Kali so I'd better start acting like it, shouldn't I?*

Priya glared at her, the demon's jaw clenched so tight Maya was sure she'd hear teeth shatter soon enough. But Maya didn't back down, even when Priya went all amber eyed on her. She raised an eyebrow in an *oh really* expression and waited. At last, the demon relented and reached for her satchel.

"Here, Maya, use this." Nik interrupted the little female power play he had clearly missed, to pass her his palm tablet. *Or had he?* Maya paused to wonder when she saw his tiny smirk. Perhaps he'd not been so unaffected by Priya's questioning of his choice of strategy. Nik leaned over and tapped a small icon and a map appeared on its smooth face. Priya glared and backed off as Joss huddled to also get a view. Then he said, "Thank you. Priya, take your team and station them outside the room while we are gone. The wards are up and nobody can get in but it's better to be safe."

Priya smiled, almost shyly, bowed, and stalked back to the demon guard. As soon as she joined them, the six guards shimmered and disappeared. Maya blinked. She so had to get used to seeing that.

"Maya, you and Joss lie down and be comfortable," said Nik.

The girls glanced at each other and Joss dropped lightly to the floor. "Whatever you want with you when you arrive must be on your person before we depart. Do not leave anything behind."

Cryptic.

"So we lie here and go to sleep?" asked Maya, unsure if she'd heard right. She had to leave her body in the underworld where the demons roamed, unattended, unsafe?

"Yes, and don't worry. The doors are locked and guarded with a spell which only Lord Yama or I can undo." Nik smiled. Maya supposed his expression meant to comfort her but the last thing she felt was comforted. Worried, a tad regretful and a little bit angry maybe. Not comforted.

"So if we die in Swargaloka . . . ?"

"We can't die there. Gods, demons and humans can be grievously injured, though. But we have enough time to return to this room and awaken you to tend to your injuries."

"Oh, okay so anything that happens there will happen to our real bodies too?" A bizarre image appeared in Maya's mind her body lying supine, unprotected, blood seeping into her clothing at her chest as an invisible weapon speared her. Maya drove the scene from her mind, such ridiculous thoughts for a warrior. Surely, she was meant to be more courageous than this, stronger, more befitting the title of the hand of Kali.

"Yes, unfortunately that is correct," Nik answered, reminding Maya she'd asked him a question.

"Oh, well we'd better get on with it right?" Maya raised her eyebrow at Nik and got an enigmatic grin and bow from him. She even allowed him to hold her hand and lower her on to the cushions. Maya snuck a quick glance at Joss to be sure she was okay. Joss threw her a ghost of a smile. *Well, seems Joss is also affected by the whole lying-around-unprotected plan. She has no idea what she's gotten herself into.*

Maya lay back and relaxed, holding tight on to her weapons. The last words she heard were in Sanskrit as Nik's voice rang around the room loud and strong.

CHAPTER 42

They awoke in a field of dreams. Maya had no words to describe the balmy beauty of the garden, green with grass and dotted with an endless variety of blooming flowers. The sky above shone the deepest bluest blue she'd ever laid eyes on, so deep she could barely pull her gaze away.

And yet other amazing sights still vied for her attention. To her right a waterfall rushed over a cliff of glistening white marble, crashing wildly into a pond far below, throwing up froth and fine sparkling spray.

Even the pool was lined with beautiful white stone, veined with silver and gold, the reflections danced in the pool's mist. The epitome of beauty.

Maya and her group rose to their feet, dusting blades of grass off themselves. Neither Nik nor Chayya looked upon the realm with the kind of awe and fascination as Joss and Maya.

They were surrounded, almost protected by a circle of trees guarding the clearing - grand old white oak trees. Oaks had always fascinated Maya, but white oaks looked more majestic than the plain brown variety.

"So, what now?" Maya asked, lowering her voice only because

the secretiveness of their arrival implied the need for silence as well.

"We head for the palace. And unfortunately we can't use our powers until we get there."

"Why?" asked Joss. "Will there be an army if they detect you?"

"No," said Nik, "Nothing that dramatic. What we want is to get inside the palace grounds undetected while doing a little recon just in case. Then get you into Varuni's room so you can get the goddess safely out."

"Cool." Joss nodded, giving Nik's plan her approval.

Good thing Nik likes Joss, and tolerated her far-out, borderline rude comments. But maybe I'm too critical of Joss in the first place.

Brought up on a tight leash, respect had always been paramount to Maya, manners just as important. There were always girls like Ria who'd never dare to express their opinions to their parents. *God forbid kids ever dared to have their own thoughts.*

A rush of pride and happiness flooded Maya's heart. Despite Joss's malfunctioning parent-child relationship at least she'd had grown up confident in herself, knowing her own identity enough not to be lost within the maelstrom of teenage hormone-hood.

"Very well. Ready yourselves," Nik addressed them. "We will have to walk. Keep to the tree line. As long as you two don't lose your glow you will be safe."

"What do you mean *glow*?" asked Maya. Nik pointed at Maya's arm and she gasped. "Oh, wow," she whispered. Her hand gleamed, iridescent, luminescent and yet ethereal.

And godly.

Yup, just like a god should glow.

But nobody else glimmered, just Joss and Maya. The girls giggled, staring at each other.

"So what happens if we lose the glow?" Maya asked Nik.

"It means you are in grave danger. That your body, back in Patala, is in some sort of physical danger."

"Danger? Danger like what?" Maya's eyes narrowed.

"Yeah, Nik, talk to us about this danger." Joss added, her words ending in a nervous lilt.

"Danger as in your body is dying, or injured." Nik said, far too calmly, especially since he calmly talked about the possibility of their physical deaths.

Maya nodded slowly. "But our bodies are safe right?"

"Yes, I'm sure they are. Other than being in a full on battle Patala is safe and in addition to the wards, your physical bodies are also being watched by our royal guard."

"But what if our bodies aren't safe? What happens to us if our bodies die?"

"Then you will remain here in Swargaloka for all eternity."

"Huh? Our souls won't go to Patala for judgment?"

"No. Not unless you want to go to Patala. But, if it does come to that, I'd suggest you don't leave. Souls who come here get to remain here in happiness and serenity. Down in Patala it's a totally different story. Trust me, you want to stay here." Nik shook his head. "But Maya. You really don't have to worry. You and Joss are safe. Believe me, nothing will happen to you."

"Okay. I guess I have to trust you on that." Maya fell into silence, giving her glowing skin a dark glare every so often. "So how did Narakasura get into this realm?" Maya frowned. The demon king certainly didn't seem deserving of entry to Swargaloka.

"Because he is allowed to," said Nik. "Anyone who yearns for the next plane of existence, can attain a higher consciousness, and can therefore enter into Swargaloka."

"One would think entry into a place like this means you'd have to be very good, or mostly good at least. A person, god or not, who goes around abducting goddesses should be barred from here," Maya said, her voice dry, her tone unforgiving.

Nik shook his head, a shade of regret coloring his features. "This time we aren't that lucky. Narakasura is special. He happens to be the son of Vishnu. And his mother is Bhumi,

Goddess of the Earth. So he's pretty powerful himself. Some say he doesn't deserve such privileges-"

"You'd think!" Joss snorted and rolled her eyes.

Maya elbowed her friend. "Shut up."

"Why? It's true. Why is he allowed to steal stuff and still live to do it again?"

Nik sighed and continued. "It seems to be the way of the world- all the worlds actually- For good to tip the scales in its favor, evil needs to gain control."

Maya nodded. "Otherwise, how will we ever know how good *good* is if it doesn't defeat evil every so often, right?"

"Well said, Maya." At the compliment, Maya blushed, turned her head and began to find the view extremely fascinating.

Maya and Joss walked behind Nik in quiet companionship. Maya loved that her friend had insisted on coming along but her heart hurt to think of the possible danger to her on this journey. Tears pooled at the corners of Maya's eyes and she blinked them away hurriedly. She threw a quick glance around her, crossed her fingers and whispered a prayer. She firmly uncrossed her fingers and marched ahead before she could begin an argument with herself about prayer and its place within religious indoctrination.

When they reached the crest of the hill they paused to take in the view. Maya sighed, blissfully happy at the entrancing scene before her. For a second she forgot everything except for what her eyes saw.

A white marble palace shimmered within the palm of the valley before them. A central square building surrounded by ever larger squares.

The shimmering sheen of the buildings seemed to have the same glow as Maya's skin. She stared in wonderment at the gleaming light, moving her hand back and forth. With a sudden gasp she stopped. For the briefest moment she was dead certain her hand had disappeared and she'd seen rocks and grass through her very body.

Bodies shouldn't be invisible. But when she looked again, the strange phenomenon had dissipated.

Must have been a trick of light.

She'd lagged behind the others so ended up jogging to join them.

CHAPTER 43

Maya's gaze remained fixed up ahead. A great stone wall enveloped the beauteous citadel of white fire and sparkly marble. The facade gleamed as if someone had stuck a hand into the center of the Milky Way, withdrawn a fistful of stars and thrown them into Swargaloka where they were drawn to every piece of solid marble in the land, leaving the remainder of the fine dust to settle within the very air of the realm.

Maya touched her face certain she'd wipe off fingers full of stardust. But her flesh remained clean. She turned her hands over and over inspecting digits and palms for certainty- and yes not a single speck of dust. How very strange. Distracted by dust that bore the power not to settle, defying gravity so strangely, Maya missed Nik's words.

A jab in the ribs courtesy of a glaring Joss brought her back to her senses. Back to her duty. She flushed as she stared to find all eyes on Nik as he outlined their plan.

Maya shook her head and tried to peek at Nik's electronics over his shoulder. The tablet blinked and flickered on, and the upper bar showed the clear lack of reception to any network. So

Swargaloka was out of range. Guess they really were in another dimension.

Maya frowned. "We appeared here straight from Patala. Why couldn't we just reappear beside the palace instead of making this long journey to get there?"

"Because I'm also doing a little recon. Checking to see what Narakasura has done to the place, how much security he has around the city and the outlying areas. Maya, should you fail the gods will have to consider leading an army into Swargaloka to retrieve the goddess." Nik gave an apologetic shrug.

She nodded. "I understand. It makes sense," Maya said despite feeling the swift tug of fear within her gut. She took a deep breath. "Priya said all the rooms on either side of Varuni's are empty?"

"Yes, her room is the fourth one on that floor. We have three balconies to pass before we get to the one leading into her quarters," said Nik

It didn't take long for Nik to detail the layout and draw a path of entry, from the corner room, to the window of Varuni's chamber. Nik turned to Maya and Joss. "So once we enter the city try to act normal. Take your direction from me - we have little knowledge of what changes Narakasura may have made within the realm. The gods are assuming he'd keep things pretty much as is but that is still speculation. Be aware in case you have to respond to an attack."

She fell into step alongside Nik, matching his large purpose-driven strides. Nik certainly did nothing in halves. Enigmatic as he was he always seemed to have a good reason for his actions and decisions.

It struck her into a strange stillness, and while her feet propelled her forward, her memory took her back to the day of her first kill. Nik had encouraged her to tell her parents. What would have happened had she ignored him, gone home and went straight upstairs or made up a suitable story to placate them? That would have been easy enough.

But something in Nik's eyes that day, the angle of his shoulders when he'd urged her to talk to them, the shiver of fear in his black, black eyes meant she'd never have considered not telling them the truth.

Nik was . . . convincing.

The truth of course had been far harder to accept but Maya had taken the lies, the deception and the reality on the chin, imploding instead on the inside. Her gut still twisted when she thought of how well she'd received Nik's lies in the end. And though the last days had only ingratiated the damned demi-god further into Maya's own good graces, she wasn't about to forgive and forget this easily.

In the first place, he wasn't supposed to even exist. Neither was the celestial plane of enlightenment supposed to exist. Maya had to get used to a topsy-turvy world where reality defied common sense.

A noise, perhaps a gleaming bird squalling overhead, drew her out of her swirling thoughts. The band gathered together and faced the marble wall. Maya must have missed the part of their debriefing on how they were to scale the beautiful monstrosity. The shimmering white wall ran along endlessly, disappearing into the distance on both left and right of the waiting group. Seemed this spot was as good as any.

The wall shivered and began to melt into nothing and Maya blinked. She waited, holding in a shocked breath for fear she'd damage this inexplicable magic.

Pure white marble dissolved providing the group with a ragged yet beautiful doorway. Nik and Maya followed Joss and Chayya, stepping over the makeshift threshold. They made it through the shimmering entrance seconds before the wall solidified barely an inch behind them. Maya at last released the breath that had turned stale and begun to burn in her chest.

Inside the wall seemed no different from being on the outside. They just faced the same silence. Swargaloka wasn't a very noisy place at all.

Yeah, considering the concentration of higher consciousness that's no surprise.

"Umm, Nik. How do we get up to the rooms in the palace?" Maya stared at the massive building in the distance.

Nik looked up from the tablet. "That's easy. We climb up."

"You are kidding right?

"Nope."

"Have you seen the palace? Look over there." Maya pointed over his shoulder. "Look, great big smooth marble walls, your highness. What magic will we need to get us up there?"

"Okay, Maya, I'm looking at the palace, but clearly you're not seeing what I'm seeing."

Maya glared at him, wanting dearly to be alone sparring with him so she could throw him flat on his back, too breathless to be pompous and condescending. "Do enlighten me."

"I'm looking at balustrades and balconies, domed parapets and spindly spires. There are lots of architectural points on the corner of the building to allow us to scale the wall up to Varuni's floor. We can do it well enough with a little rappelling equipment and a dash of bravery." Now Nik had the nerve to grin at her.

"Fine, as long as you don't end up getting me killed, *your highness*," said Maya. She may have gone a bit too far with the sarcastic tone. Nik and his father needed her more than she needed them. Maya shrugged the thoughts off and scanned the tablet face, intent on memorizing the route as well as any and all possible exits and entry points.

Their journey to the citadel had been uneventful enough to make them complacent so Maya tried to be more on guard. But there was something so calming about the place. The population seemed to have increase exponentially within the walls of the city. Everywhere around them were people dressed in pristine white, walking in calm serenity, head down, eyes lowered, moving up and down the streets.

The streets. Maya almost did a double take at their condition. Such cleanliness should be impossible, but most of the residents walked barefooted across the marble cobbles of the tree-line streets. Ancient white oaks interspersed with huge trees of jasmine or what Maya's grandmother call 'Raat ki Rani' or 'Queen of the Night'. Maya remained bathed in awe and the scent of the night blooming jasmine as the band slowly made their way in the direction of the distant spires of the pale palace.

Maya almost felt the need for a pair of sunglasses, the combination of white on white was so dazzling. In tandem with the white was the silence. There seemed to be no need for the rush of sounds people made in cities. The clatter of wheels, the patter of feet, the chatter of gossip and whispers. Here in Swargaloka, it seemed silence was golden.

From beyond the line of trees came flashes of shimmering light and the sound of rushing water. As they traveled Maya tried to peer through the trees and managed to catch a glimpse of pure white pools of clear rushing water.

Suddenly Maya felt thirsty, and reached for her flask.

"Beyond the trees are the temples," said Nik, keeping his voice to a whisper, almost shocking Maya out of her skin.

CHAPTER 44

"Temples?" she asked.

"Yes, the souls who come to Swargaloka are of the people who have given up all material wealth. They would have attained a state of supreme divine consciousness - almost a state of constant meditation, of pure peace. Or they're so adept at meditation they're able to enter this state with ease."

"Do you have to die to get here, then?" Maya said, a little sarcasm slipping through.

She didn't really expect him to answer. "Some people do, and some don't. Some yogis and spiritual masters reach this plane regularly within their lifetimes."

Maya's gaze flitted around her from face to face. Were all these people really dead? And yet it seemed harder to understand how many of them could be alive either. She looked at her glowing arms, ran a finger across the glittering surface - she was alive and she was here too. So it's not impossible that people who'd attained such purity of soul and karma could visit Swargaloka regularly, as if going on vacation.

As Maya looked up from her hand her eyes met a pair of dark and amused ones. Across from her stood a group of four monks, who gathered before an older man, a teacher perhaps. He smiled at her, the twinkle in his eyes making deep black turn to honey gold. He inclined his head and the sun caught the earring he wore, glinting sharply enough for her to look away, and when she glanced back after blinking against the tears she found him, along with his disciples, gone.

Nice vanishing trick, old man.

"Let's move. The palace is close," said Nik, putting a warm hand to Maya's back and sending little shivers up and down her spine. She clenched her jaw a bit, stiffening her resolve as well.

Now is not the time to get all romantic with the prince of the underworld.

They walked further, everyone strolling as if they weren't together. Maya hung back letting Nik walk ahead and followed in silence, since talking seemed to be not the activity of choice around here. Head down, she tramped along, giving only minor curiosity to her lack of hunger in the last few hours.

Maya walked right into Nik's back, having been deep in thought when they arrived at the palace.

And what a palace it was. Stunningly white, rising endlessly up into the clear blue sky, it looked a lot like one of those red palace frontages Maya had seen in Jaipur, hundreds of windows, with the walls carved into small almost filigreed designs. It sparkled and shone, breathtakingly beautiful.

In front of her, Nik rummaged in his shoulder pack, pulling out a great loop of rope, and a small triple hook that looked like three fishhooks welded together.

"The hooks are large enough to grab onto the balconies as you go. You will have to use your hands to bypass each window, but the carvings are perfectly designed for holding onto."

"What I want to know is if they're thick enough to take my weight or will I end up pulling away a bunch of carvings and falling to my death?" said Maya, completely serious.

"They should carry your weight; you're one of the smallest

bodies in our group anyway. If you remember to secure the hook each time you move to the next window you'll be fine."

"Easy for you to say since you're not the one climbing this monstrosity," mumbled Maya. But although she was slightly put out being the only one risking her life, she was aware of the blood thrumming through her veins, and her head felt light and free. She couldn't deny she looked forward to this.

"We're all coming with you, except maybe Joss." Nik threw a quick glance over at Joss whose face appeared paler than was possible.

Maya stepped over to her, "Are you okay Joss? You don't look well."

"Heights," Joss managed to utter in a similar fashion to an arachnophobe in response to a spider sitting on their lap.

"It's fine, wait here for us."

"No freaking way. You are so not leaving me behind. I'm coming, heights be damned." Joss spoke with such a level of vehemence Maya knew neither she nor Joss herself would be capable of changing her mind. No point in even trying.

"Right, let's get this show on the road," said Maya. She faced Nik and Chayya. "So why can't you take me in there the way Chayya brought me to Patala?"

Nik was busy coiling up the rope. "Because the palace is warded against gods and demons. Neither of us can enter. Believe me, we've tried. It's why the balcony is the smartest choice. It gets us near enough." His face darkened. "But you'll need to get Varuni outside and hand her over the balustrade and through the ward. Your body will act as a conduit and allow Varuni to pass through. Joss will need to hold onto either Chayya or me to be taken back to Patala."

With a start, Maya realized she'd almost forgotten she wasn't really here, that her real body lay asleep and prone in a random room somewhere in one of the Planes of the underworld. At the moment, Yama held her life in trust. Maya shuddered, still not at peace with the idea. She shrugged. There was really nothing she could do but get on with it.

The three of them moved to a corner of the building. Lush green grass grew at their feet, and peacocks called in the distance. The garden around her remained silent and Maya wondered at Narakasura's complacency. Surely, he would guard his newly-won kingdom.

She asked Nik that very question in hushed tones.

Again Nik said, "He does not expect an assault like ours, hence he hasn't prepared himself for such. But be aware, Maya. There is always the danger a guard may come upon us here in the garden or even once you enter the palace." Nik looked from Joss to Maya and back again. "Use these carvings on the corner of the building to maneuver yourself upwards until you reach the first row of balconies. Anchor the hook onto the first balcony before you begin moving along it. Remember, secure the hook a few feet ahead of you each time, and then release it when you approach it. It will be slow but it's also safe. Ready?"

Maya nodded, despite feeling as unready as she could possibly feel, but she had to get moving. She grabbed the anchor and hooked it in a space between two large knobs as high above her head as she could reach. She started to scale the wall, her leather covered toes moving sure and confident against the carved frontage of the fantastic white palace.

Nik and Joss followed and Maya let out a silent sigh of relief. It felt easy, the climb. As long as she ensured the anchor was in place she was safe from falling. The knowledge gave her confidence and she moved faster, more agile than she'd ever expected to be on the vertical face of a building.

When she at last reached the level of the goddess's room she anchored herself on the carved balustrade of the first over-hanging balcony, and waited for the other two to catch up. Joss needed Nik's help more than expected thus slowing him down a bit.

Just when Maya began to feel impatient and considered moving on without them, they pulled up beside her. "Right, Joss. Can you check it out?" Nik asked.

Joss nodded and clambered over the balustrade. She tiptoed across the tiled floor of the ornate balcony. She carefully parted the heavy silk curtains that blocked off the room and peeked into the darkened interior while Maya and Nik hung about outside.

A few seconds later she turned back to them and grinned. "All clear."

"Right. Joss can wait here." Nik said. "We'll need eyes on this room just in case."

"I know what you're doing Nik," Joss responded, a wry smile at her mouth. "You're making me feel useful and you're very sweet but I can take care of myself."

Nik shoved a pair of knives into Joss's hands. "Hold on to these and use them if the guards find you."

"Okay," said Joss, her eyes bulging in fear-filled surprise.

Nik threw Joss an encouraging smile as Maya gave her a firm supportive nod. An unspoken *You'll be fine, just hang in there, pal.*

Joss hesitated then retreated further into the darkness of the room.

Maya sent up a fervent prayer.

CHAPTER 45

Maya hoped her friend would be safe, hoped against hope Nik was right and the room wouldn't be entered by one of Narakasura's guards. Already Maya's stomach churned with a fear that had nothing to do with killing the Demon King.

She shrugged silently. Scanned the face of the palace wall. Pity getting into these rooms had to be so pedestrian; no magical appearances like the demons or Chayya. She stiffened her back and her resolve, trying not to concentrate on the unfairness of it all.

Bet Priya is laughing at me now. Even in her absence, the Rakshasa had a way of irritating her.

She glanced over at her destination. Two balconies to go. Just two more to the balcony leading to the room where Narakasura held the goddess Varuni captive.

Until now, they'd been heading upward, which had been easy enough. Fasten the anchor, toe-hold, finger-hold, pull up. Repeat. Moving sideways was a whole other ballgame.

Maya moved her foot slowly along the little carved lip of marble, inching along, holding her breath. She reached with her left hand for the anchor, then popped the rope attached to it between her teeth. There wasn't much choice in how to hold the contraption while all her fingers and all her toes struggled to grip onto the smooth surface of the wall.

She tried not to think about the thousands of demon hands that had used this particular anchor. She tamped down the urge to retch, trying to ignore the thick, tightly woven grimy rope, so very close to her tongue. *Harden up, Maya. You've killed demons, sucking on a filthy rope is nothing.*

Maya reached the first balcony, every muscle quivering with tension. *Don't look down, don't look down, don't look down.* Maya spoke the words, over and over, having already looked down once and knowing a second attempt would send her to her death. Automatically, she grabbed the anchor with her right hand and reached out to secure it on the next balustrade. Safe. The next balcony would be the last. But still, a shudder ran through her.

Despite her best efforts she felt her body sway away from the building, felt her stomach drop. Maya tried desperately to hold on tighter, fingers scrabbling, digging for purchase. She tried to plaster herself to the wall. But ever so slowly, the distance between her body and the palace began to increase as she tipped backward.

Fingers slippery with sweat grabbed at slippery marble, gripped hard. Maya felt three nails rip apart, felt the warm rush of blood and the slick stone beneath her fingers.

Then clean fresh air.

In the distance, Maya heard a voice calling her name. "Maya hold on." But it was no use. Too late. As she fell backward Maya studied her bloody fingerprints on the stark white purity of the palace façade. The redness was so right, so bright and so fitting as if it belonged there, as if meant to be there. Again, she heard Nik call her name and she turned to look at him. Nik stretched out his hand, fingers extended as long as he could, but it was all too late.

Maya fell, her body plummeting two stories before she was jerked back upward so hard she could have sworn she'd heard her back break in two. The anchor rope. Damn. The last she recalled was fixing the anchor. Thank the dark goddess it held. But she had little time to thank her stars or any gods before her body was again slammed into the side of the building from the force of the fall.

For long moments, she hung there, her aching muscles caring little for survival.

"Maya, wake up," Nik called, his voice low, harsh.

Maya blinked, the sun stabbing her eyes, bringing more liquid to already overflowing tears of pain.

"Maya, are you okay?" Nik spoke beside her, his tone urgent and rough with fear.

Her body on fire with agony, Maya tried to assess her limbs in order to give Nik an honest answer. Hands and legs worked fine. Hearing, sight, and voice, fine. Her back could be broken judging from the fiery pain in the center of her spinal column, but she still felt her legs so she wasn't going to panic.

Nik finally grabbed her hand. The warmth of his fingers sent a surge of comfort through her arm and straight into her heart. Dangling on the side of a palace in a dimension of higher consciousness, almost killing herself to rescue the source of the Amrita to save the gods, Maya took one small step to finally accepting perhaps this was all really happening. It was time for her to accept she'd been wrong all along. Kali and Yama were real and her parents were right, had always been right.

Nik's fingers tugged at hers. She blinked and tugged back, allowing him to pull her closer. He'd lowered himself down so he was at the same height as Maya. Only when he had his arm tightly encircling her waist was she able to swing herself upright. And take her first non-panicked breath.

"Ok, Maya. I think you need to stop playing around and scaring me half to death. Are you okay? Everything still in one piece?" Nik said with a touch of laughter in his voice and a touch of a smile on his lips.

"Yes, thank you, my lord." She grinned at him.

"Now, let's get moving, I think there is still a goddess to save?" Maya tried to tell herself Nik's expression of approval and a hint of pride in his eyes meant nothing. But for the first time she didn't bristle with indignation because he dared to be proud of her. She gave in a little and basked in the satisfaction instead.

Only a little and only for now, a small voice whispered the reality in her ear.

Maya grabbed for a finger hold and let out a hiss of pain. She'd forgotten about her fingernails.

"What's wrong?"

"Nothing, I just broke a nail."

Nik chuckled. "I never thought I'd see the day when Maya Rao fussed over a manicure."

"Idiot," said Maya, grinning as she lifted her damaged hand and showed him her three ripped and bloody fingertips. "I guess it's a little more than just a broken nail."

"Give me your hand," Nik instructed. *Let him look. Perhaps he has a first aid kit stashed in his pack.*

Suddenly her palm warmed, in much the same way as it did when Maya channeled her fire. Her three fingers began to throb with an inexplicable heat. It should have felt agonizing but was only painful instead. When he released her hand, Maya gasped.

"What did you do?" She stared from her fingers to Nik's face. A moment ago, her fingernails had barely been holding on to the flesh of her nail beds. Maya had known all three nails were lost and accepted she'd have to wait for them to grow back again, but now they were good as new. Still caked with dried blood, still sore and throbbing, but on their way to mending.

"It's my little magic trick." Maya clicked her tongue and Nik responded. "Okay, I used my own fire. Possessing the firepower means we also have the power of healing. You, as the hand of Kali will have a stronger healing power, but since you haven't honed it as yet, I thought I'd use my power and fix it for you. At least so you can climb back up to the balcony."

"Wow, okay." Maya flexed her fingers and dusted off the gritty flecks of dark red crusting her cuticles.

"As you climb you can send intermittent bursts of power to the nails, keep them warm and they won't hurt as much. Now I think we need to be going. We've been hanging around here far too long."

Maya nodded and began to haul herself up. The rest had done her body good, her nails felt better although they still hurt, and all she wanted was to get this job done and head home. She sent pulses of fire heat to her fingers as she climbed, gripping onto the rope above, pulling herself up, moving with greater confidence the closer she got to the balcony.

CHAPTER 46

At last, Maya and Nik reached the balcony where she'd slipped. Her blood still gleamed red and accusing as she grabbed the balustrade and hauled herself up. She spared seconds wondering if it would rain at any point and wash away the gore now crusted against the white marble.

One foot at a time they moved toward the next balcony; their goal, Varuni's prison. Maya paused beside the balcony, securing her anchor over the balustrade first, before turning to Nik.

"What now?"

"Now you go in and convince her you're here to save her."

"What do you mean convince her?"

"Varuni is known for her spirit. She isn't going to come quietly."

"But isn't she being held prisoner here?"

"Yes, she is Narakasura's prisoner but think about it. Someone jumps through her window and tries to take her away? She's going to think she's in danger and she may not want to leave with you."

"And what about you? Aren't you coming in with me?"

"No. Remember, if I try to enter, I will trigger the ward and he'll know we're here. We want to get in and out without detection." Nik gave a wry smile.

"You better be right the wards are not set to detect humans," Maya warned Nik. The last thing she needed was more hurdles to saving Varuni.

"We have solid and trustworthy informers."

"Okay, I'd better get on with it," said Maya as she slung one leg over the balustrade. She slipped off the ledge, landing lightly on both feet. With a nod to Nik, she turned to face a pair of burgundy drapes edged in gold silk trimmings. The curtains rustled and moved in the slight breeze and Maya took a deep breath and spent only a second wondering what the room held in store for her.

Maya slipped inside, eyes adjusting for the change in light from super-bright sunshine to medium indoor lighting. The room was well appointed. A beautiful white four-poster bed sat along one wall, both headboard and footboard intricately carved with scenes of dancing girls, shepherds, and cows. A low table stood to Maya's left, also made from either pale marble or painted wood. Maya felt confused for a moment, wondering why interior decor was even given consideration in this plane of consciousness. Clearly, this was more a world than just a transcendental meditation hotspot. Maya blinked and registered the young woman seated on the marble floor beside the table.

The goddess Varuni looked no older than Maya herself.

For a long moment Maya stood, unsure of how to get the attention of the goddess. Varuni must have heard some sound. She looked up, straight into Maya's eyes but before Maya could utter a word Varuni dived for her bed, shoved her hand under the mattress and brought forth two short slightly curved daggers.

Seriously? Please someone tell me I don't have to fight a goddess!

"Please. I'm only here to help you," said Maya as she stared into the ferocious, almond shaped eyes of the furious goddess. Her high cheekbones bloomed with anger, pitch-black hair flung across her shoulder looked angry in its disarray. And for the first time Maya saw a glow behind Varuni. Maya froze. She could have sworn she'd seen multiple arms, exactly like in the pictures she'd seen of gods and goddesses, or the statues in the temples and at home. A bright array of two sets of arms, curving around Varuni, but only if Maya didn't look directly at her. As soon as she focused on them, they disappeared.

"You have just climbed through the window of my room. What gives you the idea I will believe anything you have to say?" Her icy tone almost hid the soft music of her voice.

"Nothing, I guess I hoped you would believe it because it's true." Maya shrugged.

Varuni stared at Maya, her gaze flicking lightly at the door.

"Please," said Maya, "At least hear me out."

Varuni moved to her right, staying out of reach of Maya, all the while pointing the two deadly daggers in Maya's direction.

The goddess lunged forward with one dagger, straight at Maya's chest. Maya skipped back out of range of the sweeping blade. Varuni said, "Talk. If you have anything to say."

A burst of anger filtered through Maya. More at Nik and Yama than at the goddess who was now actively trying to kill her. "I've been sent to rescue you."

"I am sorry but I find that quite difficult to believe. I have been trapped here for a century and now someone has decided to send a rescue and all I get is a little human girl?"

Maya gritted her teeth and took a deep breath. "I'm sorry you had to wait that long, but I was asked to save you a few days ago. I'm just doing what I was requested."

"And who did the asking?" The goddess bounced low on her knees, ready to pounce.

"The God Yama and the Goddess Chayya. Oh and Nik... Nikhil, the son of Yama."

Varuni raised her eyebrows as if the list of names surprised her, but all she said was, "And who exactly are you?" A steely challenge filled the question.

"My name is Maya Rao."

"You are human," Varuni responded, a cold edge to her voice. "And how is a mere human supposed to help me?"

"I'm apparently more important than I look." Maya lifted her chin a fraction of an inch. "I'm also known as the Hand of Kali." There, she said it, even though she never thought she'd ever throw her title in someone's face. She didn't have a reason to dislike Varuni, except the goddess was quite sarcastic and a bit cold. Not that Maya could blame her after being in the captivity of a demon for decades.

"The Hand of Kali?" Varuni spoke the words slowly. Taking a small step toward Maya. "Can it really be?"

"Yes, that's what they call me. Now whether you believe me or not, you really have to come with me before we outstay our welcome. The last thing we need is for Narakasura to appear."

"Very well, if you are my only way out I will take it," said Varuni as she tucked her knives into her belt and stepped to Maya.

Maya nodded, and walked backward. She kept her eye on the door as she led the way back to the balcony. Varuni was a few feet away from slipping between the parting in the drapes when the door crashed inward and bits of mahogany went flying all over the room.

CHAPTER 47

Maya pushed Varuni behind her and growled, "Go out onto the balcony. Now. Nik's waiting to get you out of here."

Varuni froze as half a dozen demons flowed into the room, the last gripping onto Joss's arm. Maya's heart sank. She'd known Joss coming along would put her friend in danger. And she'd been right. Joss stared at Maya, a silent plea in her eyes.

Maya didn't feel in the least bit confident. She felt more hopeless than ever since she'd discovered she carried the power of Kali in her fingertips.

Maya reached into her satchel for her weapon, hoping the Madu and their sadistic spiked edges would serve her well. Slowly the chamber began to fill with the odor of demons. Maya sucked in a breath, almost choking on the thick aroma of rotting meat and incense. This time the meaty smell also contained a hint of rancid, making her stomach swirl with the desire to hurl. Perspiration dotted Maya's forehead and her hands shook.

She gave her head a swift shake and focused on the gathered guards. Joss's guard shoved her forward, sending her flying into

Maya, but she saw his intention and moved slightly out of the way, allowing her friend to stumble past.

"You okay?" she asked Joss, keeping her eyes on the demons.

"Yes," Joss responded through gritted teeth. "Let's get 'em."

"You got your knives?"

"Yup." Maya could see in her peripheral vision, the glint of light on the blades of the swords Nik had given Joss. Now she hoped Joss being a natural fighter would pay off. But still, a nagging twinge in Maya's gut spelled bad news. "Stay behind me at all times," she said.

"Yes, ma'am."

The demons surged toward them in one go, a wave of gleaming swords, amber eyes and the putrid odor of rotten meat. Maya had no time to think. It was all she could do to put her set of Madus to work, blocking a swipe of a sword there, knocking another dagger from a demon's arm.

Maya stiffened. She had an idea. She'd been close enough to knock the weapon from one of the demon guards. Close enough was perfect for Maya's plan. She waited, bouncing on her toes, blocking here, slashing there. Waited until one guard took the opportunity to lunge forward with an upward slash. But instead of allowing him to slice her open for her guts to spill on the ground, Maya dodged the attack, slammed the heel of her hand into the hilt of the guard's sword and knocked away the deadly blade. A breath later, giving him no time to think or move or breathe, Maya grabbed his arm and set off a burst of fire as strong as she could summon on short notice.

Flames ripped through his body and soon even his amber eyes flickered with the flames of Kali's fire. In a burst of burnt fabric, orange embers and the odor of cooked meat, the Rakshasa disappeared, imploded, leaving not an inch of himself behind.

But Maya couldn't waste any time enjoying the victory. She glanced back to find Varuni still frozen in place. "Go to the balcony," she whispered loudly to the goddess. Maya turned her attention back to the guards, hoping Varuni would move.

Five left and who knew how many more were on their way. She tamped down the thrilling mix of excitement and distaste at killing the demon, and bounced on her feet, looking out for the next guard to attack.

She quickly dispatched two more guards who hadn't seemed to learn their fellow demon's lesson. *Three left. Three is good.* But a movement at the door caught her attention. Priya, slipped into the room throwing Maya a hateful glare. So time apart hadn't improved Priya's feelings toward Maya. But Maya didn't waste precious seconds thinking about the beautiful demon and her unwarranted dislike.

Maya mentally crossed her fingers that Chayya and Nik were safe and hadn't abandoned her. She threw Priya a quick glance before defending herself against the thrust of another sword. Behind her Joss squeaked and Maya heard her short blade skim the edge of a demon's weapon. Maya dispatched her opponent, gripping his arm in hers until he was nothing but a puff of smoke and a residual flame.

She swung around, stabbing her Madu right into the abdomen of Joss's attacker. Joss choked, struggling for breath, a pained expression twisting her shocked features. Maya understood her reaction. The demon tipped over, and fell to the ground, groaning and shuddering. A moment later he was dead. Naga poison apparently worked at super speed.

Only two Rakshasa left. She could handle them easy enough, although Priya should certainly make things easier. But Priya just stood in place, unmoving and equally untouched by the attacking guards. Maya frowned.

"Come on Priya, let's get these guys good and dead and let's get out of here," said Maya, although her gut did that incessantly negative wobble again.

"But Maya, that is not part of the plan," said Priya, her eyes amber, her face as stiff as a poker.

"What do you mean?" Maya got the words out between gasps, dispatching one more demon, and bouncing on her feet while the last guard stared at the disappearing husk of his comrade.

Outnumbered, he gave Priya a quick glance and ran straight out of the door as if hellhounds were on his tail. *Damn, no doubt he was off to fetch reinforcements.*

Priya was light on her feet and faster than Maya had expected her to be. Maya stumbled backward from a blow to the abdomen where Priya had landed a solid kick with the heel of her foot. Maya struggled to get the breath back into her lungs and was about to rise when Joss ran at Priya, a screeching war cry echoing around the white room.

The demon was ready for her, parried each one of Joss's advances, easy as taking candy from a child. Maya, breath all back and in one piece, ran for them but it was too late. Almost in slow motion, Maya watched Priya step away then lunge, tricking Joss into moving forward and running right into Priya's vicious curved blade.

"You should have listened to me, human. This game is not for you. It doesn't matter if they call you the hand of Kali. It's not meant to be. No human should have such power," she said, all the while holding onto Joss who remained impaled on the demon's sword. Priya gave the injured girl a disgusted glance then pushed her backward, letting go of the hilt of her dagger and dusting her hands as Joss staggered backward.

And then it all made sense.

"You betrayed us," Maya said, her voice flat and devoid of all emotion as she watched Joss struggling to breathe, an expression of twisted shock contorting her features..

"Of course I did," Priya said, triumph overflowing in her tone. "Lord Nikhil was stupid to think he could trust me especially when he wanted us to support you, a mere human. He should have known better."

"So you all betrayed us?"

Priya gave her shoulder and elegant shrug. "No. Most of Yama's Rakshasas are too damned loyal for their own good. Unfortunately it's just me but I think I did very well on my own."

"Yes she did."

Those three words dropped the temperature in the room several degrees.

At the door, another small contingent of demon guards flanked a young man as he entered. He wasn't much older than Maya or Nik, tall, fine boned, with piercing green eyes.

Maya only had a moment of doubt before she said, "Narakasura."

"Well spotted, my dear girl," he said, his voice rough and low and almost sexy. *Nuh uh that cannot be possible. I'm here to smoke the dude if I have the chance.* He waved his hand and Maya followed it to Varuni who now stood stock still behind Maya.

Maya had hoped she'd listen and leave but she hadn't. Varuni stared at Maya, an unhappy look on her face. Maya's focus had remained on fighting the demons. She hadn't noticed Varuni's capture. Now, a demon held her roughly by the arm, the sharp point of his dagger threatened to rip into her jugular. Two of Narakasura's guards ran to her, grabbing her by the arms. "Take her to the cells." Once the demon with the dagger relinquished the goddess, they left.

Narakasura paced before Priya, hands folded at his back as if deep in thought. Then he said, "Thank you Priya, for your kind assistance."

"Thank *you*, my lord for giving me the opportunity to show I'm worthy."

"But Priya, my dear the last thing you showed me was how worthy you are. You've shown me very clearly you would turn on your master in an instant to fulfill your own purpose. And you've also shown me you feel jealousy and envy is a justifiable reason to betray your entire kingdom." Narakasura took a few steps and turned to Priya. "You've demonstrated precisely why I could never trust you as part of my guard. I'm sorry, my dear, but I have no further use for you."

The demon king snapped his fingers and a column of fire wound around Priya. She gasped, shock widening her almond eyes as the flames grew higher and higher and enveloped her body. She began to scream, so loud the sound hurt Maya's ears as it echoed around and around the room.

Narakasura snapped his fingers again and although Priya didn't seem to stop screaming, they could no longer hear her. While the column of fire raged behind him, he turned to Maya and smiled.

Maya's gaze shifted from Narakasura to the pillar of fire. *What a cool trick that is.* She had to stop herself from looking back to the demon king. *How could someone so bad look this good?*

It just wasn't fair.

"Well, Maya Rao, the hand of Kali," Narakasura said as he circled Maya. She wasn't at all comfortable with his inspection. His probing eyes made her feel naked, and she wasn't entirely sure what she was expected to do surrounded by guards, facing the great demon king.

Maya glanced at Joss who stood a few feet from the balcony, still teetering on unsteady legs. Maya raised her eyebrows and tipped her eyes at the drapes, hoping her friend would understand. Joss, gave a tiny, pained nod and took a little step back, and though a guard drew closer to her, he didn't do much else.

Maya faced Narakasura, lifting her chin a tiny bit. A quick glance at the balcony and Maya jumped for joy inside. Joss was gone and she hoped they didn't forget Maya was still here.

Maya shook the thoughts free and paid attention to Narakasura as he stood smiling at her. "Now where did your friend go?"

"That's for her to know and you to find out, don't you think?" Maya glared at him.

Narakasura frowned. "Do you really want to waste time playing these little games, human girl?" The demon king paced, arms held behind his back as he walked.

"My name's Maya and it's not really a game. We both know you're powerful, and certainly capable of getting what you want.

He clicked his tongue and paced again. "Well, Maya, why don't we start by you calling me Kas?" When Maya didn't respond he glanced at her and scowled. "I do not like trespassers. Especially those who enter my home to steal from me."

"Varuni wasn't yours to begin with."

"The Amrita belongs to all of the gods. Therefore so does Varuni. What gives Yama and Shiva the right to keep her for themselves?"

Somehow, Maya suspected he didn't want or expect and answer. She glanced at the drapes hiding the balcony.

Fear bolted through Maya lightning fast. Had Chayya abandoned her when she'd needed her the most?

"See, Maya. Not everyone will stick by your side even if you are the Hand of Kali."

"I guess people are the same no matter what their race or the plane of existence they occupy, right?" Maya responded, her tone dry. She didn't believe for a minute Nik would leave her here. Did she?

Chayya's disappearance threw a dark cloud of doubt over Maya's confidence. Would any of them even return for her? Who was she anyway? Just a mere human girl. She may have some of Kali's power but surely there were other people in the world like her, on whom Kali had bestowed similar powers.

Besides, she'd never believed in Kali in the first place. For that reason alone she probably didn't deserve the power. And Narakasura seemed to sense her fear. He took a step toward her and raised his hand.

Instinctively Maya blocked, siphoning her power to her palms but before she could do anything Narakasura sent a ball of spinning flames directly at Maya. She yelped and ducked automatically.

"What the hell was that?"

"Oh, I wanted to see how talented the hand of Kali is. I'm not even sure what this power is that you have. What powers has the Dark Mother bestowed upon you, my dear Maya?"

Wouldn't you like to know. Aloud she said, "I'm not here to fight you."

"But that wasn't what I was told." He moved closer.

Maya stood her ground. "Well, you really should make sure your informants are trustworthy then, shouldn't you?"

In her ear he whispered, "A beautiful young woman like you, all alone in the palace of a demon king. Imagine what fun we can have together. What a force we will be against the gods and the demons?" His voice almost lulled her into a happy calm. Almost.

Maya's hands still burned with roiling fire and she ached to release it but not yet. He was too close. And pray tell why was he so close to her? She turned her head and looked him straight in the eyes. "I will never, ever be on your side so don't waste your breath trying to control me and trying to convince me the side of a demon king who has to resort to abducting gods for his own nefarious needs, is a good side to be on. I'd rather be alone, thank you very much."

"Come on Maya show me your fire. Show me the power Kali has given you. Show me you have the power to fight me," said Narakasura as he circled Maya.

Maya wanted to grit her teeth but he was so near her, she knew he'd pick up on her frustrations. She wanted him out of her face. She'd failed her mission and the longer she stood there and waited the more she convinced herself Nik and Chayya had abandoned her. The urge to cry swept through her throat but she swallowed it down. No, they wouldn't abandon her.

The demon King, or Kas as he apparently preferred, stepped away from Maya, stopping a few feet from her. He turned his head and said, "I quite like you Maya Rao. Therefore, I won't kill you. Not this time." He spun around and sent a flash of fire at Maya.

Maya gasped and threw out her hands, eyes fixated on the flickering flames of pure white fire speeding towards her. Somehow, she knew her fire would do nothing to fight Kas's menacing flame and yet she let it fly anyway.

Two streams of flames met in a shower of orange and white sparks. Maya took a few steps backward and braced herself. White seemed to gain, moving closer to Maya, taking over the orange. She drew on everything within herself. She thought of her parents who'd taken care of her all her life, of Claudia who'd sacrificed so much for her, of Joss who'd had a knife stuck into her and might be dying, of Ria whose life depended on Maya succeeding at this task.

She breathed deep and pushed back, sending the white fire hurtling along the line to Narakasura. He stumbled backward, a look of surprise mingled with rage marring the beauty of his face.

Maya grinned, triumphant as the demon king steadied the flame at his end and began to push back at her. She readied herself, waiting for the perfect moment to give him another taste of her Kali-given power. The reassuring weight of heavy silk fabric hung right against her back, with the balcony a mere inch away.

Maya watched the king as she took one final step back pulling the drapes with her. He strode toward her, purposeful, unhurried. The edges of the fabric closed, cutting off Maya's view of the approaching demon king.

Maya was about to bolster her fire when she heard a voice behind her. Chayya waved at her. The goddess had one arm around a now unconscious Joss as they hung onto the outside of the balcony. Chayya put a finger to her lips.

They were mere feet away from the advancing Narakasura and his angry white fire. Nik hung from the balustrade too, beckoning her forward and she scrambled to climb over it to him, keeping a close eye on the drapes as Narakasura roared his anger and as his footsteps reached the balcony.

"We don't have time to scale the façade and get back down," said Nik. Maya stared at him, eyes round and larger with consternation. "We have to jump."

"Jump? Are you insane?" she hissed as the footsteps drew closer. A glance beside her confirmed Chayya and Joss had disappeared safely leaving Nik and Maya hanging from the balustrade.

"We have to. It's the only way to be free of the palace wards." Nik shook Maya's arm, pulling her into the swirling arms of panic. "Listen to me. We have to jump. Once we're free from the wards I can transport us right back to Patala safely. But we have to jump away from the wall."

Maya nodded and gulped, staring from Nik's face to her fingers as they grasped the rope. Above them, any second now, Narakasura would be upon them.

"Okay let's do this before my brain tells me it's the worst idea I've ever had in my life." Maya gulped down a breath and tried to steady her stampeding heartbeat.

"Right," said Nik. "On three okay. One two three."

And Maya closed her eyes and jumped with Nik. One moment she was flying through the air, the sound of Narakasura's furious roar ringing in her ears, the next she was lying flat on a bed of soft cushions breathing as if she'd just run a marathon.

They were back in Patala. Safe and sound.

CHAPTER 49

Adrenaline made Maya feel a little light headed as she sat up with a start, patting her hands and legs, staring around the room.

Everyone was well except for Joss.

Maya spun about looking for her injured friend. Joss lay beside her, the front of her clothing soaked through bright red and still moist. Even the dagger remained in Joss's abdomen. A stark reminder to Maya that Joss had been injured just as she'd feared.

"Someone do something." Maya sobbed, and felt Nik beside her. Tears blurred her vision as she looked at him, her eyes begging him. "Please do something. Save her. You have to save her. This isn't her fight but she came anyway. She came for me. Please, Nik."

"We will do what we can," said Nik. "And you can help."

"Me?"

"Yes, you have Kali's fire in your hand. It's time you learned how to heal as well." Nik grabbed Maya's hand and pulled her forward to sit beside him, next to her unconscious friend.

"Now, place your hands around the wound and center yourself. Then pulse your fire into the cut while I remove the knife. Your fire should prevent excessive blood loss. I'll help you as soon as I have the blade out. Maya," Nik called her name loudly, bringing her back to the present. She still felt lightheaded and her body ached. Maya gave herself a little shake as Nik said, "Ready?"

She nodded and did as he'd instructed. Her hands quivered where she held them against Joss's blood covered shirt. Terror stiffened Maya's fingers and weakened the fire. She swallowed hard, tried to regulate her breathing, tried to brush off her fear and strengthen the flow of heat into Joss's body. No easy task as images of Joss flitted through her mind.

Joss in kindergarten, helping Maya to pack away her crayons. Joss in first grade sharing Maya's lunch. Joss's tenth birthday sleepover and getting sick on too many s'mores made in the living room fireplace.

Maya was terrified of hurting Joss, but she had no choice. She had to use the fire. But a voice inside her cried out. What if she did something wrong and Joss died? What then? How did she go back home without Joss?

A tinny, clanking sound broke through Maya's concentration as Nik threw the dagger onto the marble floor. She watched it as it spun around, staring at it almost in a trance. Joss's blood gleamed bright red against the silver blade. Maya felt Nik's warm hands settle beside hers on Joss's stomach and watched as he closed his eyes and began to concentrate with her.

A dense and nervous hush filled the room. Chayya watched in somber silence. Maya settled her attention on her supine friend. Warmth simmered where Maya's skin met Joss's body. Her fingers lay against half-dried and sticky, half-coagulated blood and yet she felt no disgust. This was Joss. Her friend for most of her life. Maya would do anything for her.

The heat in Joss's abdomen began to increase slowly, spreading through her flesh and back into Maya's fingers. A shudder of fear ran through Maya. Was it too much? Nik's head dropped forward, and he'd uttered not a word in all this time. She swallowed and refocused her concentration, tamping down a sob and blinking back her tears. Every one of her muscles remained tensed and tight, and pain flowed within her. She drew in a ragged breath and stared at Joss, still unresponsive. At least it looked like the wound was no longer bleeding.

At last, Nik sat back and Maya glared at him. "What are you doing? Why are you stopping?" She sobbed as she stared helplessly at Joss's unmoving form.

"There isn't anything more we can do, Maya." His voice came out harsh and ragged as his shoulders slouched and he dragged his fingers over his face and scraped them harshly through his hair.

"No, you can't mean that." Maya cried, her voice breaking on the last word.

"I'm sorry, Maya," Nik reached out a hand to comfort her but she shrugged it off. And backed away violently. She could see the hurt in Nik's eyes but she didn't care. Why was he giving up? Maya sobbed, sucking air into her lungs. Her chest felt constricted, tight, as if all the air was being drawn out of her at once. Her abdomen hurt too, as if someone had kicked her in the gut.

She got to her knees, scraped at her tears with the heels of her hands. "That's not good enough. You brought her here so fix it," Maya spat the words out at Nik, as her head spun and she lurched to her left, a little off balance.

"Maya!" cried Chayya, staring at Maya's own abdomen. "You're hurt."

"What? No . . . I . . ." Maya looked down, noticing the large patch of bloody burned fabric where bits of charred skin and flesh peeked through revealing a rough circle of terrible burns. "When did that happen?" Maya breathed the question almost to herself as the world around her darkened slowly. She struggled against the encroaching blackness but it seemed to have a strength she couldn't counter. And she slipped into unconsciousness, finally allowing the darkness to carry her away.

THE CALL of a peacock brought Maya back to consciousness. She wondered if it was the same proud fellow she and Nik had seen in the garden.

Such a mundane thought when her body and her heart ached for the loss of Joss. Maya swallowed hard. She didn't want to cry. She'd cried enough as she'd slept fitfully for the last few hours.

She shoved back the covers and made her way to the window seat. Her legs threatened to give out from beneath her and she sat down hard on the cushions and leaned her head against the frame, taking in the spectacular view of the gardens. But the beauty of the plants and trees blurred behind a veil of tears. Maya held on to herself tightly, needing to stop feeling the ache inside of her. Feeling as if she were about to burst into a million pieces.

How did she get past the emptiness eating away at her heart? It burrowed into her belly and her heart and her soul like a living parasite, its teeth eager to gouge its way deeper to maximize the pain.

It was all for nothing. Accepting Yama's mission had been the worst thing Maya could have done. Her decision had killed Joss. No matter how much she tried to palm the blame onto Nik for bringing Joss with him to Patala, in the end her friend had come because Maya had decided to help Yama.

And in the end, Joss was dead. What a waste. She hadn't even been able to get Varuni back. Maya gritted her teeth. Did she really give a damn about Yama and Varuni and the slow death of the gods without their special elixir of immortality? The Amrita didn't mean anything to Maya. At this point, all it represented was the loss of her best friend.

But Maya had to admit Joss wouldn't feel sorry for herself.

What would Joss want her to do? How could she make it up to her friend?

And Maya heard Joss's voice inside her head, almost as if she stood right next to her. "Finish it."

Finish it.

Maya thought. It was what Joss would have wanted. Otherwise, everything really would have been for nothing.

Maya nodded to no one in particular.

Finish it.

CHAPTER 50

The next morning Maya awakened when Nik entered the room. It was too late to jump back into the bed and he found her as she'd fallen asleep in the wee hours; lying against a pile of cushions in the window seat, with her forehead plastered to the cool windowpane.

At least she hadn't been drooling. Thank the gods for small mercies.

"Hey, sleepyhead." He handed her a glass and she drank without question. Orange juice. Cold, rich, pulpy and completely tasteless.

Maya upended the glass, drank the last drops and set it on the table beside her. "When do we leave?"

Nik stared at her, looked like he was about to say something and then changed his mind. "I've had some feedback from our deep cover agents-"

"Deep cover agents?" Maya laughed, the sound harsh even to her ears. "Are you kidding me?"

"No, Maya, we have to call them something. And these are soldiers-"

"Demons you mean?" She arched an eyebrow at him, daring him to deny it.

"Yes, demon soldiers." He sighed and pulled a chair close to the window seat. "Look, we have to be sure this time everything goes as planned. We are only using the deep covers for minimal info. Not even Priya knew about these two agents. And we don't want their covers blown."

"Fine. Whatever." Maya returned her gaze to the garden, not wanting to admit she regretted her rudeness. Nik didn't deserve it but she was in no mood for a retraction. She wasn't in the mood for much besides kicking some major demon butt right now.

After a moment of silence he continued, "From their information we know Varuni was taken from her quarters to a cell beneath the palace."

"Kas has a dungeon?" Maya said. This was getting better and better.

"Kas?"

"Narakasura."

"Oh, yes. He has also spent a considerable amount of his life in your world. I see he has taken a liking to a shortened version of his name."

"Much like you," Maya said blandly still avoiding his eyes.

"True," he said, then went silent. And it was the silence that did it.

"I'm sorry." Maya turned to face Nik. She brought her feet up onto the seat and wrapped her arms around her knees. "I'm sorry, it's not fair for me to take my anger out on you. I shouldn't. But every time I open my mouth I want to say something that will hurt you. I never thought of myself as a mean-spirited person but maybe I am."

"No, don't think that. You are hurting and of course you instinctively want to hurt me. And I understand. You blame me for bringing Joss here-"

"But I don't anymore. She wanted to come. She made that so clear, Nik. How could I not respect her wishes?"

"And yet you are still angry with me." He smiled gently, and as he spoke he pulled Maya's hand free and threaded his fingers with hers.

"No," she whispered. "I'm not angry at you. I'm angry that she is gone. I'm angry she came, I'm angry I let her stay. I'm so . . . angry . . . I couldn't save her. And it hurts so much. It hurts to breathe. I just don't know how to stop it." Tears flowed harder and hotter and all Nik did was open his arms and Maya went straight to him. She wound her arms around his waist and cried into his chest. Nik held her close and let her weep, giving her his presence and his warmth while she cried.

A little while later, much of her tears spent, all her sobs quieted, Maya lay still against Nik's broad chest with the beat of his heart as an assurance that everything horrible had really happened. It also reminded her that everything good had happened too.

"Thank you." She sniffed, mortified that she needed to blow her nose and there wasn't a Kleenex in sight. She almost choked with laugher when Nik placed a travel pack of tissues in her hand.

"My mom hates cotton handkerchiefs. She's a firm believer in Kleenex and an even stronger advocate for travel packs."

"Your mom sure knows what she is talking about." Maya laughed before taking the tissues and wiping her nose. Suddenly she felt much better.

"I'll tell her you both agree on Kleenex then." Nik nodded sagely.

Maya laughed. "What else can you tell me about Kas and Varuni?"

"Apart from the fact you will have to set yourself up to get caught, not much else."

"Yeah, I see what you mean. So I materialize in the palace and the guards take me to the cells where they are keeping her. How do we know they won't take me somewhere far away from her?"

"We don't. But we just have to hope they don't. The palace was never intended to be a place to hold prisoners. Swargaloka itself it the embodiment of good and righteousness. My guess is Kas has taken some of the more ancient rooms and transformed them into jail cells specifically for Varuni and you. It would be easy to assume that Varuni was his first captive."

"So once they take me to Varuni what then? You and Chayya appear and get us out?"

"No. Well not exactly." Nik drew a sheet of folded paper from him pocket, spreading it out on the small table beside the window seat. "Here. Memorize this. At some point, you will end up in the dungeon. One level up is the ground floor. This is a plan for that floor. Follow the marked route to the garden with the fountain. It's sort of a side courtyard that has a wall running along the one edge. We'll wait on the other side."

"How will you know I'm there?"

"Use this." Nik handed her a flat black stone. "Throw this over the wall. It's a special stone. Once it lands on the ground it bursts into a black cloud of dust. We'll know you are there." Maya stared at the stone. *Weird.* Nik continued. "Chayya and I will find a way to get you out-even if it means blowing up the wall. Remember we can't enter the palace at all."

"Do we have a plan B?" Maya curved an eyebrow.

"Nope. For now it's Plan A or die trying."

"Fine with me." Maya nodded." Let's finish this."

TAKING a bath seemed the most mundane of things to do especially when Maya couldn't wait to get back to Swargaloka. But she scrubbed off the blood and traced the tenderness of her wounds before rinsing off and getting dressed.

This time she didn't care for white. She chose red and yellow. The colors seemed significant since fire was meant to be her power. Why not dress for success?

Maya wrinkled her nose at the length of plain fabric meant to go with her outfit thinking she should just leave it off. In the end, she decided to wear it anyway.

She proceeded to strap knives to her thighs and legs, hidden well beneath the long overdress, then spent a moment trying to find an appropriate place on her body to hide the poison tipped Madu. She scowled at the weapons and strapped one onto each thigh. Maya picked up the vial of Naga poison Nik had given her and stuffed it securely into her bra. There must be worse places to hide such a deadly venom.

Lastly, Nik's odd stone found its way into a small pocket sewn into the drawstring pants and then Maya left the room and paused in the waiting area to stare at Joss's door. For a second she was transported right back to the moment Joss drew her last breath. Maya struggled to take a breath and even though it hurt, she forced another rush of air through her lungs.

She had to get this done for Joss.

Maya charged into the hallway and almost walked straight into Nik. The silence stretched awkwardly between them.

Nik cleared his throat and the little sound broke the tension. "I was just coming to get you. Chayya is ready."

Maya nodded. "I'm ready when you are."

CHAPTER 51

$\mathcal{N}$ ik transported Maya to Swargaloka and the trio didn't waste any time once they arrived. With the sun high in the sky, Chayya led them around the palace to a walled off courtyard. She stopped in front of a tree whose enormous branches reached over the wall. The goddess faced Maya. "Ready?" Chayya's eyes grew darker with worry.

"As ready as I'll ever be," Maya answered giving Chayya an encouraging smile. "Let's do this."

Chayya raised her hand and whispered, "Be careful, Maya. And may Kali be with you."

Maya scrambled up the tree, and eased herself out onto the thick branch. Closer to the trunk it supported her weight well. But as Maya reached the top of the wall, the branch sagged beneath her, pulling her down. She peeked onto the other side of the wall and found a bed of pungent marigolds. She crossed her fingers, hoped for lush, soft soil and jumped.

Maya landed on her back, completely flattening the bed of gorgeous orange flowers. She scrambled to her feet, dusted herself off and made her way toward the building. Slipping inside a large airy room, she tiptoed to an open door. For a moment she hoped she wouldn't get caught, then realized being captured was her intention.

She strode through the doorway and emerged into a wide corridor. A shout went up as a guard ran toward her. Maya pretended to turn and run. The Rakshasa rushed forward, yelling loudly, calling for reinforcements no doubt. Maya's immediate reaction was to punch him in the face or better yet, incinerate his ass. But she calmed herself and did nothing. Just waited for him to grab hold of her. It was, after all, part of the plan.

As soon as he touched her, she brushed his hand off, and threw a half-hearted punch at his head. She decided it would certainly look strange and encourage suspicion if she didn't at least put up a small fight.

She ducked as the demon guard aimed a fist at her cheek, then landed a blow to his gut that sent him stumbling back a few paces. Half a dozen guards spewed into the hallway and Maya knew she couldn't possibly fend them all off without raising eyebrows so she struggled against their grip, only pretending to try and get herself free.

They barely paused to pat her down, swiftly relieving her of her knives and Madus. Maya's stomach twisted in disappointment. There had always been the possibility they wouldn't think to check her for weapons. With them gone, she was left with only her poison and her own firepower.

They grabbed hold of her before marching her out the room and down what seemed like a dozen flights of stairs. Of course, Nik had mention cells below the palace. Marble staircases and handmade wall hangings and life-size brass statues passed in a blur. She was on her way to the dungeons. *Wonderful.*

Beneath the palace, pale marble changed to off white stone; still beautiful but not as resplendent as the building above. The guards shoved Maya through a large arched doorway and stabbed a key into the lock of a gigantic wooden door.

Without a word they flung her into the room and left her to

roll over until she came to a stop against the far wall. They slammed the great door shut so hard the stones above her sent a fine shower of dust floating to the ground. Maya sniffed, then shoved herself to her feet.

She was about to take a step toward the door to test its strength when a voice emanated from the darkness at her right. "What are you doing back here? I thought you were safe."

Maya turned and faced Varuni with a grin as the beautiful goddess emerged from the shadows. "Safe is boring. I'm here to take you home."

Varuni snorted. "You will more likely die for your efforts. In case you didn't know, Kas has warded this cell. Nobody gets in or leaves who isn't accompanied by his guards. That rules out any help from Chayya or Nik."

"Oh don't worry, I wanted to be captured. There wasn't any other way to get here."

"Well I hope you have a plan. I don't think I can survive another year in this place. As lovely as it is I prefer my own home thank you very much."

"Right, we just have to find a way out of here."

"I would have hoped you would have a pretty good idea before you got yourself stuck here," said Varuni, her tone icy as she folded her arms.

"Yeah, rub it in why don't you." Maya clenched her jaw. "Nik's informants only told us where you were."

"Next time could you have a proper plan please?" Varuni said, her voice cool and her expression a bit too haughty for Maya's liking. Given Varuni also happened to be a goddess Maya controlled her tongue and began to pace the floor.

She went over everything Nik and Chayya had told her, everything she could remember about her previous visit to the palace, but nothing stood out, nothing struck her enough to figure out a better plan.

"Will you stop walking up and down? You are making me

dizzy," snapped Varuni. She rose and went to a tray holding a large pitcher and two steel glasses. She poured what looked like water into one glass and handed it to Maya. "Here, drink that. You should calm down enough to give me a chance to sleep."

Maya took the glass. "Thanks." A drink of water would probably help to rehydrate her. Lately food and water were the last things on her mind. But when she sipped she almost gagged and would have spat it out if it weren't unladylike. She shuddered. "What the heck is that?"

Varuni laughed. "You're not very strong for the Hand of Kali."

"What's that supposed to mean?"

"Just that the girl who wields the power of Kali should really have a stronger constitution."

"My constitution is plenty strong enough. What was that you gave me to drink?"

"I'm not the Goddess of Wine for nothing."

Maya gasped. "You gave me wine? What is wrong with you? I need to be aware and awake not lying here in an intoxicated heap just so you can get some sleep."

"Oh, do not fuss. You barely drank any of it. Had I known you were going to be so fussy I would never have given it to you."

Before Maya could think of a response, the door flew open and the two women didn't get to continue their argument. Two guards entered and grabbed Maya, each taking her by an arm and manhandling her out of the cell without a word.

THE GUARDS soon delivered her to another room, much larger this time, and quite beautiful in its design. The entire chamber was a full circle with alcoves set into the walls. Maya noticed stone statues of Kali and Yama in two of the alcoves. She snorted in silence. A man stood at the furthest end reading from a book set upon a table filled with lamps and incense and trays of things.

She got the impression of a hooked nose and sunken eyes, skin as pale as the marble on the palace façade.

Between Maya and the strange man, a large table occupied the middle of the room. Carved from an off-white rock traced with ebony flecks, the table stood at least to Maya's waist. The surface sank in the tiniest bit and at its center were a row of thumb-sized holes. A rim ran around the edges of the table forming a little gutter.

Maya gulped. The only thing she could think of for the purpose of the holes and the gutter was to drain blood from a victim or a sacrifice. Crap. Now she'd gone and gotten herself into something she had totally no idea how to get out of. How does one get away from an evil torturer anyway?

"Put her on the table." His voice drifted towards Maya, just loud enough to hear. His tone sounded aloof, cold.

The guards shoved her toward the table. One held her so tight she couldn't look sideways. Just the action of being pushed forward by a demon hand pissed her off royally. She swung her arm to her right and sent a burst of fire directly behind her. Maya blinked. She hadn't even considered the possibility she could be hurt by the resulting stream of flames but she didn't particularly care. Right now one of the guards was screaming like a girl. And she liked that very much.

"Get him out of here." The pale man turned toward Maya and the remaining guards as her victim was taken away still squealing. He opened his palm and a long ribbon of blackness emanated from his hand. The dark thread swam through the air honing in on Maya. When all four of her guard stepped away from her in unison Maya knew she was in trouble.

The ribbon of blackness wound around her and despite looking like it was made from air, its strength was unbelievable. It bound her as tightly as any chain ever could have and Maya's stomach clenched with fear. This sorcerer was way more powerful than she had anticipated.

With the slightest movement of his forefinger, the sorcerer lifted Maya off the ground and moved her through the air, placing her gently on the white stone table. Maya struggled against the ties of the black smoke but it was useless. Even as she felt the hard rock beneath her back, she knew struggling was a waste of her energy.

"Leave," came the icy instruction. Four sets of boots marched out of the room.

But as the door would have closed, one set of footsteps entered, a relaxed pacing indicating the owner of those feet was in no rush to get anywhere fast.

"My dear Maya. I was so hoping to run into you again." Kas moved to the side of the table and Maya glared at him, sure her eyes spit flames at his face. "Come now, why so angry with me?"

"Do you have to ask? Let me go."

"No need to be rude." Kas ran a finger along the edge of the stone and he turned to meet her eyes. *Odd. Was that a hint of sadness in his expression?* "I'm sorry it's come to this, Maya. I thought you would come to my side. But you are still resisting me."

"And I will always resist you. I'll never join the side of the demons." Maya spat her response with a more fevered vehemence than she expected.

"Very well." Kas sighed, the rush of air sounding genuinely sad. "I'll leave you to the ministrations of Balraj. I hope he'll be resourceful enough to change your mind. At the very least he should be able to find a way to drain you of your power and then it will be mine."

Kas ran a finger along the skin on Maya's arm, sighed again, and left.

The door closed behind Kas as a thick smoke began to permeate the air within the room. The threads of black shadows still bound Maya into place, her hands strapped tightly to her sides.

"Now, human girl." Balraj's voice startled Maya and she turned her head to find him standing right beside her. His bald head gleamed in the light of more than a dozen torches dotting the walls. His black eyes were flat, like dead coals in the deep pits of his eye-sockets. He'd certainly taken time in dressing up to apply a thick line of black Kohl around both his eyes. Pity they made him look more like a living corpse than anything else. "Be still."

He wore the raiment of a holy man; a wide fabric tied at his waist with a matching length wound around his body and shoulders. The dark orange color didn't seem right on Balraj whose very skin seemed to emanate evil.

He held onto Maya's arm and lifted a chain embedded into the stone, winding it around her wrist now freed from the rope of darkness. He repeated the process at the other side of the table and waved a hand across her body. With that movement, the binding shadows rose into the air and dissipated into nothing.

Maya pulled onto the chains but they encircled her wrists so tightly it hurt to even move her hand. "What are you doing?" she said, her voice ringing around the room.

"Just be silent." He answered with a serene calm as the smoke thickened. He brought a clay vessel to her side, brushing his hand over a burning pile of embers from which the thick smoke billowed. Maya's heart tightened as she recognized one item in the bowl. A bone. She didn't want to think where the bone had originated. This was a dark magic Balraj conjured and it frightened her.

The smoke filled Maya's lungs and she coughed and hacked, her body wanting to expel the foul air. From what she could tell, the smoke wasn't having any recognizable effect on her. Not yet, at least.

Balraj took both Maya's hands and laid them flat, palm facing up. Then he stood at the foot of the table and began to chant. The words were almost a song, a hypnotic melody. And Maya blinked, trying to concentrate on what he was doing. She wanted to be conscious and aware.

But when the sorcerer aimed both his hands at Maya, the pain coursing through her body was like nothing she'd ever experienced in her life. Similar to the fire in her veins when she'd first learned to control it, but also extremely different.

The violence and power in the agony sweeping through her body took her breath away and almost knocked her unconscious. Slowly she began to feel her fire swirling within her, heat building within her abdomen.

Maya breathed slowly, trying to control it, to tamp it down. She refused to let the despicable sorcerer have any of her power.

But it was useless.

No matter how much she tried, she couldn't stop it. It was as if he'd found the origin of the fire and began to pull at it with a power way beyond her own ability.

Fire coursed through her body and flowed straight into her palms. Balraj was ready, his hands outstretched to receive the continuous waves flowing from Maya's palms. She watched in desperation as he took her Fire, watched as he frowned and drew harder.

Maya's own body burned as if she were ablaze. Perspiration dripped from her face, soaking into her hair. She writhed against the heat and the agony, pulling at the chains not caring they cut into her skin or that her wrists began to bleed. Time seemed to stand still and Maya fell into a semi-conscious fugue, falling in and out of consciousness as the agony rose and fell.

At last, Balraj screamed in frustration and walked to his table. Maya dropped back onto the stone, the constant strain against the pain relieved if only for a moment. She had not an ounce of energy left. If he came back to kill her she'd be completely helpless.

But she held onto the hope he hadn't gotten what he wanted. So hopefully they'd let her live a little longer. Long enough for her to find a way out. Long enough to find a way to get Varuni out of here.

Maya tilted her head toward Balraj, watching to see if she could make out what he was doing. But he leaned on his table, shaking his head.

She slipped into unconsciousness listening to Balraj muttering about something not working.

MAYA AWAKENED as her body hit the ground and she went tumbling, only stopping when her head smacked into a wall. She groaned, listening to the tramp of boot-steps leaving and the thunk of the cell door shutting tight. She moved her head and gasped, then righted herself enough to support her weight on one elbow and hold onto her head with the other.

Her fingers came away sticky and red and she hissed at the sharp bite of pain.

"Shhh, lie still. You have a gash on your scalp." The shuffling of feet and soft crinkling of fabric brought Varuni to her. "Where did they take you?"

"Some albino sorcerer dude." Maya muttered. She didn't need to be convinced to lie back. Her body was so weak from Balraj's ministrations all she really wanted to do was sleep.

"That would be Balraj. He is Narakasura's sorcerer. A very ruthless, evil man." A tamped down fury laced Varuni's words. Maya allowed Varuni to lift her head and barely flinched when the goddess moved aside the hair above her temple. "The skin is broken. I will need to disinfect it."

Maya chuckled but it came out more like a cough. "Well, you're not the goddess of wine for nothing, right?"

Varuni laughed. She rose and went to the pitcher, bringing Maya a glass of her wine. She lifted Maya's head, put the rim to her lips and said, "I suggest you drink. You need some pain relief and some rest."

This time Maya drank quietly, not a cell in her body would have dared to say no to Varuni. At last, she lay back. Varuni pulled forward the long piece of fabric of her sari that hung at her shoulder. She tilted the cup and poured wine over the edge. The cell was silent except for Maya's ragged breathing, and intermittent hiss of pain as Varuni cleaned first the broken skin at her wrists and then the wound on her scalp.

Maya fell asleep right there on Varuni's lap. She knew she wouldn't allow herself to fail. Her last thoughts were for Joss and everything she'd sacrificed.

CHAPTER 53

Maya awakened later, lying on her side facing Varuni who sat in the lotus position looking very much like she was deep in meditation. Maya blinked. Yes, still there. She tried to moved but couldn't. Tried to swallow but found it almost impossible.

She called to Varuni but the sound emerged like something between a croak and a cough. Varuni threw herself onto her knees and crawled to Maya's side. She ran her fingers over Maya's forehead, her eyes pools of worry.

"What's wrong?"

"I am worried, Maya. You are no better than yesterday. What did the sorcerer do to you?"

"From what Kas said and from what Balraj did, I think he was trying to strip me of my powers."

"Well, whatever he was doing to you has weakened you terribly. And I am very afraid they will soon return." Varuni sighed. "I will no doubt get into trouble for this but there is one thing I can do to help you." She set Maya's head back onto the stone floor before rising and heading for the pitcher. The goddess brought the cup to Maya and sat before her cross-legged.

Varuni held the cup in front of her within her praying hands. Soon the goblet glowed and a smooth white smoke swirled around the hands of the goddess and encircled the cup. Varuni began to glow too, and even as weak and tired as Maya was, she could see Varuni's other two pairs of arms rising behind her. The goddess's skin shone a pearlescent shimmering glow.

At last, Varuni sighed and the luminous light faded. Maya was oddly disappointed. Varuni rushed forward and helped Maya to a sitting position while she supported her back. Maya looked at the contents of the cup the Varuni now held before her. A milky white liquid shimmered within the bowl.

"What is this?" Maya already suspected she knew the answer.

"It is the Amrita, the Elixir of Immortality." Varuni said in a whisper. "It will restore your strength to you and I am hoping it will help you in case Balraj sends for you again."

"Will it make me immortal too?"

"No." Varuni grinned. "The amount I am giving you is restorative and healing only."

"Won't they know you've given it to me?"

"No. I've told Kas the only place in which I can make the Amrita is on Mount Kailas. And since he can't get there yet, I've been safe and so has the Amrita."

"That was clever." Maya smiled at the goddess and sipped at the milk-like drink.

"I am not without my tricks." Varuni replied with a wink. "Now you sleep. And if for some reason you awaken somewhere else, remember to act weak and almost sickly. They will expect to be draining you of your power."

Maya emptied the cup and nodded. She closed her eyes, drifting off to sleep without the least bit of resistance. Fortunately, when she awakened she was still in her cell with Varuni. The goddess leaned against the far wall, singing a song Maya hadn't heard before. She trailed off and scrambled to her feet as Maya struggled to sit up.

"How do you feel?" Varuni's gaze flitted across Maya's face, to her body and back.

"I feel . . ." Maya assessed how she felt and was pleasantly surprised. She grinned at Varuni. "Actually I feel pretty great."

"See, my magic worked!" The goddess gloated happily. "Do you feel like eating? You will need your strength."

"Not really, considering where my food is coming from." Maya frowned. "Is it safe?"

"I have been eating it for a while and I am neither poisoned nor dead."

"Good, then I'll eat. I need to keep my strength up. I'm sure they're not done with me yet."

Varuni nodded, and went to a small wooden table beside the door. Apparently, Kas treated his prisoners very well. Three little brass pots contained a variety of vegetable curries, beside which sat a small pile of naan, still steaming. "This meal just arrived so everything is hot." She brought the tray and laid it on the floor in front of Maya, who attacked the food with a hunger she hadn't known she had.

At last, sated and satisfied, Maya followed Varuni's lead and washed up at a tiny basin in the corner of the room. A spout with running water falling constantly into a little stone bowl set with a drain. Functional yet natural.

"Right, I think I'm ready to start." Maya flexed her muscles, and bounced lightly on her toes. She scanned the cell and frowned.

"What is wrong?" The goddess's face scrunched with concern.

"I'm not sure where the best place is to practice here. No matter where I choose anyone can just come up and look through those bars and see me." Maya glanced at the iron rods set in the top of the wooden door like a little window.

"Oh pssht." Varuni waved a dismissive hand. "I can stand guard for you. It is probably for the best. We do not want them to know you have your strength back."

Maya grinned. She and Varuni hadn't gotten off to a good start, with the goddess almost snapping her head off when Maya arrived the first time to save her. Now, Varuni kept guard while Maya went through the practice routine she and Nik had developed.

The thought of Nik made her hesitate. She worried about him and Chayya. What had they done when she hadn't returned with Varuni as planned? Had they also been caught?

Varuni's high-pitched yelp grabbed Maya's attention and brought her back to reality. She stared at the goddess and gasped. Varuni dabbed at flames sticking to the door just inches from where she stood.

"Sorry," Maya said, a sheepish smile on her face.

"Concentrate. Or you might burn me up next time."

"So are you more flammable than the other gods?"

"What do you mean?"

"Well you are the goddess of wine and wine is flammable-" Maya giggled.

"Very amusing, human girl. I suggest you use your tongue less and concentrate on strengthening your powers. Or perhaps we can languish here in Kas's prison forever?"

Maya returned to her practice but not before she saw the curve of Varuni's lips and the hint of a smile. At least she had a sense of humor. Soon fireballs were flying around Maya and she began to tire. At last, she sighed, huffing out a strong breath. A breath that sent two fireballs floating off to the furthest corner of the cell.

"What was that?"

"Yes, I saw that too. Have you tested the limits of your powers?"

"Yes, with Nik. A lot. But we never tried using my breath to control the fire."

"Well, try now," Varuni ordered, grinning.

Maya drew a ball of flame and sent a soft breath at it. The

fireball responded and floated away toward the wall. Maya breathed in, almost sucking the air back into her lungs and the flame followed, floating slowly back to her.

Next, she blew the flame toward the door and the iron bars, her pursed lips directing the air in a thin stream, sending the little fireball floating through to the passage outside. Varuni gasped. "How clever. And how useful too." She nodded her approval more to herself and Maya wondered what type of plan the goddess was busy concocting.

Then Maya paid no more attention as she sank deeper into her routine, pushing herself further than ever. When she finally stopped to rest, she grinned. The stone sidewall of the cell was pock marked with overlapping black rings; remnants of the hundreds of fireballs she'd thrown at it.

But for all the physical strain she put her body under, her sleep was restless and fitful and filled with strange dreams of Kali and Yama and Nik calling for her help.

CHAPTER 54

"Maya, wake up. Someone's coming." Varuni whispered. But when Maya tried to rise the goddess pushed her back onto the pallet of blankets. "Stay down and pretend to still be weak."

Maya lay down and closed her eyes. A guard flung the wooden door open, sending it clanging hard against the stone wall. Boots stomped on the floor and two guards lifted Maya roughly from her sleeping position.

"What are you doing? She is very ill." Varuni yelled at them but they paid her no heed.

Maya peeked out every so often, as they half-dragged half-carried her, and soon confirmed she was heading back to the sorcerer's chamber. Her heart sank. She wasn't afraid, not really. It was the pain she wasn't sure she could handle.

As the guards entered the room and deposited Maya on the stone table, she prayed Varuni's Amrita had done some good.

Balraj approached Maya, tapping her on her cheek. She responded with a moan and fluttered her eyelids pretending to struggle to open them.

"Pathetic human." Balraj clicked his tongue. "*You* are supposed to be the Hand if Kali? I have to wonder what Kali was thinking." He held Maya by her chin, his fingers digging deep into her flesh and pressing into her bones. He must have spent those moments staring at her face and Maya wondered why. Was he frustrated with his attempt to take her power from her? He shoved at her face and moved to his table for a moment.

Balraj returned and went through the same procedure as the last time only now he seemed more determined, more vicious and although Maya would have loved to open her eyes and see what he was doing she pretended weakness. And her fire still refused to comply.

After a while he growled, the sound deep and visceral, ringing around the room and making her blood freeze in her veins. She felt cold steel press into her wrist then searing pain as something sharp pierced her flesh. Warmth flowed over her skin and Maya knew the knife had drawn blood. Her heart thundered but she tried to regain control.

Balraj circled the table and repeated the procedure with her other wrist. Maya recalled the holes in the stone table. The memory made her heart beat so fiercely it hurt her ribs. What was he up to?

When he moved behind her head and placed the knife against her neck, Maya almost shuddered with terror. She swallowed hard when she felt the moist heat of blood at her throat. Balraj left her, probably to return to his table and Maya shivered in terror. She was bound to the table by thick chains. How was she supposed to get herself out of here before she was killed?

It wasn't long before she heard the drip, drip of a liquid falling into a container beside the table. It wasn't long either before she began to feel faint. Maya breathed slowly, trying to remain calm despite being terrified she was soon going to meet her end.

Footsteps drew closer. Maya heard the clink of metal against the stone floor as Balraj return to retrieve the container filled with her blood. His footsteps receded and the sorcerer spent a few minutes at his table, chanting. The smell of incense and smoke filtered to Maya as she became slowly weaker.

Balraj returned, nudging her in the ribs until she opened her eyes. This time she didn't need to feign weakness. She could barely keep her eyelids open. He strode to stand at her feet and began to chant, pulling the fire from her hands with no resistance from Maya. Fire thrust from her palms and streamed toward Balraj. He laughed as the fire filled him. He drew it from her until the flames became a weak trickle. At last, he stopped and seemed very happy from the cackling chuckles coming from his table after he was done.

He summoned his guards and moments later they threw Maya back into her cell, her clothing and hair sticky with blood.

~

"WHAT HAPPENED?" Varuni rushed to Maya as the guards departed. "Are you okay? You are bleeding, Maya."

"I'm fine I think. He bled me. Then he did something with the blood. But Balraj seemed happy afterward. It was different this time when I didn't resist." Maya sat up and leaned against the stone wall behind her while Varuni prepared her a drink. She looked at her wrists where blood still seeped through the cuts Balraj made. She touched a finger to her neck, and they came away wet.

Maya grabbed her scarf and tore it into three strips, glad she'd chosen to wear it She was about to tie them around her wrists when she remembered what Nik said to her not too long ago. Healing with fire. What would it hurt if she tried?

She placed her finger on the cut and relaxed, breathing in and out slowly. Focusing her power, she aimed it in a thin stream at the wound. Nothing happened. She tried again and again, finally giving up in disgust.

"Patience and focus, Maya." Varuni said as she poured Maya's drink. "Try again."

"It's not working." Maya scowled.

"Focus your attention, Maya Rao. Before all your life's blood leaks out and you expire here on the floor of this cell. Now try again. I need to get out of here. Please." Varuni patted Maya's shoulder and handed the drink to her.

"What's this?"

"Amrita." Varuni whispered. "Drink quickly."

Maya obeyed. She watched Varuni as she moved so gracefully across the floor. This was the last place a goddess should be, locked up in a cell, held captive by a demon king. Maya handed the empty cup back to the goddess. "How did you manage for so long? He's had you for a century now. That's a very long time. I'm not sure I could manage without going insane."

"Who said I was still sane?" Varuni grinned and laughed. Then her face fell. "It's been hard. Especially when nobody came to save me. I couldn't believe all they did was wait."

Maya frowned. "You must have been very angry."

"Not so much angry as hurt." She managed a small smile. "But in the end they sent you."

"Much good I am. Look at how I got myself caught."

"I hardly think that is your fault. You did not do anything alone did you? Not until now. And now you are doing something yourself."

"What? All I'm doing is getting tortured." Maya snorted. "And having my Fire torn from me. Not much of a Hand of Kali, am I?"

"You have submitted to Balraj's torture and you are still alive. That says a lot. Most humans would have died before he finished his first round."

Joss's face appeared in her mind's eye. Joss wouldn't back down. Not now. Maya nodded and gritted her teeth. She felt a little stronger after the Amrita and at last ready to try again to heal her own wounds. She rubbed away the grit of dried blood from around the still seeping cut.

She calmed herself and concentrated, remembering how the fire felt as it filtered within her veins. She drew a breath from her belly and sent a stream slowly into her hand, focusing the power in a fine flow through to her finger. She held her fingertip to the broken skin of the wound, feeling the warmth of the flame as it seeped through her flesh. She didn't fear she would burn herself. Just that she would fail.

Maya rubbed her finger against her skin and tears blurred her vision. It worked. Her skin was clean, marked only by a thin raised line. She smiled and looked up at Varuni who grinned and nodded. Maya relaxed and repeated the process with the other hand. Her neck proved slightly more difficult, and with no mirror to guide her she roped Varuni in to place her finger on the moist wound.

When she finished she began to push herself to her feet.

Footsteps thundered along the passage outside. Varuni threw her a glance and whispered, "Pretend you are sick."

Maya obeyed and sank low, hunching her shoulders. She hung her head and closed her eyes, allowing her hair to fall across her face.

CHAPTER 55

hey stepped into the cell and dropped something onto her pallet.

"Get dressed and be quick. Lord Narakasura will see you now." The guard said, then turned and left.

Varuni rushed to Maya, grabbing the three strips of fabric she hadn't used to bind her wounds. "Lift your arms." Maya obeyed as the goddess helped her out of the blood-drenched overdress. Varuni flung the dress on the floor and rushed to the tap to wet the fabric, while Maya dug into the little pocket in the pants for Nik's weird stone. The goddess hurried back to Maya and rubbed vigorously at the dried blood at the bottom of her hair, and from her neck to her hips. "Quick, the pants too. Hurry."

Maya kicked off her shoes and tugged at the knot at her waist, pulling off the drawstring pants. She stood there in her underwear while Varuni cleaned her back and hair of as much blood as she could.

Done cleaning Maya's bloody back, Varuni turned and grabbed the pile of clothing still on Maya's pallet and clicked her tongue in disgust. "This is what they want you to wear?" She screeched.

Maya's jaw dropped. A small beaded blouse with capped sleeves that ended under her bust. And a skirt that looked likely to flare to a full circle. They were serviceable enough except for the part that women usually wore these types of heavily beaded garments for weddings. Not for what Maya planned to do. "That's it?"

Varuni nodded and Maya sighed as she assessed the dark blue and silver beaded creation. "Well, let's get it on, I don't want the guard to catch me in my underwear thanks."

Less than two minutes later Maya stood ready, tucking the stone into her unique hiding place with the little vial of poison. Without the deadly sharp Madus to deliver the venom, she'd have to rely on her fire and her wits.

"Very clever." Varuni approved. Then her face stiffened as if she'd just remembered something. She rushed to the table and poured a cup of water, then performed her Amrita creating ritual. Once done she hurried to Maya and almost thrust the drink at her. "Quickly. Before they come back."

Maya swallowed fast, and it was just in time, as she wiped at the moisture left on her lips she heard the thundering of the guard's boots as they returned for her. She sank quickly onto the pallet, feigning weakness, and waited.

THEY DRAGGED her off again although this time they were a little more careful, looping her hands around their shoulders and keeping her off the ground so her feet didn't sweep the floor. A few flights of stairs and a few marble lined passages later they approached a pair of double doors made of what Maya thought was gold.

The doors opened as the guards led Maya into a gigantic hall, much larger than Yama's in Patala. Filigreed screens covered every window, the work large enough to see the world outside, but small enough to provide privacy for the room's inhabitants.

All this beauty wasted on Kas. Maya gritted her teeth as the Rakshasas halted and let go of her. She teetered on her feet and fell lightly to her knees her head lolling forward.

"Why is she so weak?" Maya heard Kas ask and lifted her head slightly to meet his very worried gaze. She kept her lids heavy and her shoulders hunched.

"I had to bleed her before I succeeded in drawing out her Fire." Balraj's voice echoed around the room.

"I believe I told you I did not want her harmed." Kas spoke, his own voice soft, even and cold as ice. Maya raised her eyes in time to see the tamped fury darkening his face.

"I apologize, my lord but it was my last resort. The spell worked and in the end, she is weak, yes, but she is fine. She will recover soon." Balraj, dressed in his sage-like robes, now wore a dagger at his waist. He bowed to his demon king, but his posture and his expression seemed perfunctory. Maya could tell his loyalty did not lie with Kas. A shiver of fear ran through Maya. So many different people with so many agendas. And she sat right in the middle of this mayhem.

Maya dropped her head forward, hoping to hide her expression of surprise and her concern. Fabric moved and soft footsteps drew closer. An arm encircled her shoulders and she shuddered, lifting her hand to throw him off. "I'm sorry Maya, this was not what I mean to happen." The demon king helped Maya to her feet and supported her with an arm around her waist. He walked her to a stone bench beneath one of the carved windows. Maya sighed as he settled her. He was definitely convinced of her weakness and that was good.

As he rose from beside her his thigh brushed against hers and she froze with shock. "Don't worry Maya I won't hurt you." She released her breath. He'd taken her stiffened body as fear. And she couldn't be more grateful. Not that she believed him. He'd tried to hurt her before and she was pretty sure he'd try again.

He left her on the bench and returned to his throne where Balraj still stood, his face stony. "Explain how the blood worked." Balraj bowed and began to speak, his voice low. Too low for Maya to hear. Their voices rose and fell until Kas's came through loud and angry. "I said no."

Kas stood up, and Maya watched him, watched the fury flowing off of him. He stalked away from the sorcerer whose expression revealed vehemence and disgust. Clearly, he didn't agree with his master's decisions.

Kas walked toward her, visibly bringing his emotions under control as he approached. "Maya, I know I asked you this before and you refused but please can you reconsider." He stopped in front her. "Come to my side, Maya Rao. Come and join me. Let us join our powers and we can rule all the planes of existence."

Maya watched his face. He seemed so sincere; as if he truly believed what he requested of her was so easily given. Could he not see how wrong he was?

She shook her head, hesitant, slightly afraid to say no. "I can't. And -" Maya paused, her mind going over and over Kas, his behavior and now his offer. She continued "-I won't. I'm sorry Kas. You have the wrong girl. I won't come over to your side for the very fact that it represents the darkness and everything wrong with the balance of things. I am Kali's Hand. I do her bidding and her bidding only. I am not an instrument of power to you or to anyone else."

He remained still as she spoke. The hue of his face darkened as his rage threatened to overflow. Again, Maya saw his struggle with control. Saw his understanding of her choice overtaken by his anger that she'd refused his offer.

"You don't understand do you, human girl?" Kas stepped to Maya, forcing her to rise to her feet, to meet him face to face. "With me you will have everything you ever dreamed of. Riches, power, your heart's desire. With me you will reign over all of existence."

"And what if that isn't what I want?" asked Maya softly. She searched his face for that tiny part of him which seemed real and maybe even partly good. "I don't want riches and power. I didn't even want this power that I have. But I see now I do have a purpose and it's not to give my power over to evil."

Narakasura's face changed, his skin darkened, resembling the dead skin of a corpse, dark, rubbery and lifeless. His eyes lightened to almost golden before orange flames lit his irises. He turned and strode to the sorcerer, hand outstretched, spine erect. Fury rolled off him in waves and even Balraj took a moment to stare at him in surprise.

Balraj handed the demon King a golden cup, spoke a few words Maya couldn't hear, then disappeared into the shadows. Kas stood on the dais, slowly turning around to face Maya.

CHAPTER 56

She almost flinched; expecting unadulterated fury but Kas had regained control and gave her a tight smile. "You will not come willingly but I do believe we can make you come despite your reluctance."

"What's that supposed to mean?" Maya snapped.

"Balraj has created a potion to help me draw the Fire from you," Kas swirled the contents of the golden goblet. "Once I drink this you must choose - suffer the agony of having your Fire stripped from you, or join me and save yourself the pain."

"I don't think so." Maya walked toward Kas and stopped a foot away from the marble step leading up to the dais. "Go ahead and try whatever magic you have on me. You'll never win. So I say bring it on, King of Demons." She flexed her fingers and waited for the moment to come when she would pounce.

He lifted the goblet to his mouth and paused to stare at her over the rim. His eyes changed from black to brown, gold to fiery. He threw her a sad smile, raised the goblet in salute and tipped the contents into his mouth. He swallowed, his lips left the cup stained red and Maya tamped down the urge to retch. He'd just drunk her blood.

She took a deep shuddering breath and waited. It seemed he did the same. When, after a few moments nothing happened, he glanced at the shadows beside him, a questioning glare on his face. Balraj stepped forward and spoke a smattering of Sanskrit at him. The grin of satisfaction on the sorcerer's features sent chills up and down Maya's spine.

Kas turned to Maya and ran the back of his hand across his mouth, wiping off the traces of blood remaining on his lips. He stared sadly at Maya for a moment before he surrendered to the anger simmering in the flames in his eyes. Kas stepped off the dais, forcing Maya to take a number of steps backward. He held his hands toward Maya palms out, and began to chant lines of familiar words. The same ones Balraj had spoken when he'd finally succeeded in taking her fire.

Maya's stomach twisted, her fear becoming a tangible thing within her gut. She breathed, tamping down her emotions, concentrating hard on Kas. His position, his voice. Everything slowed down the tiniest bit as she began to see each element of her awareness separately. She heard Kas breathe in and out, heard his heartbeat, the staccato sound betraying his underlying emotion as he stared at her.

With the chant over, Kas raised his hands, expecting Maya's Fire to leap forth and drive into his body through the center of each of his palms. It was what Maya expected, too.

Except nothing happened.

Kas stared at her. His anger flushed his face as he thrust his palms forward, repeating the words and waiting.

"Maybe your sorcerer isn't as powerful as he thinks?" Maya suggested with a small smile as she waited, knees soft, ready to pounce if he so much as blinked in her direction.

Kas growled his anger and yelled Balraj's name. "It will take some time, Your Majesty. Just a little time." The sorcerer spoke from the shadows.

His words were certainly no comfort to Maya. Neither was

the confidence in his voice. But she wouldn't go down without a fight. She had something they didn't have. Amrita flowing thick and fast within her veins. That should certainly count. Maya hoped.

"Balraj." Kas roared. The fury of the command brought the sorcerer scurrying from the corner of the Hall. "Keep her still."

Balraj nodded and scuttled forward to Maya. He stood still then thrust his hands out, palms aimed at Maya; a movement twisting her stomach with fear at the memory of the pain she'd suffered at those hands.

Balraj's magic drove deep into Maya's body, finding the threads of her fire and drawing them out ever so slowly. Maya gritted her teeth. No way was he taking advantage of her power again. Maya planted her feet solidly onto the grounded and gathered the flames.

She poured all her anger and pain into it, recalling the agony Balraj had caused her, the amount of suffering he'd put her through. The heat built up in her abdomen, fire licking her veins, burning white hot yet comfortable, bearable. She breathed and gently pushed the fire to her fingertips allowing the heat to build there. She waited as Balraj chanted, feeling the pull he had on her Fire. His magic battled her inner control and she watched almost as an onlooker as she took a deep breath and thrust the fire out of both hands in twin streams of bright orange heat.

Straight at the sorcerer.

He cackled, thinking he'd succeeded but he was so wrong. The fire flew at him, controlled by Maya. Balraj stared at his hands. He may have realized he held no power over her. But it was too late.

The double-barreled fire penetrated the sorcerer's chest with a force that propelled him backward until the step to the dais tripped him up and he fell into a sitting position, legs akimbo, a startled, confused expression on his pale features.

Maya trained her Fire on him until she felt he'd had enough.

He was after all a powerful magician. Who knew what tricks he had up his sleeve? But Maya left it a moment too long. Her power a bit too much.

She eased back the streams of flame but in vain. An orange glow burned beneath Balraj's skin, creeping along his neck and down to his hands. The shocked sorcerer turned his palms over, his eyes bulging with unadulterated fear.

Maya's heart thudded as she watched him burn up from inside. There was nothing she could do. Not anything she knew how to do, anyway. Besides, he deserved his punishment for what he'd done to her. Still, she felt a rush of guilt run through her. She was no unfeeling killer. Nor would she ever want to be.

Now she stared in subdued horror as the fire filled Balraj's head, as it singed his clothing, turning the orange cotton fabric into bits of black soot.

Then he exploded and Maya ducked.

She raised her head a mere moment later and wanted to laugh at herself. What had she expected, chunks of cooked meat flying all over the place? She shook her head slightly and stared at the spot that Balraj had occupied only a second ago. All that remained was a charred circle in the floor where he'd stood and bits and pieces of black ash and orange fabric floating around and landing softly on the marble tiles.

And Balraj's gleaming dagger.

Maya's gaze darted around the room in front of her. Her breathing evened as she realized while she'd been intent on Balraj, she'd lost track of Kas. He was behind her somewhere, and that meant he couldn't see what she was doing.

She knelt, her fingers closing over the hilt of the weapon; Maya withdrew the vial of Naga poison and swiftly dipped the tip of Balraj's dagger in it. Her fingers shook as she closed and hid the tiny bottle again and shoved the weapon within the fall of her skirts.

She felt the vicious tip of Kas's dagger before she registered his breath at her ear. He stood close behind her as he plunged his knife deep between the ribs on her right side.

CHAPTER 57

She steeled herself against the pain, drawing immediately on her fire, urging the heat to search out the broken organs and tissue, to mend and fix her body, stem the blood loss and knit the open mouth of the wound.

Kas stepped back as Maya turned, a triumphant grin on his face. The amber fires still glowed within his eyes making Maya sad for him.

"Don't do this, Kas. Stop now while you have the chance."

He shook his head sadly. "It is done, Maya Rao. You will soon die. Whatever you are, Fire Wielder, Hand of Kali, Demon Hunter. It makes no difference because you are merely human. Just a mortal."

Maya glared at him. "Don't you think the Mother Kali would want to protect me? And where she can't protect me, don't you think she will come to my aid?"

The demon king glared at her, unhappy with her confidence. He shook his head again. "Be that as it may, Kali cannot enter this palace. No god or goddess can. Or have you forgotten that?"

"No, I haven't forgotten. I just know I'm getting out of here soon enough. And that you will pay for your crimes very soon, too."

Kas laughed, the sound deep and jovial. "You think I am afraid of consequences? I have waited a lifetime to be able to rise again and take back what is mine. And nothing, especially not a puny human girl, will stop me."

"Well, good luck to you, Demon King." Maya spoke softly, gripping the hilt of the poison tipped knife, waiting for the opportune moment to stab him.

He lunged at her, a vicious curved sword appearing in his hand out of nowhere. Maya stabbed at him and jumped back. She'd missed. But luckily so had he.

No fair. Maya readied herself for another pass. She faked a lunge, bringing Kas closer than he expected. Before he retreated Maya gouged the dagger deep into the flesh of his bicep, ripping open the hand woven sleeve, laying bare his wound.

She'd succeeded, but why didn't she feel thrilled and triumphant about it? She knew the poison in the dagger was powerful but she didn't know if it would kill him. And somehow, the thought of killing Kas didn't sit well with Maya.

She forced herself to stay focused. She couldn't afford the emotional weakness right now. He was the demon king holding all the gods hostage by taking away their immortality elixir. But Maya had Varuni to think about - the goddess waited in Kas's dungeon for Maya to free her. That was real. And Nik and Chayya? They were no doubt worried sick waiting for her. She didn't have the time or the inclination to sit around waiting to be rescued.

She had to act. Now.

Kas stumbled back, a little surprised at Maya's attack. His features settled into a hard, angry expression. His eyes flitted to his knife and Maya knew he wondered why she wasn't weak from the injury he'd inflicted. He lunged again and this time

Maya wasn't fast enough. He tripped her up but as she fell she wound her foot around his calf bringing him down with her. She used his momentum and rolled with him, curling her dagger round in one smooth move to place it at his neck.

"Go ahead." He urged. "Do it." He sounded sullen, yet his eyes taunted her. Which confused Maya all the more. She pressed the knife to his throat as she leaned over him, one knee against his chest, the other holding his hand firmly on the marble floor.

But Maya couldn't kill him. She shoved herself off him in disgust. It was too easy to slit his throat while he goaded her to finish the job.

Kas laughed as they rose to their feet, dusting himself off. "I knew you didn't have it in you." He chuckled as he began to circle her. Again, he held out his wrists and Maya stiffened. He was going to used Balraj's magic. "I've wasted enough time playing your games, human girl."

As he spoke the last word, he thrust his hands toward Maya and tugged them back, the movement fluid, graceful. But Maya didn't have time to contemplate the sinuous beauty of his potentially deadly motions. She felt a pull in her solar plexus, as if her fire were being tugged out of her body by Kas's single move.

A thrill of fear surged within her as she fought for control of that burst of fire. Could he really take her Fire from her? When the flames began to surge forward to her fingertips, Maya began to panic. Fire left her hands reaching out toward Kas as he stood there, so calm, so expectant.

She should have killed him when she had the chance. Maya wanted kick herself. Her Fire pulsed within her veins, flowing through her in answer to Kas's call. He was taking Kali's Fire.

No.

She wasn't going to let him.

She slipped her fingers into the little metal detail that curved out of the handle of the sorcerers dagger, letting the weapon rest on the tops of her fingers, blade jutting out to the side. It gave her the freedom to use her fire while still able to used the blade if needed.

Maya calmed herself, remembering what Nik had taught her. She breathed deep, letting the intake of air flow into her lungs, bringing peace and calm.

Fire spurted from Maya's fingers and flew to Kas. The demon king smiled.

Peace filled Maya's veins, calm flowing through her mind and soul. She reached for the Fire deep in her solar plexus, winding the tongues of flame together, and gathering them into a smooth skein of golden flame.

Heat bathed Maya's face as her Fire roared, leaving her body, escaping to Kas.

At last, Maya breathed again and the Fire breathed with her. Calm and content and controlled. Heat rippled within her body, flowing smoothly to her hands, when it turned to stem the tide of the flames leaving Maya's fingers.

The warmth dissipated, the Fire slowed and Kas stared at his hands, confused.

Maya shifted her weight on her feet, her toe tracing a wide circle around her. She drew her right arm anti-clockwise over her shoulder, bringing it up waist height, to join her other hand. Her father would be proud of her fluidity. The movement gave her the perfect amount of latent energy.

Maya glanced at Kas, a little sad he'd pushed her this far. But she couldn't allow anyone to take her Fire especially when they wanted to exploit it for their own needs. He met her gaze as if he knew what she meant to do.

He didn't move.

She breathed and nudged, sending Fire roaring out of the palms of her hands, a stream of heat flying at Kas with a strength and power that amazed Maya. And shocked the demon king. The barrel of fire hit him straight in the chest and sent him staggering a few feet, battling the onslaught of flame.

Maya felt a moment of victory. Which lasted only until Kas stumbled toward her, shoving back against her Fire. Maya had seen his pure white fire before, could see he was trying his hardest to summon it.

She had to finish it now. Before he drew on his own fire. The poison hadn't had any effect. But maybe she needed to get the Visha into him a second time.

Maya tipped the dagger forward, held it waist high, concentrating hard on Kas as he moved another step toward her.

The demon king grew stronger, but Maya had to take the chance. Before he could advance any further or gather any more strength Maya ran the few feet it took to get to him. She caught the startled look on his face but she didn't slow down, just kept running, slashing at his thigh as she went.

The growl of pain he uttered made her feel slightly bad. She had to remind herself he hadn't had any qualms about potentially killing her while relieving her of her Fire. She spun around behind him, as he turned to face her, one hand at the blood-ridden gash in his trousers. Kas glanced at the dagger, then at his wound.

Maya blinked, a moment wasted as she ducked to avoid the fiery ball of white fire Kas sent at her. Heat warmed her cheek as Kas's flame flew past Maya's face, singeing her hair. She ignored the bitter odor of burnt hair, and threw the dagger aside. She turned to face Kas, smoothly drawing a ball of flames of her own, and letting it fly at the demon king without a pause.

Maya's fireball glanced off Kas's shoulder, leaving behind a black patch of burnt fabric, revealing reddened, yet unhurt skin. Kas grunted, sent fire back at Maya that came with such speed she couldn't get out of the way fast enough. The ball came straight at her abdomen and the only thing she could think of doing was to grab the fire, like Nik taught her, grasp hold of it, mold it, and send it back at its owner.

The fireball hit Kas dead center of his chest and he staggered back in shock. His own fire couldn't hurt him, but the power Maya had put behind the speeding ball of flame surprised him.

And it shocked Maya.

CHAPTER 58

But she had no time to waste as Kas began to send her a volley of fireballs, each larger and hotter than the next. She dodged a few, and threw some back at him. Her fire was stronger than his but she wasted so much time deflecting his fireballs she couldn't draw on her own. Then she had a thought.

What if she imbued his fire with hers? She'd only know if she tried. If it worked then she'd at least be able to subdue him.

She concentrated on catching the next batch of pure white fireballs, gathering each in her hands, spending precious moments filling the growing ball of flame with her own Fire. Maya kept her gaze on Kas, hoping he'd keep his eyes on hers. She hoped he wouldn't notice her injection of Kali's Fire into his demon flame.

The ball grew within her palms and Kas grinned.

Maya grinned back, passing the sparking fireball back and forth from hand to hand. She drew her arm back sending the flame flying at Kas with all her might. Her body shuddered with the energy she put behind the throw.

Kas, so confident in his own fire, so sure of himself he all but reached for the fireball as it closed in on him. He blinked again at the speed at which the ball flew at him. Then caught it with a confident swagger. But the power behind Maya's throw sent him staggering, and for a moment, she wondered if her hidden Fire would fail. Until Kas screamed as Kali's flames wound themselves around his hands, setting his flesh alight with a strange shimmering flame.

Maya cringed as Kas yelled out again, staring at his flaming hands in horror. When his gaze returned to Maya's it was filled with confusion. And something else. A heavy hooded dulling around the amber glow of his eyes. Perhaps the first dose of poison had been working its way through his body all along. Perhaps her Fire had sped up the deadly strength of the venom.

He took a step toward Maya and she scrambled backward to avoid him as flames spread to his upper arms and chest. The demon king fell to his knees. Maya winced as bone connected with marble in a jarring thud. Kas sank onto his heels, his eyes almost rolling back in his head as he swayed, unbalanced and weak.

He swallowed hard. "You are very strong, Maya Rao. Perhaps my sorcerer misled me. He'd been so sure he'd weakened you with his attempts to take your Fire. It seems he was wrong about his potion too. But this is not the end. You and I are not yet done." His lips twisted into a parody of a smile as he sank to the ground. Instinctively Maya ran to him. She wasn't sure what she'd meant to do but she didn't get to do it.

The demon king Narakasura shimmered, then disappeared.

Maya stood there for a second, shocked at Kas's disappearance. She hadn't expected to defeat him with her Fire. In fact she'd bet everything on the poison being the way to overcome him. The moment felt a little anticlimactic. And the silence in the white marbled hall made it worse. Her gaze fell on Balraj's dagger lying on the floor. She made a face, reluctant to have anything further to do with the hideous sorcerers possessions but she needed a weapon. She retrieved it and headed to the door, taking one last look at the grand throne room of the white palace of Swargaloka.

At the door, Maya ducked her head into the hall, looking out for guards. Footsteps echoed at the far end of the passage. The Rakshasas were coming, although they didn't seem to be in any great hurry. Of course, they wouldn't know their Demon King was gone. Maya scurried to a nearby alcove, almost fully occupied by a gigantic brass statue of the elephant-headed god Ganesh. She tucked herself beside the figure, glad the god's huge protruding stomach hid her from the oncoming guards.

As soon as they ran into the throne room, Maya fled down the hallway without a backward glance. She paused at the end of the passage and tiptoed to the edge of the circular stairwell that would take her back to the dungeon and to the goddess Varuni.

Her heart thudded as the sound of a gong echoed around the palace. The multitude of hurried footsteps meant the guards must know something was amiss. She hoped they were hurrying anywhere but in the direction she needed to go. The hallway seemed clear so Maya descended the steps, dagger at the ready, but flight after flight all she met was dead silence. Perhaps the gong had called all the guards away? Maya hoped that was the case.

Where had Kas disappeared to anyway? He'd left before she could properly finish him off and she felt dissatisfied. But she'd come for Varuni. And now she could get her out of here.

She reached the cell door and stopped in her tracks. No guards meant no keys to open the thick wooden doors.

A shuffling sounded inside the room and Varuni came to the little barred opening. "Maya. You're safe." She smiled, relief brightening her eyes. "Come, get me out of here."

"I can't. There aren't any keys." Maya scanned the wall beside the cell and stared down the corridor of cells hoping to see a convenient hook with a jumble of keys. She'd almost incinerated a demon king but she was now unable to open a damned door.

Maya blinked.

That was it. She grinned and said, "Step away from the door and stay back until I tell you to move."

Varuni frowned, then nodded and hurried to the far wall, watching in silence.

Maya quickly drew a practiced ball of Fire and flung it at the door. All the flame did was sputter out leaving a dark scorched circle in the wood. She frown and tried again, this time training a stream of flames at the door, steadily holding it in place until the wood slowly caught alight. Soon the entire door burst into flames, burning merrily, the wood cracking and falling onto itself.

At last, Maya was able to kick the middle of the door in, providing Varuni a large enough opening to escape the cell.

The goddess grinned as she left the place of her imprisonment, and threw her arms around Maya. "Thank you, Maya. You saved me."

"Not yet. Not until we are out of the palace."

"Fine, let's get going."

Maya led the way, remembering the sketch Nik had made her memorize. The entrance to a spacious fountained courtyard, one floor up from the dungeon, toward the back of the palace. They moved fast but all that greeted them was silence.

"The place is deserted. What happened?"

"I'm not sure. I killed the sorcerer. And I injured Kas quite badly. There were some guards near the throne room. But now they all seem to be gone."

"They probably left."

"Left to go where?"

"Back to Naraka? Or to wherever Kas is hiding out. You did not kill him so he will be somewhere licking his wounds. I do not think he would have expected you to be as powerful as you are. I had no doubt you would defeat him."

"Yeah, he certainly had no idea I had so much Fire power.

Balraj seemed to have been quite mistaken in his assumption his little potion would enable Kas to take my power." Maya said as she hurried to a door along the hall they'd entered. She opened it and sighed with relief. The fountained garden.

"It seems your power makes you immune to potions and magic." Varuni said, following Maya into the garden.

"Potions and magic, except for the Amrita you mean?" Maya raised an eyebrow, keeping her gaze on the expanse of lush greenery ahead.

"The Amrita is pure. It is neither a potion nor is it magic." Varuni's tone was so solemn Maya threw a quick glance at her face.

"Okay," Maya said slowly, as they hurried to the far wall where. This wasn't the time to interrogate Varuni on what she meant about the power of the Amrita. Maya was just happy the Elixir had worked to make her healthy.

Maya patted her chest for the stone, a hysterical giggle bubbling up at the incongruity of keeping poisons and magical stones so close to her heart. "What are you looking for?"

"A weird stone Nik gave me."

Varuni laid a hand on Maya's forearm. "Wait. You do not need it. I can take you outside the wall now."

"Oh" Maya blinked then stared at Varuni, nodding her head. "Do you think the wards no longer work since Kas is gone?"

Varuni nodded and held onto Maya, and they both disintegrated, shimmering into nothingness only to appear just as quickly on the other side of the palace wall.

To find Nik pacing, wearing away the grass beneath his boots. Chayya sat cross-legged under a nearby tree, a worried expression darkening her beautiful face. They both looked up in shock as Maya and Varuni appeared.

"Oh, dear god, Maya. I was so worried." Nik hurried to her, enveloping her within his warm arms. He thrust her back, staring at her face. "Are you okay? What happened? Did you kill Narakasura?"

"Nikhil, give the girl a moment to breathe," said Chayya softly as she pushed Nik and Maya apart. She smiled at Maya. "I knew you would get the job done."

"Thanks but I'll be happy only when I get back home." Maya's lips twisted sadly. The memory of Joss and all she'd sacrificed stabbed Maya's heart and brought a moist sheen to her eyes.

"Right, let's get back to Patala, report to Yama, and then we can get you home." Nik threw an arm around Maya giving her an encouraging glance. "Ready?"

She nodded and he transported them back to the waiting room outside Yama's hall in Patala.

CHAPTER 59

*M*aya stood in Yama's chamber, slightly off balance after being awakened by Chayya in a fevered rush. She'd been sent straight to her room to rest. After having her wounds looked at, a welcome soak in the pool and a belly full of food, Maya had fallen asleep almost immediately when her head touched the silk pillow.

Now, she placed one palm against her throbbing abdomen, thankful it looked like it was healing fast. Kas's stab wound in her side seemed undetectable too. She breathed and tried to pay close attention.

Could they not have found a better time to drag her out of her bed?

Nik came to her. "Sorry to have to wake you but Yama will speak to you now."

Maya nodded. Of course. Everything in Patala revolved around Yama, considering he was a god and all.

"Are you okay?" Nik bent to her.

And though Maya's instinctive response would have been to bite out an accusation, a sense of sadness and tiredness under-lined his voice, and Maya understood.

Because the very same emotions were reflected in her own

heart. In the end all she said was, "I'm feeling much better thanks. I'm just pissed off Kas got away. I guess I'll settle for having him banished from Swargaloka forever, though." Maya still saw the shock and surprise on Kas's face as she'd blown him into another dimension. Literally.

"Yeah, I know exactly what you mean." Nik nodded, his eyes on his father. "Trust me when I say Kas will get what's coming to him."

Maya walked to stand before the dais as Yama sat on his throne. Chandragupta began to scratch away at a page in his great book, his attention seemingly diverted from her presence before Yama. Nik moved with her, reminding Maya she'd forgotten both Nik and Chayya were still dutifully by her side. She reveled a little in their show of support and made a mental note to thank them. For now, she paid attention to the god of death. The god who owed her a boon.

"Maya, you have fulfilled your end of the bargain. You have retrieved the goddess Varuni and saved the gods from dying." As he spoke Yama began to glow, encircled by a soft light. "You have restored our power and our longevity and for that we are most grateful."

"Thank you, my lord. I am grateful for all the help I was given to complete my task," Maya responded, realizing then her anger with Nik for losing Joss had made her feel ungrateful to him for his aid. She turned to look at him and Nik smiled.

"It is good you are humble. To acknowledge the help of others in one's own success is a great act, Maya. In honor of your bravery and willingness to aid the gods to fight this demon king, I believe it is suitable at this time to grant a boon."

"Ria?" asked Maya hopefully.

"Yes, Maya. When you return to your home you will find your friend alive, well and healthy."

"Will she remember what I did?"

"I am not sure, Maya," Yama said, shaking his head. "That I

cannot promise. I will do what I can to wipe her memory. Perhaps it is safest that way for her and for you."

Maya nodded. "Thank you, my lord." She hesitated, and made a small half-turn to leave when Yama's voice stopped her in her tracks.

"Maya, the boon you asked for showed an immense amount of selflessness. I have been around a very long time. Few people have the depth of selflessness and self-sacrifice as you do to use your boon for someone else. Because of that, I will grant you two more." Yama walked toward Maya and held his closed fist out to her. She opened her palm wondering what he had for her and hoping at the same time it wasn't something deadly. He dropped two stones of frankincense in her palm. "One for each of your boons. Burn it and I will come to you and grant your wish."

"Thank you my lord," said Maya. She smiled her gratitude as she felt the weight of the frankincense in her hand.

"It is time for you to return home now Maya. Time for you to continue on your path as the Hand of Kali. Things may not always be easy but remember there are those around you willing to help you along your path. You are an asset to us, Maya Rao. Don't ever forget you are more important than you know."

Yama gave her a nod and a smile and walked back to his throne.

Have I been dismissed?

"Come, we should leave," said Nik.

Maya nodded and was ready to depart with Nik. But anything else she was about to think froze in her mind as she caught sight of Joss's body lying on a flower strewn table before Yama.

Maya's heart twisted. "What the hell are they doing?" She said through clenched teeth. To Maya it looked like they were preparing for a funeral. Nobody placed flowers around living people. Ever. Well, maybe when they were being married but other than that? Nope. Didn't happen. Maya choked down a sob as she stared at Joss's serenely peaceful face. She had to remind herself she'd done as she'd promised. She'd finished it. And Joss's death wouldn't be in vain.

"Is it a funeral?" Maya almost choked on the words.

Nik nodded, his eyes dark and sad. When he moved to throw his arm around her she shrugged him off. "No." She shook with fury and anger and grief. Everything she'd done had been for Joss in the end. Maya was so angry she clenched her fists hard. And found that the palm of one hand was already occupied.

She opened it and stared at the two pieces of frankincense.

When she looked up at Nik she knew immediately he'd figured out what she wanted to do. Nik shot a look at Chayya whose expression revealed such understanding and emotion that Maya was ready to burst into tears in that instant.

"Are you sure?" He watched her, his eyes penetrating right to her soul. "You must be certain."

"Yes. I've never been more sure about anything in my life." Nik nodded almost to himself and walked toward Yama. Every step he took thudded as Maya's heart knocked against her breastbone.

CHAPTER 60

Maya dared to take another look at the pair of shiny pieces of incense. When she looked up again Nik was with Yama, speaking fervently into his father's ear.

A moment later Nik finished his discussion with his father and moved off the dais toward Maya. He drew close, and curled an arm around Maya's shoulders.

Behind her, Maya crossed the fingers of her unoccupied hand. Every bit of luck would help. "Well here goes nothing."

Nik opened his mouth then promptly shut it when Yama rose from his throne. "Maya Rao, is it true this human girl gave her life for you?"

"Yes it is, my lord."

"Is it true you will do anything to grant her life back to her?"

"I would do anything." Her hand gripped the two pieces of frankincense and Maya didn't even think about it. The words flowed instinctively from her lips. "My lord I offer one of my boons in exchange for the return of Joss's life."

Yama stared at Maya until she could no longer stand still. Her feet itched to move and only when she knew she couldn't bear it for one more second did Yama finally end his scrutiny. "Lord

Chandragupta, please find this child's life thread and give me the details."

Although Maya had seen the book move before the whole process was still incredibly fascinating. Chandragupta opened the tome and laid it flat, then moved slightly away. The gigantic pages began to flip over so fast they emitted a gusty breeze not unlike a strong electric fan. Chandragupta remained motionless and expressionless while he waited.

At last, the book fell open and silence reigned in Yama's throne room. Yama and his assistant conferred, speaking in the dulcet tones of the ancient Sanskrit language. After some intense discussion, the god of the underworld, Yama, Lord of Death and Justice, left the dais and moved toward the supine, unmoving corpse.

"My son has informed me of the lengths this human girl has gone to help you, Maya, in retrieving the goddess Varuni from Narakasura's clutches. I am further certain of this given the important fact, pointed out by my son, that it was not the girl's time to die. This is confirmed by Lord Chandragupta. I have also taken into consideration the trials of this child's life, the difficulties she has faced and the sins she has committed within her short life."

Maya bristled. What sins was he talking about? Joss had led a difficult, empty life with parents who, though they were physically around, were emotionally absent. She'd had to fend for herself most of her life anyway. And as for sins, who knew what Yama considered to be a sin. Not that Maya had any intention of clarifying that right now. Her heart thumped as she waited for Yama to speak.

"Your boon is an easy one to grant. I give life back to this child as she has earned this privilege. Let us hope she uses the time given back to her wisely." Yama moved to stand beside the table where Joss's body lay. He held both hands out toward Joss and Maya shivered.

Behind Yama, two sets of hands rose and encircled the god; bringing six palms forward to place blessings upon Joss.

Just like in all the pictures and statues. Imagine that.

A strange light began to glow, covering the god's hands and Joss's abdomen. The glow swirled and gleamed, an almost tangible viscous substance and yet it wasn't even there. Soon the light enveloped Joss although it remained brightest around her injury.

Maya waited, afraid to breathe as she watched Yama at work. It seemed strange he hadn't revived her with a simple click of his godly fingers, but who was she to question his methods. With both Nik and Chayya at either side of her, Maya knew she could get through this. She had to.

For Joss.

At last, Yama breathed deeply and stepped away from Joss. "It is done. She will awaken in a few moments. Be sure to enlighten her of the great responsibility she has to not waste this life I have given to her," said Yama, giving Maya a sharp nod as four guards came forward to carry Joss away.

～

THEY LEFT Yama's hall and walked mostly in silence back toward Nik's quarters and the rooms they'd been given. As they reached Joss's room Chayya touched Maya's hand.

"You did very well Maya Rao," said Chayya, placing her hands together and giving her a deep bow.

Maya returned the greeting, "I could never have done it without you, Mother Chayya."

"Oh, Maya you know there is no need for formalities with us. I will watch over you always. And even when I can't be around one of my shadow girls will always be nearby. Just call for me and I will come to aid you," she said. Chayya hesitated, then leaned forward and gave Maya a tight hug. Maya hugged her back, surprised and touched by the display of affection.

"Namaste, Maya. Farewell until we meet again," said Chayya and then she slowly disintegrated into a twist of shadow and light until she was gone.

Maya stared at the spot Chayya had just occupied, thinking back on everything the goddess had done for her from the day she first met her in the hallway back at school when she'd been fighting the Amber-demon. So many things would have been impossible without the help of the goddess.

"Maya." Nik's voice penetrated her fog and she glanced over her shoulder at him. He'd waited so patiently, and even now that he'd disturbed her reverie he did it with such gentleness and kindness it made Maya want to cry. "Shall we go in? Are you ready?"

Maya nodded, and Nik opened the door. Joss sat up in bed, swathed in silken sheets and a bright orange bedspread woven with patterns of peacocks and dancing girls.

"Hey guys, where have you been so long? I've been waiting for like forever already," said Joss, pale but cheerful.

"You've been hurt, you idiot. You needed rest more than you need visitors."

"Well I can't help it if I get bored. There isn't really anyone to talk to here," Joss pouted. But her expression didn't last long as a huge grin took over her face again. "So tell me, what did I miss? The last I remembered was Priya stabbing me. That traitorous b-"

Maya cut her friend off before she could complete the profanity. She didn't want to disturb Nik's sensibilities but she needn't have worried. One look at his face revealed an appreciative grin as he smiled at Joss. "Yes, you missed the interesting punishment Kas had in store for poor Priya."

"Poor Priya?" Maya scoffed. "As far as I am concerned she got exactly what she deserved. What made her think the demon king would trust her in the first place?" Maya's mind returned to Priya's tortured face as she burned within Kas's fiery column.

Maya quickly relayed the events to her speechless friend. When she came to the part where Joss had died, the blonde girl couldn't have gotten any paler. "What did you say?" Joss asked, her voice a mere whisper.

"Yama gave you your life back. He said you must make sure to live a life worthy of his decision to return your life to you. But Nik here was smart. I think it all came down to the fact it wasn't your time to go."

"Oh, okay," Joss replied softly, her forehead scrunched.

"What's wrong?" Maya suspected Joss's expression meant she was worried, almost afraid.

"So does this mean I am in debt to the god of the dead?"

"No Joss, he has cleared the debt. For helping Maya success-fully retrieve the goddess Varuni," answered Nik as he smiled at her.

"Okay, phew. That's good. I don't think I could have slept in peace knowing I owed the big cheese of the underworld big time." Joss grinned. "So what now? Can we go home?"

Maya never thought she would hear Joss ask about home with such happiness, but she suspected her friend technically wasn't referring to her own home.

"We're ready whenever you are." Maya grinned.

Joss flung off the covers, revealing herself fully dressed in a baby blue baggy Indian pants and a cerise knee length overdress embroidered in deep blue and gold trim. For someone who'd been certified dead not too long ago, Maya thought she looked fabulous.

Maya and Nik laughed as Joss shoved her feet into a pair of beaded slippers. "Will you two quit laughing and let's go before some other god finds something we need to do for them that will really kill us for good."

"Right, let's go home," said Maya.

CHAPTER 61

They arrived in Maya's house, right into the center of the entrance hall. In full view of Maya's mom and dad who'd been in the sitting room, worry lining their faces as they bided their time for their daughters return. They rose to their feet, enveloping Maya within their arms, asking a ton of questions Maya felt too overwhelmed to answer.

"I'm okay." Maya gave her mom another squeeze before stepping back. She glanced at Joss who looked a little pale after the teleportation. "For now, I need you to look after Joss."

"What happened to Joss? Are you okay dear?" Maya's mom asked as she placed an arm around Joss, drawing her to the nearest sofa.

"Mom, Joss was injured. She's fine but she's a bit weak and I think she needs rest," Maya said. It earned her a belligerent glare from Joss, but Maya ignored it as she also noticed the lines of fatigue marking her friend's face.

"So what happened?" Dev's concern was clear in his voice and his face. "Did you see Yama?"

"Yes, we saw Yama and completed the mission to his satisfaction, too," Maya grinned, throwing a glance at Nik.

"Details, Maya? We've been waiting here, counting the seconds until you got back."

"Okay." Maya laughed as she and Nik sat on the sofa by the door. Maya and Joss took turns to relate the story from the moment they arrived in Patala. Her parents listened in shocked silence until the tale was told. At last, she said, "And now I need to check on Ria."

"But Maya, if you were injured shouldn't you rest?" Her mom frowned.

"Leela, Maya has grown both in the power she wields and in the strength of her body. Maya is fully healed and as strong as she ever was." Nik spoke with a certain air and Maya did a double take. For a moment, he'd sounded just like Yama.

"Very well, Nik. If you say so," Maya's mom answered, before sending him a threatening look. "And you'd better be right, young man. Or you'll have me to answer to if Maya gets sick."

Nik smiled. "Don't worry. She'll be fine. Besides, even the hounds of hell won't keep Maya from seeing Ria so we all might as well play along."

Maya punched Nik's arm. "We'll be back soon." With that, she grabbed Nik's hand and almost dragged him out of the house before her father decided to stop them.

They walked in silence before Maya realized she still held Nik's hand. When she tried to tug free, his fingers tightened around hers. They stopped under the overhanging branches of an ancient oak, cloaked in shadows and silence.

Maya stared at Nik, unsure of what to say. Things had gone from strained to tolerant to strained again and it was high time they ended the emotional seesaw ride. But she wasn't sure how.

At last, she sighed. "Nik, what is this? What do we have?"

She'd almost expected he'd pretend not to know what she meant but he said, "We have something incredibly special. And what it is now is what we've made of it so far. What it will be tomorrow will be what we intend to make of it."

"Stop being so cryptic and godly." Maya glowered.

"Maya, I'm just saying that relationships like ours can work. I was born of such a relationship. although my parents did have a hard time of it."

"So what now? Are you even going to be around anymore? Once you're done training me won't you go home?" Maya tried to keep her voice calm, tried to keep back the tears burning her eyes.

Nik shook his head, a frown creasing his forehead. He held her shoulders following her gaze even as she tried to look away. "Maya I will always serve Yama in whatever way he deems necessary. That is my job. But that doesn't mean I won't have time to be with you. Besides, you still have a whole lot more learning to do when it comes to your Fire. And there is nowhere else I'd rather be while you are honing the intricacies of your power."

"So you will stick around?"

"Yes. If anything things are going to get more interesting now the Hand of Kali is gaining power," he teased.

Maya punched him lightly in his abdomen and he grabbed her hand and pulled her close. "Don't you worry. I'm not leaving you anytime soon. Unless of course you want me to leave." He leaned closer and Maya inched forward.

"No. I don't want you to leave." She whispered. She'd almost said 'ever' before she bit the word off. No matter how she felt about him she couldn't ask him to give up his entire life for her. Not yet. Not while everything was so new and unknown.

When Nik's lips touched hers she forgot about past and future, about ifs and buts. All that mattered were their bodies so close together as Maya entwined her arms around his neck. Their lips seeking each other's heat and need driving them to distraction. At last, he pulled away.

His voice was hoarse as he whispered, "Maybe you should go see Ria and then maybe we can continue this later."

Maya blushed as they moved apart. She tucked her hair

behind her ears and nodded before setting off in the direction of Ria's house.

At the Gupta's doorstep, Maya turned to Nik, unsure how to express herself. "Look Nik, I need to do this alone-"

"Absolutely, Maya. I'm here for support. I'll be waiting outside for you." He nodded at the door, then began to shimmer like a mirage until he disappeared into thin air.

"You so have to teach me that trick."

A disembodied chuckle emanated from the empty air a few feet from Maya and she grinned as she turned and walked to the Gupta's front door.

SHE TOOK a deep breath and knocked, blood thundering in her ears as she waited. At last, footsteps pattered to the door and Mrs. Gupta opened it.

And Maya received a bright and welcoming smile from Ria's mother. *That's strange. The only time she ever got this kind of welcome was when Ria's dad was out of town on business.*

"Hello Maya, it's so nice to see you." Ria's mom ushered her inside, calm and comfortable and not once looking over her shoulder in fear. Yes, the tyrant had left the building. "Ria is in the living room, go right in and I'll bring you all some kulfi I made."

Maya smiled, actually looking forward to a taste of Mrs. Gupta's Indian style iced sorbet, which Maya secretly thought was even better than her mom's. Maya entered the room, wincing at the hideously green, hideously paisley carpet Ria's dad so loved.

Ria looked up from a book she'd been reading and let out a shriek. "Maya, where have you been?" She hurled herself off the couch and flew straight into Maya's arms, hugging her for dear life. "Ohmygod, Maya I have so much to tell you."

"Okay," said Maya, laughing. "Take it slow, you don't want to tire yourself out." Maya swallowed her shock at the words she'd uttered. What if Ria didn't recall being sick? What exactly did Ria know anyway?

"Don't worry, I'm fine. Ma said the doctors couldn't find anything wrong with me. They did all kinds of tests. MRI's. CT's. Nothing could explain it. And then a few days ago I woke up just like that." Ria smiled. Her smile flickered to a frown for the briefest second. "I remember you, Maya. You were really upset about something. It was like I'd had a dream you'd come to help my but you were crying and then you left. "Are you alright?" Ria held onto Maya's arm.

Maya had no idea how to answer her friend. What was she supposed to say? *Oh yeah, apart from having recently fought head to head with an invincible demon king, and oh yes apart from having just had my best friend die on me and then be brought back to life, apart from that I'm hunky dory.* Instead, Maya held her tongue and gave Ria another hug.

Ria returned the hug then held Maya away, searching her face. "No more knockouts by your dad?" Ria giggled as she traced Maya's cheek where no proof remained of the injury she'd received not so long ago.

"I'm good, Ria. Just a bit tired."

"Oh, look at me," said Ria. "Such a bad hostess. Come sit. I'll go get you a drink."

"Ria, wait. Your mom said something about kulfi."

"Oh, okay, she won't be long." Ria nodded smiling from ear to ear.

"So tell me, what's this news you have?"

For the briefest moment, a shadow flitted over Ria's bright expression and then it was gone. Maya hid a frown. "I must introduce you to someone. I'm very excited, Maya." Ria paused, then took a deep breath as if to quell her excitement, and said, "I'm getting married."

CHAPTER 62

"*H*is name is Viren and he's studying medicine. We are to be married as soon as the arrangements can be made."

Maya's face fell. The shock was so much she even forgot to maintain a polite smile in case she offended Ria.

But instead, Ria laughed and moved to sit beside Maya. She gave her a quick comforting squeeze and said, "Don't worry for me Maya. This was *my* choice. Viren is . . . very kind to me. We . . . make a good match for each other. Really we do-"

"Did I hear someone mention my name?" A voice cut Ria off and she grinned even wider.

"Yes, you did, and we were talking about you, too," Ria said, laughing happily as she stared up at the handsome young man. Viren entered the room placed the tray of kulfi on the table and was about to find a seat when Ria rose and went to him, taking his arm. "Viren, I want you to meet my dearest friend in all the world, Maya Rao. And Maya, this it Viren Sen, my betrothed."

Maya rose to shake his hand, shocked to recognize Ria's fiancé. He'd attended to Ria when she'd fallen into her coma. He'd also been there to hear Mr. Gupta's horrible words about his very own daughter. And yet he still agreed to marry Ria? Why? Now, Viren had his arm around Ria and smiled down at her quite happily. As far as Maya could tell his affection seemed genuine, so she calmed down a tad.

Until Viren's gaze left Ria's and settled on Maya and the smile in his eyes disappeared. "I am very happy to meet you, Maya. Ria has told me so much about you." Maya's heart tightened. There was a hardness in his eyes that seemed to be a warning to her. A hardness that worried Maya. He continued, his voice neutral and almost friendly, "It seems you have been a protector to Ria on more than one occasion, am I correct?"

Maya shared a glance with Ria, the unspoken question of how much Viren knew about Ria's situation with her father hung between them, almost palpable. "Er . . . I did what I could," was all she was able to muster.

"And I'm grateful. I know Ria hasn't had the best of childhoods and I hope I can give her the kind of marriage where she will feel safe and happy and loved."

The words nice enough but they fell like blows upon Maya's heart. What would happen to her poor friend? She'd have to leave school and without a proper education she'd be bound to this marriage forever, no chance of ever escaping. Bound to the man who Maya's gut was telling her had a hidden agenda. And Maya suppressed a shudder. Who knew what type of man Viren truly was. Would he turn on Ria once they're married? Show his true side? Become exactly like her father as he grows older? The coldness in his eye scared Maya.

How could she be happy for Ria? Her friend was giving up her life and Maya wanted to sob because it was so clear Ria was blind to it all. Did she see this marriage as an escape route? Did she not realize she could be running from one cruel controlling male to another? And this time the decision may well be forever. No turning back for Ria.

Ever.

Maya swallowed her tears. She ached to get up and run away and leave Ria and Viren and just flee. But she couldn't. Because Viren said, "Maya there is one thing I meant to ask you."

"What is that, Viren?" Maya asked as politely as she could, as she placed a spoonful of kulfi in her mouth. The cool, mango goodness calmed the tears in her throat a bit, for which Maya was incredibly grateful.

"I want you to give me your blessing."

Maya almost choked on her kulfi which suddenly became hard and icy and impossible to swallow.

He dared ask me for his blessing? Even when he's giving me that cold look that's telling me he doesn't give a damn about my opinion?

Maya stared at Viren, wondering what she could possibly say that would allow her to get out of the situation without offending her best friend's future husband. But his eyes told her all. His eyes were saying he couldn't care less about her blessing. His cold hard eyes told her in no uncertain terms she wasn't welcome in the least.

Maya had always abhorred the tradition of arranged marriage. She'd seen the sadness in Ria's mother's eyes. And in the eyes of many of the girls she knew whose families still practiced the tradition even after immigrating to the States. Now she faced it head on in the form of Viren and Ria. Her heart ached for what Ria may endure, and Maya prayed Viren's coldness was because he didn't like her, and not an indication of his nature, not a suggestion of his treatment of her friend.

"Er . . . I'm not the person you should be asking," Maya replied shaking her head.

"I think *you* are the best person. You are Ria's best friend, and staunchest protector." Maya stiffened. He wasn't letting it go. Apparently he seemed to expect an answer, seemed to want this farce to be acted out to the end. Was he trying to prove something?

"But I don't know anything about you, Viren. I don't think you should be making me part of this . . . arrangement."

"Then maybe you can get to know me?" Viren offered Maya his hand. "Why don't you give me a chance and let's be friends."

Maya took his hand, although still filled with doubt. "Viren, look, it's not easy to just be someone's friend, it takes time-"

"We have plenty of time," he replied, not taking any of Maya's excuses for an answer. He seemed adamant and open. But his eyes still lacked warmth.

Maya scoffed in silence. They didn't have a lot of time. They'd be getting married soon. "So when is the wedding?" How did he expect her to get to know him when within no time Ria would be plucked out of school, married and gone to live with her brand-new husband to her new life, cooking, cleaning and popping out sons?

"We've decided to set the date for after Ria completes her schooling," he said, moving again to Ria's side.

That surprised Maya, but it still wasn't a long way off. She rose to her feet. She really couldn't take this anymore. Sitting there pretending she was fine with Ria being shipped off to marry a stranger. "Look, I really have to be going. My mom and dad will be wondering where I've gotten to."

Viren and Ria both rose and followed Maya as she left the sitting room and went to the door. She turned to take in Ria's expression. Disappointment.

Viren reached out and Maya took his hand giving it a firm shake. "It was nice to meet you, Maya. I hope we can meet again sometime soon." He smiled at Ria and held onto Maya's hand a little too long. Squeezed it a little too hard. A warning sent and taken, Maya thought. Then he left the hall, heading upstairs giving Maya and Ria some privacy.

"Thank you for coming Maya," Ria smoothed her dark hair back.

Maya reached out to hug her. "I'm glad I came. I'm glad you're well and healthy."

"But you aren't happy about my choice to marry?" Ria snorted. "Maya, I can read you like a book. You're upset with me and you're taking it out on Viren."

"What do you mean?"

"He was kind enough to offer you friendship. He even asked for your blessing. Maya, if you can't find it in your heart to give us your blessing how can you really be my friend?"

"Ria, no. It's not like that." Tears filled in Maya's throat, threatening to spill again. "I just . . . how do you know you're not making a mistake?"

"I know. I've gotten to know him, Maya. And he is a good person. He wants what's best for me. And if you can't see it, if you can't accept it maybe our friendship is not as strong as I thought."

"Ria." Maya had seen the hardness in his eyes. This was not a man who had Ria's best interests at heart. There was cruelty in the hardness. With everything that had happened, with all the power Maya had gained, she knew she had to follow her gut. And her gut was saying Viren isn't the warm and loving fiancée he's pretending to be.

"No, Maya. If you can't accept Viren is right for me, and if you can't support me in this then please don't visit me again. I ask you to please leave me alone."

"Ria, how can you ask me to do that?" The words came out as a whisper.

"Then can I count on your support? Can Viren count on your blessing?" Ria pushed for an answer. *When did Ria develop this type of strength?* Maya wondered.

"I . . ." Maya could not say it. Wouldn't ever let a blessing for their marriage pass her lips. Even the thought of such a thing was like a curse on Maya's own soul. She grabbed Ria's hands and squeezed them. "You know I love you. And you know how I feel about arranged marriages. But how could I abandon my best friend just because I don't agree with her decision? You know I will do everything in my power to help you. Fine, maybe I don't adore Viren and maybe I won't even after I get to know him better, but this is your choice and I will stand by you. You will always have my support."

"Oh, Maya." Ria grabbed hold of Maya and squeezed her into a bone-crushing hug. "Thank you. I know you don't know Viren and maybe you two won't get along." Ria tilted her head, a shadow of sadness darkening her features. Then she smiled. "I can live with that. I just can't live without you in my life."

The girls grinned at each other and Maya sighed, relieved. "I have to go. See you at school?" Ria nodded.

Maya stepped off the porch and turned to wave at her friend as she closed the door.

On Maya and a chapter of their lives spent entirely with each other. Maya wasn't looking forward to adding Viren into the mix.

CHAPTER 63

As Maya turned away from the Gupta's darkened doorstep, her heart felt like a stone in her chest. She knew deep down she'd never be able to accept Ria had just given up and agreed to an arranged marriage to escape her father. Maya had agreed to support Ria despite her gut feeling about Viren. But why did it all seem so wrong? Why did it feel like Maya was the one doing the wrong thing?

She thought of her own parents. Would they ever impose a marriage on Maya? Force her to marry someone she didn't love? Maya blinked away the tears. No. They wouldn't. They'd always been understanding and patient with her, even when she'd thrown their faith back in their faces. She'd denied to them and to herself that the gods ever existed.

And now, today, she knew she'd been wrong all along. It did seem surreal. Everything she'd been through in the last few days seemed like a rather tragic, dramatic dream. But it had been real.

She even felt like a different person. More aware. More accepting. More trusting. She trusted Nik and even Chayya and Yama and Kali too. She even trusted her powers, believed in them. But her trust didn't extend to Viren. Not when he'd warned her off with those cold hard eyes.

She'd made the choices that brought her here today. And her choice for Ria was bittersweet. She'd saved her friend from death. Had given her a second chance. Only to find Ria about to be imprisoned in an arranged marriage, and no matter what Ria tried to say she hadn't been able to convince Maya the choice had been wholly, happily hers to make.

Maya descended the steps, her throat tight, tears singeing her eyes.

"Are you okay, Maya?" A disembodied voice spoke close to her, warmth of his breath kissing her cheek and making her smile.

"Yes, you can become visible now if you don't mind."

Nik shimmered into existence beside her, keeping pace as they walked the few blocks back to Maya's house.

"To answer your question, no, I'm not okay but I'll get over it." Tears tightened Maya's throat. "Ria is getting married. He's a doctor. Viren Sen. And it's an arranged marriage. Not that I'm abandoning her, but I can't believe she gave in. After everything she'd been through with them she just allowed her father to control her even more. And now, Viren will be in control of her for the rest of her life. And she's happy to be with him. Is she really that blind?"

"Sometimes duty does blind us to reality. Perhaps it is a road she is meant to travel. Perhaps it is part of her destiny to experience the life her husband has offered her. Things happen in strange and mysterious ways sometimes." Maya sighed. Nik's words had a truth to it she couldn't deny. Then he chuckled. "Well, I can tell you one thing," Nik looked over at her and grinned, "Life will never be the same again for Maya Rao."

Maya snorted. "Yeah, tell me about it."

"But you do have a bunch of people looking out for you, you know?" Maya met Nik's gaze, eyebrows raised in question. "Your parents, Claudia, Kali, Chayya, even Varuni said to send you her eternal gratitude. And you have two boons from the God of the Underworld."

"One boon," Maya reminded him with a grin.

"Oh, yes, one boon." Nik nodded, his dark locks falling over his forehead. "And there is one more thing you do have."

"What's that?" Maya's voice was soft as the question left her lips.

Nik linked his fingers with hers, warm skin entwined with warm skin setting off a million tiny sparks. "You have me."

~ TO BE CONTINUED ~

Thank you for reading. The Hand of Kali Series continues with Blood & Gold.

ACKNOWLEDGMENTS

Fire is a labor of love. It explores parts of Hindu mythology that even I was entranced to discover. I hope you have as much fun reading this book as I did writing it

It took a long time to finish Fire. Not that it was a difficult task, but that it was peppered with hospital stays and parts of it were actually written while I was on morphine. I will admit it is interesting what a writer can produce on a drug-induced high. Personally, I wouldn't recommend it ;)

To Cassie Hart, Leigh K Hunt, Melissa Pearl & Brenda Howsen. The Inklings- our amazing writing group who are always there for me no matter what. You chicks rule!

To Annetta Ribken – thank you for your fine editing skillz.

To my fab family. Mum & Dad, Vin and Namo. Thank you for picking and dropping my offsrping, for delivering food to my door when I so needed it, and for peppering my mindless work (and pain) with much needed laughter.

To Sel, Dharsh and Dhivs. I could never thank you enough.

To Eduardo Priego- for you amazing cover art for Fire.

To Patti Larsen. Dearest friend - for being willing to drop everything to help little old me.

FREE STARTER LIBRARY - JOIN MY NEWSLETTER

Get the following titles FREE when you subscribe to my newsletter.

Tee's Newsletter

http://smarturl.it/TeesMailingList

ABOUT THE AUTHOR

I have been a writer from the time I was old enough to recognize that reading was a doorway into my imagination. Poetry was my first foray into the art of the written word. Books were my best friends, my escape, my haven. I am essentially a recluse but this part of my personality is impossible to practice given I have two teenage daughters, who are actually my friends, my tea-makers, my confidantes… I am blessed with a husband who has left me for golf. It's a fair trade as I have left him for writing. We are both passionate supporters of each other's loves – it works wonderfully…

My heart is currently broken in two. One half resides in South Africa where my old roots still remain, and my heart still longs for the endless beaches and the smell of moist soil after a summer downpour. My love for Ma Afrika will never fade. The other half of me has been transplanted to the Land of the Long White Cloud. The land of the Taniwha, beautiful Maraes, and volcanoes. The land of green, pure beauty that truly inspires. And because I am so torn between these two lands – I shall forever remain cross-eyed.

Stalk Tee here:
www.tgayer.com
tee@tgayer.com

facebook.com/TGAyerAuthor

twitter.com/TGAyerAuthor

bookbub.com/profile/t-g-ayer

www.ingramcontent.com/pod-product-compliance
Lightning Source LLC
Chambersburg PA
CBHW021222060726
47590CB00005B/1597